JUMPER

Steven Gould is the author of *Jumper*, *Wildside*, *Helm*, *Blind Waves*, *Reflex*, and *Jumper: Griffin's Story*, as well as several short stories. He is the recipient of the Hal Clement Young Adult Award for Science Fiction and has been on the Hugo ballot twice and the Nebula ballot once for his short fiction. Steve lives in New Mexico with his wife, writer Laura J. Mixon and their two daughters. As he is somewhere between Birth a̶̶̶̶̶ he considers himself to be middle-aged.

D1353335

By Stephen Gould

Jumper
Jumper: Griffin's Story

Steven Gould

JUMPER

HARPER
Voyager

Harper*Voyager*
An imprint of HarperCollins*Publishers*
77–85 Fulham Palace Road,
Hammersmith, London W6 8JB

First published in Great Britain by HarperCollins*Publishers* 2008

This paperback edition 2008
3

A catalogue record for this book is
available from the British Library

ISBN-13: 978-0-00-727599-1

Set in Times

Printed in Great Britain by Clays Ltd, St Ives plc

Mixed Sources

Product group from well-managed
forests and other controlled sources
www.fsc.org   Cert no. SW-COC-1806
© 1996 Forest Stewardship Council

FSC

FSC is a non-profit international organisation established
to promote the responsible management of the world's forests.
Products carrying the FSC label are independently certified
to assure consumers that they come from forests that are managed
to meet the social, economic and ecological needs
of present and future generations.

Find out more about HarperCollins and the environment at
www.harpercollins.co.uk/green

For James Gould, soldier, craftsman, sailor, father
and
Laura J. Mixon, engineer, teacher, writer, wife

PART 1:

BEGINNINGS

ONE

The first time was like this.

I was reading when Dad got home. His voice echoed through the house and I cringed.

"Davy!"

I put the book down and sat up on the bed. "In here, Dad. I'm in my room."

His footsteps on the hallway's oak floor got louder and louder. I felt my head hunching between my shoulders; then Dad was at the door and raging.

"I thought I told you to mow the lawn today!" He came into the room and towered over me. "Well! Speak up when I ask you a question!"

"I'm gonna do it, Dad. I was just finishing a book."

"You've been home from school for over two hours! I'm sick and tired of you lying around this house doing nothing!" He leaned close and the whiskey on his breath made my eyes water. I flinched back and he grabbed the back of my neck with fingers like a vise. He shook me. "You're nothing but a lazy brat. I'm going to beat some industry into you if I have to kill you to do it!"

He pulled me to my feet, still gripping my neck. With his other hand he fumbled for the ornate rodeo buckle on his belt, then snaked the heavy Western strap out of his pants loops.

"No, Dad. I'll mow the lawn right now. Honest!"

"Shut up," he said. He pushed me into the wall. I barely

3

got my hands up in time to keep my face from slamming nose-first into the plaster. He switched hands then, pressing me against the wall with his left while he took the belt in his right hand.

I twisted my head slightly, to keep my nose from grinding into the wall, and saw him switch his grip on the belt, so the heavy silver buckle hung on the end, away from his hand.

I yelled. "Not the buckle, Dad! *You promised!*"

He ground my face into the wall harder. *"Shut UP!* I didn't hit you near hard enough the last time." He extended his arm until he held me against the wall at arm's length and swung the belt back slowly. Then his arm jerked forward and the belt sung though the air and my body betrayed me, squirming away from the impact and . . .

I was leaning against bookshelves, my neck free of Dad's crushing grip, my body still braced to receive a blow. I looked around, gasping, my heart still racing. There was no sign of Dad, but this didn't surprise me.

I was in the fiction section of the Stanville Public Library and, while I knew it as well as my own room, I didn't think my father had ever been inside the building.

That was the first time.

The second time was like this.

The truck stop was new and busy, an island of glaring light and hard concrete in the night. I went in the glass doors to the restaurant and took a chair at the counter, near the section with the sign that said, DRIVERS ONLY. The clock on the wall read eleven-thirty. I put the rolled-up bundle of stuff on the floor under my feet and tried to look old.

The middle-aged waitress on the other side of the counter looked skeptical, but she put down a menu and a glass of water, then said, "Coffee?"

"Hot tea, please."

She smiled mechanically and left.

The drivers' section was half full, a thick haze of tobacco smoke over it. None of them looked like the kind of man who'd give me the time of day, much less a lift farther down the road.

The waitress returned with a cup, a tea bag, and one of those little metal pitchers filled with not very hot water. "What can I get you?" she asked.

"I'll stick with this for a while."

She looked at me steadily for a moment, then totaled the check and laid on the counter. "Cashier will take it when you're ready. You want anything else, just let me know."

I didn't know to hold the lid open as I poured the water, so a third of it ended up on the counter. I mopped it up with napkins from the dispenser and tried not to cry.

"Been on the road long, kid?"

I jerked my head up. A man, sitting in the last seat of the drivers' section, was looking at me. He was big, both tall and fat, with a roll of skin where his shirt neck opened. He was smiling and I could see his teeth were uneven and stained.

"What do you mean?"

He shrugged. "Your business. You don't look like you've been running long." His voice was higher-pitched than you'd expect for a man his size, but kind.

I looked past him, at the door. "About two weeks."

He nodded. "Rough. You running from your parents?"

"My dad. My mom cut out long ago."

He pushed his spoon around the countertop with his finger. The nails were long with grease crusted under them. "How old are you, kid?"

"Seventeen."

He looked at me and raised his eyebrows.

I shrugged my shoulders. "I don't care what you think. It's true. I turned seventeen lousy years old yesterday." The tears started to come and I blinked hard, got them back under control.

"What you been doing since you left home?"

The tea had gotten as dark as it was going to. I pulled the tea bag and spooned sugar into the cup. "I've been hitching, panhandling a little, some odd jobs. Last two days I picked apples—twenty-five cents a bushel and all I could eat. I also got some clothes out of it."

"Two weeks and you're out of your own clothes already?"

I gulped down half the tea. "I only took what I was wearing." All I was wearing when I walked out of the Stanville Public Library.

"Oh. Well, my name's Topper. Topper Robbins. What's yours?"

I stared at him. "Davy," I said, finally.

"Davy . . . ?"

"Just Davy."

He smiled again. "I understand. Don't have to beat me about the head and shoulders." He picked up his spoon and stirred his coffee. "Well, Davy, I'm driving that PetroChem tanker out there and I'm headed west in about forty-five minutes. If you're going that way, I'll be glad to give you a ride. You look like you could use some food, though. Why don't you let me buy you a meal?"

The tears came again then. I was ready for cruelty but not kindness. I blinked hard and said, "Okay. I'd appreciate the meal and the ride."

An hour later I was westbound in the right-hand seat of Topper's rig, drowsing from the heat of the cab and the full stomach. I closed my eyes and pretended to sleep, tired of talking. Topper tried to talk a little more after that, but stopped. I watched him out of narrowed eyes. He kept turning his head to look at me when the headlights from oncoming traffic lit the cab's interior. I thought I should feel grateful, but he gave me the creeps.

After a while I fell asleep for real. I came awake with a start, unsure of where I was or even who. There was a tremor running through my mind, a reaction to a bad dream, barely remembered. I narrowed my eyes again and my identity and associated memories came back.

Topper was talking on the CB.

"I'll meet you behind Sam's," he was saying. "Fifteen minutes."

"Ten-four, Topper. We're on our way."

Topper signed off.

I yawned and sat up. "Jeeze. Did I sleep long?"

"About an hour, Davy." He smiled like there'd been a joke. He turned off his CB then and turned the radio to a country and western station.

I hate country and western.

Ten minutes later he took an exit for a farm road far from anywhere.

"You can let me out here, Topper."

"I'm going on kid, just have to meet a guy first. You don't want to hitch in the dark. Nobody'll stop. Besides, it looks like rain."

He was right. The moon had vanished behind a thick overcast and the wind was whipping the trees around.

"Okay."

He drove down the rural two-lane for a while, then pulled off the road at a country store with two gas pumps out front. The store was dark but there was a gravel lot out back where two pickups were parked. Topper pulled the rig up beside them.

"Come on, kid. Want you to meet some guys."

I didn't move. "That's okay. I'll wait for you here."

"Sorry," he said. "It's against company policy to pick up riders, but my ass would really be grass if I left you in here and something happened. Be a sport."

I nodded slowly. "Sure. Don't mean to be any trouble."

He grinned again, big. "No trouble."

I shivered.

To climb down, I had to turn and face the cab, then feel with my feet for the step. A hand guided my foot to the step and I froze. I looked down. Three men were standing on my side of the truck. I could hear gravel crunching as Topper walked around the front of the rig. I looked at him. He was unbuckling his jeans and pulling down his zipper.

I yelled and scrambled back up to the cab, but strong hands gripped my ankles and knees, dragging me back down. I grabbed onto the chrome handle by the door with both hands as tight as I could, flailing my legs to try and break their grip. Somebody punched me in the stomach hard and I let go of the handle, the air in my lungs, and my supper all at once.

"Jesus fucking Christ. He puked all over me!" Somebody hit me again as I fell.

They grabbed my arms and carried me over to the open tailgate of a pickup. They slammed me down on the bed of the truck. My face hit and I tasted blood. One of them jumped up on the truck bed and straddled my back, his knees and shins pinning my upper arms, one hand gripping my hair painfully. I felt somebody else reach around and unbuckle my belt, then rip my pants and underwear down. The air was cold on my butt and upper legs.

A voice said, "I wish you'd gotten another girl."

Another voice said, "Who brought the Vaseline?"

"Shit. It's in the truck."

"Well . . . we don't need it."

Somebody reached between my legs and pawed my genitals; then I felt him spread the cheeks of my butt and spit. His warm saliva splattered my bottom and . . .

I pitched forward, the pressure off my arms and hair, the hands off my bottom. My head banged into something and I struck out to hit my hand against something which gave. I turned, clutched at my pants, pulled them up from my knees, while I sobbed for air, my heart pounding and my entire body shaking.

It was dark, but the air was still and I was alone. I wasn't outside anymore. A patch of moonlight came through a window six feet away to shine on bookshelves. I tasted blood again, gingerly touched my split upper lip. I walked carefully down to the patch of light and looked around.

I pulled a book from the shelf and opened it. The stamp on the inside cover told me what I already knew. I was back in the fiction section of the Stanville Public Library and I was sure I'd gone mad.

That was the second time.

The first time I ended up in the library, it was open, I wasn't bleeding, my clothes were clean, and I just walked away . . . from that building, from that town, from that life.

I thought I'd pulled a blank. I thought that whatever my father did to me was so terrible that I'd simply chosen not to remember it. That I'd only come back to myself after reaching the safety of the library.

The thought of pulling a blank was scary, but it wasn't strange to me. Dad pulled blanks all the time and I'd read enough fiction to be familiar with trauma-induced amnesia.

I was surprised that the library was closed and dark this time. I checked the wall clock. It read two o'clock, an hour and five minutes later than the digital clock in Topper's truck. *Jesus Christ.* I shivered in the library's air-conditioning and fumbled at my pants. The zipper was broken but the snap worked. I buckled the belt an extra notch tight, then pulled my shirt out so it hung over the zipper. My mouth tasted of blood and vomit.

The library was lit from without by pale white moonlight and the yellow glare of mercury streetlamps. I threaded my way between shelves, chairs, tables to the water fountain and rinsed my mouth again and again until the taste was gone from my mouth and the bleeding of my lip had stopped.

In two weeks I'd worked my way over nine hundred miles from my father. In one heartbeat I'd undone that, putting myself fifteen minutes away from the house. I sat down on a hard wooden chair and put my head in my hands. What had I done to deserve this?

There was something I wasn't dealing with. I knew it. Something . . .

I'm so tired. All I want is to rest. I thought of all the snatches of sleep I'd had over the last two weeks, miserable stolen moments on rest-stop benches, in people's cars, and under bushes like some animal. I thought of the house, fifteen minutes away, of my bedroom, of my bed.

A wave of irresistible longing came over me and I found myself standing and walking, without thought, just desire for that bed. I went to the emergency exit at the back, the one with the ALARM WILL SOUND sign. I figured by the time any alarm was answered, I could be well away.

It was chained. I leaned against it and hit it very hard, an overhand blow with the flat of my hand. I drew back, tears in my eyes, to hit it again but it wasn't there and I pitched forward, off balance and flailing, into my bed.

I knew it was my bed. I think it was the smell of the room that told me first, but the backlit alarm-clock face on the bedside table was the one Mom sent the year after she left and the light from the back porch light streamed through the window at just the right angle.

For one brief moment I relaxed, utterly and completely, muscle after muscle unknotting. I closed my eyes and felt exhaustion steal over me in a palpable wave. Then I heard a noise and I jerked up, rigid, on the bedspread on my hands and knees. The sound came again. Dad . . . snoring.

I shuddered. It was strange. It was a very comforting sound. It was home, it was family. It also meant the son of a bitch was asleep.

I took off my shoes and padded down the hall. The door was half open and the overhead light was on. He was sprawled diagonally across the bed, on top of the covers, both shoes and one sock off, his shirt unbuttoned. There was an empty bottle of scotch tucked in the crook of his arm. I sighed.

Home sweet home.

I grabbed the bottle neck and pulled it gently from between his arm and his side, then set it on the bedside table. He snored on, oblivious. I took his pants off then, pulling the legs alternately to work them past his butt. They came free abruptly and his wallet fell from the back pocket. I hung the pants over the back of a chair, then went through the wallet.

He had eighty bucks plus his plastic. I took three twenties, then started to put it on the dresser, but stopped. When I folded the wallet, it seemed stiffer than it should, and thicker. I looked closer. There was a hidden compartment covered by a flap with fake stitching. I got it open and nearly dropped the wallet. It was full of hundred-dollar bills.

I turned the light off and carried the wallet back to my room, where I counted twenty-two crisp hundred-dollar bills onto the bed.

I stared down at the money, four rows of five, one row of two, my eyes wide. My ears were burning and my stomach suddenly hurt. I went back to Dad's room and stared at him for a while.

This was the man who took me to the mission and the secondhand stores to buy clothes for school. This was the man who made me take peanut butter and jelly to school every day rather than part with a crummy ninety cents' worth of lunch money. This was the man who beat me when I'd suggested an allowance for doing the yard work.

I picked up the empty scotch bottle and hefted it, shifted my grip to the neck. It was cold, smooth, and just the right size for my small hands. The glass didn't slip or shift as I swung it experimentally. The glass at the base of the bottle was extra thick where the manufacturer had chosen to give the impression of a bigger bottle. It looked very strong.

Dad snored away, his mouth open, his face slack. His skin, pale normally, looked white as paper in the overhead light. His forehead, receding, domed, lined, looked egglike, white, fragile. I felt the base of the bottle with my left hand. It felt more than heavy enough.

Shit.

I put the bottle back down on the table, turned off the light, and went back to my room.

I took notebook paper, cut it dollar-bill-size, and stacked it until it felt as thick as the pile of hundreds. It took twenty sheets to match the stiffness of the money—maybe it was thicker or just newer. I put the cut paper in the wallet and put it back in the pocket of his slacks.

Then I went to the garage and took down the old leather suitcase, the one Granddad gave me when he retired, and packed it with my clothes, toiletries, and the leather-bound set of Mark Twain that Mom left me.

After I'd closed the suitcase, stripped off my dirty clothes, and put on my suit, I just stood looking around the room, swaying on my feet. If I didn't start moving soon, I'd drop.

There was something else, something I could use. . . .

I thought of the kitchen, only thirty feet away, down the hall and across the den. Before Mom left, I'd loved to sit in there while she cooked, just talking, telling her stupid jokes. I closed my eyes and pictured it, tried to feel it.

The air around me changed, or maybe it was just the noise. I was in a quiet house, but just the sound of my breathing reflecting off walls sounded different from room to room.

I was in the kitchen.

I nodded my head slowly, tiredly. Hysteria seethed beneath the surface, a rising bubble that threatened to undo me. I pushed it down and looked in the refrigerator.

Three six-packs of Schlitz, two cartons of cigarettes, half a pizza in the cardboard delivery box. I shut the door and thought about my room. I tried it with my eyes open, unfocused, picturing the spot between my desk and the window.

I was there and the room reeled, my eyes and maybe my inner ear just not ready for the change. I put my hand on the wall and the room stopped moving.

I picked up the suitcase and closed my eyes. I opened them in the library, dark shadows alternating with silver pools of moonlight. I walked to the front door and looked out at the grass.

Last summer, before school, I'd come up to the library, check out a book or two, and then move outside, to the grass under the elms. The wind would ruffle the pages, tug my hair and clothes around, and I would go into the words, find the cracks between the sentences and the words would go away, leaving me in the story, the action, the head of other people. Twice I left it too late and got home after Dad did. He liked supper ready. Only twice, though. Twice was more than enough.

I closed my eyes and the wind pushed my hair and fluttered my tie. The suitcase was heavy and I had to switch hands several times as I walked the two blocks to the bus station.

There was a bus for points east at 5:30 A.M. I bought a ticket to New York City for one hundred and twenty-two dollars and fifty-three cents. The clerk took the two hundreds without comment, gave me my change, and said I had three hours to wait.

They were the longest three hours I've ever spent. Every fifteen minutes I got up, dragged the suitcase to the bathroom, and splashed cold water in my face. Near the end of the wait the furniture was crawling across the floor, and every movement of the bushes outside the doors was my father, belt in hand, the buckle razor-edged and about the size of a hubcap.

The bus was five minutes late. The driver stowed my suitcase below, took the first part of my ticket, and ushered me aboard.

When we passed the tattered city-limits sign, I closed my eyes and slept for six hours.

TWO

When I was twelve, just before Mom left, we went to New York City for a week. It was a terrible and wonderful trip. Dad was there for his company, all his days spent in meetings and business lunches. Mom and I went to museums, Chinatown, Macy's, Wall Street, and rode the subway all the way out to Coney Island.

At night they fought, over dinner, at the one play we went to, and in the hotel room. Dad wanted sex and Mom wouldn't, even after I was asleep, because the company was footing the bill for one room only and I was on a rollaway in the corner. Three times during that week he made me get dressed and go down and wait in the lobby for thirty minutes while they did it. The third time, I don't think they did, though, 'cause Mom was crying in the bathroom when I came back and Dad was drinking, something he never did in front of my mother. Not usually.

The next day I saw that Mom had a bruise on her right cheekbone and she walked funny—not limping on any particular side, but like it hurt to move either leg.

Two days after we got back from New York, I came home from school and Mom was gone.

Anyway, I really liked New York. It seemed a good place to start over—a good place to hide.

"I'd like a room."

The place was a dive, a transients' hotel in Brooklyn, ten

blocks from the nearest subway stop. I'd picked it with the help of the Pakistani cabdriver who drove me from the Port Authority Bus Terminal. He'd stayed there himself.

The clerk was an older man, maybe my dad's age, reading a Len Deighton novel through half-glasses. He lowered the book and tilted his head forward to look at me over the glasses.

"Too young," he said. "You're a runaway, I'll bet."

I put a hundred down on the counter, my hand still on it, like Philip Marlowe.

He laughed and put his hand on it. I lifted my hand away.

He looked at it closely, rubbing it between his fingers. Then he handed me a registration card and said, "Forty-eight a night, five-buck key deposit, bathroom's down the hall, payment in advance."

I gave him enough money for a week. He looked at the other hundreds for a moment, then gave me the room key and said, "Don't deal here. I don't care what you do away from the hotel, but if I see anything that looks like a deal, I'll turn you myself."

My jaw dropped open and I stared at him. "You mean drugs?"

"No—candy." He looked at me again. "Okay. Maybe you don't. But if I see anything like that at all, you're history."

My face was red and I felt like I'd done something wrong, even though I hadn't. "I don't do stuff like that," I said, stammering.

I hated feeling like that.

He just shrugged. "Maybe not. I'm just warning you. And don't bring any tricks here either."

A memory of rough hands grabbing me and pulling down my pants made me cringe. "I don't do that either!" I could feel a knot in my throat and tears were dangerously close to the surface.

He just shrugged again.

I carried my suitcase up six flights of stairs to the room and sat on the narrow bed. The room was ratty, with peeling wallpaper and the stench of old cigarette smoke, but the door and the door frame were steel and the lock seemed new.

The window looked out on an alley, a sooty brick wall five feet across the gap. I opened it and the smell of something rotting drifted in. I stuck my head out and saw bagged garbage below, half of it torn open and strewn about the alley. When I turned my head to the right I could see a thin slice of the street in front of the hotel.

I thought about what the clerk had said and I got mad again, feeling small, diminished. Why'd he have to make me feel like that? I was happy, excited about being in New York, and he jerked me around like that. Why did people have do that sort of shit?

Wouldn't anything ever work out right?

"I don't care how talented, smart, bright, hardworking, or perfect you are. You don't have a high school diploma or a GED and we can't hire you. Next!"

"Sure we hire high school kids. You seem pretty bright to me. Just let me have your social security number for the W2 and we'll be all set. You don't have a social security number? Where you from, Mars? You come back with a social security number and I'll give you a try. Next!"

"This is the application for a social security number. Fill it out and let me see your birth certificate. You don't have your birth certificate? Get it and come back. No exceptions. Next!"

"I'm sorry, but in this state, if you're under eighteen, you must have parental permission to take the GED. If you're under seventeen it takes a court order. You come back with your mother or father, and a birth certificate or New York driver's license, and you can take it. Next!"

There is a point where you have to give up, at least for a while, and all you want to do is shut down. I rode the subway back to Brooklyn Heights, and walked numbly in the direction of my hotel.

It was late afternoon, heavily overcast, and the dingy, gray street seemed entirely appropriate to my mood.

God damn them! Why did they have to make me feel so little? With every interview, every rejection, I'd felt guiltier and guiltier. Ashamed of something but I didn't know what. I kicked out at a piece of trash in the gutter and stubbed my toe on the curb. I blinked rapidly, my eyes blurring, the breath harsh in my throat. I wanted to just crawl into bed and hide.

I took a small cross street to get over to the avenue the hotel was on. The street was narrow, making it even darker, and there were plastic bags of garbage piled on the sidewalks, up against the stoops of old brownstone buildings. I didn't know why they called these row houses brownstones; most of them were painted green or red or yellow. The garbage was piled so high before one building I had to step out into the street to pass. When I stepped back on the sidewalk, a man stepped out from a doorway and came toward me.

"You got a subway token to spare? Any change?"

I'd seen lots of panhandlers that day, mostly around the subway stations. They made me nervous, but those hungry days hitching away from Dad were still fresh in my memory. I remembered people walking past me as if I didn't exist. I dug into my pocket for the sixth time that day while I said, "Sure."

My hand was coming out of the pocket when I heard a noise behind me. I started to look around and my head exploded.

There was something sticky between my cheek and the cold, gritty surface I was lying on. My right knee hurt and there was something about the way I was lying that didn't seem right, like I'd been especially careless in going to bed. I tried to open my eyes but my left one seemed stuck shut. The right one looked at a rough concrete surface.

A sidewalk.

Memory and pain returned at the same time. I groaned.

There was the sound of footsteps on the sidewalk and I thought about the muggers. I jerked heavily up onto all fours, my head throbbing like the dickens, my sore knee becoming even more so as I put weight on it. The sticky stuff on the sidewalk was blood.

Standing seemed impossible so I turned over and sat, my back to a row of garbage cans. I looked up and saw a woman carrying two grocery bags slowing down as she walked around the giant pile of garbage bags and saw me.

"My *gawd*! Are you okay? What happened to you?"

I blinked my open eye and put my head in my hands. The effort of sitting up made a sharp, throbbing pain stab at the back of my head.

"I think I was hit from behind." I felt for my front pocket, where I'd been carrying my money. "And robbed."

I pulled the lids of my left eye apart with my fingers. My eye was okay, just stuck shut with blood. I carefully touched the back of my head. There was a large lump there, wet. My fingers came away red.

Great. I was in a strange city with no money, no job, no family, and no prospects. That stabbing pain at the back of my head didn't compare with the hurt of somehow feeling I deserved this.

If I'd only been better as a kid. Maybe Mom wouldn't have gone, Dad wouldn't drink so much. . . .

"My apartment is just two doors down. I'll call nine-one-one." The woman didn't wait for a response. I watched her hurry past, a container of Mace in her hand, connected to her key chain. As she walked down the sidewalk, she stayed away from the buildings, checking the doorways as she went by.

Smart. Much smarter than me.

911. That meant police. *I'm a minor and a runaway. I have no ID and I don't want my parents notified.*

I thought about my hotel room, still three blocks away. I didn't even feel like standing, much less walking three more blocks. I knew I'd feel safer there. I thought about my arrival there, of the steel door with the good lock, of the torn wallpaper. It was even paid up for three more days.

I closed my eyes and *jumped*.

The hotel floor was warmer than the sidewalk and I felt much safer. I edged over to the bed and pulled myself up, slowly and carefully.

I got blood on the pillow but I didn't care.

Around midnight I went down to the bathroom, walking carefully, like my Dad after a night of drinking. It was empty. I locked the door, then ran a bath while I peed.

In the mirror I looked like something out of a slasher movie. Blood had run across my hair from the scalp wound, matting it and making the light brown stuff black and nasty. The upper left side of my face had also lain in the blood where it pooled and it was patchy, flaking off and leaving the skin underneath discolored. I shuddered.

If I'd felt well enough to walk back to the hotel, I doubt I would have made it without the police being called every block.

I got into the tub, amazed that there was hot water. The last two days it had been tepid at best. I eased onto my back and lowered the back of my head into the water. There was a slight stinging but the heat felt good. I worked soap into the hair gently, and washed my face. When I sat up, the water in the tub was brownish red. I rinsed the soap and residual blood out of my hair with the tub's faucet, and was drying off when someone tried the door.

"I'm almost done," I said.

A voice from the other side of the door said loudly, "Well hurry it up, man. You got no right to be hogging the toilet all night."

I scrubbed harder and decided to let the hair dry by itself.

There was a loud noise, like someone hit the door with the flat of their hand. "Come ooooonnnnn. Open the fucking door!"

"I'm getting dressed," I said.

"Fuck. I don't care about that—let me in, you little faggot, so I can pee."

I got angry. "There are bathrooms on the other floors. Go use one of them!"

There was a brief pause.

"I'm not going to no other bathroom, shithead. And if you don't let me in right now, I'm going to hurt you *real* bad."

My jaws hurt and I realized I was grinding my teeth together. *Why can't they leave me alone?* "So," I finally said. "You gonna wait there, with a full bladder, or you gonna go find someplace to pee?"

"I'm not going anywhere, little fucker, until I carve a piece of your ass."

I heard a splashing sound and yellow liquid began running under the door. I picked up my clothes and, without dressing, jumped back to my hotel room.

My heart was pounding and I was still angry—"pissed off," you might say. I opened my door a crack and looked down the hallway to the bathroom.

A tall Anglo, heavily muscled and wearing nothing but jeans, was zipping up his pants. Then he hit the door again and shook the doorknob.

From one of the other rooms, someone said, "Shut up already!"

The man at the bathroom said, "Come and fucking make me!" He continued to pound on the door while he reached into his back pocket for something. When he brought it out he flicked his wrist and something shiny flashed in the hall's dim light.

Jesus Christ.

I still felt scared, but the more I looked down the hall, the angrier I got. I put my clothes on the bed and jumped back into the bathroom.

The pounding on the door was deafening. I flinched away from the force of it, then picked up the trash can from the floor and dumped its few paper towels out onto the floor. Next I filled it with bloody, soapy water from the tub and propped it above the doorway, on the arm of the spring-loaded mechanism that closed the door. I studied it critically, my heart still beating, my breath hard to catch. I shifted it slightly to the right.

Then, one hand on the lock catch, I turned off the light, unlocked the door, and jumped back to the hotel room.

I opened the door just in time to see him rattle the doorknob, find it was loose, and push forcefully into the room. There was a dull thud and water splashed out into the hall. In the middle of that he yelled and slipped on the floor, his head and shoulder coming into view as he slammed down on his back. He grabbed at his head with both hands in a manner I could identify with, if not sympathize. I didn't see where the knife had gone, but he wasn't holding it at the moment.

Other doors opened slowly in the hall and heads cautiously peered around doorjambs. I shut my door softly and locked it.

For the first time since I arrived in that hotel, I smiled.

Well, it was time to face it. I was different. I was not the same as my classmates from Stanville High School, not unless some of them were keeping a pretty big secret.

I saw several possibilities.

The first was that Dad had really given it to me that last time, inducing brain damage or other trauma to the point where I was dreaming the whole mess. Maybe even my mugging was just a detail added by my subconscious to correlate with the "real" injuries. I could be lying in the St. Mary's Hospital intensive care unit back in Stanville, a little screen going beep, beep, beep over my still form. I doubted this, though. Even in my most terrifying nightmares I've had an awareness of the dream state. The stench of the garbage from the alleyway seemed too real.

The second possibility was that I'd done most of the things I remembered and most of the bad things that had happened to me had. My mind just warped reality in dealing with the results, giving to me the more palatable alternative of escape by a singular paranormal ability. This seemed more likely. Each time I'd "jumped" there was a feeling of unreality, of disorientation. This could be my shift into an irrational psychosis, an adjustment to a nasty reality. On the other hand, it could be the result of every sense reeling as the environment surrounding me changed completely. Hell—the very nature of the jump could be disorienting.

It was this third possibility that I distrusted the most. The one that meant I might finally be someone special. Not special in the sense of special education, not special in the sense of being a problem child, but unique, with a talent that, if anybody else had it, they hid. A talent for teleportation.

There, I'd thought the word. Teleportation.

"Teleportation."

Aloud it vibrated in the room, a word of terrible import, alien to normal concepts of reality, brought into existence only under special circumstances, in the framework of fiction, film, and video.

And if I *was* teleporting, then how? Why me? What was it about me that made me able to teleport? And could anybody else? Is that what happened to Mom? Did she just teleport away from us?

Suddenly my stomach went hollow and I began breathing rapidly. *Jesus Christ! What if Dad can teleport?*

Suddenly the rooms seemed unsafe and I pictured him appearing before me, the belt in his hand, anywhere, anytime.

Get a grip. I'd never seen him do anything like that. Instead, I'd seen him stumble down the street a half mile to the Country Corner, to buy beer when he'd run out, hardly able to walk or talk. If he could teleport, surely he'd have used it then.

I sat on the narrow bed and dressed myself, putting on my most comfortable clothes. With extreme care, I combed my hair, checking the result in the tiny mirror on the wall. The bump, still large and aching, looked like a barber's mistake. There was some slight seepage of blood, but it wasn't really visible through the hair.

I wanted some aspirin and I wanted to know if I was crazy. I stood up and thought about the medicine cabinet in our house. It was funny that I still thought about it as *our* house. I wonder what my dad would say about that?

I didn't know what time it was, other than after midnight. I wondered if Dad was asleep, awake, or even home. I compromised and thought, instead, of the large oak tree in the corner of the backyard. It was another place I used to read. It was also a place I used to go when Mom and Dad fought, where I couldn't hear the words, even though the volume and anger still carried that far.

I jumped and my eyes opened on a yard that needed mowing. *I'll bet that pisses him off.* I tried picturing him behind the mower, but I just couldn't. I'd done the lawn since I was eleven. He used to sit on the back porch with a beer in his hand and point out the spots I missed.

The house was dark. I moved carefully along until I could see the driveway. His car wasn't there. I pictured the bathroom and jumped again.

The light was out. I flipped the switch and took a bottle of ibuprofen from the medicine cabinet. It was half full. I took a bottle of hydrogen peroxide and some gauze pads as well.

I jumped to the kitchen then, because I was hungry and to see if I still could. He'd bought groceries since the night I'd left for New York. I made myself two ham-and-cheese sandwiches and put them and the stuff from the bathroom in a paper bag I took from the pantry. Then I carefully cleaned up, trying to make it no more clean or messy than I'd found it. I drank two glasses of milk, then washed the glass and put it back in the cabinet.

There was the sound of tires in the driveway, that old sound of dread and tension. I picked up the bag and jumped back to the backyard. I didn't turn off the light, because he would have seen it through the window. I hoped he'd think he'd left it on himself, but I doubted it. He used to scream at me enough for leaving the lights on.

I watched the lights go on down the length of the house—front hall, living room, back hallway. The light in his bedroom went on, then off again. Then the light in my room went on and I saw him silhouetted in the window, a dark outline through the curtains. The light went out then and he walked back to the kitchen. He checked the back door to see if it was locked. I could see his face through the window, puzzled. He started to open the door and I ducked around the trunk of the oak.

"Davy?" he called out, barely raising his voice above conversational level. "Are you out there?"

I remained perfectly still.

I heard his feet scrape on the back porch and then the door shut again. I peered around the trunk and saw him through the kitchen window, taking a beer from the refrigerator. I sighed and jumped to the Stanville Library.

There was a couch with a coffee table in Periodicals that was away from the windows and had one of the lights they left on above it. That's where I ate my sandwiches, feet propped up, chewing and staring off into the dark corners. When I was done eating I washed three ibuprofen down at the water fountain, then used the bathroom.

It was a relief not having to worry about someone crashing through the door. I soaked a few gauze pads with hydrogen peroxide and dabbed at the cut on the back of my head. It stung more than the time before and the pad came away with fresh blood. I winced, but cleaned it as best I could. I didn't want to end up in a hospital with an infection.

I bagged the ibuprofen, gauze, and peroxide, then flushed the used gauze down the toilet. I jumped, then, back to my hotel room in Brooklyn.

My head hurt and I was tired, but sleep was the last thing in the world on my mind.

It was time to see what I could do.

THREE

In Washington Square Park I appeared before a bench that I'd sat upon two days previously. There was a man lying on it, shaking from the cold. He had newspapers tucked around his legs and his fists knotted in the collar of a dirty suit jacket, pulling it close around his neck. He opened his eyes, saw me, and screamed.

I blinked and took a step away from the bench. He sat up, grabbing for his newspapers before they blew away in the light breeze. He stared at me, wild-eyed, still shivering.

I jumped back to the hotel room in Brooklyn and took the blanket from the bed, then jumped back to the park.

He screamed again when I appeared, shrinking back onto the bench. "Leave me alone. Leave me alone. Leave me alone." He repeated it over and over again.

Moving slowly, I put the blanket on the other end of his bench, then walked away down the walk to MacDougal Street. When I'd walked fifty feet or so, I looked back at the bench. He'd picked up the blanket and wrapped it around himself, but he wasn't lying down yet. I wondered if someone was going to steal it from him before morning.

As I neared the street, two men, dark figures silhouetted by the streetlights, blocked my path.

I looked over my shoulder so I wouldn't be taken by surprise again.

"Give us your wallet and your watch." There was the

gleam of a knife in the streetlight; the other man hefted a length of something heavy and hard.

"Too late," I said. And jumped.

I appeared in the Stanville Library, back in front of the shelf that went from "Ruedinger, Cathy" to "Wells, Martha." I smiled. I hadn't had any particular destination in mind when I'd jumped, only escape. Every time I'd jumped from immediate, physical danger, I'd come here, to the safest haven I knew.

I mentally listed all the places I'd teleported to and considered them.

They were all places I'd frequented before jumping to them, either recently, in the case of Washington Square and the New York hotel, or repeatedly over a long period of time. They were places I could picture in my mind. I wondered if that was all it took.

I went to the card catalog and looked up New York. There was a listing under guidebooks, Dewey decimal 917.-471. This led me to the *1986 Foster's Guide to New York City*. On page 323 there was a picture of the lake in Central Park, in color, with a bench and trash can in the foreground, the Loeb Boathouse to one side.

When Mom and I were touring New York, she wouldn't let us go farther into Central Park than the Metropolitan Museum on the park's east side. She'd heard too many stories of muggers and rapes, so we didn't get to see the boathouse. I'd never been there.

I stared at the picture until I could close my eyes and see it.

I jumped and opened my eyes.

I hadn't moved. I was still standing in the library.

Hmph.

I flipped the pages and tried the same thing with other places I hadn't been—Bloomingdale's, the Bronx Zoo, the interior of the base of the Statue of Liberty. None of them worked.

Then I hit a picture of the observation deck of the Empire State Building.

"Look, Mom, that's the Chrysler Building and you can see the World Trade Center and . . .

"Shhhh, Davy. Modulate your voice, please."

That was Mom's expression, "Modulate your voice." Much kinder than saying "Shut up" or "Pipe down" or my dad's "Shut your hole." We'd gone there the second day of that trip and stayed up there an hour. Before I hit the picture I hadn't realized what an impression it made on me. I thought I only had hazy memories of it at best. But now I could remember it clearly.

I jumped and my ears popped, like they do when you take off and land in an airliner. I was standing there, the cold wind off the East River blowing my hair and ruffling the pages of the guidebook I still held in my hands. It was deserted. I looked down into the book and saw that the hours were listed as 9:30 to midnight.

So, I could jump to places I'd been, which was a relief in a way. *If* Dad could teleport, he wouldn't be able to jump into my hotel room in Brooklyn. He'd never been there.

The view was confusing, all the buildings lit, their actual outlines nebulous and blurring together. I saw a distant green floodlit figure and things fell into place. Liberty Island was south of the Empire State and I looked down Fifth Avenue toward Greenwich Village and downtown. The twin towers of the World Trade Center should have clued me in.

I could remember Mom feeding quarters into the mounted telescope so I could see the Statue of Liberty. We didn't go out to the island because Mom was queasy on boats.

I felt a wave of sorrow. Where had Mom gone?

I jumped, then, back to the library and replaced the guidebook on the shelf.

So, was it just any place I'd been?

My granddad, my mother's father, retired to a small house in Florida. My mom and I visited only once, when I was eleven. We were going to go again the next summer, but Mom left in the spring. I had a vague memory of a brightly painted house with white tile on the roof, and a canal in the back with boats. I tried to picture the living room but all I could picture was Granddad in this indefinite, generic sort of room. I tried to jump anyway, and it didn't work.

Hmph.

Memory was important, apparently. I had to have a clear picture of the place, gained from actually being there.

I thought of another experiment to make.

I jumped.

On Forty-fifth Street there is store after store specializing in electronics. Stereo equipment, video equipment, computers, electronic instruments. Everybody was closed when I appeared at the corner of Fifth Avenue and Forty-fifth, including the vendor of Italian ice that I'd patronized the day before.

I could see into the stores, though, their interiors lit for security or display purposes. There were steel bars lowered over most of the windows, secured with massive padlocks, but you could peer between them.

I stopped before one store with wider bars and better lighting than most. I studied the floor, the walls, the way the shelves were arranged, the merchandise closest to the window.

I had a very real sense of location. I was here on the sidewalk just six feet from the inside of the store. I could picture it clearly in my mind. I looked up the street both ways, closed my eyes, and jumped.

Two things happened. First, I appeared inside the store, inches from hundreds of bright, shiny electronic toys. Second, within an instant of my appearance, a siren, very loud and strident, went off both inside and outside the store, followed by the blinding flash of an electronic strobe which lit the interior like a bolt of lightning.

Jesus! I flinched. Then, almost without thought, I jumped back to the Stanville Library.

My knees felt weak. I sat, quickly, on the floor and shook for over a minute.

What was the matter with me? It was just an alarm, some

sort of motion detector. I didn't have this reaction when the two thugs in Washington Square accosted me.

I calmed down. That hadn't been so unexpected, so abrupt. I took several deep breaths. I could probably have stayed there, transferred several VCRs back to my hotel room, before the police showed up.

What would I do with them? I wouldn't know who to sell them to, not without getting ripped off or busted. The very thought of dealing with the kind of people who bought stolen goods made my skin crawl. And what about the store owner? Wouldn't he be hurt? Or would insurance cover it? I started feeling guilty just picturing it.

Another thought set my heart to beating harder and faster. *Maybe that flash was for photos? Maybe they have closed-circuit TV cameras set up?*

I stood up and started pacing across the library, breathing faster, almost gasping.

"Stop it!" I finally said to myself, my voice loud in the quiet building. *How the hell are they going to catch you, even if they had your fingerprints, which they don't? If they did catch you, what jail would hold you? Hell, no merchandise was stolen, no locks forced, no windows broken. Who's going to believe there was someone in the store, much less press charges?*

Suddenly, like a weight descending on my shoulders, I was exhausted, weaving on my feet. My head began to ache again, and I wanted to sleep.

I jumped to the hotel room and kicked off my shoes. The room was chilly, the radiator barely warm. I looked at the thin sheets on the bed. *Inadequate.* I thought about the man in Washington Square Park. *Is he warm enough?*

I jumped into the dark interior of my room in my father's house, scooped up the quilt from the bed, and jumped back to the hotel room.

Then I slept.

It was midday when noise from the street, a horn I think, woke me. I pulled the quilt higher and looked at the cheap hotel room.

It was Wednesday, so I thought my dad should be at the office. I stood up, stretched, and jumped to the bathroom in the house. I listened carefully, then peered around the corner. Nobody. I jumped to the kitchen and looked out at the driveway. His car wasn't there. I used the bathroom, then, and had breakfast.

I can't live off my father forever. The thought made my stomach hurt. What was I going to do about money?

I jumped back to the hotel room and sorted through my clothes for something clean to wear. I was running out of underwear and all of my socks were dirty. I considered going to a store, picking out a selection of clothing, and then jumping without paying the bill. The ultimate shoplifter.

Real class, Davy. I shook my head violently, gathered up all my dirty clothes, and jumped back to my father's house.

There—more and more, I was thinking of it as *his* house, not ours. I considered that a good step.

Well, *he* had left some of *his* clothes in the washing machine without moving them to the dryer. From the smell of the mildew, they'd been there a couple of days. I piled them on the dryer, then started a load of my clothes.

If it was *his* house, then why was I there? *He owes me at least the odd meal and load of laundry.* I refused to feel guilty for taking anything from him.

Of course, while the washer ran, I paced through the house and felt guilty.

It wasn't the food, or doing laundry. I felt guilty about the twenty-two hundred I took from his wallet. It was stupid. The man made good money but made me wear second-hand clothes. He drove a car that cost over twenty thousand dollars but kept me, so he wouldn't have to pay my mom child support.

And I still felt guilty. Angry, too.

I thought about trashing the place, tearing up all the furniture, and burning his clothes. I considered coming back tonight, opening his Cadillac's gas tank and lighting it off. Maybe the house would catch fire, too.

What am I doing? Every minute I stood in that house

made me feel angrier. And the angrier I got, the more guilty I felt. *This is not worth it.* I jumped to Manhattan and walked through Central Park, until I was calm again.

After forty minutes, I jumped back to Dad's house, took the clothes out of the washer and put them in the dryer. Dad's mildewed clothes I put back in the washing machine.

There was something else I needed from the house. I went down the hall to Dad's den—his "office." I wasn't supposed to go in there, but I was a little past caring about his rules and regulations. I started in the three-drawer filing cabinet, then moved to his desk. By the time the clothes were finished drying, I was finished, too, but I hadn't found my birth certificate anywhere.

I slammed the last drawer shut, then gathered my dried clothes up and jumped back to the hotel room.

What am I going to do about money?

I put the clothes on the bed, then jumped to Washington Square, in front of the park bench. There was no sign of the sleeper from the night before. Two old women sat there, deep in conversation. They glanced up at me, but kept on talking; I walked down the sidewalk.

I'd tried to get honest work. They wouldn't take me without a social security number. Most of them also wanted proof of citizenship—either a birth certificate or a voter's registration. I had none of these. I thought about illegal aliens working in the U.S. How did they get around this problem?

They buy fake documents.

Ah. When I'd walked down Broadway in Time's Square, several guys had offered me everything from drugs to women to little boys. I bet they'd also know about fake IDs.

But I have no money.

I felt very third world, caught in a trap between needing money to make money and no superpower's loan in sight. If I didn't pay my hotel bill the next day, I was also back out on the street. I would need some form of debt relief.

The shriek from the Forty-second Street burglar alarm seemed less frightening in broad daylight. I thought about stealing VCRs or TVs and hocking them at pawn shops, then using the money to try and buy fake ID.

The thought of carrying a VCR into a pawnshop frightened me. I didn't care that I was uncatchable. If someone was itchy enough I might take a bullet. Perhaps I was being paranoid. If I stole something worth more? Jewelry? Go to the museum and rip off paintings? The more expensive the item, the more chance I had of not making any money from it, getting ripped off or killed.

Maybe the government would hire me?

I shuddered. I read *Firestarter* by Stephen King. I could imagine being dissected to find out how I did this thing. Or drugged so I wouldn't do it—that's how they controlled the father in that book. Kept him on drugs so he couldn't think straight. I wondered if they already had people who could teleport.

Stay away from the government. Don't let anyone know what I can do!

Well, then—I guessed I'd have to steal money itself.

The Chemical Bank of New York is on Fifth Avenue. I walked in and asked the guard if there was a bathroom in the bank. He shook his head.

"Up the street at the Trump Tower. They have a rest room in the lobby."

I looked distressed. "Look, I really don't mean to be a problem, but my dad's meeting me here in just a few moments, and if I'm not here he'll *kill* me, but I really got to pee. Isn't there an employees' rest room somewhere?"

I didn't think he'd buy it, but the lie, plus any mention of my father, was making my distress real. He looked doubtful and I winced, knowing he was going to send me away.

"Ah, what the hell. See that door there?" He pointed to a door past the long line of teller's windows. "Go through there and straight back. The bathroom is on the right at the end of the hall. If anyone gives you a problem, tell them Kelly sent you."

I let out a lungful of air. "Thanks, Mr. Kelly. You've saved my life."

I went through the door as if I knew what I was doing. My stomach was churning and I felt sure that everyone who passed me could read my intentions and knew I was a criminal.

The vault was two doors before the bathroom. Its huge steel door hung on hinges larger than myself, open, but a smaller door of bars within was shut and a guard sat before it, at a small table. I paused before him, looking past him to the interior of the vault. He looked up at me.

"Can I help you?" His voice was cold and he stared at me like a high school principal looks at a student without a hall pass.

I stammered, "I'm looking for the bathroom."

The guard said, "There are no *public* rest rooms in this bank."

"Mr. Kelly said I could use the employees' rest room. It's kind of an emergency."

He relaxed a little. "End of the hall then. It's certainly not *here.*"

I bobbed my head. "Right. Thank you." I walked on. I really hadn't gotten a good enough look. I went into the bathroom and washed my hands.

On the way back I stopped and said, "That sure is a huge door. Do you know how much it weighs?" I stepped a bit closer.

The guard looked annoyed. "A lot. If you're quite through using the bathroom, I would appreciate it if you returned to the lobby!"

I pivoted. "Oh, certainly." I stared at the door again from my new angle. I saw carts and a table up against one of vault's interior doors. The carts had canvas bags on them, as well as stacks of bundled money. Another step and I glimpsed gray steel shelves against another wall.

Got it!

The guard started to stand up. I looked away from the door and saw his face color.

"On my way," I said. "Thanks for your directions."

He growled something, but I walked briskly down the

hall. As I walked past the lobby guard, I smiled. "Thanks, Mr. Kelly."

He waved and I went out the door.

I spent the rest of the afternoon in the library, back in Stanville, first reading the encyclopedia entries under Banks, Bank Robberies, Alarm Systems, Safes, Vaults, Time Locks, and Closed-Circuit Television, then skimming a book on industrial security systems that I found in Applied Technologies.

"David? David Rice?"

I looked up. Mrs. Johnson, my geography teacher from Stanville High School, was walking toward me. I looked at the clock—school had been out for an hour.

I hadn't been to school in three weeks, ever since the first day I had jumped. I felt my face get hot and I stood up.

"It really is you, David. I'm glad to see you're all right. Have you gone home then?"

For some reason I was surprised that the school knew I'd run away. I started to agree. It was so much easier to lie, to say I'd come back and that I'd be in school tomorrow. I know that's what I would have done a month before. Take the path of least resistance. Avoid fuss. Say whatever was necessary to keep people from being mad at me.

I hated for people to be mad at me.

I shook my head. "No, ma'am. I haven't. And I'm not going to."

She didn't seem shocked or even surprised. "Your father seems very worried. He came up to the school and talked to all your classes, asking if anyone had seen you. He's also put up those posters . . . well, you've probably seen them around town."

I blinked, then shrugged. *Posters?*

"What about school?" she asked. "What are you going do about classes? How are you going to go to college? Or get a job?"

"I . . . I guess I'll have to make other arrangements." I felt good about not lying to her, but was still afraid she was going to disapprove of me. "I tried to take the GED," I said. "But they won't let a seventeen-year-old take it without parental permission or a court order."

Mrs. Johnson licked her lower lip, then asked, "Where are you staying, David? Are you getting enough to eat?"

"Yes, ma'am. I'm okay."

Her words seemed chosen very carefully. It dawned on me that she wasn't going to bawl me out for missing school or for running away. It was as if she was trying to avoid spooking me—avoid scaring me off.

"I'm going to phone your father, David. It's my duty. However, if you like we can talk to the county social worker. You don't have to go home if you don't want to." She hesitated and then finally said, "Does he abuse you, David?"

The tears came then, like an anvil falling out of a clear blue sky. I thought I was fine up until then. I squeezed my eyes shut, and my shoulders were shaking. I kept quiet, stifling the sobs.

Mrs. Johnson took a step toward me, I think to hug me. I recoiled, stepping back and turning away, wiping furiously at my eyes with my right hand.

She dropped her arms to her side. She looked unhappy.

I took a deep, shuddering breath, then two more, the shakes gradually diminishing. "Sorry," I said.

Mrs. Johnson spoke then, softly, carefully. "I won't call your father, but only if you come see Mr. Mendoza with me. He'll know what to do."

I shook my head. "No. I'm doing okay. I don't want to go see Mr. Mendoza."

She looked even more unhappy. "Please, Davy. It's not safe on the street, even in Stanville, Ohio. We can protect you from your father."

Oh, yeah? Where were you for the last five years? I shook my head again. This was going nowhere.

"Do you still drive a gray VW, Mrs. Johnson?" I said, looking over her shoulder.

She blinked, surprised by the change of subject. "Yes."

"I think somebody just hit it."

She turned her head quickly. Before she figured out that

you couldn't see the parking lot from where we were standing, I jumped back to the Brooklyn hotel.

God damn it all to hell! I threw the industrial-security book across the room, then scrambled to get it, a wave of guilt washing over me, both about getting angry and about mistreating a library book. Books didn't deserve to be abused . . . did people?

I curled up on the bed and pulled the pillow over my head.

It was dark when I sat up, dazed and uncomprehending, waking in slow, confusing stages. For a moment I looked around, expecting to find Mrs. Johnson standing over me and telling me many fascinating facts about western Africa, but I woke up a little more and the dim light coming through the thin shade revealed the room, my condition, my state of being.

I stood up and stretched, wondered what time it was, and jumped to the Stanville Library to look at their wall clock. It was 9:20 P.M. in Ohio, and the same in New York. Time to get to work.

I jumped to my backyard, behind the oak tree. Dad's car was in the driveway, but the only lights on were in his room, the den, and my room. *What's he doing with my room?* I felt panic rising, but forced it down. *Ignore it. You'll be able to get to your room.*

The gardening stuff was in the garage, on a shelf above the lawn mower. Rakes, shovels, and a hoe hung on nails across the wall below the shelf. I appeared before this collection and groped past insecticides, fertilizer, grass seed until my hands closed on the old gardening gloves. I put them on, then jumped to the front driveway.

Dad's Caddy gleamed in the streetlight, a huge, hulking beast. I walked to the passenger side and tried the door, gently. It was locked. I looked in, at the plush upholstery and the gleaming dash. I could vividly remember the smell of it, the feel of the seats. I closed my eyes and jumped.

The car alarm went off with a whooping shriek, but I was expecting it. I opened the glove compartment and took the

flashlight. The porch light came on and the front door
started to open. I jumped to my room.

The alarm sounded a great deal quieter from here, but
still unpleasant. I was sure that porch lights were coming on
all over the neighborhood.

The ski mask was in the bottom drawer of my dresser,
buried under several pairs of too-small long underwear. I
found it just as the car alarm stopped. I started to jump,
then realized I didn't have the flashlight in my hand. I
looked around the room and saw it on the dresser.

The front door shut and I heard footsteps in the hallway.
I picked up the flashlight and jumped.

The gloves were leather, old and stiff. They hurt my
fingers just to bend them. The ski mask was large enough,
even though it was four years old. All the stretch was gone
and it was pulled out of shape, but I thought it would work.
Positioned right, it covered all of my face except my eyes
and the bridge of my nose. The bottom half hung loosely
over the rest of my face, but it concealed it.

It itched like hell.

I jumped.

I appeared in a pitch black room with dead air and a
smooth floor. I waited a moment before I turned on the
light, steeling myself for the scream of an alarm. I was also
afraid I wasn't in the right place and didn't want to rush the
moment of failure's discovery.

I didn't hear any alarms, though, for all I knew, lights
could be flashing on a dozen monitor consoles from the
bank all the way to the police station. If there were other
teleporters in the world, wouldn't banks know about them
and take measures? Like flooding the'vault with poison gas
when it was locked? Or booby traps? The air around me
turned thick, and the darkness pressed in on me until I
thought that perhaps the very walls were moving in. I
flicked the flashlight switch without conscious volition.

So much money!

The carts I'd seen earlier were stacked high—either with
neatly bundled piles of money or with trays of rolled coins

or rough canvas bags with "Chemical Bank of New York" stenciled on their sides. Most of the shelves held bundled stacks of new bills.

I closed my eyes, suddenly dizzy. By the vault door there was a light switch. I turned it on and fluorescent lighting lit the room. There didn't seem to be any TV cameras in the vault, and I couldn't see any little boxes on the wall that looked like any of the heat sensors I'd read about that afternoon. No gas flooded from vents. No booby traps sprang into action.

I turned off the flashlight and went to work.

The first cart I came to was obviously from the previous day's deposits. The money was definitely used, though bundled neatly. I picked up a stack of one-hundred-dollar bills. The paper band wrapped around the middle said "$5,000" and was stamped with the Chemical Bank's name. There was a cardboard box on another cart. It was filled with packets of one-dollar bills, each packet holding fifty bills. I tried to estimate how deep the stack went, then shook my head. *Count later, Davy.*

I picked up the box and jumped to the hotel room. I dumped it on the bed, then jumped back.

I started at one end and moved to the other. If the packets looked new, I checked to see if the bills were in serial-number order. If they were I left them. If they weren't I put them in the box. When the box was full, I jumped to the hotel room, dumped the contents on the bed, and jumped back.

When I was done with the loose money on the carts, I checked the bags. They seemed to be transfer deposits from subbranches, all in used bills. I took all the bags, without checking the contents of the others. Money was already spilling off the edges of the bed so I put the bags on the floor, under the bed.

The shelves held new bills, the range of their serial numbers neatly written on their paper bands. I left them and took a last look around. Still no ringing alarms. The door was solidly shut.

It didn't matter. If what I had read about time clocks was

true, it would take a very special set of circumstances to open the door before the next morning, even if alarms were ringing.

For one brief second I considered leaving a thank-you note, perhaps even some spray-painted graffiti, but decided against it.

I imagined there would be enough excitement the next morning without that.

I jumped.

FOUR

On Times Square the big electronic billboard said it was
eleven o'clock. I blinked. I'd done the whole thing in under
forty minutes, and that included getting the gloves and the
flashlight.

People still swarmed the square, young adults mostly, in
pairs and groups. Some of them lined up at movie theaters,
others just walked along Broadway looking into the stores
that were still open. There was a festival atmosphere like the
midway of carnival.

I walked into a shop filled with T-shirts, most of them
extolling the virtues of New York City. "Welcome to New
York City—Now Leave," said one. I smiled, even though I
was trembling and reaction was making me nauseated.

In my pocket was a packet of twenty-dollar bills, fifty of
them. I'd taken off the paper wrapper and made sure I could
pull them out one at a time, but I was still nervous. The
back of my head, where the muggers had hit me, was aching
and I kept looking over my shoulder in almost involuntary
twitches.

*Christ, Davy, you're broadcasting victim like crazy. Calm
down!*

The T-shirt store also sold luggage—cheap nylon bags,
duffles, overnighters, sports bags, and backpacks. That's
what I really wanted. I picked up one of each kind and
color.

The clerk stared at me, then said, "Hey, kid, unless you're going to buy all of those, look at one at a time, okay?"

I kept on picking up bags and he came around the end of the counter, an angry expression on his face. "Didn't you hear me? I said—"

"I heard what you said!" My voice was shrill and loud. The clerk took a step back and blinked. I took a deep breath, then said in a quieter voice, "I've got twenty bags here. Ring them up." I walked over to the counter and put the bags on it.

The clerk still hesitated, so I took some of the twenties out of my jacket pocket—more than I meant to, in fact. Probably half, around five hundred dollars.

"Uh, sure. Sorry I yelled. You know we get some kids in here who shoplift. I've got to be careful. Didn't mean nothing by it. I—"

"Fine. Don't worry about it. Just ring it up, please."

As he rang up each bag, I stuffed them into the largest one, a duffel with a shoulder strap.

He must have felt bad about misreading me, because he gave me a ten-percent discount for quantity. "So that comes to two twenty-two fifty with tax."

I counted off twelve twenty-dollar bills, then said something I've always wanted to say. "Keep the change."

He blinked, then said, "Thanks. Thanks very much."

I walked out the front of the store, turned right, and jumped.

I sorted the money by denomination first, piling the packets against the wall opposite the bed. I had to move the cheap dresser across the door to give me room, but I didn't mind. I was feeling pretty paranoid by now, so I hung the quilt over the window shade, completely blocking the window.

By the time I cleared the bed and had reached the bagged money, I had two piles of ones over two feet high, twenty-five packets to a layer. I didn't stop to figure amounts yet. I continued my sorting, throwing the empty bank bags on the bed. Once, I jumped to the Stanville Library to check the time.

Finally, I finished sorting and stacking. I hadn't figured amounts yet. That would come later.

I gathered the empty bank bags, then, and put my ski mask and gloves back on. It was 2 A.M.

I took several deep breaths and tried to keep calm. Nervous exhaustion was setting in, though I wasn't in the least sleepy. I concentrated on the interior of the vault and jumped, trying at the same time to keep the Stanville Library in my mind in case they'd opened the vault.

They hadn't.

Jeez, I left the light on. I dropped the bank bags on one of the empty carts and turned to turn off the light. *Light? Christ! Where's the flashlight?* My heartbeat increased and I felt panic in my throat. *Oh, God. I don't need this.* I sagged against the wall when I saw the flashlight on the first cart I'd emptied. I knew it didn't have my fingerprints but it might have Dad's. *And where were you, Mr. Rice, last Friday night?*

Right here in Ohio, of course. But I don't know where my son is. . . .

I picked the flashlight up, turned off the vault's lights, and jumped back to the hotel room.

I'd been hurrying, stacking the money so I could take the bags back before morning. I didn't want them in my possession. I realized that I could get rid of them anywhere. I could even put bricks in them and drop them into the East River, but I thought that there'd be more confusion if I left them in the vault.

As if there isn't going to be enough confusion as it is.

Still, I'd been in a hurry, so I hadn't really looked at how much money I'd stolen. I sat back on the bed and stared.

Each layer of the piles was five packets by five. Call it a little over a foot along the wall by two and a half feet out from the wall. There were more ones than any other denomination, three stacks each over four feet high. There was one stack of fives just under two feet high, one stack of tens about a foot and a half high, one stack of twenties about nine inches high, almost one layer of fifty-dollar bills, and seventeen packets of hundred-dollar bills.

I jumped to the Stanville Library and borrowed a calculator from behind the circulation desk. I counted the layers and did all my calculations twice. I did them more than twice if the first two times didn't match.

There were twenty-five packets per layer. That meant there were, for instance, twelve hundred and fifty dollars per layer of ones and twenty-five thousand dollars per layer of twenties. I had one hundred and fifty-three layers and six packets of ones, which gave me, in singles alone . . . I dropped the calculator onto my lap and fell back onto the bed shaking.

I had one hundred and ninety-one thousand and four hundred dollars in one-dollar bills. When all the calculations were done and redone, I had a nine hundred fifty-three thousand and fifty dollars, not counting the seven hundred and sixty dollars in my jacket pocket.

Nearly a million dollars.

Since there were seventeen packets of hundred-dollar bills, I divided the five-through-hundred-denomination packets into seventeen of the nylon bags. This gave me almost fifty thousand per bag, give or take a year's salary. Then I stuffed enough one-dollar packets in each one to fill it the rest of the way up. In some bags this added as little as seven hundred dollars. In some of the bigger bags it added as much as thirty-two hundred dollars. Then I stuffed the last three bags, the larger duffels, with one-dollar packets, until they were almost too heavy to pick up. There was still a pile of ones two feet high. I counted the layers and put it at thirty thousand dollars. Even when I refilled the cardboard box from the vault there was twenty-five hundred dollars left.

Jesus! Where am I going to put this stuff?

From the street outside there was the sound of a siren, an almost continual noise in New York, but this one was closer than most. I stopped breathing. When the sound continued past, I drew in a shuddering breath and cold sweat beaded my forehead. It reminded me how dangerous this neighborhood was. It reminded me of the bathroom incident just down the hall and of my mugging.

Here I was, a rich man for only an hour, and I was paranoid already. *Money doesn't solve all problems,* I thought. *It just makes new ones.*

I wondered what time it was. *I've got to get a watch!* I jumped to the Stanville Library and saw that it was 3:30 A.M. I put the calculator back behind Circulation and was about to jump back when I glanced up.

The Stanville Library was built in 1910, a large granite building with fourteen-foot-high ceilings. I knew this because Ms. Tonovire, the librarian, used to practice her tour on me. When they added air-conditioning to the library, in 1973, they put in a suspended ceiling to cover the ductwork. This was about ten feet high.

I climbed the magazine shelves back in Periodicals and pushed on one of the foot-and-a-half-by-three-foot panels. It lifted up and slid to one side. It was dark above.

I jumped back to the hotel room and moved ten of the bags to the top of that duct, spacing them out to distribute the weight. I also put the box of ones there.

The hotel room seemed empty without the piles of money or the jumble of filled nylon bags. The one bag that was left I zipped shut and slid under the bed. Then I took off my shoes, turned off the light, and lay down.

My body was tired but my brain raced, nervous, excited, exalted, guilty. *I don't want to get caught. Don't let me get caught!* I shifted, trying to make my body comfortable. My mind wouldn't stop. I kept hearing noises in the street and couldn't sleep. I tried to reassure myself. *How would they catch you? If you spend the money carefully, you're home free. Besides, they couldn't keep you, even if they had a clue that you'd done it.*

I rolled over on my side.

The library? What if they decide to clean the tops of shelves? Won't they be suspicious when they find my footprints in the dust? I shook my head and tried to burrow deeper into the pillow.

I tried deep breathing. It didn't work. I tried counting backward from a thousand but that brought up images of the money-stacks and stacks of money. The fifty or so thousand dollars under the bed seemed to push at me through the bed, seemed to have a presence that was almost animate. *Dammit, it's just a bag of paper!* I pounded the pillow, pushing and rearranging it, then firmly closed my eyes.

An interminable amount of time later, I sighed, sat up, put my shoes back on, and jumped to the library.

Only when I'd dusted the top of every shelf in the building and dawn sunlight was coming in the windows of the library could I put the duster away, jump back to Brooklyn, and fall asleep.

"Well, what kind of watch are you looking for?"

"I want one that lets you see what time it is in several different time zones. It should also have an alarm of some kind, be waterproof, and look classy without being pretentious. I want it to look nice in dressy situations, but I don't want to be hit over the head every time I walk through a questionable neighborhood, just because I'm wearing it."

The clerk laughed. He was a wearing a closely trimmed beard and a yarmulke, the little circular hat some Jews wear. It was new to me—I'd only seen them before on TV. He spoke. "Given it some thought, I see. What was the price range you wanted?"

"Doesn't matter. I just want those features."

The store was on Forty-seventh Street, a jewelry/electronics "boutique." I'd come here first thing, jumping to the subway at Grand Central Station, then walking the remaining six blocks.

The clerk pulled three different watches out of the case.

"All three of these do what you want—the time zone thing and alarms. This is the cheapest—it's fifty-five ninety-five."

I looked at it. "Not very dressy."

He nodded, very agreeable. "Yeah. These other two are much classier. This one"—he pointed at a watch in gold metal with a gold and silver metal strap—"lists for three hundred and seventy. I think we have it on special for two ninety-five." He pointed at the other one, a slim watch with a lizard-skin strap. "This one doesn't look as flashy as the other one, but it's gold-clad silver where this guy"—he held up the gold-metal-banded watch,—"is anodized stainless steel."

I prodded the slim watch. "How much?"

He grinned. "Thirteen ninety-six and thirty-five cents."

I blinked. He started to put the expensive watch away. "I love to watch a customer's eyes when I tell them that. It's not as if we're up on Fifth Avenue. I don't know why it's even in the inventory."

I held up my hand. "I'll take it."

"Huh. This one?" He reached for the flashy gold watch with his other hand.

"No. That one, the fourteen-hundred-dollar job. What's that with tax?" I thought for a moment, then reached into my right front pocket—that's where I'd put twenty hundred-dollar bills. When I started counting them out onto the counter, he grabbed his calculator quickly.

Behind him a row of televisions of varying size and shape all showed the same program, an afternoon soap opera. It ended and a "News Before the Hour" logo came on, then showed the outside of the Chemical Bank of New York. I stared. Reporters poked microphones at a grim-faced man who was reading from a sheet of paper. None of the sets had the volume on.

The clerk noticed and looked over my shoulder. "Oh, the bank robbery. Won't be long before they get them."

My stomach was hurting and I felt like my knees would collapse. I managed to say one word: "Oh?"

"A million dollars gone from the vault from the time they closed it to the time they opened it again? It had to be an inside job. If that money wasn't there when they opened the safe then it wasn't there when they closed it."

"I hadn't heard."

"The news broke at eleven-thirty," he said, counting my change out on the counter. "Apparently a teller tipped the press. There, fifteen hundred and eleven fifty-five out of fifteen twenty leaves eight forty-five." He looked back at the TV. "Whoever did it is going to have to hold that money for a long time."

I carefully stowed the change. "Why's that?"

"Well, all the employees with access are probably going to be watched like hawks. When they spend one penny they can't account for, whammo!" He handed me the receipt and warranty card for the watch. "You need anything else? A nice VCR? A camcorder? Computer?"

All that neat stuff—but I didn't have any place to put it yet. "Perhaps later."

"Any time. Any time at all."

I ate at the Jockey Club in the Ritz Carlton, just south of the park. The bell captain looked at me funny when I walked through the lobby and down the stairs to the restaurant, but the hostess saw me to a table and acted like it was a pleasure. I picked the most expensive thing on the lunch menu.

While I waited for the food I played with the controls on my watch and watched the other patrons to see how they were dressed and how they acted in a fancy restaurant. There were fresh flowers on each table and the waiter brought hot rolls and butter automatically.

I didn't have much experience in restaurants—not since Mom left. She'd tried to do more than show me how to eat with my mouth closed, but I was self-conscious.

When the food came, I only ate half of it. There was too much of it and I wasn't too hungry. The news program had upset me, made me paranoid again.

I tried to pay the waiter when he brought the bill, but he gently corrected me. "I can take this up to the cashier for you, if you wish, or you can just pay on the way out."

I said I would do that and thought for a moment how he'd guided me without making me feel stupid. If it had been my father he would have said, "Pay the cashier, dipshit. Don't you know anything?" The difference was considerable. I left the waiter a twenty-dollar tip.

Paying for a fifty-dollar lunch seemed unreal, just as buying the watch earlier seemed a game. It was like playing with Monopoly money, like playing make-believe.

What would you do, Davy, if you were rich?

I'd be happy. I walked across the street and into Central Park, green and lush, and somehow *alien* in the middle of all the concrete and steel.

Well, I can try.

PART 2:

THE PURSUIT OF HAPPINESS

FIVE

I met Millie during the intermission of a Broadway revival of *Sweeney Todd, The Demon Barber of Fleet Street.* It was my sixth time to see it. After paying the first time, I just popped to an alcove at the back of the mezzanine five minutes after eight. The houselights are off by then and I would find a seat without any trouble. If it looked like someone arrived late and was headed for my claimed seat, I would bend down as if to tie my shoe and jump back to the alcove. Then locate another empty seat.

I don't mind paying, but I often don't decide until after curtain time that I want to see it. Then the box-office attendant will waste my time trying to get me to buy a ticket for another night. Too much trouble.

This was a Thursday-night show and the crowd was surprisingly heavy. I was pressed against the balcony railing drinking overpriced ginger ale and watching the lines at the bathrooms.

"And what are you smiling about?"

I jerked my head around. For a moment I thought it was one of the ushers about to evict me as a gate crasher, but it was this woman, not much older than me but apparently over twenty-one—at least, she was drinking champagne.

"Are you talking to me?"

"Sure. Maybe that's presumptuous of me, but in a crowd this dense, intimacy is a foregone conclusion."

"Well, yes it is. My name is David."

"Millie," she said with a vague wave of her hand. She was wearing a dressy blouse and black slacks. She was pretty, wore owl-like glasses, no makeup, and had her shiny, black hair cut long on top, then tapering in to the neck. "So what were you smiling about?"

I frowned. "Oh . . . I guess I was feeling a little superior, not having to wait in line. Does this temporary intimacy extend to talking about bathrooms?"

She shrugged. "Why not? I'd be in line myself, but I ducked out in the first act. I'll probably have to do it again later. What's your secret? Bladder of iron?"

I turned red. "Something like that."

"Are you blushing? Wow, I thought teenage males talked about bodily functions continuously. My brothers certainly do."

"It's hot in here."

"Yeah. Okay. We won't talk about excretory functions anymore. Any other taboo subjects?"

"I'd rather not give you any ideas."

She laughed. "Touché. You a local?"

"Sort of. I travel a lot, but this is home for now."

"I'm not. I'm here for a week of the touristy stuff. Gotta go back to school in two weeks."

"Where's that?"

"Oklahoma State, majoring in psych."

I thought for a moment. "Stillwater?"

"Yeah. I guess you do travel."

"Not to Oklahoma. My grandfather went to school there, back when it was Oklahoma Agricultural and Mechanical."

"Where do you go to school?"

"I don't. Haven't the aptitude."

She looked over her glasses at me. "You don't sound particularly stupid."

I blushed again. "I'm just taking my time."

The lights began dimming for the second act. She finished her champagne and dropped the plastic glass in the trash. Then she stuck out her hand.

I took it. She pumped it twice firmly and said, "Nice talking to you, David. Enjoy the rest of the show."

"You too, Millie."

I cried during the second act. Sweeney's wife, who's had her child stolen away from her and has been driven mad by rape, is revealed to be the mad, dissolute street beggar/prostitute, but only after Sweeney kills her when she witnesses the murder of her rapist, Judge Turpin.

The first time I saw this scene I decided I didn't like it. I went away, in fact, with a very negative impression of the show. It was only after I found myself examining the face of every bag lady on the street to see if she was my mother that I realized why I didn't like the scene.

Still, I didn't stop looking at bag ladies and, after a while, I started returning to *Sweeney Todd*.

I skipped the finale and jumped to Grand Central Terminal. It's one of the places you can find a cab late at night. I stuck my hand out and this black man, perhaps twenty-five and raggedly dressed, jumped out in the street. "Cab? You need a cab? I'll get you a cab."

I could have walked to the regulated taxi stand on the Vanderbilt Avenue side, but what the heck. I nodded.

He stuck a chrome police whistle in his teeth and blew it, two sharp piercing blasts. Down the block a cab pulled over two lanes and pulled up. The black guy held the door for me. I handed him a bill.

"Hey, man. Two dollars to get a cab. Two dollars."

"That's a ten."

He stepped back, surprised. "Oh. Yeah. Thanks, man."

I had the cabbie go back across Forty-fifth to the theater where *Sweeney* was showing and had him park it on the curb. I stood on the sidewalk, one foot still in the cab, and fended off people who wanted the cab. "I'm picking someone up. This cab is taken. I've already got this cab. Sorry. No, I don't want to share this cab. I'm waiting for someone. Go away."

I was beginning to question this endeavor when Millie finally appeared, looking very New York with her purse around one shoulder and her neck, her face very determined and purposeful.

"Millie!"

She turned, surprise on her face. "David. How did you get a cab?"

I waved my hands and shrugged. "Magic. Let me give you a lift."

She came closer. "You don't know which way I'm going."

"So."

"I'm staying down in the Village."

"Close enough for government work. Get in." I held the door for her and told the driver, "Sheridan Square." I frowned. *Close enough for government work.* My dad used that phrase. I wondered what other things I did that were like my father.

Millie frowned. "Where is that?"

"It's in the heart of the Village. It's also near some really great restaurants. You hungry?"

"What is this? I thought we were just sharing a taxi." She was smiling, though. "How much is the fare going to be? I was going to take the subway back. I didn't exactly budget for a cab. I'd heard how impossible it is to get one after the theaters let out."

"Well, it's true. It felt like planet of the zombie taxi-seekers there while I waited for you."

"You were waiting for me?" She looked nervous for a moment. "My mother told me not to talk to strangers. How much is the cab going to be?"

"Forget the cab. I offered a lift, not half a taxi. And I'm good for something to eat if you want."

"Hmmm. Just how old are you, David?"

I blushed and looked at my watch. "In forty-seven minutes I'll be eighteen." I looked away from her, at the passing lights and sidewalks. I remembered the events surrounding my seventeenth birthday and shuddered.

"Oh. Well happy almost birthday." She stared ahead. "You act older than that. You dress awfully nice and you don't talk that young."

I shrugged. "I read a great deal . . . and I can afford to dress like this."

"You must have some job."

I wondered what I was doing in this cab with this woman. Lonely. "I don't have a job, Millie. I don't need one."

"Your parents are that rich?"

I thought about Dad, the skinflint, with his Cadillac and his bottle. "My dad does all right, but I don't take anything from him. I have my own money—banking interests."

"You don't go to school and you don't work? What do you do?"

I smiled without humor. "I read a lot."

"You said that."

"Well . . . it's true."

She looked out the window on the other side of the cab. Both her hands clutched tightly around her purse. Finally she turned back and said, "I ate before the show, but some cappuccino or espresso at one of those sidewalk cafés would be nice."

A couple of days after the bank robbery, when my nerves had settled somewhat, I moved into the Gramercy Park hotel. This was nice for a while, but the atmosphere of the hotel and the size of the room got to me after a month.

I started looking for an apartment in the Village, first, but, even though I could afford things there, most of the places wanted references and ID and bank accounts—stuff I didn't have. Finally I found a place in East Flatbush for half the money with half the hassle. I got a year's lease and paid the landlord in postal money orders for the deposit and three months' rent.

He seemed happy.

Shortly after I moved in, I did some minor repairs, added iron brackets on both sides of the doors to hold two-by-four drop bars, and walled up a walk-in closet off the hall. When I was done, it was just another blank wall, a room without an entrance.

Except to me, that is.

And, except for the odd pounding, which I was careful to

do during the day while my downstairs neighbors were at work, nobody was the wiser since I'd jumped the materials directly into the apartment from a lumberyard in Yonkers. Nobody saw me carry the lengths of two-by-fours or Sheetrock into the apartment.

I moved the money from the library after that, stacking it neatly on the shelves in the hidden closet and devoting an entire week to replacing the Chemical Bank paper straps with rubber bands and then burning the paper straps in the kitchen sink.

Before that, I just knew that I was going to show up at the library and find a policeman waiting for me. Now the worst I feared was the landlord coming in and wondering what I'd done with the closet.

Covering the wall so cleanly really did something for me. It wasn't something I bought with money. It wasn't something someone else did for me. It left me feeling good about myself.

I resolved to do more work with my hands in the future.

To furnish the apartment I bought only furniture that I could lift. If something was too big for me to lift, it had to break apart into liftable pieces. That way I could jump them directly to the apartment.

Most of my furniture purchases were bookshelves. Most of my other purchases were books.

Millie was in town for four more days. She let me follow her through several traditional New York sights—the Bronx Zoo, the Metropolitan Museum, the Empire State Building. I took her to see two more Broadway shows and to a dinner at Tavern on the Green. She accepted them reluctantly.

"You're really sweet, David, but you're three and a half years younger than me. I don't like you spending money on me under false pretenses."

We were walking in Central Park across the Sheep Meadow on our way to the mall. Kites, bright daubs of flitting pigment, tried to paint the sky. Bicyclists went by in clumps on the sidewalk on the other side of the fence.

"What's false about it? First of all, I am not trying to create an implicit contract between the two of us. I have this money and I like spending time with you. The only thing I expect from it is the time itself. Time that I'm not alone. I wouldn't *mind* something else, but I don't expect to buy it.

"And this age thing is a crock of sexist shit. I'm surprised at you."

She frowned. "What's sexist about it?"

"If I were three years older than you, romantic involvement would be possible, even probable. Have you ever dated someone that much older than you?"

She blushed.

I went on. "I think it's acceptable in society because older men have accumulated more worldly goods. Therefore they make better suitors. Perhaps that's the original reason. Perhaps it's that alpha male crap. Older bulls have survived longer, making their genes worth coveting. Aren't you above those outdated factors? Are you going to let a male idea of what and who you should be make your choices for you?"

"Give me a break, David!"

I shrugged. "If you don't want to spend the time with me for other reasons, just say so. Just don't use that age thing." I stared down at my feet and said in a quieter voice, "I have to put up with enough shit because of my age."

She didn't say anything for a long time, until we were walking past the fountain café. My ears started to burn and I was mad at myself—almost ashamed for some reason. I wished I'd kept my mouth shut.

"It's not particularly fair, is it," she said, finally. "We get this conditioning, this mind-set. It's pumped into us from the time we're little kids." She stopped walking when we were back on the sidewalk, and sat on a nearby bench. "Let me try it another way. It's not fair to get involved with you, not for either of us, when I'm flying back to Stillwater tomorrow."

I shrugged. "I already travel a great deal. OSU isn't that far out of the way."

She shook her head. "I just don't know."

"Come on." I grabbed her hand and pulled her up. "I'll buy you an Italian ice."

She laughed. "No. I'll buy *you* an Italian ice. My budget will stretch that far." She held on to my hand after she was up. "And I'll try to keep an open mind about things."

"What sort of things?"

"Things! Just things. Shut up. And quit smiling."

It wasn't until after I got the apartment that I went back to Dad's house. While I was staying in the Gramercy Park, I had the hotel do my laundry and I ate room service if I didn't want to go out, so I had less reason than usual to jump back to Stanville.

My second day in the apartment, though, I needed a hammer and a nail to hang a framed print I'd bought in the Village. I could have jumped to a store, but I wanted to hang it right then.

I jumped directly to Dad's garage and rummaged through the shelves for a nail. I'd found one and was picking up the hammer when I heard footsteps. I glanced out the garage door windows and saw the top of Dad's car.

Oh. It's Saturday.

The door from the kitchen started to open and I jumped back to my apartment.

I hit my thumb twice while pounding in the nail for the picture. Then, when I hung it, I found that I'd put it too low and had it to do all over again, including hitting my thumb.

Damn him, anyway!

I jumped back to the garage, threw the hammer down on the workbench with a loud clatter, and jumped back to the apartment.

Serve him right, I thought, to come running back in again and find nothing.

The next week I jumped to the house and, after determining he wasn't home, did a load of laundry. While the washer ran I walked through the house, seeing what was changed.

The house was much neater than when I'd done laundry four weeks previously. I wondered if he had hired someone since I wasn't there anymore to do the housework. His room was not quite as neat, socks and shirts thrown in a pile in the corner. A pair of slacks hung crookedly over the back of a chair. I remembered finding Dad's wallet when I'd pulled a pair of pants like those off him. That was when I'd found the hundred dollar bills.

The back of my head throbbed, as usual, when I remembered that money. Most of that money had been taken from me when I was mugged in Brooklyn. I felt a twinge of guilt.

Hell.

It took me less than half a minute to jump back to my money closet, pull twenty-two hundred-dollar bills, and jump back. The money made a nice pattern on his bedspread, five rows of four, with a single hundred dollar bill for each side.

I thought about him coming back into the house and finding them there, laid out. I savored the surprise, the shock, and thought about the language he'd use.

When I took the clothes out of the dryer, I resolved to find some other place to do my laundry. I liked the feeling of being out of debt to him.

The only things I would take from the house from now on, I resolved, would be things from my room, things that belonged to me. Nothing else from him. Not a solitary thing.

I started looking for other jumpers in the places I was most comfortable—libraries. My sources were books I used to laugh at, shelved in the occult/ESP section. There wasn't much I could credit as anything more than folklore, but I found myself reading them with a desperate intensity.

There were an awful lot of books in the "woo-woo" section of the library: pretty bizarre stuff—rains of frogs, circles in wheat fields, hauntings, prophets, people with past lives, mind readers, spoon benders, dowsers, and UFOs.

There weren't very many teleports.

I moved from the Stanville Library to the New York Public Library's research branch, the one with the lions out front. There was more stuff, but lord, the evidence wasn't very convincing. Well—actually, what evidence?

My talent seems to be documentable. It's repeatable. It's verifiable.

I think.

To be honest, I only knew that *I* could repeat it. I knew that *my* experience seemed repeatable. I hadn't performed it several times before unbiased witnesses. And I wasn't about to, either.

The only objective evidence I could point to, was the bank robbery. It made the paper, after all. Maybe my hunt for other teleports should pursue reports of unsolved crimes?

Right, Davy. How does that help you find other teleports? It doesn't even guarantee that there are other teleports, just unsolved crimes.

I dropped the search for a while, discouraged, and instead thought about *why*.

Why could I teleport? Not how. Why? What was it about me?

Could everybody teleport if they were put in a desperate enough position? I couldn't believe that. Too many people were put in those positions and they just endured, suffered, or broke.

If they escaped the situation it was by ordinary means, often—like my encounter with Topper—running from the frying pan into the fire. Still, maybe there were a few who escaped my way.

Again, why me? Was it genetic? The thought that perhaps Dad could teleport made my blood run cold, made me look in dark corners and behind my back. Rationally I doubted it. There were too many times he'd have jumped if he could. But no matter how many times I told myself that, the gut feeling still remained.

Could Mom teleport? Is that what she did? Jump away from Dad, like I did? Why didn't she take me? If she could teleport, why didn't she come back for me?

And if she couldn't teleport, what happened to her?

All my life, I'd wondered if I was some sort of alien— some sort of strange changeling. Among other things, it would explain why Dad treated me the way he did.

According to many of the more extreme books, the government was actively covering up all this information—concealing evidence, muffling witnesses, and manufacturing spurious alternative explanations.

This behavior reminded me of Dad. Facts constantly shifted around our house. Permissions changed, events mutated, and memories faded. I often wondered if I was crazy or he was.

I didn't think I was an alien, though . . . but I wasn't sure.

My landlord gave me a funny look when I asked if I could pay him the monthly rent in cash.

"Cash? Hell, no. Those postal orders are bad enough. Why don't you get a bank account? I thought it was strange when you paid with those postal orders, but I put it down to you being new in town. You want to have the IRS down on me?"

I shook my head. "No."

He narrowed his eyes. "The IRS really frowns on large cash transactions. I wouldn't want to think there's something funny about your income."

I shook my head. "No. I just have a lot of cash left over from a trip I took." My ears were burning and my stomach felt funny.

Later in the day I gave my landlord another postal money order for the rent, but I could see him thinking about it.

A woman on the phone told me that to open an account with her bank I would need a driver's license and a Social Security number. I had neither. Even talking to her I had to use a public phone. I was afraid to try and get a phone without I.D.

I put a thousand dollars in my pocket and jumped to Manhattan, west of Times Square, where the adult bookstores and porno theaters line Forty-second Street and Eighth Avenue. In two hours I was offered drugs, girls, boys, and children. When one of them said they *could* provide a driver's license, it was only to lure me down an alleyway, so they could "jump" me. I jumped first and quit trying for the day.

* * *

The Stanville Public Library is just off the downtown district, a three-block-by-two-block area of public buildings, restaurants, and dying stores. The Wal-Mart at the edge of town and the big mall twenty miles away in Waverly were taking the downtown business.

I walked along Main Street and thought about how different this stupid little town was from New York City.

The boarded-up front of the Royale movie theater had graffiti on the plywood, but the message was "Stallions Rule!" In New York the graffiti on theaters was obscene or angry, not high school athletic bragging. On the other hand, there were over fifty movie theaters in the midtown section of Manhattan and that didn't count the porno houses. Here in Stanville the only theater was closed, done in by the video business. If people wanted a real movie theater, they had to drive to the sixplex in Waverly.

It was pointless to compare restaurants, but the variety and range of them hit home when I came to the Dairy Queen. It was brick with high glass windows and bright fluorescent lighting. It had all the atmosphere and charm of a doctor's examining room. I thought of seven spots in Greenwich Village that would serve me anything from gourmet ice cream to "tofutti" to frozen yogurt to Bavarian cream pie. I could be at any of them in the blink of an eye.

"I'd like a small dip cone, please."

I didn't know the elderly woman behind the counter, but Robert Werner, who used to be in biology class with me, was flipping burgers. He looked up from the grill, saw me, and frowned, as if I was familiar but he couldn't place me. It had been over a year, but it hurt that he didn't recognize me.

"That will be seventy-three cents."

I paid. In the Village it would have been considerably more. As I walked back to one of the plastic laminated booths I saw myself in the mirror that ran along the back wall. No wonder Robert couldn't place me.

I was wearing slacks from Bergdorf's, a shirt I'd gotten from some snotty clerk on Madison Avenue, and shoes from Saks Fifth Avenue. My hair was cut neatly, slightly punkoid, far different from the untrimmed mess I'd worn a year before. Then I would have been wearing worn, ill-fitting jeans, shirts with clashing patterns, and three-year-old tennis shoes. There would have been holes in the socks.

I stared for a moment, a ghostly overlay of that earlier, awkward me causing me to shudder. I sat down, facing away from the mirror, and ate my ice cream.

Robert came out from the kitchen to bus a table near me. He looked at me again, still puzzled.

What the hell.

"How's it going, Robert?"

He smiled and shrugged. "Okay. How about you? Long time no see."

He still didn't place me.

I laughed. "You might say that. Not for over a year."

"That would have been at . . .?" He paused, as if remembering, inviting me to fill in the blank.

I grinned. "You're going to have to remember all on your own. I won't help you."

He glared then. "Okay. Dammit. I know you, but where from? Give me a break!"

I shook my head and nibbled on my cone.

He turned to finish bussing the table, then straightened up suddenly. "Davy? Christ, Davy Rice!"

"Bingo."

"I thought you did a milk carton."

I grimaced. "Poetically put."

"Did you go back home?"

"No!" I blinked, surprised at the force in my voice. More softly I said, "No, I didn't. I'm just seeing the old home-town."

"Oh." He put his hands in his pockets. "Well, you look really good. Really different."

"I'm doing all right. I . . ." I shrugged.

"Where are you living now?"

I started to lie, to tell him something misleading, but it seemed petty. "I'd rather not say."

He frowned. "Oh. Is your dad still putting those posters up?"

"Christ, I hope not."

He started wiping the table. "You going to be here on Saturday? There's a party at Sue Kimmel's."

I felt my face turning red. "I was never in with those guys. Half of them are college kids. They wouldn't want me there."

He shrugged. "I don't know. Hell, maybe they think too much about clothes and things. They only invited me because my sister's close to Sue. You look more like you'd fit in now than I do. If you want to go with me, I'll vouch for you."

Christ, I must've changed a lot.

"Don't you have a date?"

"Nah. Nothing definite. Trish McMillan will be there and we sort of have this thing, but it's not a date."

"It's nice of you, Robert. You don't really owe me anything like that."

He blinked. "Well . . . it's not like I hang out with a high-class group. Maybe you'll add something to my image."

"Well . . . I'd like to. You working here all week?"

"Yeah, even Saturday until six. That old college-fund grind."

"When do you think you'll be ready to go?"

"Eight, maybe."

"You driving?"

He pointed out into the parking lot. "Yeah, that old clunker's mine."

I took a deep breath. I didn't want to go to his house. I didn't know what his parents would say to me or about me to Dad. The thought of going to that party, though . . . that really tempted me. "Could you pick me up here?"

"Sure. Eight sharp, Saturday night."

I spent some time that evening talking to Millie on the phone. It was frustrating because I kept having to put quarters in the pay phone.

"So, how's school so far?"

"Okay. Haven't really had to struggle yet. It's just the first month."

A recorded message asked me to add more money. I shoved several quarters in. Millie laughed.

"You really need to get a phone."

"I'm working on it. Getting a phone in New York . . . I'll call you with the number when I get it."

"Okay."

I was standing at the phones in the back lobby of the Grand Hyatt by Grand Central, a small mountain of quarters on the ledge in front of me. People swept past, going to the bathrooms. Occasionally a Hyatt security man in a suit would roust nonguests out of the bathroom. They were usually black, poorly dressed, and carrying plastic bags filled with miscellaneous belongings.

For some reason it bothered me that the security guard was black, too.

"What did you say?"

Millie was indignant. "I said there's a party I've been invited to in two weeks. I don't want to go because Mark will be there."

"Mark's your old boyfriend?"

"Yeah. Only he thinks I'm still involved with him."

"How's that? I thought you didn't return his calls or let him in your apartment."

"I don't. He's amazing. Oblivious. And the sonofabitch keeps it up even though I know he's dating someone else."

"Hmmm. You sound like you'd really like to go to this party."

"Well. Shit. I don't want to make decisions based on avoiding or seeing him. It pisses me off."

"I could—"

The recording had me put more money in.

"What did you say, David?"

"I could go with you if you like."

"Get real. You're in New York."

"Sure. Now. In two weeks I could be in Stillwater."

She was quiet for a moment. "Well, it would be nice. I'll believe it when I see it, though."

"Hey! Count on it. Will you pick me up at the airport? Or should I take a taxi?"

"Christ! A taxi won't run sixty miles to Stillwater. I'll come get you, but it will have to be after classes."

"Okay."

"What, you mean it?"

"Yes."

She was quiet again. "Well, okay then. Let me know."

That took care of my next two Saturday nights. I said good-bye and hung up. The security guard came out of the rest room following closely behind another street person. I swept the rest of the quarters off the ledge and dropped them in one of this guy's plastic bags. He looked at me, startled and, perhaps, a little frightened. The security man glowered at me.

I walked around the corner and jumped away.

Leo Pasquale was a bellboy at the Gramercy Park, the nice hotel I'd stayed at before I got my apartment. He was the winner in the hotel-staff dominance due over who waited on me.

I tip well.

"Hey, Mr. Rice. Nice to see you."

I nodded. "Hello, Leo."

"Are you back with us? What room?"

I shook my head. "No. I've got an apartment now. I could use your help with something, though."

He looked around at the bell captain, then tilted his head to the elevator. "Let's ride up to ten."

"Okay."

On the tenth floor he led me down the hall and opened a room with a passkey. "Come on in," he said.

The room was a suite. He opened a door and we walked out onto a large balcony, almost a terrace. The afternoon was pleasant, warm without being muggy. The traffic noise rose up from Lexington Avenue in waves, almost like surf. Buildings rose around us like mountain cliffs.

"What do you need, David? Girls? Something in a recreational drug?"

I took the money out of my pocket and counted out five hundred-dollar bills. I gave them to him and held the remaining five hundred in my other hand where they were still visible.

"Down payment. The rest you get on delivery."

He licked his lips. "Delivery of what?"

It was my turn to hesitate. "I want a New York State driver's license good enough to pass a police check."

"Hell, man. You can buy a fake driver's license for less than a hundred . . . a good one for under two-fifty."

I shook my head. "Your money is just a finder's fee, Leo. I'm not paying for a fake ID with this thousand. I'm paying to be hooked up with an expert. I expect to pay for his services myself."

Leo raised his eyebrows and licked his lips again. "All of the thousand is mine, though?"

"If you come up with the product. But if it's hackwork, if it's no good, forget the second five hundred. Find me a wizard and the rest of the money is yours. Can you do it?"

He rubbed the bills between his fingers, feeling the texture of the paper. "Yeah. I'm pretty sure. I don't know anyone directly, but I know a lot of illegals with really good papers. You got a number I can reach you at?"

I smiled. "No."

"Cagey."

I shook my head. "I don't have a phone. I'll check back. When will you know something?"

He folded the money carefully and put it in his pocket. "Try me tomorrow."

I paid a homeless man twenty dollars plus cost to go into a liquor store and buy a magnum of their more expensive champagne. He came out with the large bottle in one hand and a jug of wine under his other arm.

"Here, kid. Have a hell of a time. I certainly intend to."

I thought of Dad. I considered taking this guy's wine away from him, grabbing it and jumping before he could do anything. Instead I said "Thank you" politely and jumped back to my apartment as soon as he'd turned away.

The champagne barely fit in the tiny refrigerator lying down, but not standing, and even then it bumped against the door. I leaned a chair against the door to keep it shut.

I spent the next two hours up on Fifth Avenue, buying clothes and shoes. A few of the clerks even remembered me. After that I went to my hairstylist in the Village and got a haircut.

You don't even like those people, Davy. Why all the fuss?

I shaved carefully, scraping the few whiskers from my face with only a few nicks. I resolved to buy an electric razor. *Hope the bleeding stops before tonight.* The face in the mirror was a stranger's, quiet and calm. There was no trace of the shaky stomach or the pounding heart. I wiped at the tiny bright beads of blood with a damp finger, smearing them.

Hell.

I still had three hours before the party, but I didn't want to read or sleep or watch the tube. I dressed in some of the old, comfortable clothes, the ones I brought with me to New York, and jumped to the backyard of Dad's house.

The car wasn't there. I jumped to my room.

There was a thin film of dust on the desk and windowsill. There was the faint smell of mildew. I tried to open the door to the hall, but the door was stuck. I pulled harder, but it wouldn't budge.

I jumped to the hallway.

There was a bright, shiny padlock hasp screwed into the wood on the door and frame. A large brass padlock held it secure. I scratched my head. What on earth?

I walked down the hall to the kitchen and found the note on the refrigerator.

Davy,

What do you want? Why don't you just come home? I promise not to hit you anymore. I'm sorry about that. Sometimes my temper gets the better of me. I wish you wouldn't keep coming into the house unless you're coming home for good. It scares me. I might mistake you for a burglar and accidentally shoot you. Just come home, okay?

Dad

It was held to the refrigerator by a magnet I'd decorated in elementary school, a clay blob in green and blue. I slipped the note out and crumpled it into a little ball.

More promises. *Well, there's been enough broken promises in the past.* As an afterthought I uncrumpled one corner of the note and stuck it back under the magnet. It hung there, a ball of paper held to the refrigerator by the blob of colored clay.

Let's see what he thinks of that.

I was angry and my head hurt. *Why do I keep coming back here?* I picked up the flour canister from the counter. It was a large glass jar with a wooden top. I tossed it up, high above the floor. It slowed, just below the ceiling, hung there, and then dropped. Before it hit the floor I jumped.

SIX

"Christ, where do you get your clothes?"

I shrugged instead of answering and climbed into Robert's car. The springs creaked and I had to slam the door twice before it would catch. I put the champagne bottle on the seat between us, a white ribbon tied around its neck.

Robert eased out of the parking lot gingerly, the springs rocking excessively as we went over the gutter. "Shocks are shot," he said. "But it's ugly."

"Great. How many people are going to be at this party?"

He waved his free hand. "Oh, fifty, a hundred, who knows. They got band for it, I think. She can afford it."

"What will her parents be doing?"

"They're out of state."

Good.

We had to park half a block down the street because of the accumulated cars. There was a crowd of Stanville High football players standing around the front door, beer cans and cigarettes in hand and mouth. We threaded our way between them.

One of them called out, "Who's your date, Robert?"

Robert just kept on walking like he hadn't heard, but I saw his neck turn red. I paused at the door and looked around. They were all grinning. The one who spoke was Kevin Giamotti, who used to extort lunch money from me in junior high. I looked at him, my stomach knotting for a second, my heart beating faster.

Christ, he's just a kid!

I shook my head and started to laugh. Compared to those guys in the alley near Times Square, Kevin was a baby. And I'd been scared of him? It seemed ridiculous.

Kevin stopped grinning. "What?" He started to frown.

"Nothing," I said, waving my hand. "Absolutely nothing." I turned, laughing even harder, almost uncontrollably, and went into the house.

Sue Kimmel stood at the end of the hall talking with a couple who seemed far more interested in touching each other than listening to her.

"You two in heat or what?" she said. "The bar's in the living room. If you're going to drink, give your keys to Tommy. He's behind the bar."

The couple moved on, joined permanently at hip and lip.

"Hello, Robert. Who's this?"

Robert opened his mouth and I said quickly, "I'm David." I brought the bottle from behind me and presented it with a slight bow. "So nice of you to let me come."

She raised her eyebrows and took the bottle. "The pleasure, Miss Doolittle, is all mine, I'm sure. Bollinger? They don't sell this around here. Folks around here think Andre's is hot shit." She touched the bow and ran her finger down the condensation on the bottle. "Where did you get it?"

I swallowed and said, "My refrigerator."

She laughed. "Subtle. Well, I shan't stare down the horse's mouth any longer." She looked at Robert. "Trish was looking for you. She's out on the patio."

"Thanks, Sue." He turned to me. "You want to meet Trish?"

I started to say something but Sue Kimmel said, "I'll bring him along in a minute. After we open this."

I found myself being gently steered down the hall and into a large room crowded with men and women my age or older. The temperature was several degrees higher than in the hallway. I loosened my tie and followed as Sue pushed her way through the crowd, using the cold, wet champagne bottle as a shepherd's crook, steering people right and left by touching exposed skin or thin cloth.

We finally ended up at a long bar running the length of the far wall. A big man, perhaps six feet four, stood behind the bar, using a built-in tap to fill a beer mug for one of the guys pressed up against the bar. He wore a strap over his shoulder festooned with car keys.

"Yo, Tommy!"

"Yo, Sue."

She put the magnum of Bollinger on the counter. "Glasses."

"Yo."

He pulled two wineglasses off a rack behind the bar.

"Not those . . . the flutes. Christ, Tommy. Champagne flutes."

She looked over at me and rolled her eyes. Tommy blushed.

"I use mason jars myself," I said. I smiled at Tommy and he nodded after a minute, then moved down the bar to fill another beer mug.

"Well?"

I turned to Sue and raised my eyebrows.

She gestured at the bottle.

"Oh, well, okay."

I'd read up on opening champagne, just in case this happened. The lead foil came off pretty much like it should and I started on the wire, untwisting and lifting it gently away from the cork. The way Sue had swung it around, I was afraid it might go off like a bomb.

The book I read said to ease the cork out gently, keeping a firm grip on the cork, to prevent it from flying off and hitting someone. Shooting the cork off, the book said, "was for buffoons and fops."

I tried to ease it out, but the thing seemed immovable. I resorted to tugging and twisting, but it still wouldn't move. I lifted it off the bar and put it between my legs, so I could get a better grip. This put my head down at the level of Sue's breasts.

"My, David? What's that between your legs?" She put a

hand behind my head and pulled me slightly closer. My forehead bumped against the hollow of her throat and I stared straight down her dress. She smelled of perfume and skin.

I tried to straighten up, my ears and face burning. The cork loosened slightly in the neck of the bottle. I managed to pull away from Sue.

Sue was laughing, watching me blush. Then her smile died and I felt a hand grab my shoulder and pull me around. A voice, loud and deep, shouted in my ear. "What the fuck you doing with my girl?"

He wasn't as big as Tommy, but he still towered over me, large, blond, bearded. I stared at him, blank, still holding the unopened bottle. He shoved me and I took a step back, bumping into the bar and Sue, and inadvertently shook the champagne. That's when it went off.

The cork caught him on the chin, snapping his mouth shut on his tongue. Champagne geysered forth, soaking both him and me. I stared in horror, trying in vain to stop the flood with my thumb. This just caused the foam to spray rather than gush.

Beside me I heard Sue say, almost under her breath, "Premature ejaculation . . . again."

"You little shit!"

He lunged for me, his hands going for my throat. I dropped, collapsing into a ball, his weight coming down on top of me, covering me, hiding me.

I jumped.

The champagne-soaked tie and shirt made a wet *thwack* as it hit the wall in my bathroom. "Dammit. Dammit. Dammit."

Why does this shit always happen to me?

There was an ache in my throat and I wanted to punch something, break things. I stared at myself in the mirror.

Wet hair plastered my forehead and my jaw was clenched tightly shut. The muscles stood out on the side of my face and neck. I relaxed my jaw and found that my teeth had been aching. I took deep breaths, leaning forward on the counter.

After a minute I ran cold water and washed my face and rinsed the hair in front, to get rid of the wine smell. I combed my hair back in a slick, smooth shell.

The difference in my appearance was striking. My hair looked much darker and the shape of my head was changed. I frowned, then went into the bedroom and picked out a black shirt with a stiff, upright collar. I put it on and checked out the result in the mirror.

I looked very little like the boy who walked into Sue Kimmel's with the champagne.

I jumped.

The football players had abandoned the front porch, but their spoor, crushed beer cans and cigarette butts, dotted the walk and grass. Even before I got to the house I could tell that the band had started—bass and drumbeat shook the sidewalk and made the windows rattle. I opened the door and the sound struck me with almost palpable force.

I considered jumping home again, but took a deep breath and leaned into the noise.

The hall was more crowded than before, but when I finally won free to the room with bar, it was less so. The wall of noise came from the other end of the room. I could see people dancing like they were insane.

There were only a couple of people at the bar, though Tommy was still behind it, drumming on the surface in time with the music. There were twice as many keys around his neck as before.

I hooked a foot on the bar rail and leaned my elbows forward. He glanced at me, then looked again. He came down to the end of the bar and shouted over the music. "Christ. You sure changed quick. I thought I knew everybody who lived in this neighborhood."

I shook my head. "You probably do. I'm not from around here."

"Well, you sure faded fast. Sue was looking for you."

"Oh?"

He reached down behind the bar and came up with the magnum of Bollinger's. "There's some left. You probably could have drained a quart from Lester's shirt, but that would taste rancid." He pulled down a tulip glass and filled it, draining the bottle to do so.

"Was Lester the guy who jumped me?"

"Yeah. Sue sent him home. She was furious."

I smiled. "Maybe I shouldn't have come back myself. I'm glad he's not here though."

Tommy nodded. "He could fall down a hole for all I care."

I blinked. "Don't like him, eh?"

He nodded, grinned, and went down to the other end of the bar.

The champagne tasted like unsweetened ginger ale, its aftertaste unpleasant. I looked in the bar mirror and un-wrinkled my nose. I shifted my grip on the glass, trying to look more sophisticated, less awkward. I sipped at the champagne again and shuddered.

Some sophisticate.

I took the glass and wandered out onto the veranda, away from the music. There were tables and chairs, white, wrought-iron. Three of them were occupied. One was off by itself, in the shadow of the hedge. I sat down.

The band started playing oldies, songs from the early sixties. They'd been hits before I was born, but I'd heard them often enough. My mom would listen to nothing but old rock and roll, songs from her teens. I grew up listening to them, wondering what they were about. Didn't particularly like them, didn't particularly dislike them.

I knew all the words.

"There you are."

Sue Kimmel pulled up one of the patio chairs and put down a glass of something with ice. "Tommy said you were back, but I walked past you three times before I realized you'd changed clothes."

I licked my lips. "I didn't mean to cause problems."

She rolled her eyes. "Lester is the one who caused problems."

"He must love you very much."

She laughed. "Love? Lester doesn't know the meaning of the word. Lester stakes territories. Lester would piss on fire hydrants if he thought other people had a keen enough sense of smell."

I didn't know what to say so I took another sip of the champagne. Ugh.

She swallowed some of her drink and smacked her lips. "I wanted to apologize to you, actually, for Lester's behavior. He doesn't realize it, but we're in the process of breaking up."

"I'm sorry."

"You've nothing to be sorry about. I'd been thinking about it all week. He's pissed me off too many times."

I took another sip. The taste was bad, but it didn't seem quite as bad as before. I lifted my glass to her, but didn't say anything.

She lifted hers and drained it. "Come on," she said. "Let's dance."

I felt a rush of panic. Dance? I set the glass down. "I'm not very good."

"Who cares. Come on."

"I really rather not."

She grabbed my hand and pulled me out of the chair. "Come on." She didn't let go of my arm, pulling me toward the music.

The band was playing something very fast, very loud. We threaded our way between gyrating bodies until a few square feet of floor space opened up. I felt closed in, threatened by all the close bodies and flying limbs. She started to dance. I stood there for a moment, then started moving. The music pounded on me like waves at the beach. I tried to find a rhythm that matched it, but the tempo was too fast.

Sue was oblivious, her eyes closed, her legs pumping in counterpoint to the music. I tried not to stare at the parts of her that bounced up and down. I felt miserable.

I waited until she was spinning around, facing away from her, and jumped back to the patio. Someone gasped to my right. I looked over and saw a girl staring at me from one of the other tables. "Jesus! I didn't see you walk up, dressed in all that black."

"Sorry. Didn't mean to startle you." I picked up the champagne flute and took it back to the bar.

"Yo, Tommy."

"Yo, David. No more champagne, man."

"Fill it with ginger ale. And put a head on it."

He grinned and filled it from the fountain gun. "Ze ginger ale, monsieur."

"Thanks."

I moved back onto the porch and reclaimed my seat. After a moment, Sue came out, looking puzzled, and a little angry.

"What's the big idea? Don't you know how many guys at this party want to dance with me?"

"I can see why. You're very attractive and you dance like a dream."

She blinked, her mouth half open to say something. She closed it and sat down. "That was good. Very good. Almost too good. Why don't you want to dance with me?"

I shrugged. "I feel foolish. You know what you're doing out there. I feel like a clumsy jerk. The contrast is painful. I'm shallow, I guess, but I don't want everybody to know just how shallow."

"Yeah. Real shallow. Compared to Lester, you're a bottomless pit."

"I'll bet Lester can dance."

"In a fakey, self-centered kind of way. More John Travolta than Baryshnikov."

I shrugged again and felt stupid. Is shrugging the only expression I know?

"I'm going to get a drink. You need anything?"

I held up my ginger ale.

"Don't disappear on me."

"Yes, ma'am."

She came back with her glass filled with some amber fluid. Behind her came Robert and a pretty redhead I vaguely recognized from high school. She was Trish McMillan, the girl Robert "sort of had a thing" with.

"Hell, man. I've been looking all over for you," Robert said. "You okay? I heard Lester climbed all over you."

"I'm fine."

"How'd you change so quick? You have a bag with you?"

I smiled and resorted to the ever popular, multipurpose shrug.

He looked like he wanted to ask more, but Trish spoke then. "Robert said he brought you to the party, but I didn't realize that you were David Rice. How long ago did you run away?"

Sue looked from Trish to me. "What do you mean, run away?"

I picked up my glass and drank some more ginger ale. I didn't think a shrug was going to work. "I left home one year and two months ago."

Trish wouldn't leave it alone. "Well, jeez. You look like you came out all right. Do you recommend it?"

"It would depend."

"On what?"

"On how bad you had it at home. It's got to be pretty awful before being a runaway is better."

"Well, what about in your case?"

I put my glass down. "I'd rather not talk about my case."

She blinked. "Well, I'm sure I didn't mean to pry. Sorry."

"No problem. Nice weather we're having."

Robert looked uncomfortable. "Yeah, some weather. David, I'm going to run Trish home. I can come get you after."

I shook my head. "Thanks. I can get home from here."

They got up to leave. Sue said, "Contraception, Trish. That vital conversation before."

Trish and Robert blushed in unison.

"Yeah, right," said Robert.

When they were gone Sue turned back to me.

"Nice kids. Where do you live?"

I saw no reason to lie. "New York City."

"Oh. So you're just visiting the old hometown."

"I do that."

She laughed. "What else do you do?"

"I read a lot."

She swallowed some more of her drink.

"What is that you're drinking."

"Glenlivet."

I shook my head, not understanding.

"Scotch."

"Oh."

"Want some?"

An image of a man in his underwear, black socks, hairy legs, unshaven, an empty bottle of scotch cradled in his arm like an infant, mouth open, eyes shut—Dad.

"No. Thank you for asking."

She leaned forward, her neckline drooping. I looked away. She straightened, pulled up a shoulder strap. I sipped at my ginger ale.

"So, have you seen the house, David?"

I shook my head.

"Come on. We can find someplace quieter to have a conversation."

She stood and, staggering slightly, led me back into the house and up the stairs. Her tour consisted of "this is the upstairs hall. This is my bedroom."

Oh my God.

"Uh, Sue. What are we doing up here?"

She shut the door behind us.

"Conversation. That conversation that I was talking about earlier. You know, to Trish and Robert." She walked up to me; I took a step back and fetched up against the closed door. She kept coming.

"You don't know me from Charles Manson, Sue. I could have every STD in the book."

She put her hands on my shoulders. In her heels she was slightly taller than me. "Do you?"

"Do I what?"

"Have any sexually transmitted diseases."

"Uh, not to my knowledge."

She pressed her mouth hard against mine. Her tongue

flicked along my lips, darted between my teeth. I felt the skin crawl along the back of my head and down my back, an eerie, not unpleasurable sensation. Her mouth, though, tasted of scotch. I pushed her gently away.

"Uh, hold up." *Oh God, she's beautiful.* I didn't know what to say. I wanted to sleep with her. I wanted to run. I wanted to just jump away.

What about Millie?

She molded her body to mine. "What? You don't like me? Is this something else you don't do?"

"Uh, uh . . . where's your bathroom?"

She pointed to a door on the other side of the room and followed me over to it. I went inside and found a small bathroom with no other exit. *Oh shit.*

She turned on the light.

"Condoms," she said. "Are in the bottom drawer." She shut the door with a snap, not unlike the popping noise a mousetrap makes when it trips.

I opened the bottom drawer. One box of Trojan Gold condoms sat among hair ties, curlers, and a tube of K-Y jelly. Only one box? Does that make her conservative or easy? I pushed it shut and looked at the window. It was two feet square, to the right of the sink. It opened inward. I stuck my head out. There was a drop of twenty feet on a sheer brick wall.

It would have to do.

I took some of her lipstick and wrote on the mirror, "SORRY, I CAN'T." Then I flushed the toilet, made sure the door was unlocked, and jumped home to Brooklyn.

"They found someone who matched your physical stats and duplicated his license with your picture. The name may be a little different, but close. Of course the address is his, but if they run your license, the dispatcher will find everything agrees in the computer." He paused and looked at me. "Oh. They also have access to the real plastic, and stock, and embossers. Your license is real."

"What about the signature?" I asked Leo.

"Well, you'll have to practice that."

I walked in silence thinking about it, glancing occasionally at the card.

We reached Lexington and started up it.

"It's really a good deal, Mr. Rice. Honest."

"Relax, Leo. It's okay. I agree." I paid him the fee, plus a bonus, and we parted.

Later that day, I put thirty thousand dollars in a share draft account at Liberty Savings & Loan for David Michael Reece. That was the name on my newly acquired driver's license. I made up a Social Security number. The girl offered me a choice of a toaster oven or a food processor. I took the toaster.

With my new checks I bought a ticket, first-class, one-way, to Will Rogers World Airport, Oklahoma City.

"Are you sure you don't want a round-trip ticket? If you buy a one-way ticket back, it'll cost you over three hundred dollars more . . . first-class."

"No thank you. I don't need a return ticket."

"Oh, you're not coming back?"

I shook my head. "No. I'm coming back. Just by other means."

"Oh. You must be driving."

I shrugged. Let her think what she wanted.

Since I didn't have a "major credit card" she said I'd have to pick up the ticket after the check cleared.

My ears started to burn and I felt like I'd done something wrong. "Why don't I just pay in cash then?" I took out a roll of fifties.

She stared. "Uh, we prefer not to deal in cash. Are you in a hurry to get the ticket?"

"Yes." I bit off the word. *What's wrong with me?*

"Let me check with my boss."

She walked back through a door. I felt, for some reason, like I was sitting outside the principal's office, waiting to be lectured on proper behavior. I felt like walking out. I felt like smashing things. I felt like crying.

I'd just about decided to jump back to my apartment and blow off the whole experience when she came back through the door with an older woman.

"Hello, Mr. Reece, I'm Charlotte Black, the owner."

"Hi." My voice was colorless, listless.

"We normally don't take cash, because our accountant frowns upon it. Also, I take the deposits to the bank and, frankly, it makes me a little nervous to carry cash in this neighborhood."

"Ah. I can understand that," I said. The back of my head twinged. "I don't want to make a big issue of this, but I'm going to be traveling a great deal. I'd like to make all my arrangements in one place." I paused. "But I don't want these waiting-for-the-check-to-clear hassles."

She frowned. "You could establish credit with us and we could open an account, billing you at the end of each month."

"How would that work?"

"You'd fill out a credit application and we'd have our credit agency check you out."

Oh, great. That's all I need, inquiries into my past.

"How about this instead," I said. "I'll write you a check for ten thousand dollars. When I've used up that, you tell me and I'll write another check. And," I added, "I'll wait until the check clears to pick up my ticket to Oklahoma City."

She blinked and inhaled sharply. "That would be acceptable."

I scribbled out the check, trying to make the signature look casual as well as resemble the one on my driver's license. She picked it up and looked at it. "Oh. We bank at Liberty. I'll take this over at lunch. Can we call you this afternoon?"

I shook my head. "My next stop is the phone company. I don't have a phone right now. How about I drop back by around three."

"Very good, Mr. Reece."

Millie met me at the gate with a smile that didn't touch her eyes. I felt something shrink inside.

"Hi," I said. I made no move to touch her. She seemed relieved.

"Wow, you got out fast. You must have been sitting near the front."

I shrugged. "They only had three rows in first class."

"Oh." She started walking and I fell into step beside her. "Do you have any luggage?"

"Just this," I said, hefting the carry-on.

"We go this way to the car."

We walked down the length of the concourse, took a turn to the right.

"Hold it a second, please."

"Huh." She stopped.

We'd come to a sign that said OBSERVATION DECK. There was a turnstile that took dimes and a stairway leading up. "Can we go up there for a second?"

She raised her eyebrows, surprised. "Well, it's no Empire State Building, but if you want."

"Thanks." I had to get change for a quarter from the concourse bar before we could go in and ascend the three flights of stairs. The view was of runways and distant trees and brown grass. I looked around, memorizing details, so I could jump straight to the airport, next time.

Millie still seemed remote, unsure of herself. I hoped there would be a next time.

"What's wrong," I asked casually, while I looked out at the airport. I glanced sideways at her. She was biting her lip.

She saw me looking at her. She closed her mouth. I smiled at her. "Am I a problem, Millie? Are you sorry I came?"

She frowned then, opened her mouth, closed it again without saying anything. Then, "Damn it. I don't know! I hate this! I feel like I'm being a jerk and being pressured and I don't know what you want."

She seemed ready to cry.

I held up my hand. "What do *you* want?"

She turned and stared out the window. "I'm not sure."

"Well . . . why don't we try to find out? Are you glad or sorry I'm here?"

"Yes."

"Oh. Some of both. Better than completely sorry, I suppose." I felt a little less like crying myself. "Why do you feel pressured? And to do what?"

She shook her head, almost angrily. "It's not right! If we were sleeping together, maybe I could justify you spending the money to fly out here. But we're not. Since you did spend the money, it's almost as if I have to sleep with you to balance things out."

"And you don't want to do that, do you?"

She shook her head.

I couldn't help ask, "Not ever?"

She narrowed her eyes. "See? Even you think that's how things are supposed to be."

I blushed. "No. I'm sorry. I don't expect that. I would be lying if I said I wouldn't like to, but I don't expect it. I flew out here to go to this party with you. I'm not trying to pressure you into anything."

"Well, the pressure is there. It's situational."

"Hmmm. Seems like you've spent more time thinking about sleeping with me than I have. I find that very encouraging."

She glared at me. "Give me a break."

"Well, you give me one. Try to assume responsibility for only your own actions. All you've done is agree to go to a party with me. It seems like you're taking responsibility for my actions, too. I'm an adult—at least, I'm able to vote. I know I'm younger than you, but that doesn't make you obligated to 'take care of me.' "

She frowned again. "I can't help how I feel."

"Well," I said, "Do you want me to go away? I'm sure I can find things to do for the weekend in Oklahoma City. Where are the cabs?"

"Is that what you want?"

I blew out my breath abruptly. "What I want is to be with someone who wants me to be there! I've spent enough time with people who didn't want me with them. I don't like it."

This stopped her for a moment. After looking blindly out at the runway she said, "Okay. Let's go."

I hung back. "Where?"

She grabbed my arm, the one with the bag, and pulled me

along. "To the party, damn it!" She linked her arm in mine on the stairway. "And yes, I do want you to be here. And stop smiling!"

Because of the timing, we got dinner on the road and went straight to the party. I felt a strange sense of déjà vu as we walked up the sidewalk to the house. Football players wearing letter sweaters or letter jackets stood outside the front door, drinking beer. Fewer of these smoked, but then, you'd expect that of collegiate-level athletes. Still, their presence and the throbbing of music from inside the house made me think of last Saturday's party.

Millie introduced me to the host, a graduate student in anthropology named Paul something. I shook hands.

"So," he asked. "What's your major?" He looked at my clothes and face. "Let me guess. Art history, freshman."

I shook my head. "Sorry. I'm from out of town. No major. No grade level."

"Oh." He sounded disappointed. "Where from?"

"New York City."

"Oh. You related to Millie?"

Millie, who'd been talking to someone else during this conversation, overheard the last bit. "No. He's my date." She said it firmly.

Paul something blinked. "Yes, ma'am. I just thought he seemed like a younger cousin or something."

Millie shook her finger under his nose. "You sexist pig! If he were three years older than me you wouldn't say anything. What a load of hypocritical bullshit!"

Paul took a step back. "Okay! Okay." He was grinning. "He's your date. It's not without cultural precedent."

Millie looked at me. "Shut your mouth. Something will fly in it."

She pulled me off to the kitchen, where the bar was set up. I decided not to comment.

She introduced me to a series of persons. I smiled and shook hands, but said very little. Millie had a glass of wine. I followed her with my ginger ale.

Sometime later, I found myself on the patio with Millie

and two of her acquaintances. We were talking about New York, its crime, and its poverty. The one person who hadn't been there had the strongest opinions.

"I don't buy the homeless thing," this woman was saying. "I think they're on drugs or lazy. They don't want to work so they beg."

I raised my eyebrows. "That's pretty black and white."

"What are you saying, that it's a racist thing?"

Millie hid her mouth behind her hand.

"No. I'm saying your viewpoint is too simplistic. Sure there are people like you describe. But I've also seen women with kids who can't get work because the only address they have is a street corner and . . ."

Millie put her hand on my arm. "That's Mark," she said quietly.

I looked over at the door. The guy standing there was a little taller than me with wide shoulders. He had blond hair and a beard. There was a girl under one of his arms with her arms around his waist. He was looking our way, at Millie.

I looked back at the woman with the opinions. "You would be surprised at the number of people on the street who don't fit your profile." I let it drop.

Millie pulled in on herself, crossing her arms.

Mark continued to stare.

The band started a slow number, Otis Redding's "Sittin' on the Dock of the Bay." "Come on, Millie. Let's dance."

She turned her head sharply, as if she'd forgotten I was there, and gave me a small smile. "Okay."

"Please excuse us," I said, and led her across the patio, to the door that led to the dance floor. Mark seemed to watch us the whole way.

"Jesus Christ," Millie said in my ear after we were on the floor. "Did you see the way he was staring?"

"Yeah. Don't let him bother you."

"Easier said than done."

I stroked her back and she relaxed a little, swaying mechanically to the music.

"How long does it take?"

"Huh?" I pressed her a little closer. She didn't seem to mind.

"To get over somebody? Especially when they won't leave you alone."

"Who broke up with who?"

She stiffened slightly. "I broke up with him. He was sleeping with Sissy."

"Sissy."

"Yeah. The limpet mine under his arm."

"Ah. But you still cared about him. And he betrayed you."

Her body stiffened and she buried her face in my neck.

I felt a hand on my shoulder. It was Mark.

I shrugged his hand off and continued dancing.

He grabbed at my arm. Millie saw him and stepped away. I turned to face him.

"Just want to cut in, man," he said, arms spread. There was a smile on his face, but it was mean.

I took Millie's arm and walked off the dance floor. He followed, tried to turn Millie around by the shoulder. I felt sick to my stomach, remote, the way I did when I knew Dad had been drinking and was going to punish me. I stepped between him and Millie. He shoved me back into Millie. She was wearing heels and one of them caught in the door sill. She flailed her arms to keep from falling.

I steadied her, then looked around.

We were standing by the door to the room. There was a row of light switches behind me. Mark was standing with his legs spread wide apart, his hands raised. The closest dancers had stopped and were watching us.

I felt like throwing up. I felt like running. I felt like killing Mark for making me feel this way, for treating Millie the way he had.

I turned abruptly and used both hands to switch off the lights. The room went dark, the only light coming from the patio door. I jumped behind Mark, a position I'd marked before hitting the switches, grabbed him around the waist, and lifted him from the floor. He flailed his arms and one of his elbows smacked me in the eye, but I didn't let go.

I jumped to the observation deck of Will Rogers Airport, sixty miles to the southwest of Stillwater, and dropped him. He staggered away from me, falling to his knees in the suddenly different, brightly lit place, putting his hands out before him to catch himself. Before he could regain his feet and turn around, I jumped away, back to the dark spot on the dance floor. Somebody turned the lights back on.

Millie was looking at me with wide eyes. I felt my face and winced. She came forward and tilted my head back, so she could look at my eye.

"Ouch. We better put some ice on that. Where's Mark?"

I looked around. People started dancing again. I stuck to the truth. "I think he left while the lights were out."

"Did he hit you?"

"His elbow, I think."

She pulled me to the kitchen, her arm intertwined in mine. As we walked she kept looking around her, looking for Mark.

We passed Sissy in the hall, talking on the phone, one ear plugged with a finger against the noise of the band. She was speaking loudly into the receiver.

"You're where? Don't give me that! You were just here a minute ago! No, I won't come get you! You want me to drive to someplace you couldn't possibly be? If you don't want to tell me the truth, don't tell me anything. Fuck you!" She slammed the receiver down and stomped off toward the dance floor.

Millie raised her eyebrows and smiled. "Well, I guess he's started lying to her, too. What did you do to him?"

I blinked and kept my mouth shut.

In the kitchen she filled a dish towel with ice cubes and eased it against my face. It hurt, but I was enjoying the attention too much to complain.

"Does that feel better?"

"Well, no, but it's probably keeping the swelling down." She laughed.

We went back to the patio then, with fresh drinks and the towel-wrapped ice. After a bit, I did another slow dance with Millie. Then she danced a couple of fast dances with Paul and another friend. Then we left.

"I'm glad I went," she said in the car, "but I'm really sorry about your eye."

"It's okay. I had a good time. It was worth the trip."

She looked at me over her glasses. Then she sighed and returned her attention to the road. We drove down by the university; then she pulled into a block of apartments.

"Whoa. What about my hotel?"

She smiled a little smile. "Waste of money."

"I have the money."

She turned off the ignition and stared straight ahead for a moment. Then she turned to me and said, "I want you to stay at my place." She averted her eyes as she said it.

"Are you sure?"

She nodded.

"Okay."

She had a two-bedroom apartment, which she shared with a roommate. When I asked, she said, "Sherry went home for the weekend, to her folks in Tulsa."

I dropped my bag by the couch and sat down. The room was filled with plants, hanging, on stands, and on the floor. The couch, a small coffee table, and a large wicker chair sat among the greenery like clearings in a jungle. Leaning back, I studied a large, frondy thing in a clay pot over my head.

My heart was pounding very hard.

"What do you call this potted plant of Damocles?"

She finished hanging up our coats.

"It's a Boston fern and it's hardly hanging by a thread."

"My mother used to keep them. I never knew the name."

I had a dark memory, a vivid flash of Dad heaving pot after pot out the back door to smash on the patio tiles, all the time raging while a small boy cringed in the corner, crying because his mother was gone.

"Would you like something to drink?"

My mouth was very dry suddenly, or maybe it was all along and I just realized it. "Water, please. Lots of water."

She brought it in a sixteen-ounce tumbler with ice. I

drank half of it at once, chilling the back of my throat so it ached.

"You were thirsty."

"Yeah."

She sat down beside me, but didn't lean back. She reminded me of a bird, perched for instant flight.

I sighed. "Maybe this isn't such a good idea, Millicent."

She looked at the floor. "Am I being too pushy? You were the one who talked about sexist assumptions."

I remembered her speech, back at the party, to Paul. I smiled. "No. That's not the problem. I like that. I like you. But I'm really nervous and, well, there's something you should know."

She edged away from me on the couch. "Don't tell me you have herpes!"

My eyes opened wider and I blushed. "No." I lowered my voice, put my elbows on my knees, and stared at the floor. "I'm a virgin," I mumbled.

She leaned forward. "A what? I couldn't hear that."

"I'm a virgin! All right?"

She flinched and I realized I'd shouted. "Sorry." I looked back down at the floor. I could feel my ears getting hotter and hotter.

She moved on the couch. I glanced sideways and saw that she'd leaned back. Her mouth was open and she was staring at me. "You've got to be kidding."

I looked back down at the floor and shook my head. I felt miserable, ashamed.

"How old are you?"

"You know. Eighteen years and two months. You helped me celebrate, remember?"

Her tension, that impression of impending flight, was completely gone. She sat back, her hands in her lap open and relaxed. She shook her head slowly. "Wow. A virgin."

"Yes! Is it such a crime?"

I felt her move on the couch again, felt her arm move around my shoulders and pull me back to lean against the couch. She was smiling at me, gently and tenderly.

I started crying.

I clenched my eyelids shut and held my breath. Water leaked down my face. Stop it! I felt so small, so ashamed.

Her arm pulled away from me, from my back, for just a moment and I felt her rejection like a stabbing knife. *That's torn it,* I couldn't help thinking. *Now she knows what a screwup I am.* Then her arm came back and her other arm surrounded me, gathered me in, pulled me to her.

"Oh, Davy. It's all right." She rocked me and the sobs broke free, ragged and hard. She pressed her lips against my hair. "It's all right, let it out. Go ahead and cry."

I couldn't stop then. Between the sobs I kept saying, over and over again, "I'm sorry, I'm sorry."

"Shhhh. It's okay to cry. It's okay." And she rocked me and rocked me.

But while she was saying it was okay, I could hear my Dad's voice, *Crybaby, crybaby. Stop feeling sorry for yourself. I'll give you something to cry about.* And I couldn't help saying, "I'm sorry." Still, the tears and sobs went on and on.

Oh, God, it hurt.

Finally the sobs lessened and the tears slowed. Millie kept rocking me gently until I straightened up. "I need to blow my nose."

She handed me a box of tissue from the coffee table, keeping one hand on my shoulder. I didn't feel ashamed anymore, but I was embarrassed. It took three tissues to clear my sinuses. Millie leaned back and pulled her legs up underneath her.

I held the used tissues in my hand, clenched into a sodden little ball. "Sorry about that," I said.

"You don't need to apologize. You obviously needed it. I'm glad you could do it with me."

I looked at her. The expression on her face, concerned, tender, threatened to bring the tears back. I sighed. "I'm not used to doing that. It seems wrong to inflict it on you."

She looked exasperated. "Men! Why the hell is our culture so screwed up? It's all right to cry. It's a blessing, a benefit. You've got just as much right to cry as anybody."

I leaned back, exhausted. Mom used to hold me when I cried.

It was hard to look at her, but I didn't want to leave. This surprised me. It would have been so easy to jump back to New York. To run away. There was a great deal to be said for escape.

"I'm going to make some tea," she said. She stood and ruffled my hair briskly, messing it.

I looked up at her and she changed the motion to a caress, a gentle motion that trailed off as she walked to the kitchen. It left a ghost feeling of her hand, warm and light, in my hair.

I got up and shuffled to the bathroom. My eyes were red and puffy and my nose still ran. I washed my face in warm water and toweled it dry. I ran wet fingers through my hair where Millie had mussed it.

"Why is it, Davy, that you know everything about my family and I know nothing about yours?" She brought the tea into the living room on a lacquered tray. The pot and cups were Japanese with unglazed rims. She poured.

"Thanks," I said.

"Well?"

"Huh?"

"Your family," she reminded.

I sipped the tea. "This is really good. Really delicious."

She raised her eyebrows. "That's what I thought. You're a good listener, Davy, and you can change the subject on a dime. You've hardly talked about yourself at all."

"I talk . . . too much."

"You talk about books, you talk about plays, you talk about movies, you talk about places, you talk about food, you talk about current events. You don't talk about yourself."

I opened my mouth, then shut it again. I hadn't really thought about it. Sure, I didn't talk about the jumping, but the rest? "Well, there's not much to say. Not like those stories of growing up with four brothers."

She smiled. "It's not going to work. If you don't want to

talk about it, that's fine. But I'm not going to be distracted again, nor fooled into talking about those idiots again."

She poured more tea into my cup.

I frowned. "Do I really do that?"

"What? Not talk about yourself? Yes."

"No, try and distract you."

She stared at me. "You are fucking amazing. I've never seen someone so good at changing the subject."

"I don't do it on purpose."

She laughed. "Sure. Maybe you don't do it consciously, but you sure as hell do it on purpose."

I sipped my tea and stared at the wall. She set the tea pot down and scooted closer to me. "Look at me, Davy."

I turned. She wasn't smiling and her gaze was calm, serious.

She spoke, "I won't force you to talk about things you don't want to talk about. You have a right to privacy. If you don't want to talk about things, fine. From the way you've changed the subject, I don't think you've ever lied to me. Would you say that's true?"

I thought about it, remembering our time in New York and the phone calls. "I think that's true. I certainly don't intend to lie to you. I don't remember ever lying to you."

She nodded. "That wasn't the case with Mark. I couldn't trust him not to lie. If I ever find out that you have, whatever we have together is over. Got that?"

I stared at her. "Yes, ma'am, I've got it." I looked at her out of the corner of my eye, sideways. "Uh. Does this mean we actually have something? Like a relationship?"

She looked at the carpet. "Well, perhaps." She turned and looked straight at me again, levelly. "Yes. We have a relationship. We're about to see if it's going to become an intimate one."

I shifted on the couch. My ears were hot and I couldn't help smiling.

She sighed and looked at the ceiling, but the corners of her mouth twitched. I slumped down on the couch and curled into her, my head on her shoulder. She put her arm around me and squeezed. She didn't say anything, just sat there, holding me gently.

After a while I started talking. I told her about Dad, Mom, and running away from home. I told about getting mugged in New York City. I told her about the hotel in Brooklyn and the incident in the bathroom. I told her about the trucker who wanted to rape me. She listened quietly, a hand on my shoulder. My voice seemed remote as I talked, not really mine.

I didn't talk about jumping and I didn't talk about the bank robbery. A part of me still felt bad about stealing the money. I still had dreams about getting caught. Telling her about the jumping would just confuse things.

I stopped talking finally, my voice sort of trailing off. I felt ashamed, like I'd just confessed doing terrible things. I couldn't look at her, even though she was there, right next to me, hand rubbing my shoulder, the warmth of a breast against my right arm, the feel of her shoulder against my cheek.

I also felt ashamed for the things I hadn't said, and less than worthy of her concern and attention. I felt like crying again, but didn't want to. I still felt bad about that.

She hugged me then, and pulled my head up into the nape of her neck. I glanced at her face. Her eyes were squeezed shut and a single tear streaked her left cheek.

That also made me want to cry.

She took me to bed after that.

"It's okay. It happens like that the first time. The second time will be better."

"See, I told you. Wow." She took a large breath. "That was more than better."

"Oh my God! Where on earth did you learn that? Are you sure this was your first time?"

"I told you," I said truthfully, "I read a lot."

3

ADJUSTMENTS

SEVEN

Love stinks.

Millie wanted to see me no more than a weekend at a time and no more than two weekends a month. She didn't want me spending the money. I offered to move to Stillwater, but she was adamant.

"No way. Wait. I know you're rich as Midas, but, dammit, I have a life, too! I have classes to study for, a part-time job, and a rich, full part of my life that doesn't include you." She held up her hand. "Now, maybe it will include you later, but not right now. Let's take it slow."

"You don't have to work. I could pay you a salary."

Her mouth dropped open. "There's a word for that. I don't believe you said that!"

"Huh?" I thought about it. "Sorry. I just want to be with you as much as possible."

It was a matter of hard negotiation to get her to agree to two weekends a month instead of one.

Love stinks.

A magician called Bob the Magnificent had an act on Forty-seventh Street. The act featured an escape that baffled the *New York Times* entertainment reviewer, so I bought a very expensive front-row ticket and went.

Bob, a short dumpy man with a beard and a tuxedo, kept the audience entertained with pretty good sleight of hand, card tricks, and magically appearing pigeons. He was also good with rings and fire. Still, in preparation for this performance, I'd been reading Houdini's *Magician Among the Spirits* and there wasn't anything about the act that made me suspect the paranormal.

As you might infer from his name, Bob the Magnificent (B.M. for short) did a lot of comedy as part of the act. He also featured these two assistants, Sarah and Vanessa; they were clad initially in long gowns, but, as the act proceeded, more and more of their clothing was "borrowed" for this trick or that. By intermission they were wearing the sequined equivalent of a one-piece bathing suit with net stockings. At least for the men in the audience, they became more and more of a distraction for Bob's sleight of hand.

During the break, I jumped home, used the bathroom, and drank a Coke. I didn't mind paying the outrageous prices charged at the theater but I did hate standing in line. Besides, the cups they use are so small. I was back in my seat when the curtain opened.

Bob started the second act by bringing various audience members on stage and pulling animals out of their ears, pockets, and necklines. I was most impressed by the six-foot python that he pulled from a woman's coat pocket. The woman, however, was *not*.

For his next trick Bob wanted to make one of his assistants disappear—he called for another audience volunteer to verify the ordinariness of his materials. He picked me.

I hesitated, then stood. Previously I'd resigned myself to jumping back to the theater after the show and finding a backstage hiding place to watch tomorrow's escape—to determine if Bob the Magnificent *was* teleporting. If I could see enough of the offstage area while up there, I could hide myself in time to witness tonight's great event.

Bob the Magnificent said, "Let's give our volunteer a big hand." Applause followed me on stage. As I topped the stairs I acquired a jump site just off side of the stage.

"Tell me," Bob said, "what's your name, young sir?"

"David." I was blinking from the bright lights, and the directional mikes set on the edge of the stage threw my voice back at me, louder than life, echoing through the auditorium.

"Just David? No last name?" I swear he smirked.

I blushed. "Just David."

Bob turned to the audience and said, "Isn't it sad when cousins marry?" He got a big laugh. He turned to me again, talking slowly, like he was talking to an idiot. "Well, David the Ordinary, I'm Bob the Magnificent." He got a small laugh. "Do you think you could remember where this came from?" He took a drape from his assistant Vanessa. The piece of cloth had begun the act as the skirt of her full gown.

I nodded.

"I knew you could." He paused for laughter. "With this ordinary piece of cloth, I intend to make Sarah, here, vanish from this stage. I want you to verify that it is an ordinary piece of cloth. An ordinary job for an ordinary fellow." He paused. "David the Ordinary."

Me ears burned hotter. With his wit directed my way, Bob seemed less and less magnificent. In fact, I'd come to the conclusion that he was an asshole, and I was hoping that he *wasn't* a teleport.

I held up the drape, shook it out. It was velveteen, cut very full and large enough to cover Sarah since it was no longer gathered into the waistline of her gown.

The audience burst into laughter and I glanced up in time to catch Bob making faces behind my back. Very funny. I flipped the drape over my head and, as it settled, hiding me from both the audience and Bob, I jumped to the spot I'd chosen, stage left.

On the stage the drape collapsed and fell to the floor.

The audience gasped, then burst into wild applause. Bob, after a moment of staring blankly at the cloth, said, "Well where the hell did *he* go?" The audience thought this was very funny and Bob, startled by their reaction, took a bow, then picked up the drape, gingerly, like it might bite him. He stamped on the floor where I'd been standing, then with a small catch in his voice said, "Uh, I guess we need another volunteer."

I couldn't tell if he was stunned for normal reasons or

because he knew what I was. No progress made, no knowledge gained. I was sorry I'd done it, but a magic act was probably the safest place to have it happen.

I backed away and stood behind a flap of curtain. My end of the stage seemed deserted though I could see a man at the fly rail for the drop curtain and another man watching the act from the far side. He was staring at the spot on the stage where the drape had fallen. The backstage area was dark and I felt relatively safe from detection.

Back on stage, Bob proceeded to disappear Sarah. I saw her drop into a trapdoor from my vantage point, but it wasn't anywhere near where I'd been standing. A little later, he reappeared her from an empty box hanging from the ceiling. It was pretty impressive, but I saw her enter the suspended box from a platform behind the curtain, moving through a slit very carefully. It was impressive—the box hardly moved.

I looked around for another hiding place. The apparatus for the grand escape was set up behind the curtain and when they flew the curtain out, I'd lose my spot. I found a stack of equipment boxes stacked to the left and crouched behind them, arranging a smaller box to sit on.

While I was doing this there was more of Bob's shtick and laughter, but I missed most of it. After a minute, though, they raised a section of the curtain and brought some spotlights up to reveal the apparatus to the audience.

"Ladies and gentleman—the Hammers of Doom!"

Sitting in the spotlight was a gray platform suspended three feet above the floor by four massive and rigid cables. The cables ran straight up from tie-downs on the stage, to the corners of the platform, then up into the fly rails above the stage. On either side of the platform two enormous pistons were poised, round steel plates about three feet in diameter and ten inches thick. These were welded onto shiny steel rods a foot in diameter that gleamed as if oiled. These rods each ran back a few feet to disappear into huge steel cylinders mounted on steel girders and fastened to the floor by massive bolts.

On the other side of this apparatus, Sarah was shoveling

coal into the firebox of a steam boiler. On the face of the boiler, a huge pressure gauge showed a needle creeping upward as the steam pressure increased. I noticed the pipes, then, that ran from a levered valve on the side of the boiler to each of the pistons.

Bob's other assistant, Vanessa, came back on stage, wheeling a hospital gurney with a sheet-covered form on it.

"And you guys wondered what happened to David the Ordinary," said Bob, his hand gripping the edge of the sheet. "Well, keep wondering." He yanked the sheet off to reveal a dummy of the kind used in car crash tests. "Meet Larry." He pulled the dummy into a sitting position, legs dangling. Larry's torso was hollowed out, leaving an oblong hole perhaps two feet tall and a foot wide. A large watermelon was wedged into the cavity.

Vanessa and Bob carried "Larry" over to the platform and locked its wrists to manacles that hung shoulder-high from the cables, so it stood, arms stretched diagonally across the middle of the platform and, incidentally, squarely between the pistons.

"Well, it doesn't look good for Larry, does it?" Bob said, stepping off the platform. He walked over to the boiler. The needle was approaching the red zone on the dial. "Sarah, did we get that safety valve fixed?" Sarah shrugged her shoulders, as if she didn't know.

"I could tell you how many tons of force these two steam hammers produce when they collide but I'll let you see, instead, with this graphic example. Lower the splash shield, please!"

A ten-foot-by-ten-foot frame, stretched tight with transparent plastic, was lowered between the audience and the platform. A recorded drumroll came from the sound system. The needle on the boiler neared the red zone. Bob pulled even more of Sarah's costume off to feed the fire, leaving her in a sequined thong bikini and halter.

Then he threw the lever.

A tremendous gout of steam shot from vents in the cylinders, briefly obscuring the platform from the audience, and then the two pistons came together with a tremendous clang and thunderclap. Watermelon sprayed forward and backward, spattering the splash shield and looking unpleasantly like blood as it dripped down.

Bob pulled the lever in the other direction and the two pistons withdrew. As they did, the lower half of Larry, from the shoulders down, dropped onto the stage, pinched off by the impact. The head flipped down and hung, upside down, still suspended by the manacled arms.

"Tough luck, Larry," Bob said.

The splash shield withdrew and Bob's assistants took the remains of Larry out on the gurney, covered in the watermelon-stained sheet. A recorded dirge played and Bob held his hand over his heart.

Sarah shoveled more coal into the firebox, and the steam gauge crawled back toward the red. Bob added parts of Vanessa's costume to the fire so that she was clad as briefly as Sarah; then Vanessa brought another audience member on stage to handcuff Bob to the platform and check the integrity of the manacles.

"Nervous?" Bob asked the man, who kept glancing sideways at the two pistons. "You should be. The last guy who volunteered disappeared and hasn't been seen since."

I had to admit he was taking my disappearance well. I made up my mind to reappear before the act was over.

Vanessa escorted the volunteer back off the stage and then Bob said, "If you guys think I'm lowering the splash shield, you're crazy. If I'm between these pistons when they connect—well, let's just say I hope to make quite an impression on the audience."

The needle moved closer to red and the drumroll began. Vanessa moved to the lever and Sarah joined her, each woman putting a hand on the lever. The stage darkened, and a broad spotlight illuminated Bob and the apparatus. A more tightly focused light lit the two women. In the sudden darkness, the mouth of the firebox spilled an orange glow onto the stage and a third spotlight flicked on and tightened on the steam pressure gauge.

I blocked the light with my hand, looking, instead, into the shadows around Bob, trying to see what they didn't want the audience to see. The tension was getting to me and the possibility that Bob would get crunched seemed more and more likely.

The raised platform eliminated the possibility of him dropping through another trapdoor. While the spotlight did cast shadows, it also wasn't so tightly focused that he could dodge to either side without being seen.

The drumroll increased in volume and the women each held up three fingers, then two, then one; then they shoved the lever hard over.

I kept my eyes on Bob. At the count of two, he shifted his hands and grabbed the chains of the manacles hard. As he did this the sleeves of his tux jacket slipped back and I saw that he had some sort of metal sleeve around his wrists, between the manacles and his skin. As the women counted one I saw something happening to the cables that the manacles were attached to. Thin wires, dull black, pulled out from the surface of the cables and tightened. I saw the ends of the manacles come free of the cable and draw slightly upward, obviously attached to the thin wires.

Bob preserved the illusion by holding his arms out stiff, so they still seemed to be pulled tight by the cuffs. Then the women shoved the lever over and the steam shot out in front of the platform. As the steam shot out, the wires tightened and Bob literally flew straight up so fast that he was in the shadows above the stage before the pistons came together.

Then they slammed together with a frightful clang and I jumped to the top of the pistons, where they pressed together, and sat there, in that brief instant before the steam cleared.

The applause was terrifying.

Bob reentered the stage, then, from the other side of the boiler and slammed the firebox door shut. With this cue, the stage lights came up and he stepped forward to take a bow. It wasn't until he motioned for his assistants to take a bow as well that he noticed they were staring at me, perched on the "Hammers of Doom."

He walked toward me, eyes wide, mouth tight. I jumped

down, first to the platform, then to the stage. The applause increased and I took a half bow. Bob turned back to the audience again and said, "Thank you for coming." Then he made a gesture with his right hand and the curtain came down.

I wondered if it might not be a good idea to leave.

Bob turned around then, hands at his side, balled into fists. "All right, asshole. How'd you do it?" His voice was harsh and loud, and I took an involuntary step back. He started walking toward me.

I looked nervously around and saw four of the backstage crew come forward, watching me, wondering who the hell I was. Some of them also looked angry. Sarah and Vanessa just watched, faces impassive.

"Bob," I said loudly, "you're a poseur."

Then I raised my hands, snapped my fingers, and jumped.

The morning after my encounter with Bob the Magnificent, I decided, out of the blue, to go to Florida, to see my grandfather. My travel agent got me a seat on a jet leaving La Guardia in less than twenty minutes. I walked aboard during the final call.

From Orlando, I switched to a small commuter flight for the last leg to Pine Bluffs. It was noisy, cramped, and it jumped around a lot in the afternoon thermals. At one point, after a particularly vicious downdraft pulled me up against the seat belt for seconds, I nearly jumped away.

The only thing that stopped me was that I didn't think I could jump back into a moving vehicle, not one out of my sight. If I was going to jump away from the plane, I decided I'd wait until we were closer to the ground and even more out of control. The flight lasted a half hour of real time and a lifetime of subjective time. Things were better when it was back on the ground.

The airport building was only slightly bigger than the first floor of my brownstone and the ticket agent was the ground crew, baggage handler, and security. The five other passengers on my flight were met by friends or relatives, leaving me to the tender mercies of the airport car service, a beat-up

blue station wagon with a driver whose face was all seams.
"Where to?"

"Oh. Hang on a second. I need to get it out of the phone book." I went back into the building, to the pay phone in the corner.

There was no Arthur Niles listed. *Shit*. I glanced around the building—no one was looking my way. I studied my corner and "acquired" it, then jumped to my old room, in Dad's house. The dust was thicker than ever. I rustled through my desk until I found one of Granddad's old letters, a birthday card with the envelope. The address was on it. I tucked it in my pocket and shut all the drawers.

There were steps in the hallway that stopped outside the door. I froze, stood still as stone. If the door handle moved, I could be gone in seconds. A voice, Dad's, with a quaver I didn't remember, said, "Davy?"

I don't know why, but after hesitating a second I said, "Yes, it's me."

I don't think he expected an answer. I heard him gasp and the floor creak as he shifted his weight from one foot to another. Then he was fumbling at the padlock. When I heard it click open, I jumped back to the Pine Bluffs airport.

The ticket agent/baggage guy at the counter glanced up as I sagged against the wall. *Well, let him wonder,* I thought, thinking of Dad, not the ticket agent. My stomach was churning, but there was a curious satisfaction, not unlike the feeling I'd gotten when I broke the flour container. Though that hadn't been as satisfying as it could have been. I didn't get to see the results, but I also didn't leave footprints.

The card and envelope were still in my hand when I walked outside to the cabby. "345 Pomosa Circle," I told him.

I got in the back and sat, quiet, as a lot of white houses and greenery went by. Dad had sounded different, *old*. I tried not to think about it.

"Here you are: 345 Pomosa Circle. That's four bucks."

I paid him and he drove off.

The house was mostly as I remembered it, a small white

bungalow with date palms and a canal that ran behind every house. The name on the mailbox said JOHNSON.

The woman who came to the door spoke Spanish and very little English. When I asked after Arthur Niles, she said, *"Un momento, por favor."* She vanished back into the house.

Another woman, blond, with a deep Southern accent, came to the door. "Mistuh Niles? He passed away four years ago, I buhlieve. Yes, it was four years ago in August. He had him a stroke, in the worst heat, and died later that same day." She put a finger on her lips as if thinking. "We lived down the street then, at 330 Pomosa. We bought the house from his daughter."

I blinked. "Mary Rice?"

"Well, I think that was her married name. I think the paperwork said Mary Niles."

"Does she live here in town?"

"I don't buhlieve so. She was here for the funeral, down at the Olive Branch Cemetery, but at the closing, she was represented by a lawyer with a power of attorney."

"Do you remember the lawyer's name?"

She looked at me. "Uh, I don't suppose you'd care to tell me why you need to know all this?"

I paused. "Well, I'm David Rice, Mary's son. When she left my dad, she, uh, left me, too." I felt my face flush and my palms were sweating. Well, hadn't she? *Didn't she leave you behind because you weren't worth taking?* Lamely, I added, "I'm trying to find her."

Silence. "Hmmm. Well, let me look at the paperwork and see what the name is. You come in out of the sun while I look." She led me back into the house and showed me a chair in the front room. "Roseleeeenda? *Aqua frío, por favor, por el hombre."* Then she vanished into the back of the house.

In a minute, the maid brought me a glass of ice water. I said, *"Gracias."*

She said, *"Por nada,"* smiled briefly, and left.

The front room was strange to me, as all the furniture was different. It wasn't until I glanced out the window and saw the way that it framed the house across the street that I had any sense of being in there before. Then the memory was sharp, clear, and painful.

"Darn you, Davy! That's the third time you've given me the queen of spades."

"Now, Davy, you be kind to your granddad. After all, he's old and feeble."

"I can still lay you across my knee and spank you, young lady. Take that!"

"Oh, Dad, not another heart! Well, I guess Davy wins again."

We'd played a lot of hearts that summer visit. Granddad and I would fish early in the morning, and some days Mom and I went to the beach.

It was a good trip.

"The deed is down at the bank, so I called my husband. He remembered the lawyer's name. It was Silverstein, Leo Silverstein." She carried a phone book with her when she came back into the room. "The phone book says his office is down on Main. It'll be overlooking the square by this address—Fourteen East Main."

I thanked her and left. When she closed the door I jumped back to the local airport, appearing by the pay phone. There was a gasp from the counter, but I just walked out through the door as if nothing had happened. I glanced over my shoulder and saw that the ticket agent was following me through the door.

Damn.

I walked around the corner and jumped back to New York.

Whereas Millie had forbidden me the touch of her body but twice a month, she still let me call her every night.

"Hi, it's me."

"What's wrong?"

"Huh?"

"You call me every night. You don't usually sound like an undertaker."

"Oh. Well, I've been trying to find my mother. I went to Florida, to see my grandfather."

"What? Are you in Florida right now?"

"Huh? Oh, no. I came back. My grandfather died four years ago."

The line was quiet for a moment. "And you just found out?"

"Yeah."

"I wonder if your father knew?"

"I don't know," I said tiredly. "I wouldn't put it past him."

"Were you close to your grandfather?"

I thought about it. Hearts and fishing and the odd birthday card with a twenty-dollar bill taped carefully inside. "Once, I was. A long time ago."

"It's rough to lose somebody. I'm sorry."

"Yeah, well . . ."

"You couldn't have known."

I stared at the phone. "How did you know?"

"What? That you feel guilty about not knowing he was dying? For not knowing when he died?"

"I should have!"

She took a deep breath. "No. I know you feel that way, Davy. You can't help it. It's all right to feel that way. *But there was no way for you to know!* We all feel guilty, now and then, about things that aren't our fault. Trust me—this wasn't something you could do anything about."

I was angry then, at her presumption, at her perception, for putting a name to the feeling I'd been fighting all day. "I should have known when I didn't get a birthday card on my fifteenth birthday. I could have written. I could have sent a letter from school. Dad wouldn't have stopped that one!"

"Your father used to read your mail?"

"Well, I'm pretty sure. We were rural so we had a postbox in town. I didn't have a key for it. I once found an envelope in the car addressed to me with no return address."

"Christ! Why did he do that?"

"I don't know. He didn't let me write relatives, though."

"No wonder, the way he treated you."

I didn't say anything for a while. She didn't press me, just stayed on the line, a companionable breathing, barely heard. Finally I said, "I'm sorry, Millie. I'm not very good company tonight."

"It's okay. I'm just sorry you're having a rough time. I wish I could hold you right now."

I screwed my eyes shut and felt the phone squeak under my suddenly increased grip. *I could be in your arms in seconds, love. I could. . . .* I made myself say, "I wish you could, too. I'll hold you to that on Friday."

"Okay. You sure you don't want me to meet your plane?"

"No. That's okay. I'll get to your door before seven P.M. Just don't eat without me."

"Okay. Sleep well."

"Thanks, I'll try. Uh, Millie?"

"Yes?"

"I . . . I . . . I'm going back to Florida tomorrow, but I'll still call, okay?"

She sounded slightly disappointed about something. "Yeah, Davy. That's fine."

I jumped to the corner of the Pine Bluffs airport building, outside, on the sidewalk. When I looked around the corner, the beat-up blue station wagon was there with the ancient cabbie. He seemed surprised to see me.

"How'd you get out here? The Orlando flight doesn't get in for another fifteen minutes."

I shrugged. "I need to go to the Olive Branch Cemetery, and then I need to go to Fourteen East Main Street."

"Ohhhhhkay. Hop in."

He tried to engage me in conversation a couple of more times, but I answered his questions in monosyllables or shrugs. He tried once more in the long curving drive of the cemetery. "I knew most of the people buried here. You looking for any body in particular?"

It was a large cemetery. "Arthur Niles."

"Ah. Well that explains your trip out to Pomosa Circle."
He pulled the car around to the far side of the cemetery and
parked in the shade of a tree. "See that white marble stone
there, fourth from the end?" He pointed down a row of
gravestones that ran to the edge of the cemetery.

"Yes. Is that it?"

"Yeah. Take your time, I'll wait." He picked up a newspaper.

"Thanks."

"Arthurs Niles, born nineteen twenty-two, died nineteen
eighty-nine, beloved of wife, daughter, and grandson."
Grandson? Oh, mother, why didn't you tell me? There were
flowers on the grave, old and withered, in one of those rusty
iron hoops attached to a stake. I pulled the flowers from the
holder and removed the few dead leaves from the grass.

*Sorry, Granddad, I didn't get to say good-bye. I would've
preferred to say hello.* I felt sad . . . incredibly sad.

After a while I consciously acquired the site for jumping,
then carried the dead flowers and leaves to a wire trash can
by the drive.

The cabbie was still reading so I stepped behind a tree
and jumped to the flower market on Twenty-eighth Street,
Manhattan. I bought a prepared bouquet with roses and
astemarias and mums and orchids. It cost thirty bucks. I
jumped back to the grave and left it in the iron holder.

The cabbie put down his paper when I climbed into the
backseat. He didn't say anything, just started up the car and
drove me into town.

He did speak, though, when he stopped the car on Main
Street. "Will you need a ride after this, Davy?"

I looked at him. *How . . .? Ah.* "How well did you know
my grandfather?"

He shrugged. "Well enough. We played pinochle at his
house every Wednesday, a bunch of us old codgers. He was
a good man—a lousy pinochle player, but a good man."

I sat back in the seat. "Do you know where my mother
is, Mr. . . .?"

"Steiger, Walt Steiger. I don't know where Mary is. After
she left your father she was here for about a year, what with

one thing or another." His expression was grim and he looked away for a moment. Then he said, "Art said that she was working out in California, I think, after that, but I'm not sure. I think he also told me she was moving again, but that was right before the stroke. I don't recall where." He twisted in the seat. "I got to talk to her for a moment at the funeral, but we just talked about Art."

"Oh." I sat there for several more heartbeats. "Thanks for the information. What's the fare?"

He shrugged. "Five bucks."

"But you had to wait over thirty minutes. . . ."

"I was reading. Give me five bucks."

He wouldn't take a tip.

Leo Silverstein's office was on the second floor, over a drugstore. I went up narrow stairs and through a glass door, where a middle-aged woman typed rapidly at a word processor while she listened to headphones. I stepped into her field of vision. She started and pulled her headphones off.

"Dictation?" I asked, smiling.

"Grateful Dead," she said. "Can I help you?"

"I'd like to see Mr. Silverstein, please. My name is David Rice. I'd like to talk to him about my mother, Mary Niles."

"Ah. Did you have an appointment, Mr. Rice?" She asked it the way people do when they know damn well you don't have one.

I shook my head and swallowed. "Sorry, no. I'm just in from New York for the day. I didn't know Mr. Silverstein handled my mother's affairs until yesterday and I wasn't sure I'd be in Pine Bluffs today."

She looked skeptical.

"I only need a moment of his time. Uh, by the way, why do they call this town Pine Bluffs? I haven't seen a pine tree or a cliff since I got here."

In a dry voice she said, "The bluffs are upriver ten miles by the original townsite. They logged the pine trees out in the early eighteen-hundreds. Have a seat," she added, pointing at the couch across from her desk. "I'll ask Mr. Silverstein if he can see you."

I sat down while she talked quietly into the phone.

I *hated* this. I've never liked meeting new people. Well, that is, I hate reaching out to strangers. *What are you scared of, Davy? Think they'll take your hand off?* I squirmed on the couch, trying to get comfortable. *Yes, they might take my hand off or, worse, not like me.*

The door to the inner office opened and a man came through, perhaps fifty, my height, gray hair. He was wearing the vest and pants of a three-piece suit and his tie was loosened at the collar. "Mr. Rice? I'm Leo Silverstein. I've got an appointment in ten minutes but I can give you until then."

I stood and shook his hand. "Kind of you," I said as I followed him into the office.

He shut the door and pointed to chair. "So you're Mary Niles's son?"

"Yes."

"What can I do for you?"

"I'm trying to locate her."

"Oh." He picked up a paperweight on his desk and shifted it from hand to hand. "I was wondering if it might be something like that."

I frowned. The plush seat seemed suddenly hard. "What do you mean?"

He took a deep breath. "Your mother showed up here six years ago with three broken bones in the face, lacerations, bruises, and severe trauma. She'd been physically and mentally abused. She went through a year of inpatient psychiatric therapy for severe depression and two operations to reconstruct her face."

I stared at him. My stomach churned.

Leo Silverstein watched me carefully, the paperweight poised in one hand, ready to drop into the other, but not yet. "Is this a surprise to you?"

I nodded. "Well . . . I knew of at least one time when my father hurt her. But, when she left, I came home from school one day and she was gone. My dad wouldn't talk about it." *I should have known!* "I was only twelve at the time."

He nodded his head. "I tried several times to talk your mother into bringing charges against your father. She refused. She said she never wanted to get near him, to be in the same state as him. She was absolutely terrified of him." He started shifting the paperweight again. "I also think that she was afraid of what he might do to you. Apparently, he made threats to this effect."

A goddam hostage. He got away with it because of me. I felt like throwing up.

"Where is she now?" I asked. *I'm sorry, I'm sorry, I'm sorry. . . .*

"Well, that's the point. I can't say. My client has instructed me to keep that information completely confidential. I don't have a choice in the matter. She made no provisions for exceptions."

"Not even for me? For her son?"

He shrugged. "How is she to know that you aren't working in concert with your father?"

"I ran away from that son of a bitch over a year ago. I am *not* working with him!"

He shifted back in his chair and I saw him grip the paperweight suddenly, almost like a weapon. *Relax, Davy.* I let a breath out slowly and sat well back in the chair, laying my hands in my lap. More slowly I repeated, "I am not working with him."

"I think I believe you," Silverstein said, loosening his grip on the paperweight and relaxing slightly. "However, that has no bearing on the matter. I still can't tell you where she is."

I folded my arms tightly across my chest. I knew that my ears were burning and I felt ashamed and angry and on the verge of doing or saying something stupid.

"I would be willing, however, to forward a message or a letter to her."

What would I say? What does she think of me? How could I write a letter without knowing that? She doesn't really want to hear from me. . . .

I stood abruptly. "I'll have to think about it," I said shortly. I noticed that Silverstein had shifted back again and was gripping the paperweight tightly. *What is it in my face that is scaring him so?* I went to the door and jerked the door open, then stopped. I was still angry at him, but part of me realized that it wasn't his fault, but that didn't take away the anger. *How would you like to be jumped to a truck stop in Minnesota, Mr. Silverstein?* Without turning I said, "Thanks. Please excuse my bad temper." Then I walked past the receptionist, out the glass door, and down the stairs.

I was about to walk out onto the street when I saw Walt Steiger, the cabbie, still parked out front, reading his paper.

I did not want to talk to him.

I jumped to Brooklyn.

The apartment was too small to contain my mood. I tried to sit, but I couldn't stop moving. I tried to lie down, but there was no way to hold still. Downstairs the Washburns were fighting again, shouting at each other. I heard dishes break and flinched as I paced.

I was still dressed for Florida, but I didn't want to change. I grabbed my coat, the long soft leather one, and jumped to the walkway of the Brooklyn Bridge.

The clock on the Watchtower building said it was forty-five degrees, and the wind off the East River bit like teeth. The sky had a low, dirty overcast that fit my mood exactly.

One year in the hospital . . . oh my God, ohmigod, ohmigod. I clenched the lapels of the coat together and stared blindly south, away from the wind, into the harbor. I remembered standing over my dad, a heavy scotch bottle in my hand, torn with indecision and doubt. I remember deciding not to kill him. *Or was it that you couldn't kill him?*

Whatever. Whatever it was that kept me from crushing his head in, I regretted it. I was sorry that I hadn't killed him.

Kill him now? I pulled my head down, between my shoulders. The wind howled past my ears, rocking me on my feet. *Maybe.*

I spent the rest of the afternoon thinking of ways to do it, most of which involved jumping. *I could grab him, jump to the top of the Empire State Building, and drop him over the edge.* I looked down at the cold waters of the East River. *The drop from here isn't so bad either.* I pictured things, played them out in my head, a hundred different violent acts. Instead of calming my anger, each one made me feel guiltier, more ashamed of myself. This made me even angrier. I found myself clenching the railing and grinding my teeth. My jaw hurt. *Damnitalltohell! I'm not the one that broke her face!*

It was when I realized that I *could* kill him, *and* get away with it, that I began to calm down. That's when I realized that I wouldn't.

I still wanted to hurt him, though. I wanted to smash things, to feel flesh under my fists. I wanted to break a few bones myself.

I remembered what I considered doing to the lawyer in Florida. I was going to jump him to that truck stop in Minnesota, where Topper Robbins, the truck driver who tried to rape me, had bought my trust with a lousy meal.

Topper Robbins. Now there's someone who deserves some punishment.

I pulled my coat tighter around me and jumped.

Topper pulled into the truck stop at 10:30 P.M., twenty minutes later than what one of the waitresses had said was his usual time. I'd been waiting for over an hour, moderately comfortable despite the snow because of newly purchased long underwear and gloves.

Waiting in the cold, though, gave me second thoughts, and I'd just about talked myself out of it, when he arrived. My hands clenched suddenly and I could feel my lips draw back from my teeth. Going home became the last thing on my mind.

He fueled up at the pumps, then pulled over into the semitrailer parking area, locked his cab, and went inside. I watched him take a seat in the drivers' section, then walked over to his truck.

His tractor cab was small. There was no bed behind the seats, just a rear window for checking blind spots. I looked around, then climbed up between the tank trailer and the cab. There was a locked storage box welded there and the air hose connections for the pneumatic brakes on the trailer. I found I could sit there with my head below the window. If I stood on the box, I could look in the window. I acquired the place for jumping, then went to the back of the truck.

A ladder was welded to the back, running past the Petro-Chem logo and the FLAMMABLE warning sign and the THIS TRUCK MAKES WIDE RIGHT TURNS sign. I climbed up it and found that there was very little to hang on to atop the tank, but at the back of the trailer, between the ladder and the tank, was a ledge formed by the hose storage boxes. I swung around the ladder and sat there. The metal was very cold, but one could ride there.

I jumped to Café Borgia, in Greenwich Village, and had hot chocolate with whipped cream and cinnamon. Between the chocolate, the warmth of the café, and the long underwear, I was nicely warmed, almost sweating, when I jumped back to the truck stop, to the edge of the asphalt.

Topper was still eating.

I walked then, back and forth, occasionally crunching the thin crust of snow on the grass. When I got chilled, I jumped back to my apartment for a few minutes. It occurred to me that I hadn't called Millie, but I didn't want to take the time now. Topper might leave, and I'd have to wait another day.

After several of these walk, jump, get warm, jump cycles, Topper finally left the restaurant. I watched him walk to the truck, open the cab, and take a hammer from behind the seat. Then he walked all the way around the truck hitting the tires. Apparently satisfied, he put the hammer back, climbed into the truck, and started it up.

I jumped to the box behind the cab before the truck could move. Once it started moving, I could jump away from it, but I probably couldn't jump back onto the truck. Not from out of sight.

The wind whipped around the edges of the cab as Topper slowly worked his way up through the gears. I pulled my coat collar higher. When the truck pulled onto the interstate, I tried jumping to the back of the truck, on the ledge formed by the hose boxes. No problem, though it was much windier back there. I jumped back to behind the cab. Again, no problem.

I'd hoped this would be the case. Even though this was a moving vehicle, I knew the distance between myself and my target. I suspected I'd be able to jump onto this truck from off of it, even if it was moving, as long as I could *see* it. If I jumped back to my apartment right now, though, I was sure I wouldn't be able to jump back.

Before I got too cold to concentrate, I started my "game."

I stood upright on the storage box, roughly behind the passenger's seat, and held on to one of the pneumatic pipes with my left hand. With my right hand, I took a small flashlight and shone it on my face as I looked in the rear window.

I couldn't see Topper, but my face was reflected in the window, seemingly floating without support. The low angle of the flashlight cast dark shadows up my face and made it look unnaturally white. The dark coat didn't reflect at all.

It took Topper a moment to notice. Perhaps he glanced at the right rear mirror and caught a glimpse of light out of the corner of his eye where no light should be. So he turned to take a good look. Probably a second and a third, as well. That's speculation, but I do know the next thing he did was put the brakes on, hard.

I switched the light off and jumped to the back platform.

The tanker took several seconds to stop. At the last minute he pulled off onto the shoulder. I heard the cab door open, and heard his steps as he climbed down. There was a sweep of light on the tarmac and I realized I wasn't the only one with a flashlight.

The diesel engine's rattle muffled his voice, but I heard him cursing, then I heard him walk toward the back of the truck, the beam from the flashlight preceding him on the asphalt. I waited until he was almost to the rear of the truck, then jumped to the back of the cab again.

I couldn't hear him, this close to the running engine. The driver's door was slightly ajar so the cab interior light was on and I could see inside. I jumped into the driver's seat and turned off the ignition. The diesel died with a rumble. I looked at the side mirrors. Topper came running up the driver's side of the vehicle. I jumped to the rear ledge again.

I heard him swearing. I climbed the ladder to the top of the truck and peered forward. He was standing by the driver's door, staring at the ignition keys, the flashlight pointed at the ground. He shut and locked the cab; then, carefully putting the keys in his jacket pocket, he started to walk back around the truck, shining the light under and around the tires as well as over the entire structure. I let him get halfway back to the rear and jumped back to the interior of the cab.

It was warm in the cab.

After marching the entire perimeter of the truck, Topper walked out to the low scrub bushes off to the side of the road and swung the flashlight this way and that. He marched back shaking his head.

I laughed. As he unlocked the door, I jumped to the rear of the truck. When he started up the diesel and started the truck rolling again, I jumped back to the storage box behind the cab.

Get the picture?

Over the next hour, I did the whole thing five more times. He didn't get twelve miles up Interstate 94. The sixth time, he began wheezing as he walked around the truck. "Goddam it! What do you want? Who the hell are you?"

I waited until he was at the rear of the truck, then stepped down off the truck and walked along the road, until I was a hundred feet or so away from the truck. There was a culvert there, marked by reflectors, that ran right to the edge of the shoulder and went under the highway. It was a concrete ditch four feet across and six feet deep. I walked farther down the road and acquired a site for jumping, a road marker, then jumped back to the culvert.

In the distance, I could see the spot of light bobbing

slowly around the tank truck. I positioned myself on the
edge of the shoulder, my collar pulled close, my hands in my
pockets, and, coincidentally, standing in front of the first
reflector that marked the culvert.

Topper finally pulled himself up into the cab and started
the engine. When he turned on the headlights, they hit me
square in the face.

I didn't flinch. I stood there. The truck didn't move for
a moment; then it started with a lurch. It made no effort to
turn back onto the road, but continued to pick up speed. I
stared at the driver's-side windshield, and held still. The
truck continued to gain speed, Topper revving the engine
quite high, but still, the truck was only going thirty mph or
so as it approached me. I held still and waited until I could
feel the heat radiating from the engine before I jumped to
the road marker, up the road.

The right front wheel of the tractor dropped into the
culvert and slammed into the far edge with the sharp punc-
tuation of the tire blowing out. The rear of the tractor cab
swung around to the right, pushed by the tank trailer. Then
the whole rig rolled over on its side in ponderous slow
motion, sparks flying as the cab scraped across the concrete
edges of the culvert accompanied by glittering arcs of glass
as bits of broken window splashed through the truck headlights.

I readied myself to jump, afraid that the tank would
explode, but it stopped shortly after that, the cab twisted
and crumpled, one of its headlights out, the other pointed
at a low angle into the sky. The tank didn't even seem to be
leaking.

I walked closer.

Topper had one arm tangled in the steering wheel and
was hanging across the stick shift down into the passenger
side of the cab. His face was flecked with spots of blood. His
eyes stared at me, followed me, as I walked around to the
front of the cab for a better look. He made small keening
noises and his one free hand tried for a purchase on the
steering wheel, to relieve the strain on his other arm.

Across the median cars were pulling to a stop. I heard doors slam and excited voices. I ignored them.

I smiled slowly at Topper. He made that small sound again and frantically pawed for the steering wheel. Then, while his eyes were on me, I jumped.

EIGHT

"Hi."

"Uh, what time is it?"

"Eleven-thirty. Did I wake you up?"

"I fell asleep on the couch. I was waiting for your call."

I grinned foolishly into the phone. "Sorry I called so late. I was busy." I was lying on my bed, under the covers, trying to warm up after my little affair in Minnesota.

"Hunting for your mother?"

"Well, no. I was evening an old score."

Her voice changed, became more wary, awake. "What do you mean? You didn't do anything to your father?"

My grip tightened on the phone. I'd managed to forget about Dad for a while. "No. I didn't. He deserves it, but I haven't." I paused. "I found out something bad today, something awful."

"What?"

"My mother spent a year in a psychiatric hospital immediately after she left my dad. She also had two operations to have her face rebuilt."

I heard her sharp intake of breath. "Oh, Davy, how awful."

"Yeah. Millie, they won't tell me where she *is*. They think I'll lead Dad to her."

"Whoa, Davy, calm down. Take a deep breath."

I closed my eyes, exhaled, inhaled. "Sorry," I said a moment later.

121

"It's all right to be upset. You've heard a lot of nasty stuff today. It must be hard for you. Now, who won't tell you where she is?"

"Her lawyer won't. She left instructions not to reveal her address to anybody, not even me."

"Oh, Davy. That must hurt." She hesitated. "I wish I could be there."

"Christ, I miss you, Millie."

We were both quiet for a moment, but it was almost like being with her.

"What on earth should I do? The lawyer said he'd forward a letter to her."

"Oh. So you could write her?"

"I guess."

"Well, don't you want to?"

"I don't know! I mean, if she doesn't want to see me, what's the good of writing?"

There was silence on the other end of the line. "Davy, you don't know what she wants. I think she's just frightened of your father. Write to her. Tell her how you feel. Tell her what *you* want."

"I don't know what I want. I can't write."

Millie let out a breath and was quiet. "What is it, Davy? Is real rejection worse than your imagined rejection? As long as you don't write, you can pretend that she'd want to see you if she heard from you. Is that it?"

Oh, Christ! I squeezed my eyes shut. Tears leaked from them. I couldn't say anything.

"Are you there, Davy?" she asked softly. "Are you all right?"

"No, I'm not," I managed to say. "That is probably too close to the mark." My throat was tight and my grip on the phone was painful. "Look, I have to think about it. I'll call you back tomorrow, okay?"

Her voice, when she answered, was small. "Okay. See you tomorrow. I really care about you, Davy."

I hung up the phone, pulled the pillow across my face, and wished I could die.

* * *

I'd felt so good after Topper crashed his truck. Why did it seem so petty in the morning light? So mean? Didn't he deserve it? I was getting angry again. I tried to pick up a book that I'd been reading the day before, but it was no good. I couldn't concentrate and the words crawled on the page.

I put on my coat and jumped to Minnesota.

"I saw a tanker truck on its side west of here. Strange accident."

The waitress put my coffee down. "Yeah, one of our regular customers. Apparently he fell asleep and went off the road."

"Was he killed?" There, I'd said it, and I didn't know whether it was a fear or a hope.

"No. He got cut up a little and I believe he sprained a shoulder. They kept him in the county hospital overnight for observation."

Alive. I felt relief and was surprised.

A busboy was cleaning the next table. "Four state troopers was in here this morning for doughnuts. I heard one of them say that they drug tested Topper. Topper claimed he didn't fall asleep—said he was after a ghost, that a ghost decoyed him into the ditch."

The waitress shook her head. "There's always been something strange about Topper, something not quite right. What was he on?"

The boy stopped wiping. "Nothing. They said he was clean. But that's why they kept him overnight, to look for brain damage. They also X-rayed his skull to see if he broke it."

"Huh! Isn't that something." She looked at my cup. "You want some more coffee, sugar?"

I smiled and said, "Yes, please."

Dear Mom,

I ran away from home a year and three months ago. I now live in New York City and I am doing well. I would like to see you, though I don't know if this is something you wish. I miss you, but I would under-

stand if you do not want to see me. In any case, I
would appreciate hearing from you.

You can call me at 718/553-4465 or write me at PO
Box 62345, New York, NY 10004.

Your son. . . .

It was awkward, rude, and simpleminded, but it was my
sixth try and I didn't want to do this letter again. I gave the
command to print and the laser printer silently produced
the page. I signed it, then put it in an envelope with Mom's
single name, Mary Niles, on it.

I jumped to the stairway below Leo Silverstein's office.
Upstairs, I gave the envelope to his secretary and asked her
to give it to him. She said she would without asking any
questions. I guess she knew the situation.

I don't want your pity! I was tempted to teleport home
right in front of her, just to take that expression of sympathetic understanding off her face. However, I'd done that
too much already. I thanked her and jumped, instead, from
the privacy of the stairwell.

I called Millie and told her about sending the letter.

"That's good, Davy. I know it's a frightening step, but at
least you'll *know.*"

"What if she doesn't want to see me? What if she doesn't
care?"

She took her time answering. "I don't think you have to
worry about that. But, even if that's the way she feels, at
least you'll know and can go on from there instead of being
stuck."

"Stuck? Well, I guess that's one way to describe it. I'm
stuck somewhere between having a mother and not having
one."

Millie said carefully, "Davy . . . you haven't had a mother
in six years. You're really stuck between knowing if she's
going to be part of your life again, or not."

I shook my head angrily. "I don't get the distinction."

"You are not the same person you were when your
mother left. Time alone would account for that, not to

mention an abusive father. Your mother is not the same person. Psychiatric counseling can bring about great changes in a person. Neither of you will be able to drop back into the relationship you had, not without a lot of pretending. It just won't *fit*."

"Damn it, Millie. It's so hard."

"Yeah."

I changed the subject. "What do you want to do this weekend?"

"I hadn't really thought about it. Maybe just lie around."

A small smile. "In bed?"

"Well, some," she said. "But not all of it. That's a really good way to ruin a relationship."

"Sex?"

"Nothing but sex. Let's have more between us than a thin film of moisture."

"Uh, don't you like it? I thought . . . well, you seemed to . . ."

"I love sex. I enjoy it enough that my Protestant upbringing gives me twinges now and then. I love sex with you, Davy, because, well . . . I love you."

There was something wrong with my face and my stomach was churning. I couldn't see the phone, the chair, the bookshelves. Only her face. "Oh, Millie—let me fly out there tonight." My voice was rough and the hand holding the receiver wouldn't stop shaking.

I heard her exhale. "Even if there was a flight, you couldn't get here until morning. I have classes."

I could be there in a heartbeat. The silence was warm with shared longing. I felt miserable and elated.

"You can come on Thursday, though, if you like."

"Are you sure?"

"I get out of my last class at four-thirty. I can be at the airport by six. No, six-thirty—that's rush hour."

"No. I'll be at *your* apartment at four-thirty, Thursday." Then, before I could lose my courage, I added, "I love you, too."

She was quiet for a moment; then, almost too softly to be heard, she said, "Oh, Davy, I'm going to cry."

"Well, you're allowed."

Go to her. Go to her now. I wanted to jump so badly, but another voice said, *Wait. She loves you, but will she love the jumper?*

I heard her blow her nose. "God, I hate the way my nose runs when I cry."

"I'm sorry I made you cry."

"Oh, shut up, you idiot. I told you, tears are a blessing. You gave me a gift and it made me happy, not sad. Tears don't always mean grief. And you're not an idiot and I love you."

Go to her. Wait. Aaaaaaagg.

"I love you. I wanted to tell you that, I started to tell you that, when I called you about my grandfather being dead."

"Well, I wondered. . . ."

"I was scared to say it. I'm still scared."

Her voice was serious. "I'm relieved to hear it. It's not something to be said lightly."

"Then why do I want to keep saying it, over and over?"

"Perhaps you feel it deeply. I've got a theory about that phrase. It should be said as long as it's true, but not so frequently that it becomes automatic, meaningless, cheap. It should not be like 'good morning' or 'excuse me' or 'pass the butter, please.' You know?"

"I think so."

"But you can say it again, now, if you like."

"Oh, Millie. I love you."

"I love you. I'm going to go to bed now, but I may have trouble sleeping. Think of me."

"How can I avoid it?" *Go to her, go to her, go to her.*

She laughed. "Good night, sweetheart."

"Good night, love."

She hung up and I stared at the receiver in wonder. Then I jumped to Stillwater, outside her apartment, and watched her bedroom window until the light went out.

I was looking for a present for Millie and I remembered something I'd seen at the Metropolitan Museum of Art gift shop. I tried to jump to the steps of the museum and nothing happened. Quickly, before I lost all confidence, I jumped to Washington Square.

No problem.

I'd only been to the museum once, with Millie, and, though I'd intended to return many times, I hadn't got around to it.

You just don't remember it well enough, I thought.

The more places I jumped, the more places I had to remember, if I wanted to jump there again. *Am I going to have to jump to every site I know once a week, to keep them fresh in my mind?*

I decided it was time to buy some more toys.

On Forty-seventh Street I found it easy to spend two thousand dollars on: one video camera, small, using eight-millimeter tape; one video player for the same size tapes; one case of twenty-minute tapes, ten enclosed; two extra NiCad power packs; and an external fast charger for the power packs.

An hour later, after I'd charged a battery pack and read the camera's instructions, I jumped to Central Park, by the croquet green, on the west side of the park, and walked across it and up to Eighty-first, where the Met is. Then I spent a few minutes filming an out-of-the-way alcove by the doors of the museum, first recording the alcove, then standing in it and recording a panoramic view. I talked about the images and smells as I did it, into the microphone.

Then I jumped home, took the tape out and carefully labeled it, "New York Metropolitan Museum of Art, Front Steps." I watched it on the video player connected to my twenty-five-inch television. The video quality was excellent.

Now, obviously, I wasn't going to have any trouble jumping back to the museum. I'd just been there and I'd paid attention. However, in six months, when I hadn't been there for a while and the memory had faded, I hoped the videotape would give me the necessary "reminder."

We'll see.

After buying Millie's presents, I spent the rest of the day recording my more infrequently used jump sites. Sometimes, when the site was a little too public, I changed it to an out-of-the-way corner. In Florida, for instance, I acquired a new site at the Orlando airport, a nook formed by two columns. In Pine Bluffs I found a spot between two bushes in the town square across from Leo Silverstein's office. In Stillwater, I found an alleyway two houses down from Millie's house. In Stanville, I chose an area behind the dumpster at Dairy Queen, between a hedge and the building at the public library, and the backyard at Dad's house.

I had to buy two more cases of videocassettes, plus a rack to store the tapes in.

This took me through the end of Tuesday. On Wednesday, early in the morning, I jumped to the Orlando airport and caught the shuttle to Disney World. The bus got there twenty minutes before it opened. I found a space between two bushes, acquired it, jumped home to get the video camera, jumped back, and recorded the place. I also recorded a site inside the park. The security at Disney World is very good, so I was careful to select a place not covered by monitor cameras. I had this weird image of Mickey Mouse coming up to me and saying, "The jig is up! The jig is up! Hee, hee! Cuff him, Goofy."

I was pretty careful.

Several times during the day I was tempted to jump where people couldn't help but see me, to skip ahead in the longer lines. I hate long lines, but I didn't risk it. I could always jump back, first thing in the morning, before the crowds got there, or near closing, after they'd cleared out.

Millie should be here, I thought. *I wouldn't mind waiting in line with her.*

A memory, long forgotten, surfaced. Mom was going to take me here, to Disney World, on our next trip down to see Granddad.

I gave up around six in the evening, my feet hurting and my head aching from the heat.

Back in my apartment I napped for a couple of hours, then called Millie. We talked for over an hour; then like previous nights, I jumped to Stillwater to watch her window until the light went off.

Midnight EST found me staring at a photo-booth picture of Millie and arguing with myself.

Why don't you tell her?

What, tell her that I'm a bank robber? That I do nothing productive with my life? That I steal people's hard-earned money?

Just tell her about the jumping.

Sure. If I tell her about the jumping, think of all the other questions she'll ask. She loves me now. I don't have to be a freak to win her love. I can be myself.

Oh, yeah? She loves what you've chosen to show her. Isn't omitting the rest just as much a lie as manufacturing false-hoods? Aren't you living a falsehood? The longer you go without telling her, the more betrayed she'll feel when she does find out.

Does she have to find out, though?

Do you love her?

Ouch. *Okay, she has to be told. Eventually. When the time is right.*

I stared at Millie's picture and shivered.

At two in the morning the Washburns started fighting again, only this time it got physical. In a period of twenty minutes, her voice went from loud, angry comments to cries of fear and then finally, shrieks of pain.

It sounded like Mom.

I jumped to the corner, by the deli, my jeans pulled hastily on, my coat over bare shoulders. I dialed 911 at the pay phone and reported an assault in progress at that address and that apartment. When they asked for my name and whereabouts I said, "I was just walking by. I don't want to get involved, but it sounds like he's killing her." I hung up.

Unable to stand the screams, I didn't jump back to the apartment, dancing back and forth on the cold pavement in my bare feet. Even from here, I could hear her screaming faintly.

Hurry, dammit.

The police took five minutes to get there, a car pulling up

with flashing lights but no siren. I couldn't hear her screaming anymore. The two cops rang the doorbell for the Washburns' apartment and spoke into the intercom. I heard the door buzz and they pushed on through and went inside.

I stood by the phone, in shadow cast by the streetlight. My feet were getting colder by the minute. *So jump someplace warm.* I didn't move. I didn't want to go back to the apartment and I didn't want to go away. It was not unlike having a sore spot in my mouth, painful to the touch, but still the tongue keeps poking and prodding at it.

The two policeman stayed in the building less than two minutes, then walked out, got in the car, and drove away.

Shit.

I jumped back to my apartment and listened carefully. She was crying, but apparently he'd stopped hitting her. I turned the radio on to hide the noise, and went back to bed.

The weekend was magic, marred only by a nagging voice that said, over and over again, *tell her or you'll regret it,* and the fact that her roommate hadn't gone home for the weekend.

I gave her the cast-marble head, first.

"Oh my God, it's beautiful. What is it?"

"It's a reproduction of a detail from Michelangelo's *Pietá.* It's called *The Head of the Virgin.* I thought it highly appropriate."

She blushed and laughed. "Your second gift of virginity? Well, it's absolutely gorgeous and I love it. I'm afraid to ask how much it cost."

I shrugged and brought out the next box.

She looked at me accusingly. "I told you it makes me feel guilty when you spend money on me!"

"Apologies, in advance, then. I've kept myself in check, mostly, but I failed. You deserve much, much more."

She stared distractedly at the wrapped box. "Humph. Trying to get out of it with sweet talk isn't going to work." She shook the box, considered its dimensions, and bounced it on her palm to get some idea of the weight. "It better be a book."

"It's not."

She opened it slowly, carefully, keeping the paper intact. She got to the jewelry case and gave me another dark look.

"Open it."

She did and her mouth dropped open. Surprise and obvious pleasure. "You remembered."

It was a copy of the "Princess Necklace," the original of which had belonged to Sithathoryunet, daughter of Sesostris II, king of Egypt during the twelfth dynasty. It had drop-shaped beads of lapis lazuli, carnelian, aventurine, and gold plate over silver, separated by round beads of amethyst. I'm sure the original had solid-gold beads instead of electroplate, but you can't have everything. Two hundred and fifty dollars plus thirty for the matching earrings.

"Well, yes. I almost offered to buy it for you then, but you were so touchy about money."

She put the box down and pushed me back onto the couch. "I still am touchy about money. Stop buying me expensive gifts." She kissed me softly, taking her time. "I mean it." She kissed me again. "And thank you."

We went out that night to the nicest restaurant in Stillwater, so Millie could dress up and wear the necklace and earrings. Three different women asked about them, leaving her to flounder through a brief history of twelfth-dynasty Egypt. She glared at me after the last encounter.

"Stop laughing! I'm a psychology major, not an archaeologist." But she kept smiling through her complaint and she kept fingering the necklace throughout dinner.

There was an uncomfortable moment when she asked me how I'd kept my suit from wrinkling in my tiny overnight bag. I'd jumped back to my apartment from her bathroom, to grab the suit off a hanger. It hadn't been in my bag. It hadn't been folded at all. "Do you believe in paranormal powers?"

"Oh, like you have the power to iron men's suits with your mind?"

"Well, it would come in handy, wouldn't it? Tele-press-esis? Psycho-iron-etics?"

She laughed and I changed the subject.

On Friday she had three classes, so I jumped back to Brooklyn, read a while; then, when Disney World opened, I jumped to Florida and rode Star Tours three times in a row.

I didn't have to wait in line at all.

I've got to bring Millie here.

We spent the afternoon in Millie's bed, warm and safe, a fortress defending us from October's chill. We walked half a lazy mile afterward, to a café by the campus. Woodsmoke was drifting from some of the chimneys and it reminded me of Stanville.

At supper she asked, "Have you heard anything from your mother?"

"No, not yet, but it's only been three days. I checked the answering machine today, and there wasn't anything."

"Ah, you can do that over the phone?"

"Yeah, you can. All it takes is a touch-tone phone." I hadn't used the remote feature, but you can. *Half-truths and omissions. You call this an honest relationship?* I covered my mouth for a moment with my napkin. Then I countered with, "Have you heard from your ex?"

"Ugh. Why'd you bring him up?"

"Sorry."

"Sissy broke up with him."

I blinked. "What, over that incident at the party?" I couldn't resist. I'd wondered what had come of his story.

"Well . . . he got pretty weird right after that. He came up with this UFO-abduction story right out of the twilight zone. Sissy is really into New Age shit and she ate it up." She shook her head. "He was never that weird when I dated him. However, Sissy skipped class one day and found him in bed with her roommate." Millie grinned. "Now *that's* the Mark I know."

"What a sleaze!" *I should've jumped him to Harlem or Central Park—it was after dark. No . . . he's no Topper Robbins.* Still, I was glad I'd done as much as I had.

We saw a bad movie after dinner, so bad it was funny, and amused ourselves with whispered alternative dialogue.

We walked back through the campus and sat on a bench counting stars until the cold forced us to walk again, back home, and to bed. Surprisingly, we didn't make love, but slept, nestled like spoons, arms entwined.

And that was all right.

I milked my stay until Monday morning, explaining that I wasn't scheduled to depart until then. She wanted to know flight times and I nearly told her everything right then. Instead, I spilled a glass of water on the both of us by "accident" and in the ensuing cleanup, the question was forgotten.

Actually, I think she knew I didn't want to talk about it. So she didn't push it.

Back in New York the indicator on my answering machine showed three messages. I shrugged, then pushed the replay button and sat, cross-legged, on the floor, my head in my hands.

The first message said, "Have you ever considered the security of life insurance? The problems of—" It was a taped computer-driven ad. I stabbed angrily at the advance button and the machine forwarded to the next message.

"Have you ever considered the security of life insurance? The prob—" I hit the advance button again, swearing under my breath. I fully expected the next message to be the same stupid ad.

"Hello, this is Mary Niles, calling for Davy Rice. It's Sunday night around eight o'clock on the west coast, uh, I guess that's eleven, your time. I'd rather not leave a number, but I'll call again tomorrow, that is Monday, evening at the same time."

Mom.

The voice was heartrendingly familiar, unaged, just as I remembered it. Her tone was hesitant at first, then simply matter-of-fact.

What do I say to her? I played it again, to hear her voice. I found tears streaming down my face and my nose was running, but, instead of getting a tissue from the bathroom, I played the message over and over and over again.

* * *

Waiting through the day was bad. I hovered around the phone all morning, on the off chance that Mom might decide to call early, but the tension kept building and building. Finally, I jumped to the Embassy 2, 3, 4 at Times Square and watched two movies in a row, just to turn my mind off.

When I jumped home, the indicator showed one message. I swore and pushed replay, but it was some guy named Morgan asking about a girl named Sheila—a wrong number. Mixed feelings, relief and disappointment at the same time.

I called Millie at seven, six her time, which was early, but I didn't want to miss Mom when she called. I didn't want her to find a busy signal or the answering machine.

Luckily, Millie had just gotten home.

"Your mom called? That's great! What did she say?"

"It was just on the answering machine. She wouldn't leave a number, but she's calling again tonight. That's why I'm calling now, so I'm off the phone later."

"Ah. I'm really glad for you, Davy. I hope it works out."

"Well . . . we'll see." I was scared shitless, but hope was there, too. "I wouldn't have sent her the letter without your help, Millie. I wouldn't have had the courage. Thanks."

"Hey! You don't give yourself enough credit. Don't put down the man I love."

"I love you. I'm going to get off now. Okay?"

"Sure. I love you, too. Bye."

"Bye." I set the receiver down in the cradle with exaggerated care, softly, tenderly. It was silly, but since she wasn't there to touch like that, I expressed it in hanging up the phone. I laughed at myself.

I was still scared.

The wait from seven o'clock to eleven was worse.

At eight-thirty the phone rang and I snatched it up.

"Have you ever considered the security of life insur—" I slammed the phone down.

Five minutes later it rang again.

"Hi, this is Morgan. Is Sheila home?"

"There's no Sheila here. You've got the wrong number."

"Oh. Sorry." He hung up.

Almost immediately it rang again.

"Hi, this is Morgan. Is Sheila there?"

"It's still the wrong number."

"Oh." Irritation. "I must be misdialing it. She was very careful when she gave it to me. Sorry."

Dickhead. She probably didn't give you her real number.

There was a pause of two minutes; then the phone rang again.

"Hi, this is Morgan. Is Sheila there?"

I paused. Then, in my best Brooklyn accent, an octave below my normal speaking pitch, I said. "Oh, jeez. I'm sorry man. Sheila's dead!" I hung up.

That wasn't very nice, Davy.

I felt guilty, but he didn't call back again.

At nine the phone rang again.

"Have you ever considered the security of life insurance? The problems of protecting your loved ones from an uncertain future?"

This time I let the ad run until I'd written down the name of the company and their phone number. Then I hung up and thought dark thoughts about the misuse of voice-mail system while I looked up their address in the phone book.

At 10:55 the phone rang again.

Oh God ohgodohgod.

I picked it up, licked my lips. "Hello?"

"Davy? David Rice."

I exhaled a shuddering breath. "Hi, Mom," I said in a small voice. "What's happening?"

It was straight out of the past, a slice of childhood. I'd get off the school bus, run up the driveway, pop in through the kitchen door, and say, "Hi, Mom. What's happening?" And she'd say, "Oh, not much. How was school?"

The voice on the other end of the line became as small as mine. "Oh, Davy . . . Davy. How can you ever forgive me?"

Is there no end to tears? My eyes stung and I blinked rapidly.

"Mom—I know about the broken bones in your face. I

know about the year in the hospital. I don't see that you had much choice. It's okay."

Well, it might become okay.

I could hear the receiver brush her cheek as she shook her head. "You never answered my letters . . . I must have hurt you terribly."

"I never *got* your letters. How many letters?" I had the old sensation in the pit of the stomach, like when Dad was going to hit me, or when I faced up to Mark, Millie's old boyfriend.

"God *damn* your father! I only sent a couple of long letters from the hospital, but I sent one once a month the year after I got out. Then, when I didn't get answers, I tapered off to four or five a year. The last few years, I just sent presents on your birthday. Did you get those?"

"No."

"That *bastard*! And I left you with him . . ."

I shifted on the couch, uncomfortable. I wanted her to stop talking about him, to stop reminding me. I wanted to throw up, run away, hang up the phone, or jump. Jump away to Stillwater, jump away to the Brooklyn Bridge. Jump away to Long Island and walk on the sand while the Atlantic rolled storm breakers at the beach.

"It's okay, Mom," but my voice convinced neither of us.

She paused, then said carefully, with a catch in her voice, "Did he hurt you, Davy?"

Don't tell her. Why make her feel worse? But part of me wanted her to feel worse, wanted to make her feel bad, wanted her to feel some of the pain that a twelve-year-old boy felt. "Sometimes. He used to hit me with his belt, with the rodeo buckle. I missed a few days of school." My voice was matter-of-fact.

She broke then, her voice dissolving into sobs, uncontrollable, and I regretted saying anything. I felt overwhelming guilt.

"I'm sorry," she said between the sobs. "I'm sorry" and "Please forgive me." Over and over again until the words blended with the sobs, like cries of pain and grief themselves, a litany that seemed never ending.

"Shhhh. It's okay, Mom. It's okay." I don't know why, but I'd stopped feeling like crying. A melancholy sadness, almost sweet in its intensity, filled me, and I thought about Millie holding me while I cried. "Shhhh. I forgive you. It's not your fault. It's not your fault. Shhhh."

Finally, she ran down and I heard her blow her nose. "I have a lot of guilt about leaving you. I thought I'd worked through it with my therapist years ago. I *hate* the way my nose runs when I cry!"

"It must be hereditary."

"You too? Do you cry much?"

"I don't know, Mom. I guess some lately. I'm not very good at it. I guess I haven't practiced enough."

"Is that a joke?"

"Sort of."

"What do you do, Davy? To make ends meet?"

I'm a bank robber. "Oh, I have banking interests. I do okay—I get to travel a lot." *Lies.* More guilt and self-contempt. "What do you do?"

"I'm a travel agent. I get to travel, too. It's very different from being a housewife."

"Travel is a good escape, isn't it?" I said. *As one runaway to another. Do you teleport, too?* I wanted to ask but if she didn't she'd think I was mad.

"Yes. Sometimes escape is what we all need. I've missed you, Davy."

Ah, there were my tears again, just when I thought they'd gone away. "I missed you, Mom." I held the mouthpiece away, but she heard my sobs. I quelled them, though, quickly.

The distress in her voice was palpable. "I'm sorry, baby. So sorry."

"It's okay. I just get like this sometimes. And you're right. I hate the way my nose runs."

A nervous laugh. "You still try to cheer me up, Davy. My own court jester. You're very special."

More special than you can imagine.

I wanted to ask something, but I was still scared, terrified, of rejection. Then she asked it and I didn't have to.

"Can I see you, Davy?"

"I wanted to ask that. I can fly out there this week."

"Don't you have to work?"

"No."

"Well, maybe next time, but I'm going to Europe in a week on a tour, but we fly out of New York and I could take an extra day and lay over."

I laughed.

"What's so funny?"

"Nothing. Well . . . a friend of mine said if you got back in my life, we couldn't step back into our old relationship, but would have to redefine it."

"He sounds very wise."

"*She* is. But the instant you said you could come here, I started worrying about cleaning up my room."

She laughed. "Ah. Well, maybe some things stay the same."

We talked for an hour more. I learned about a man she was seeing, some college courses she'd taken, and the beauty of the upper California coast. In turn I talked about Millie, my apartment, Millie, New York, and Millie.

"She sounds wonderful," Mom said. "I'll call you when I've got my flight information. Are you sure you have room? I've heard about New York apartments and I can afford a hotel."

"Those are Manhattan apartments you heard about. I've got lots of room." *And I'll buy a new bed*, I thought. "If I'm not here, leave the information on the answering machine."

"Okay, Davy. I was really glad to hear from you."

"Me, too, Mom. Good night. I love you."

She started crying again and I hung up.

NINE

I had a bonded cleaning service come in on Wednesday. It had been so long since I'd opened the door to the apartment that it stuck and I had to get them to lean on it from outside before it would open. There was a funny expression on their faces when the door finally came open.

"Jesus!" I said. "What's that smell?"

The first of the three women pointed over her shoulder in answer to my question. I looked around her.

Someone had built a nest in the hallway outside my door with newspapers and old couch cushions. There was a coffee can buzzing with flies beside it. By the smell, it was a makeshift toilet, well used.

"Oh, wow," I said, embarrassed. "I don't come in this way."

"No wonder," said the woman. She was a tall black woman with wide shoulders and a streak of gray that went back over her right ear. "I'm Wynoah Johnson, from Helping Hands. Are you Mr. Reece?"

"Yes."

"Okay. I understand you want the deluxe treatment. You want us to start with the stairwell? That'll be extra since it's not in the apartment. It's also what we call 'excessive filth.' "

I felt ashamed for some reason. "Uh, I guess so. I don't care what it costs. I really didn't know about it."

She shrugged. "Okay. You really ought to talk to your landlord. This building got a super?"

I shook my head.

"Charlene," said Wynoah, "get this shit out to the trash."

"Ahhhhhh," said one of the other women, a young Hispanic, "why do I always get stuck with the pee-pee?" She put down her bucket and broom and went downstairs, holding the coffee can at arm's length.

Wynoah was sizing up my living room. I pointed at the outside hall and asked her, "You see that sort of mess often?"

"Too often. When an apartment is empty for a while in some of these buildings where the doors don't shut right, you get squatters and they can't get the water turned on because they don't have a lease. They get chased out and we get called to clean up." She was nodding at the room with its video and stereo equipment, couch, recliner, and bookshelves. "Hell, the way the hall looked, I thought this was gonna be one of those *nasty* jobs. This ain't nothin'. Let's see the rest."

I showed her the spare room, with the computer desk and the bookshelves and the brand-new futon couch I'd bought the day before as a spare bed. My bedroom with a futon platform bed, bookshelves, and a padded antique rocker I bought in Soho. The bathroom and kitchen were both tiny.

"Well, it looks like a lot of dust to me, but nothing too bad. Books collect dust," she informed me in a tone that implied distaste.

It occurred to me that they were the first humans in my apartment other than myself. Even when I'd viewed the apartment, before renting it eleven months before, the broker just sent me over with the keys, not bothering to come herself.

Of course, part of it was paranoia. I still had three-quarters of a million dollars in my money closet. I didn't want people to wonder about that empty space between the kitchen and the bedroom. But another part of it was that it was much easier to bring a book home than a person. A book or a video or a sandwich from the deli . . . all of these things were comfortable, undemanding things.

But they didn't make the place alive, not like people did.

I visited the Hamilton Insurance Company that afternoon, after the cleaning service left. Hamilton Insurance used recorded automated telephone ads, the one that started, "Have you ever considered the security of life insurance?" I stuck my head in their reception area, acquired a jump site, and left without speaking to anyone.

Later, after all of the company's employees had left, I returned and located their automated telemarketing equipment set up in a corner office. I found an employee roster with home phone numbers in the reception area.

An hour later, the equipment was calling the company's employees and playing the ad for them. Over and over and over again.

I went home, to bed, a smile on my face.

At 11 P.M. Mr. Washburn began beating his wife again. There was very little escalation, just two angry sentences and then she started screaming again and I could hear his fists hitting her, wet, meaty sounds.

I jumped to their landing and began pounding on the door, hard, rapidly. "Stop it! Stop it!" I shouted.

Her screams stopped and I heard heavy steps cross to the door. It opened and he stood there, red-faced, eyes narrowed, teeth bared. "What the fuck do you want?" One hand was closed in a fist and his right hand was behind the door.

I'd seen him before, on the steps, leaving or coming in. He was taller than me, and heavy in the middle. He was barefoot in dark slacks and a white tank-top undershirt. He brought the other hand out from behind the door. There was a gun in it.

I froze.

He asked again. "What do you want?"

In the background I heard his wife moaning. A familiar smell came to my nose, the smell of scotch. My stomach hurt.

I jumped behind him, grabbed his waist and heaved. He was heavy, very heavy, and the second he felt my arms around him, he threw himself back. I lost my balance and started to fall, all of his weight coming down on me. Before we landed, I jumped to Central Park, at the playground near 100th on the West Side.

We went down in the sand pit, next to the concrete hill with all the tunnels. Washburn's body drove all the air out of my lungs and he twisted, quick as a snake, to grab at me, to point his gun at me.

I jumped away, reflexively, then gasped for breath in the Stanville Public Library. *God, he was heavy.* After five minutes I could breathe without stabbing pain.

I jumped back to the Brooklyn apartment and looked in the Washburns' front door, still standing open. There was a sound from their front bedroom and I called out, "Hello? Are you all right?"

Great. You know she's not all right. Idiot!

I walked in hesitantly. She was lying on the floor by the bed, trying to pull herself up. I forgot about trespassing and went to her. "Don't try to move. I'll call an ambulance."

"No. No ambulance." She was still trying to pull herself up, trying to get onto the bed. I gave up and helped her onto it, but she wouldn't lie down. She wanted to sit.

"Where is he?"

"Manhattan."

"How long?"

"Huh?"

"How long has he been gone?"

"Oh. He just left."

Her face was swollen. Both her eyes had been blacked, but the way the color spread, I figured they'd been done the day before. She was bleeding from her mouth and there was a cut on her forehead that also seeped blood.

"My purse."

"Ma'am?"

"Please. Get me my purse. I think it's in the kitchen."

I looked at her dubiously. For all I knew she was about

to have a brain hemorrhage from the beating she took. She should be in a hospital.

"Please . . . it's got the address of the shelter. The shelter for battered women."

I went and found her purse, came back, and dug through it at her request. The address was written on a small piece of lavender stationery. There were hearts and flowers at the top.

Jesus.

I called a taxi and helped her pack some things—some clothes, some money stashed away in a book, and an album of old photographs. Then I eased her down the stairs to meet the cab.

She was moving better by the time we got downstairs and I was beginning to believe she just *looked* like death. I paid the cabbie—overpaid him—in advance and made sure he knew the address. I also told him that if she got worse to go straight to the nearest emergency room.

The cab pulled away and drove down the street, getting smaller and smaller and smaller. I hoped she'd make it, but to help, I'd put two thousand dollars in her purse while I helping her pack.

I was scared to stay in the apartment Thursday and Friday, scared I'd mess it up and scared of Washburn.

On impulse, I jumped to the Delta terminal at Dallas–Fort Worth International Airport and hopped a flight to Albuquerque, where I played tourist for most of the day, including taking the aerial tramway to the top of the Sandia Mountains. I wore myself out enough to sleep after I jumped home.

The alarm went off at 10 P.M. and I called Millie.

"What did you do today?"

I hesitated. "I piddled around, played tourist, played with some computers." I smiled to myself. "I was trying not to think about Mom's visit."

"Nervous."

I exhaled. "Very." The weight of my anticipation was heavy, like an undone chore with no time to do it before my dad got home. It didn't feel like eagerness at all. It felt like dread.

"Well, I can understand that. You have every right to be nervous."

"What? You think it's going to go bad?"

She took a quick breath. "No, sweet. I think it will be fine, but it's been so long since you've seen her, you don't know what to expect. You've had a lot of bad things happen since she left—it doesn't surprise me that you don't know what to expect. That would make anybody nervous."

"Ah. Well, I was wondering if I wasn't weirding out. . . ."

"No more than the circumstances dictate." She was quiet for a moment and then said, "You surprise me, Davy, sometimes, at how well you do handle these things, given all that's happened to you."

I swallowed. "You don't feel it from this side, Millie. I don't know if I can stand it, sometimes. It *hurts*."

"Most people in your circumstances wouldn't even know it hurt, Davy. They would have built a wall of unfeeling so thick that they wouldn't know when they were sad or in pain or even happy. The pain would be so great and so close that they could only hide from it and all feelings.

"To know that it hurts is the only way to get past it, to heal."

"Humph. If you say so. Sounds like those other people have the right idea. To not hurt sounds like a good idea."

"You listen to me, David Rice! You go that route and you won't feel joy or love, either. What happened between us would never have happened. Is that what you want?"

"No, never that," I said quietly, hastily. "I do love you. That hurts sometimes, too."

"Well good. It's supposed to." She took a ragged breath. "At least it hurts me sometimes, too. I think it's worth it. I hope you *feel* that way too?"

"Yeah. I do."

"Are you coming a week from tomorrow?" she asked.

"I could come on Thursday again."

"Oh . . . I've got a test on Friday. I've got to study for it—but you can stay until Tuesday if you like."

I smiled a small, satisfied smile. "Okay. I will."

Later, I jumped to Stillwater and watched Millie's bedroom window for a while. Then I jumped to the Albuquerque airport, let my ears equalize, jumped to the parking lot at the base of the tramway, let the ears equalize again, and jumped to the observation deck atop the mountain. This time there was some pain, but the ears cleared after a second.

I have to find someplace halfway between, somewhere around 7800 feet, as another stepping stage.

The city was scattered below, like stars fallen to earth, grids of streets and parking lots, punctuated by pillars of building lights. It was two hours earlier than New York, so there was still a slight glow on the far western horizon that shaded from light blue to black, with stars directly above almost as dense as the city lights below.

There was a light wind, but the air was very cold, making the light from above and below somehow distant, remote, and not at all warm. Looking at them, beautiful as they were, made me feel cold within. They weren't the sort of things one should watch alone, because the scale of them, the vast numbers, made one feel diminished. They made me feel very small.

I held my nose and jumped home in stages.

I met Mom at the airport with roses and a limousine.

There was a large crowd waiting outside the security gate at La Guardia. The airport is so crowded that they don't let anybody but passengers into the actual gates. Naturally, this didn't stop me. I just jumped past security to a spot I could see down the long corridor, well past the metal detectors and carry-on luggage scanners.

Her connection from Chicago was twenty minutes late, increasing my anxiety. I thought about plane crashes, mixed signals, missed planes. It would really be something if she turned out not to be on the plane. I smelled the roses for the twentieth time—the scent had gone from a light perfume to a cloying scent, almost rancid. I knew it wasn't the flowers, only my anxiety.

Stop smelling them, then!

I paced from one end of the gate's waiting area to the other, occasionally sniffing the flowers.

When the flight did arrive she was among the last off, walking slowly, a briefcase in her hand.

She'd changed. I don't know why this surprised me. Before she left, Mom had black, shiny hair, long and thick. She'd also been plump, talking endlessly about dieting, but never turning down a dessert. She'd also had a nose one might call aquiline if one was kind, or beaklike if one wanted to be nasty. I shared that nose with her and with her father, so I knew well enough what people could say about it.

Her hair was short now, cut close around her face, shorter than Millie's, and it was white, as were her eyebrows. She'd lost at least fifty pounds and was wearing a narrow-waisted dress. I saw at least two businessmen turn to watch as she walked past. And her face had changed. Certainly not beyond recognition, but it took me a minute to realize what it was. Her nose was smaller, slightly turned up, and I felt a moment's sharp grief, a feeling that I'd lost another connection to her. For a paranoid moment I wondered if I'd made up the shared features, that I really wasn't related to her—alien. Perhaps *really* alien.

Then I remembered the hospital stay, and the surgery to repair her face after she'd left us.

She was scanning the crowd at the gate, all of them, except me, waiting to board the continuation of her flight to D.C. Her eyes crossed over me, a young man wearing a (new) expensive suit, then looked quickly back, a tentative smile on her face.

I advanced, the flowers held before me, almost like a shield. "Welcome to New York," I said.

She looked from my face to the flowers and back to my face. She set the briefcase down, took the flowers from me, and opened her arms wide. Tears were streaming down her face . . . and mine. I stepped into her arms and squeezed her nearly as hard as she held me.

It felt wrong. She was shorter than me and the ample plushness of her hugs that I remembered from my childhood was also gone. It felt uncomfortably like holding Millie. I let go after a minute and stepped back, profoundly disturbed, confused. Who was this person?

"God you've grown," she said, and it was all right again.

That voice was there, the voice of my past, the voice that said, *Oh, not much. How was school?* The voice that said, *Your father can't help it, dear, he's sick, sick.* The voice hadn't changed.

"Well, I suppose I have. It's been six years."

I picked up her briefcase and swore at myself. *She knows how long it's been. Why'd you say that?* "You look really good, Mom. I like your hair and you lost a lot of weight." I didn't mention her face because I didn't want to talk about the events that caused her operations, that drove her away in the first place.

She just nodded and walked along beside me, sniffing occasionally at the roses. She held then in both her arms, cradled, as if they were an infant.

I used a pay phone in the baggage area to call the limo's cellular phone. The limo was waiting up on Ninety-fourth Street, just on the other side of the Grand Central Parkway from the airport. By the time we'd claimed Mom's luggage and got out on the sidewalk, it was sitting at the curb. The driver, a small black man in a black suit, was leaning against the hood.

I'd met him at the limo agency the day before, so he recognized us right off, coming forward and saying, "I'll carry that, ma'am."

Mom looked at me, surprised, and perhaps a little frightened.

"It's okay," I said. "This is Mr. Adams, our driver."

She relaxed and handed him the case. "A limo? A limousine?" she said, looking at me.

"Well, yes. I think that's what they're called."

Mr. Adams held the rear door for her, his body tilted

forward solicitously, a hand ready to help her in. After Mom was in, he continued to hold the door, looking at me.

"Oh." I put the suitcase I was still holding down beside the other cases and climbed in. Mr. Adams shut the door and put the cases in the trunk.

"A limousine?"

"You keep saying that, Mom. Would you like something to drink?" I opened the small refrigerator. "There's a split of champagne in here." I'd make her open it if that's what she wanted—I wasn't going to open any more champagne bottles without practicing first in private.

She settled on mineral water. I took ginger ale. We used the champagne flutes anyway. Mr. Adams took the Van Wyck to the Belt-Parkway. The Saturday-afternoon traffic was light, so it was only thirty minutes before the limo pulled up before my brownstone. "This is the right address, sir?" He sounded doubtful.

"Yes," I said, blushing. I was seeing my neighborhood through his eyes—the trash and graffiti and groups of sullen Hispanic and black men who stood on corners. I never saw this side because I always jumped straight to my apartment. If I wanted to go for a walk, I'd jump to the Village or the south end of Central Park or downtown Stanville, Ohio. Places that weren't so nervous-making.

Still, it was *my* building I was really worried about. I hoped we wouldn't run into Washburn. We didn't.

Mr. Adams made sure the limo was locked and its alarm activated before he carried the bags up to my apartment. Once he'd put the bags down in the spare room, Mom tried to tip him.

"Oh, no ma'am. I've already been paid a more than adequate gratuity for the weekend."

"The weekend?"

"Mr. Adams will be driving for us during your visit. It can be hard to get cabs out here sometimes."

She blinked. "Oh."

Mr. Adams tipped his hat. "I'd best be getting back to the car. May I suggest, sir, that I move it until you need me? You have a lot of nice things here in your apartment—it might be best if the limousine wasn't downstairs to draw the wrong sort of attention to it. You could reach me on the car phone."

"That's very thoughtful of you." I saw him to the door. Before he left I said, "There's a precinct house three blocks toward Flatbush Avenue. Perhaps that would be a good place to park . . . for the car that is."

"Yes, sir," he said, relieved. "I hope this isn't inconvenient."

"No," I answered. "It's probably best for *both* reasons."

Mom spent some time in the bathroom, freshening up. I sat in the living room, in the recliner, my feet up, and listened to the sound of running water. She hummed to herself as she washed, another reminder of the past, comforting and disturbing at the same time.

"I see you managed to 'clean up your room,' " she said, coming into the living room and standing before the bookshelves.

"Well . . . yeah." I added almost convulsively, "I had a cleaning service in."

She laughed quietly. "I'm glad to see you're still reading. Your father never was much of a reader."

I didn't say anything for a moment. She turned to me with raised eyebrows. "Yes, reading is very important to me," I said into the awkward silence. "I think if I hadn't been a reader, I would have gone mad."

The small smile on her face died. "Escape?"

"Yeah—escape and a feeling that the rest of the world wasn't mixed up or crazy. That people could really have lives that didn't involve . . ." I shut my mouth. *Stupid, stupid, stupid.*

Mom took a deep breath. "I need to say some things to you, Davy. I need to say some things I've been thinking about for years." She looked scared, but somehow determined.

I sat up in the recliner, the footrest folding beneath with a little *click*. My stomach started to churn. "Okay," I said.

She sat down on the end of the couch closest to the

recliner and leaned forward, her elbows resting on her legs, her fingers interlocked. "Have you ever heard of Alanon?"

I shook my head.

"Alanon is an organization modeled after Alcoholics Anonymous. Its emphasis is not on alcoholics themselves, but on their family members, their spouses or children. I started going to their meetings after I moved to California." She paused a second. "When a person lives with an alcoholic, with any abusive person, they start to have the same kind of arrested emotional development that the alcoholic does. For the same reason, the techniques for treating alcoholics also turn out to be effective for treating the victims of their abuse."

I nodded. I didn't know what she was getting at and I suspected I didn't want to know, but she was my mom.

"The thing that both organizations depend on is something called the twelve-step program. The steps are things one has to accomplish or accept to overcome and heal what has happened to them. Without going through the whole list, I need to do what is called a ninth step with you."

This was not my mother. This wasn't the woman who joked with me, comforted me, looked after me. I didn't know who this serious, determined woman was. Reluctantly, I said, "What is a ninth step?"

"Making amends. Acknowledging the harm and damage that one has done to the person that was harmed and damaged."

"Oh, Mom. You didn't do it, . . ."

"Shhh. This isn't easy. Let me finish what I have to say."

I slumped in on myself, my arms crossed tightly, and looked at the floor between us.

"I did terrible things to you, Davy. I abandoned you for six years with a man I knew was an alcoholic, capable of terrible emotional and physical abuse. Before I left, I silently abetted emotional abuse. I let him destroy your self-esteem. I let him 'punish' you for things that didn't warrant punishment. I was a silent partner in his abuse of you."

As she spoke I curled in on myself, as if my stomach were

cramping, as if to curl around my pain, my hurt, and shield it from the world.

She went on. "I failed to confront his abuse of you out of fear, out of doubt, out of uncertainty. I failed to take action after I abandoned you, action to protect you from his abuse, action to recover you from him. And, worst of all, I abused you directly, by abandoning you, by taking my love and care away from you, by treating you like lost luggage, that one doesn't have an obligation to, a responsibility to."

She took a deep breath of air and I looked at her face, not lifting my head, but peering through my hair, where the bangs fell forward. Her cheeks were wet, but her eyes watched me, blinking to clear the tears.

"I pray," she said, "that one day you'll be able to forgive me."

"Oh, Mom . . . it wasn't your fault. You were driven away!"

She shook her head violently. "I'm just as responsible. I acknowledge that responsibility even if you don't want to think of me in that way. Someday you will, and I fear that your anger at me will be far greater than what you feel toward your father."

"Oh, never! I . . . I can't even talk about him without . . . without, ah shit." I started crying myself. Mom came to me, quickly, and perched on the armrest of the recliner. I leaned into her and she held me, silent, one hand patting awkwardly at my back.

After a minute I tried to wipe my tears from my face with my fingers. My nose was drippping so I mumbled, "Excuse me," and stood, Mom's arms dropped. I brought a box of tissues back from the bedroom. We both knew our noses and laughed a little.

"Genetics is wonderful," I said.

"You're entirely welcome." She blew her nose hard, alike a mezzo-soprano foghorn. "Thanks for listening to me."

It wasn't you. It wasn't your fault. "You're welcome, I guess, . . ." I wanted to argue the point, but even more I wanted to drop the subject, to talk about anything else. "Are you getting hungry yet?"

"A bit."

"I have a reservation in the Village for six-thirty. It will take us about forty-five minutes to drive there so we need to leave in about thirty-minutes. I also have theater tickets to *Grand Hotel.*"

"My God. Are you bankrupting yourself for my visit?"

I thought about the money chest, ten feet behind her. "Not even close, Mom. Not even close."

"Well," she said with a kind of artificial gaiety, "I'd better change then.

We are at I Tre Merli, an Italian restaurant on West Broadway. People stared when we got out of the limo. I tried to act nonchalant. Mom thanked Mr. Adams warmly for holding the door. We arranged a time for him to pick us up with enough leeway to get to the theater.

Our table was ready immediately, a consequence of eating early, though the hostess had seen Mr. Adams hand us out of the limo, so perhaps that helped as well.

During dinner, the waiter suggested wine from the restaurant's own vineyard. Mom agreed. I drank a glass of red that seemed to go well with the food. It made me lightheaded and nervous. I spoke to her about it.

"Do you drink much, Davy?" She looked sideways and leaned closer. "I guess, technically, you're still underage in New York, aren't you? Though you don't look it."

I shrugged. "That's not it. I can always pay somebody to buy it for me. I just don't know . . . I mean, Dad . . ."

"Ah. You wonder if you're an alcoholic, too. I shouldn't worry about it too much, not if this is the first alcohol you've had in . . . how long?"

"I tasted some champagne about six weeks ago. I didn't think much of it."

She nodded. "Well, it's something to keep an eye on, but don't be too paranoid. It was one of my fears, too, after I got to California. My therapist convinced me my problems had different causes."

I wondered if there was a secret organization out there: Teleports Anonymous. *Hi, my name is David Rice and I'm a teleport.* Mom didn't look like a teleport, did she? What does a teleport look like? I wanted to tell her, but things were going so well—I didn't want to blow it by revealing my alienness. Or the bank robbery, for chrissakes. The only time I remember her punishing me was when I stole a neighbor's toy.

Grand Hotel was good, brilliantly staged, with wonderful music. My favorite character was Mr. Kringelein, the terminally ill Jewish accountant. The Jimmies, two black entertainer/waiters, were also good, but while I liked the way the play ended, there was one thing that disturbed me greatly.

The aging ballerina, expecting the young and handsome Baron to meet her at the station, isn't told by her manager and companion that he's died the night before. I hated that. It seemed like the harshest bit of kindness I've ever seen, like betrayal—like manipulation, to make her go on dancing. I hated that.

Mom shrugged. "It's life. It's too much like life, perhaps, but it's realistic."

Neither of us had slept well the night before, in anticipation or dread of the visit, so Mr. Adams drove us back to the apartment and we turned in.

The next morning as we were getting into the limo I saw Washburn watching us from his window. I ignored him, acting like he wasn't there, but I couldn't help but remember the gun in his fist. *I wonder how he got back from Central Park?*

We ate breakfast on the Upper West Side; then Mr. Adams dropped us over at the Metropolitan Museum of Art, where we took in the Russian traveling exhibit of French Impressionist paintings.

"You're a member of the museum? How often do you come here?"

I shrugged. "More, since I joined. I spent some time here when I was still living in Manhattan."

"Oh."

We enjoyed the exhibit, though the Sunday crowd was thick and obnoxious.

After a woman stepped directly between Mom and the painting she was looking at, she took me aside and asked with a smile, "Do they *train* people how to be New Yorkers? I don't see how they could be so rude otherwise." She frowned then. "Well, I guess they do. Family behavior is training. Dysfunctionality passes down through generations. God, I hope all New Yorkers aren't products of dysfunctional families."

"I've met lots of friendly New Yorkers," I said. "Me, for instance."

"Ha! You're an import. Definitely foreign material."

"Well, Mr. Adams, then."

She nodded. "I'm sure there are plenty."

I called Mr. Adams from the pay phone and he picked us up out front. It would probably take us an hour to get to Kennedy Airport. "I know we have plenty of time," Mom said, "but I want to double check my aisle seat. I can't stand to sit in the middle or at the window. I hate it."

On the way out to the airport Mom tried to talk to me about getting into therapy.

"Are you saying I'm crazy?" I was a little angry—upset. I'd been trying to work up the courage to tell her about the teleportation—to ask her if she could or anyone in our family. If she thought I needed therapy *now*. . . .

"No. Not crazy. However, you just can't shrug off what you've been through. We all carry this baggage around with us, this emotional garbage. We have to work through it, or we'll end up inflicting it on our children." She avoided looking at me when she said this. "Seeing a therapist doesn't mean you're crazy, or bad, or sick. A therapist is like a . . . a guide. He knows the signs, the roads, the pits. He can help you find the pain inside, acknowledge it and its cause, and get past it."

I looked out the window.

She kept talking. "You ran away from your father and that was a good thing. But the damage is there and you can't run away from it. It's a part of you."

No problem is so big that it can't be teleported away from: Linus, paraphrased.

I found myself getting angrier and angrier. *Cool it, Davy. It's not worth it.* "I'll think about it," I lied, finally, to get her away from the subject.

She looked, for a moment, like she was going to keep on it, but she smiled after a minute and said, "Tell me about your job."

I shrugged. *Maybe I should have let her go on about therapy.* "It's more like banking interests. Nothing really to talk about. I'd rather hear about your trip to Europe."

I don't think I fooled her. I think she knew there was something about my "job" that I didn't want to talk about, but she didn't press it.

"We're spending four days in London, two days in Paris, three days in Rome, two days in Athens, three days in Istanbul, and then home again. It's crazy, but it's one of these travel agents–only tours to evaluate hotel facilities. I've done it twice before and you're always so tired that you really haven't a clue about the facilities. Still, it helps to be able to tell a client what they have to do to get a cab in Lisbon or change money in Amsterdam. And I've never been to Turkey before, so that will be nice."

"Sounds wonderful. If I had a passport, I'd go with you."

She smiled. "Well, I'd like that. Next time. And did you say you were going to come out to California?"

I nodded. "Count on it. I'll give you a week to rest up after your trip, then I'll be out after that."

She smiled and I smiled and for one brief second I felt like things were okay, that we'd done the impossible and put the paths of our lives back together. Maybe not on the same road, but so they'd cross each other occasionally and maybe run alongside of each other for a short time. I felt like I had a mother again.

Before she boarded her plane she cried and held me very tight. I felt empty as I walked back to the curb and to Mr. Adams's limo.

He held the door for me, but I raised my hand. "No, thanks, Mr. Adams. The ball is over and I'm going to turn back into a pumpkin." I gave him a hundred-dollar bill and said, "Enjoy the rest of the weekend, what's left of it. You were very good to us."

"Are you sure I can't drop you back at your place?"

"No, thanks. I'll make my own way. I mean it," I added when he started to insist. "Thanks again."

He nodded. "If you need a limo . . ."

"I know who to call."

He drove off into the afternoon traffic, a sleek, black whale cruising smoothly through a school of darting, fractious fish.

I jumped home.

PART 4:

CHINESE CURSE

TEN

On Monday I dropped my dirty clothes off as usual, jumping to the alley behind the laundry, and leaving them to be done, seventy-five cents a pound, no starch, shirts on hangers. When I stepped out on the sidewalk again the sun was shining brightly, the air felt cold and, for a change, clean. It felt *crisp* like a bite out of a new apple, fresh from the refrigerator. I decided to walk the six blocks back to the apartment.

Over the weekend, with Mr. Adams driving us, I'd seen more of my neighborhood than usual. It wasn't without its pleasant aspects, but in early November, with all the leaves gone from the trees and bushes, it looked bleak and dirty. Amazing what a touch of green will do. Also, the nearer I got to my block, the more prominent the graffiti got, the more trash there was.

I wondered if I should move. *How would I feel if Millie was staying here, if she had to walk through this area?* I found myself looking at the men sitting on the stoops or standing on the corners. They stared back, challenging, until I looked elsewhere. *If Millie visits, we'll stay in a hotel in Manhattan.*

It was because I was looking at everyone on the street that I noticed the guys in the car. They were parked three buildings down from my apartment, reading newspapers, the windows halfway down. A paper cup of coffee on the dashboard put a circle of condensation on the windshield.

As I passed them, I heard the crackle of a dispatch radio, the kind you hear on cop shows.

I looked at the man on the passenger side. It was Washburn.

He was sipping from another cup of coffee and reading the paper, but at the sound of my footsteps he glanced toward me. When our eyes met, he jerked his head back, surprised. A large dollop of steaming coffee dropped onto his chest and he jerked again, swearing and patting ineffectually at his chest with newspaper. As he did this, I saw his jacket gape open and saw the wood-inlaid grip of his pistol in a shoulder holster.

Christ, he's a cop? That explained the gun and it explained why the patrol cops didn't do anything the night I called 911.

I walked on, with hardly a break in step, pleased that he'd spilled the coffee, but not wanting to acknowledge him. Nothing makes a person madder than being stared at when they've done something clumsy.

Since they were there, I went through the alley, toward the back gate, and jumped up to the apartment from a private space by the garbage cans. I looked out the window and saw Washburn, complete with coffee stain, get out of the car and walk up the sidewalk until he was directly below. He peered around the corner, into the alley.

I went into the bathroom and took some Alka-Seltzer.

What does he want?

It couldn't be the bank robbery, could it? The only other crime I'd committed was using a false driver's license, unless opening a bank account with false ID was fraud or something.

Hell, are they even watching me? Maybe I'm being paranoid.

At 1 P.M. the two men in the car were still there.

I jumped to Forty-seventh Street, bought a tripod, returned, and mounted the video camera on it, at the window. I ran an RCA jack across the room to my television and watched them at maximum zoom, in living color, on my twenty-five-inch screen. A couple of different times one or the other would take a bathroom or coffee break at the Korean deli on the corner.

Are they watching me?

I jumped to the landing outside my apartment door, went down the stairs and out the door. I ignored the car and walked down the block away from them. The street was fairly still, just then. In the distance, I heard a car door shut and then a car start its engine.

At the corner I took a right, then jumped back up to my apartment in time to see Washburn walk briskly up the sidewalk. At the corner, he looked to the right, then held one hand over his ear and moved his lips. I heard the car's tires squeal, then catch. It went past the apartment and around the corner.

Well, I guess there's no doubt. I looked around at the apartment, sad. I knew they couldn't arrest me. I'd be gone before they could open the door, but all my stuff—all my precious books . . .

Dad wouldn't let me keep books.

"What's the big deal—you've read it, haven't you?" Then he'd take them down to the used-book store and sell them for peanuts. He never got anything close to what they were worth. He didn't like them cluttering up the house, or even my room.

They weren't going to get my books.

Millie's apartment complex, on the edge of the OSU campus, had a vacancy. They were surprised to get a tenant in the middle of the semester. The rent, for a second-story, two-bedroom apartment, was less than half of my New York rent and the deposit was only two hundred dollars. To simplify things, I paid the rent through the end of the spring semester, eight months' worth, explaining that I'd just cashed the scholarship check and that if I didn't pay for the rent, I'd probably spend it on pizza. They accepted my New York license and my dad's address in Ohio and let me move in immediately.

I started in the living room of the New York apartment, with my shirt off and my hands sweating. I looked at a bookshelf, then jumped to the Stillwater apartment and chose a wall for it. Then back to the New York apartment. I stepped in to the bookshelf, three feet wide and shoulder-high, gripped one of the lower shelves, and heaved. The ligaments and tendons connecting my shoulders to my neck strained and I felt a strain in my lower back, but the book-shelf, one of my largest, didn't seem to move. I exhaled and leaned back. The shelf tipped, came off the floor.

I jumped.

In the Stillwater apartment I leaned forward quickly. The bookshelf hit the floor and tipped back, banging into the wall and knocking seven books off the top shelf and onto the floor.

I left them there. The shelf was off the floor for just a second, but it came with me when I jumped. This bore thinking about, but I didn't want to take the time.

The other bookshelves were easier, but by the time I finished, my shoulders were aching. I took the entertain-ment center in sections, much smaller loads than the book-shelves. The computer desk was also easy, but I took all the drawers out of my dresser and jumped them separately. I'd done my hanging clothes and I was about to take the bed apart when I thought about the money.

Oh. I started laughing. The more I laughed, the funnier it seemed. There was over seven hundred thousand dollars in the closet and I wanted to save my books. I leaned against the wall and shook, tears streaming down my face, almost breathless with laughter. *There may be hope for you yet, Davy.*

I jumped to Stillwater and found a linen closet in the hallway. It had shelves, but didn't seem big enough. I looked up, thinking to add a shelf above, and saw an attic access hatch. After retrieving a step stool and a flashlight from the Brooklyn apartment, I found that there was a three-foot crawlspace between the roof and my apartment ceiling. It reminded me of the library back in Stanville.

The attic was blocked off from the other apartments by fire walls, making it private enough for my purposes. I transferred the money in stages, ignoring the rest of my belongings until every dollar was stacked neatly in the crawlspace.

What will they think of my doorless closet? Should I open the door back? I remembered a pointless television special involving the basement of a Chicago hotel and a hotshot broadcast "journalist" who thought he'd found Al Capone's missing vault. It would be interesting to see their reaction when they broke through. I almost considered leaving a little money, just to confuse them.

I took a break, then, and had supper at Fraunces Tavern, in the financial district. This was a mistake. The service is leisurely, and by dessert my back had stiffened and my body seemed one dull ache from the top of my neck to the calves of my legs.

I tried walking along the water in Battery Park, to loosen up, but the cold wind off the mouth of the Hudson seemed to make things worse, adding a headache to my other ills.

Stupid police!

I jumped directly to the bathroom of the Brooklyn apartment, to take some ibuprofen. The room was dark, and I reached out to flip the light switch, but stopped.

Someone was in the apartment.

How'd they get past the drop bars?

The bathroom door was half open and I stepped quickly behind it, to peer though the crack by the hinges. The front door was six inches ajar and there was a blackened, irregular oval hole cut in the steel door. On the floor, just inside the doorway, was an acetylene-oxygen rig, with small tanks and a cutting torch. A decal on the oxygen tank said PROPERTY NYPD.

Down the hallway a uniformed policeman was helping a man in a suit examine my bed. They were probing the mattress with something that looked like hat pins, thin needles about six inches long. From the kitchen I could hear pots and pans clanging as someone moved them around.

I wondered if they had a search warrant.

Do you want to ask them, Davy? "Oh, excuse me, *Officer. Do you have a piece of paper that lets you perform acupuncture on my bed?"*

I decided to get the ibuprofen someplace else. I stood there, though, fascinated in some perverse way. I felt, almost, as if I was witnessing my own violation. I heard dishes clatter together and clenched my fists. The dishes in the kitchen were handmade pottery that I'd bought for five hundred dollars from a specialty shop in the Village.

At least the books are okay.

The phone rang. I looked at my watch.

Oh, Christ! Millie.

I hadn't moved the phone or the answering machine. There hadn't been a reason—there wasn't even electricity at the Stillwater apartment, much less phone service.

The phone was in my bedroom, just visible on the bedside table. The man in the suit picked up the phone before the answering machine switched on.

"Hello," he said, tilting his head toward the hallway. It was Washburn. He'd managed to change his shirt since the morning.

"No, you have the right number. This is David's apartment. This is Sergeant Washburn of the New York City Police Department. Who am I speaking to?" He held his hand over the mouthpiece and said to the uniformed cop, "Call dispatch and get a trace." The uniformed cop took a radio from his belt and went into the living room.

Washburn uncovered the mouthpiece. "No, to the best of my knowledge, David is all right. He left this apartment sometime this morning. He doesn't seem to have been back. Have you known David long?" He listened. "Trouble? Well, that remains to be seen. We want to talk to Mr. Reece about a couple of things." He listened again, then said, "Well, we have a search warrant—that's why. Could you please give me your address and phone number, Ms. Harrison?" He wrote in a pad that he took from his jacket pocket. "Oklahoma? But you're in the city right now? . . . No? Well, if you hear from Mr. Reece, could you please have him call Sergeant Washburn at the Seventy-second Precinct." The uniformed cop came back into the bedroom and showed Washburn something written on a pad. Washburn compared it with his own pad and nodded.

"No, you have the right apartment. David's rental lease says Rice, but his bank account says Reece. We don't know whether Reece or Rice is correct. That's one of the things we'd like to talk to him about. Please have him call. Goodbye."

He hung up the phone. The other plainclothes cop stuck his head out of the kitchen. "Well?"

"Girlfriend, maybe. In Oklahoma. Talks to him every night. She seemed surprised and upset. Sounded like she didn't know anything about his Reece persona. The number she gave us was legit."

"I wonder if she knows where he gets his money?"

"Well, we can get hold of her later, if we don't find out here," said Washburn.

"Are you sure this is worth all this trouble? I mean, the only thing we have on the kid is illegal identification."

"Shit, Baker! What about assault? Where does he get his money? The Social Security number he gave belongs to some grandmother in Spokane, Washington. The IRS wants to know about that. None of the people named David Rice or David Reece on their books have this address, so he's probably never paid income tax. To me, that says drugs—drugs and drug money."

The uniformed cop said, "I don't find nothing in this mattress. What put you onto this guy, anyway?"

Washburn said, "Shut up and keep searching."

"Jeez, Sergeant. What's the big deal?"

Baker stuck his head out of the kitchen. "Washburn has the apartment downstairs. He's been watching this Reece/Rice kid for a while, and the kid must have got wind of it. He and some of his friends jumped Washburn, knocked him out, and left him in Central Park."

"Christ, Sergeant, why didn't you press charges?"

Because it didn't happen.

Washburn shrugged. "I'd rather he went down for something big. Besides," he admitted, grudgingly, "there were no witnesses and I didn't see his help. They jumped me from behind. But there's something going on here. I checked with the landlord. The kid paid the deposit and first several months' rent in postal money orders. Finally, he starts paying by check, but the name is different from the one on the lease. Last Saturday they see a limo drop the kid and a woman here. A limo, in this neighborhood? We check the license number on the check and, lo and behold, this isn't the address on the license, so we check that address and we find another David Reece—one with a different face, but the same driver's license. So, we put a tag on this David starting Sunday, but he loses us at Kennedy. We were afraid he'd skipped, but he comes walking back to his apartment Monday morning. Later that afternoon he walks out of the apartment, around the corner, and disappears again."

Baker, in the hallway, said, "Next time we see him, we're arresting him. He's too good at dropping a tail. That's why Ray and your partner are downstairs." He went back into the kitchen.

The uniformed cop asked, "Who was the woman?"

"His mother. That's what the limo driver told us. The kid paid in advance, in cash, for the weekend, and tipped the driver an additional hundred at the end. They picked her up at La Guardia and dropped her at Kennedy. The driver didn't get her name or either of the flight numbers. Says the kid just told him what terminal and when. Possibly she brings his drugs in."

Leave my mother alone! I considered jumping down to the street and torching their cars, perhaps smashing the windshields. The anger just made my head hurt more.

I jumped to Stillwater, where I bought ibuprofen at a convenience store and washed it down with 7UP.

What am I going to do about Millie?

Sherry, Millie's roommate, answered the door. The expressions that her face went through when she recognized me told me volumes.

"Hang on a second," she said. She didn't ask me in. She didn't say hello or ask how I was doing. She pushed the door closed in my face.

The headache and the anger returned. When Millie

opened the door, my face was red and my pulse was pounding in my ears. She looked scared.

"Davy, what are you doing here?"

I shrugged. "I need to talk to you. Since I'm not welcome inside, perhaps we could take a walk."

She swallowed. "I'm not sure I want to walk with you."

"Oh for Christ's sake!" She flinched and I went on in a quieter voice. "Sergeant Washburn didn't say I was violent, did he? Surely he would have told you if I was suspected of murder or something."

"How did you know . . .? Well, okay. I'll get my coat."

She joined me on the porch a minute later, her hands stuck deep in the pockets of her coat, her eyes remote, her face still.

I walked out to the street and she followed a few paces behind. We started slowly down the sidewalk. The sky was cloudy, the temperature right above freezing, and a thin mist, more than fog and less than rain, left surfaces slick and wet. I could smell woodsmoke.

She broke the silence first. "Why are you walking like that? Are you hurt?"

"I was lifting furniture. I overdid it a bit, but I was in a hurry."

"Right. . . ."

Her tone of voice stung. "It's the truth!"

She turned her head sharply, her jaw set. "Ah, truth! That's an interesting subject. Let's talk about truth!"

I exhaled. "All right. Why don't we."

"Let's start with names, Mr. Rice, or should I call you Mr. Reece. What is your name?"

"Rice. I've never lied to you."

She jerked her head up, her mouth open. "Oh? And who do you lie to? Do you confine your lies to bank tellers? Are girlfriends exempt from lies?"

I lowered my head and repeated stubbornly, "I've never lied to you. Everything I've told you has been true."

She didn't believe me. "There's lying and there's lying. Do you know what lying by omission is? Do you know what lying by implication is? Why do the police want you? What did you do? Why did you keep it from me?"

"Because I wanted you to love me!"

She took a step back, the scared look on her face again.

"Because I wanted you to love me. . . . Oh, fuck it!" I stopped and stared up into the clouds, tears mixing with mist.

She looked away, unwilling to watch me. I stifled the tears, clenched my eyes shut, squeezed them out.

"What do you want?" I asked. "What can I do to make it all right?"

"You lied to me. You betrayed me. I told you what that means."

I shook my head, disbelieving. "You said that if you ever found that I lied to you, we were through. Is that what you want? Shall I just go away and never bother you again?"

She looked at me, her eyes narrowed, her mouth a thin, uncompromising line. "Yes."

I looked at her disgust, her anger, her hate, and I couldn't stand it.

"Good-bye, then."

Out of spite, then, while she watched, I jumped away, to escape, without thought, without direction. Then, on the floor of the Stanville Public Library, I curled up in a ball and cried and cried and cried.

I spent the night in my recliner, in the Stillwater apartment, my long leather coat as a blanket. There was no heat or light because I'd yet to have the utilities turned on. I had nightmares about Dad, when he'd hit me for crying. Millie was there, standing at the side and nodding at everything Dad said. I awoke in the gray of dawn, shivering, my back aching. I chose not to go back to sleep.

After putting on my shoes, I jumped to the landing outside my apartment door in Brooklyn. There was a fresh hasp and padlock locking the door and a sign that said, SEALED BY NYPD. FOR INFORMATION, CONTACT D. WASHBURN, 72ND PRECINCT.

I jumped to the bedroom. The bed was stripped, all the

linens tossed in the corner. I cautiously checked the rest of the apartment.

At some point they'd realized that there was too much dead space between the kitchen and living room. They'd torn through the covered-up door of the money closet, but I knew there wasn't a thing to find in there.

The kitchen was a shambles, dishes stacked precariously on the counters. Several of them had been taken aside and dusted with fingerprint powder. The garbage had been dumped in the sink and examined closely.

I ignored the mess and began jumping items to the Stillwater apartment, sorting the pots and dishes into the cabinets. I was surprised to find they hadn't broken anything, but it didn't seem to matter.

Nothing seemed to matter.

Still, I handled each delicately glazed piece with reverential care, wiping the dust from it with a dish towel before consigning it to its place in the cabinet. I'd bought the dishes at the end of the summer with Millie's help. Mom had liked them very much.

By midmorning I'd transferred all the kitchen and bathroom stuff, as well as the bed and its frame. The only things left in the apartment that I had any interest in were the drapes and miniblinds, but I was sure the police were still waiting for me outside and I didn't want them to know I was in the apartment.

Back in Stillwater, I went through the motions of having the water, electricity, cable, and gas turned on. I also decided against starting a new bank account. If I couldn't pay for something with a postal money order or cash, I wouldn't buy it.

None of the utilities seemed to blink at receiving cash for deposits. Maybe things are different in college towns. They all promised to activate services by the end of the next day. While I was out, I passed the phone company, but I also decided against a phone. I was not feeling very sociable.

One of my windows looked out on the street running between the campus and the apartment complex. I stared out of it for most of the afternoon, watching people walk by, their steps quick in the rain. I jumped to a deli in Manhattan for coffee and a sandwich about midafternoon, but I ate them at the window in Stillwater.

At 4:15, Millie crossed from campus at the light and walked up the street. She was moving more slowly than those around her, staring down at the sidewalk, her face remote. She was carrying an umbrella that she'd bought from a street vendor in New York City back when I'd first met her.

"Four dollars, miss. Only four dollars." She'd shaken her head. *"Three dollars, three dollars."* In the end, they'd settled on two and a half. I'd commented that it would probably dissolve in the rain, but there it was, proving me a liar.

I wanted to jump to the sidewalk and stand in front of her, but the memory of her face from the night before was too much.

So, why am I in Stillwater, then?

I watched her walk slowly out of sight.

I tried to write Millie a letter, to explain why the police wanted to talk to me. To explain that I'd purchased a fake ID with money that I robbed from a bank using an ability that people didn't have. Every time I saw the words on screen, I found myself deleting the document. Hell, I found myself doubting the story. How could I expect Millie to believe it?

I wanted to get away, to hunker down, to wait out the storm. I visited Serendipity Travel and went through their brochures. I ignored all the places that showed people smiling and having a good time. Smiling was not compatible with the image in my head. Finally I found the place, a retreat, located in West Texas. The brochure talked about isolation and wilderness and meditation. It was perfect.

It took me most of the day to get into El Paso. From there I boarded a bus just before it left, and sat near the front, away from the smoking section. I carried the camera in one of the backpacks bought for the Chemical Bank robbery, and stuffed in the pockets of my coat were antihistamines, ibuprofen, and tissues.

I had a cold.

We went east on I-10, winding along the Rio Grande and into a thunder-and-dust storm. I dozed, my sleep troubled by weird, half-remembered dreams that didn't quite stop when I awoke. At the rest stop, before we turned south at Van Horn, on U.S. 90, I stumbled off the bus to buy something to drink, my mouth dry and my skin hot. It hurt to swallow.

The storm's intensity worsened and the bus took four hours to do the next leg of the journey. My fever seemed worse, but I didn't want to waste the time I'd spent so far. If I jumped away now, I'd have to start over at the rest stop, outside Van Horn. I blew my nose and dozed.

At Marfa the bus turned south on U.S. 67, a road which stretched across the desert before climbing through the Cuesta Del Burro and Chinati mountains before making the long drop down to the Rio Grande at Presidio, elevation thirty-three feet. The bus made a meal stop here, at the Presidio Tastee-Freez, but I jumped to Greenwich Village for a falafel pita. I only ate part of it—no appetite. I jumped back for the last leg of the journey, down Farm to Market Road 170.

It was late afternoon and the sky was cloudy, but it was *hot* in Redford. I thanked the bus driver, recorded a jump site, and jumped directly to the Stillwater apartment with only a slight ear pain.

My lover had rejected me, the police were after me, I had a fever of 102°F, my right ear wouldn't stop aching, and I was having trouble breathing. So I felt guilty for feeling sorry for myself.

It's easy enough to say, *Hey, Davy, you're entitled. You've got every right to feel sorry for yourself.* Understanding that didn't make me feel any less guilty. If anything, it made it worse, because the guilt made me angry, made me defensive. So, I was feeling sorry for myself, guilty, and angry.

'Cause deep down inside, I knew I deserved it all.

At 8 P.M. I jumped to a twenty-four-hour clinic in midtown Manhattan. I lied on the sign-in forms about my name and address and said I would pay in cash. The doctor, a Hindu named Patel, listened to my symptoms, took my temperature, peered in my ears, then listened to my lungs.

"Oh, my," he said. I went into a spasm of coughing. He held the stethoscope away from my chest for its duration, then listened again when I was still. "Oh, my."

He took a bottle out of a refrigerator and loaded an unpleasantly large syringe. "You have no known allergies, right?"

"Right."

"Drop your pants."

"What is it?"

"Antibiotics. Ampicillin. You're on the edge of pneumonia. I am giving you this shot and prescriptions for oral antibiotics, cough medicine, antihistamines, and eardrops. If your lungs were any more congested or your fever any higher, I would put you into a hospital bed. As it is, you are to go straight to a drugstore and fill this, then home to bed."

He stuck the needle into the upper part of my right buttock. It didn't hurt at first, but when he depressed the plunger, the muscle cramped severely. "Owww!"

"Don't walk," he added. "Take a cab. Don't exert yourself. Drink plenty of liquids. Drink liquids until you think you will burst."

I nodded, rubbing the muscles below the injection.

He looked at me with narrowed eyes. "Are you sure you understand?"

I laughed weakly. "Do I look as bad as all that?"

"Very bad. Yes."

"Okay. Drugstore, home, bed, lotsa liquids, lotsa rest. Take a taxi. What else?"

He looked less worried. "Come back in two days. Have a seat while I write out the prescriptions."

"I'd rather stand," I said, still rubbing my butt.

He pointed at the couch. "Lie down, then. Doctor's orders. It is very important you rest."

When he'd finished writing out the prescriptions, he asked me how I felt. "My butt hurts."

"You are not having itching, or apprehension? Are you

feeling puffy around the eyelids, lips, tongue, hands or feet?"

"No. Why?"

"Just to make sure you are not having an allergic reaction to the injection. Well, off with you, and don't forget to come back in two days."

I paid in cash, jumped to a twenty-four-hour drugstore that I knew in Brooklyn, and had the prescription filled. The pharmacist took forever. There was no place to sit. I leaned against the end of a display and coughed. When he finally finished, I paid, staggered out the door, and jumped, no thoughts in my head but bed.

The room I appeared in was empty and dark, bare of all furniture except the miniblinds on the window. It was the Brooklyn apartment, still sealed by the NYPD.

Stupid! I concentrated, remembered the Stillwater apartment, its view of the campus where I'd watched Millie walk in the rain. I jumped again, and got it right.

I took all of the appropriate drugs, in the right quantities, making myself check everything twice. The way I felt, I was likely to OD by mistake. The antibiotics were the worst, horse pills, but at least they made me drink several glasses of water before the lump in my throat was gone. If I understood the directions, I wouldn't have to take the next dose until morning.

It took all my willpower to undress before falling into bed.

The next thirty-six hours were blurred, distorted by fever, antihistamines, and restless sleep. When I wasn't asleep, my thoughts turned inevitably to Millie. If I managed to avoid thinking of her, I thought about the police. Every sound I heard outside my apartment made me think they were about to break in, and I would stumble to the windows and look desperately around, paranoid. Once the mailman walked by and for an instant I took the uniform to be police blue.

The fever broke sometime Thursday evening and I

dropped into a deeper, more restful sleep, though I had dreams.

Friday morning, I showered, dressed, and jumped to the clinic in Manhattan. There was an awkward moment as I struggled to remember what name I'd given on my previous visit, but I managed, in the end, to dredge it up.

"Well," Dr. Patel said, listening to my chest, "that is much more like it. How do you feel?"

"Weak, but my ear doesn't hurt now."

"And is there any pain in the chest?"

"No."

"Well, I am thinking that we caught it in time. Be sure and complete the full course of antibiotics. You may take or leave the antihistamines and cough medicine as your symptoms require, but, to be on the safe side, keep up the eardrops for two more days. If the pain does not return, you may discontinue application."

I thanked him and paid for the visit.

Back in Stillwater I wandered aimlessly about the apartment, restless. I tried to pick up several different books but found it difficult to concentrate. Finally, I spent some time hooking up the entertainment center, running all the cables from VCR to TV to stereo to 8-mm videotape player (for the camera's tapes) to the wall cable outlet.

I watched the last half of an old movie classic on one of the movie channels, then flipped around, looking for something interesting. There were several soap operas, a few game shows, and movies that I'd already seen or thought were stupid. Then I hit CNN and paused.

"The hostage crisis at Algiers Airport is over, leaving one hostage dead and several others wounded. The three hijackers and fourteen of the hostages were driven from the airport in a truck and passed through Algerian Army checkpoints. Five hours later, a bus with the hostages aboard pulled up outside the Swiss consulate. The fourteen hostages taken from the aircraft were the only Americans aboard after the death of Mary Niles."

What . . .?

"There has been no response to American and British

demands that Algeria arrest and try the hijackers. We go now to Athens Airport, where the hijacking of Pan Am flight 932 began."

The screen switched from the female news anchor to a blond male reporter standing in an airport concourse. He said, "Luggage crew on the ground saw three men carrying duffel bags board the Pan Am 727 from a food service truck, shortly before the plane taxied away from the gate. According to one of the British passengers, these men hid themselves in the aft lavatories, bursting out, after the plane was airborne, with grenades and Uzi submachine guns. They made all passengers put their hands behind their heads and their heads between their knees. Those in first class heard one of the hijackers screaming into the cockpit intercom in broken English that he would start killing the flight attendants if the cockpit door was not opened.

"Captain Lawrence Johnson, pilot of flight 932, reported the hijacking to Athens radar control and changed his transponder code to read 7500, the international signal for hijacking. Then he had his copilot open the door."

The scene on the TV changed to an exterior control tower while a voice-over, heavy with radio static, said, "This is Pan Am 932. We have a hijacking and are diverting to Beirut." A message that said RECORDING appeared at the bottom of the screen.

The scene changed back to the CNN news anchor. "Four hours later, Pan Am 932 attempted to land at Beirut Airport, but Syrian Army forces in control of western Beirut refused permission to land, blocking the runway with fire trucks and airline buses. After threatening to crash the plane or land in the sea, they were told, 'Doesn't matter to us. You will not land here.'

"The hijackers then diverted the plane to Nicosia Airport in Cyprus, which also refused permission to land, but, in consideration of fuel problems, allowed the hijackers to land in Larnaca, where the hijackers demanded the plane be fueled. Cypriot authorities refused, but relented when the hijackers threatened to kill passengers one by one, until they received fuel. During fueling, airport antiterrorist personnel, dressed as fueling crew, affixed small radio-controlled charges to the landing-gear tires."

The camera showed the aircraft taxiing away from the fuel pits, and then, when it was in the middle of the taxiway and almost to the runway, small puffs of vapor came from each of the wheels and the aircraft shuddered to a halt.

The next scene was of a woman in a hospital bed. Her face was swollen and there was a dressing covering one cheek. A voice-over explained that this was Linda Matthews, flight attendant on Pan Am 932. She began talking.

"When the tires blew the hijackers started screaming, very angry. They began beating the copilot and screaming at Captain Johnson to 'Take off, take off!' He tried to get the aircraft moving twice more, but the airframe just shook. Finally he said, 'I can't. The landing gear is gone.' They opened the door, then, and had some of the passengers hang me out the door to look at the landing gear. I told them that all the tires were flat. I told them there was no way the aircraft could take off. That's when he began hitting me with the barrel of his gun. That's when they started hitting Captain Johnson, too."

The screen switched back to the anchor. "The hijackers demanded a new aircraft then, immediately. Authorities refused. Negotiations stretched out for seven hours. During this time, the hijackers demanded the release of several Shiite Muslims being held in Jordan, Saudi Arabia, and Italy. Finally, in the first apparent breakthrough, the hijackers said they would release all but the American passengers in return for a new plane. Authorities countered with an offer of a new plane if all hostages were released. The hijackers said, 'Wait for our answer.' "

The screen switched back to Linda Matthews, flight attendant.

"During the flight from Athens they moved everybody out of first class and put them in empty seats in coach. The flight wasn't very full, so this wasn't a problem. The leader, the hijacker who always made the demands, came out of the cockpit. He looked very angry. I'd been moved to a seat at the back of first class where I pretended to be unconscious.

I didn't want them hitting me again. The leader called out to the hijacker standing at the back of coach in Arabic. The man at the back of coach brought a briefcase forward. On his way I could hear him hitting at anybody who wasn't completely bent forward, face on their lap. They pulled a female passenger from the first aisle seat in coach and handcuffed the briefcase to her wrist. Then I heard the leader say, 'Take message to Americans.' The woman, the one they'd pulled from coach, she looked very frightened, hardly able to stand. I heard the leader say to her, 'You are much luck. You leave plane.' "

The scene changed to an exterior view of the aircraft, zooming in on the door as somebody kicked out the yellow inflatable emergency slide. Then somebody was pushed from the door, almost ejected, to fall onto the chute sideways. They slid down and ended up sprawled on the concrete.

It was Mom.

She picked herself up with difficulty and limped as she walked away from the plane. The case was apparently heavy and she tried to shift it to her other hand, but the handcuff wouldn't let her, so she held it with both hands on the handle, hanging to one side and bumping her knee as she walked.

The scene shifted back to Linda Matthews, in her hospital bed.

"All three of the terrorists were looking out the window. The leader had this box in his hand. I thought it was a radio. It had an antenna, anyway. He pushed a button on it."

The scene shifted back to the tarmac and Mom, now several hundred feet away from the aircraft. An airport jeep in the foreground had just started moving forward to pick her up when the suitcase blew up in a blast of fire and smoke.

Mom was blown several feet away and ended up in a heap, like a pile of bloody rags, one arm flung out to the side, one arm missing. Just before the camera cut back to the news anchor, there was a voice in the background, probably the cameraman's, saying, "Oh my God! Oh my God!"

The news anchor continued, a grim expression on her face. "Shortly after the bloody death of Mary Niles, Cypriot authorities delivered a fueled 727 to the terrorists. Herding the fourteen American passengers and crewmen ahead of them, they boarded the plane and flew to Algeria. Once in Algeria, negotiations with a joint team of Algerian, PLO, and Saudi representatives continued for fifteen hours. At the end of this time, the hostages were released and the terrorists were taken from the airport under army escort."

The camera changed to a different angle on the anchor. She said, "In the European Community today, talks between . . ."

I turned the TV off with the remote control.

"I can't stand to sit in the middle or at the window."

I let the remote control drop through limp fingers. *I guess she couldn't teleport—I wish she could. I wish I'd been there. I should have been there!*

Well, you got your aisle seat, Mom.

In the corner of the apartment I came back to myself, seated on the floor, wedged between the end of the couch and a bookshelf. There was a book on the floor, with half the pages torn out and crumpled, individually, into tightly packed balls. My hand was in the process of tearing out yet another page when I realized what I was doing.

Mom . . .

I looked at the book, *Pudd'nhead Wilson,* from the Twain collection Mom gave me. I felt terrible. Dad tore up books. I didn't want to be like Dad. I threw the book across the living room and pulled myself up on the couch armrest. I felt like there should be tears and there weren't any.

It didn't happen. It was fever. It was delirium.

I turned on the evening news and the camera footage was there again, on ABC. I turned the TV off quickly, before the explosion.

Millie . . . Millie has to help me.

It was too much for one person to stand. Too much to

stand alone. I walked out of the apartment and around the corner, intending to make her listen to me, to tell her about Mom, but I paused at the corner, uncertain.

Two different images—the explosion and Millie's face as she told me to go away and never bother her again—those images flipped back and forth in my mind, jostling for my attention, struggling against each other, sometimes merging to stab twice as deep.

The exterior of the apartment was red brick. I leaned against it, the brick cold and rough against my face. The wind was cold, out of the north, the sky clear with tiny, cold stars, like pieces of flint, like shards of broken glass.

There were footsteps on the walk and I turned, hunched over in the shadow of the hedge that lined the walk. A man passed by without seeing me, heading down the walk toward Millie's building. He passed into the direct glare of the streetlight and I saw his face.

It was Mark, Millie's old boyfriend, the man I'd jumped a hundred miles and left on the observation deck of Will Rogers World Airport.

Has he come to bother Millie again?

I could be a hero again, wait until he started bothering Millie, then jump him to Brooklyn, to Minnesota, far away, where he wouldn't bother her. Would she listen to me then?

Mark knocked firmly on her door. I jumped to the side of her walkway, behind an evergreen bush that was chest high. My hands flexed and unflexed, anxious to have something to grab, something to hit at. I thought of the walkway at Battery Park, of the railing between land and cold, cold water.

How easy just to jump him to the edge. . . .

The door opened and I gathered myself to jump, to grab, to hurt. I listened carefully, waiting for the angry words to come, but though I heard Millie's voice, there was no anger, no outrage in it.

"Ah, Mark. Thanks for coming," she said.

The door swung wide, Mark stepped inside, and the door shut. The door shut. The door shut.

Oh, God! I felt like a fool, like an idiot. I flinched away, jumped back to my apartment several hundred feet away. *Oh, God!* I saw my antibiotics on the counter and, by reflex, glanced at my watch. It was time to take another pill and put the eardrops in. I leaned against the counter for a moment, my eyes shut tight, thinking, *Where are the tears? Where are the goddamned tears?*

The cap on the antibiotics was childproof, requiring more of my attention to open it than I felt like giving. I finally managed the lid and tried to swallow a pill dry. It stuck in my throat, like a piece of bone, like a stiff and stale piece of bread. I pulled open the nearest cabinet and revealed the dishes, the wonderful handmade dishes. The glasses were at the other end of the cabinet and I couldn't be bothered.

I took a large mug, filled it with water from the tap, and washed the pill farther down my throat, but not far enough. It seemed stuck still, at the bottom of my esophagus, uncomfortable and unpalatable. I filled the mug again, angry at the pill, angry at Millie, angry at Mark, angry at myself.

The second cup of water pushed the pill on down and I set the mug on the edge of the sink, carelessly. It toppled over and fell, handle first. The handle snapped with a noise like a dry stick broken between one's hands.

God damn it all to hell!

I picked up the two fragments and started to piece them together, but it seemed so pointless. I threw the cup back into the sink with great force and it shattered, the noise both startling and pleasing me, a piece of the ceramic flying past my ear to hit the refrigerator.

I picked another mug out of the cabinet and threw it even harder.

The tears came then, great racking sobs that didn't stop until long after I'd smashed every dish in the set.

ELEVEN

Leo Silverstein told me over the phone that it would be a closed coffin, and it was.

I arrived an hour early, jumping to the airport and taking the airport car service. It was Walt Steiger's station wagon but the driver was younger. "Where's Walt," I'd asked. "He's got a funeral" was the answer.

Inside the Calloway-Jones Funeral Parlor a grave-faced man with white hair and a dark suit glided up to me quietly and asked my relation to the deceased.

"I'm her son."

"Ah, you'd be Mr. David Rice? Mr. Silverstein told us to expect you. I am Mr. Jones. Through here, please."

He led the way through a pair of double doors to a churchlike room with stained-glass windows. Her coffin was at the front of the room, on the right. A man stood facing it, his head bowed, his back to us. When he heard us enter he took out a tissue and blew his nose before turning around. I'd never seen him before.

He looked blankly at us for a moment, then turned his attention to me. He took a step forward and said tentatively, "Davy . . .?"

I nodded. I didn't like looking at him particularly. The pain on his face made me want to run and hide. "I'm sorry," I said. "I don't remember your name."

"We've never met. My name is Lionel Bispeck."

"Oh! You're Mom's, er, boyfriend." I felt like a fool calling a forty-five-year-old man a "boyfriend."

He turned suddenly and blew his nose. "Sorry. Oh, Christ, I'm out of tissues."

"Here," I said, groping inside my jacket. I pulled out a new, extra-large linen handkerchief. "I brought four." I needed them for the lingering symptoms of my bout of near-pneumonia, as well as for the tears.

Mr. Jones cleared his throat and said, "When you are ready to sit, these first two rows are for family." He pointed at the first two pews nearest the coffin. There were neat white placards on the end which said FOR THE IMMEDIATE FAMILY.

"I think I'm the only family there is, Mr. Jones."

He raised his eyebrows. "A Mr. Carl Rice phoned and asked for the time and place of the ceremony."

I swallowed. "Oh. I didn't expect my father to attend." *I'll kill him!* "In any case," I said, "my mother divorced him several years ago and he is *not* family."

Mr. Jones looked pained. "If he should make his identity known to me, I will try and seat him elsewhere, but it's not something we have control over."

"I understand, Mr. Jones. Does Leo Silverstein know that my father is coming?"

"I shouldn't think so. Not unless your father phones Mr. Silverstein directly."

"Do you expect Mr. Silverstein?"

"Definitely."

"When he comes, would you tell him about my father?"

"Certainly." He glided away, a white-topped shadow, oozing propriety.

I shuddered.

The pain on Lionel Bispeck's face was gone, replaced by anger.

"Ah . . . you know about my father."

He nodded, started to say something, then just shook his head angrily.

"Well, you better come sit with me."

He hesitated. "It's not right."

"No," I agreed. "He has no business here."

"No, I mean for me to sit up front."

I looked at the ceiling. "Did you love her?" I asked, exasperated.

"Yes."

"Then come sit down. Do you think she wouldn't have wanted those who loved her to sit together? Besides, if Dad shows up, I'll need all the support I can get."

"Oh. All right." He almost smiled then.

"What?"

He shrugged as he sat down. "You're a lot like her. She used to bully me into doing all sorts of reasonable things."

I set my mouth. "Bully? You don't know the meaning of the word. You haven't met Dad yet."

The almost smile died. "No . . . I'd like to beat his face in!"

I nodded. "Maybe you don't need to meet him after all. But he's an angel compared to terrorists."

"Oh, fuck!" Lionel was twisting the handkerchief between clenched fists. "I thought I was a pacifist. I was a conscientious objector during Vietnam, but I'd gladly pull the trigger if I could get those *bastards* in my hands." He pounded his knees, then let out a deep breath. "I don't see that much difference, though, between them and your father. Terrorism always targets the innocent."

I took a deep breath, then another, the room swimming. I wanted to kill them myself. The rage sickened me, made my stomach hurt and heart race.

"Easy," I said, more to myself than Lionel. "Calm down."

He blew his nose again. "Sorry."

"Quit apologizing, dammit! You didn't do anything wrong." I remembered Millie saying the same thing to me and I had to turn my head away, struggle with the tears. I took out another of the new linen handkerchiefs.

Leo Silverstein came in then. I introduced him to Lionel.

"Could I talk to you a minute, David?" He led the way over to an alcove with coat hooks at the back of the room.

"Is it about Dad?"

"Oh. No—I don't know what to do about your father. I'd like to get him arrested but the chief witness is . . ."

"Dead. She's dead. Okay, what is it?"

"Before you called yesterday, I tried to get hold of you at your New York number."

"How'd you get that number?"

"When you gave me that letter for your mother, I phoned her. She asked me to open it and read it to her."

"Oh. What about it?"

"A New York police operator answered your phone. They asked where you were. I told them about the funeral."

Great. I shrugged as if it didn't matter. "Okay. Anything else?"

He stared at me. "Why do they want to talk to you?"

"That's not your concern." I started to walk away, but he grabbed my arm.

"Wait a minute. It *is* my concern. I'm the executor of your mother's estate. You're a beneficiary."

Estate. Dead people have estates. Mom was dead. That's the thing about it—I was constantly forgetting that she was dead. My mind was trying to protect me, but it kept coming back. *Oh, Mom . . . why are you always leaving me?* The image from the TV played in my head again. I stared at Silverstein.

He dropped my arm like it was red hot and stepped back.

"Anything else?" I repeated.

"The press is outside, television and newspaper. Mr. Jones is keeping the cameramen out, but he can't keep the reporters from coming in and watching. If they try for any interviews in here, though, he'll have them escorted out by the police."

"The police are here?"

"Just the usual—two off-duty motorcycle cops to escort the procession. They're keeping an eye on the press, though."

"Oh. Thank you, Mr. Silverstein," I said. "You've been a great help. I'm sorry I keep snapping at you."

He shrugged uncomfortably.

More people were coming in. Walt Steiger, the taxi

driver, clapped his hand on my shoulder for a moment, then went and sat in the back. Mrs. Johnson, the lady who lived in Granddad's house, came up, expressed sympathy, and introduced her husband before taking a pew in the back.

Leo Silverstein came back after a while. He had a man with him wearing a dark suit.

"David, this is Mr. Anderson, from the State Department."

I stood slowly and shook his hand. "I want to thank you, Mr. Anderson, for having her body shipped home."

"No thanks are needed. It's my job, but the deceased are usually tourists who've had a heart attack or a car accident. It don't like my job very much, when it involves violence."

I nodded slowly.

He continued. "This isn't the time, but if you have any questions, here's my card."

I thanked him again and he went away.

Lionel stirred on the seat beside me. "Christ, there's Sylvia and Roberta and . . . it's the whole office." He waved his arm.

A group of women who had just entered saw him and walked quietly up the side aisle. They hunched over in that strange protective posture that people take when they talk in church or to the bereaved. Lionel introduced them.

"This is Sylvia and Roberta and Jane and Patricia and Bonnie. They're the staff of the Fly-Away Travel Agency. Sylvia was your mother's boss. Patricia and Bonnie were on flight 932."

They ranged in age from almost elderly to Millie's age. Comfortably fat to thin.

I shook hands with all of them, soaking up their sympathy and grief like a sponge. "It was very good of you to come from so far."

Sylvia muttered something about travel agents and cheap airfare.

"Look," I said, "could you sit up here with us? They gave the family two whole pews and I'd just as soon not be all alone up here."

That was agreeable. They filled in the rest of the first pew and sat quietly, eyes straying about the room but always returning to and dwelling on the coffin.

Their presence comforted me, made me feel less alone, less small. The six years Mom spent away from me seemed less wasted. She'd made these people care for her, love her.

At ten minutes before the hour, ten minutes before the ceremony was to start, I saw sergeants Baker and Washburn enter the back of the room and stand there, scanning the crowd. They were dressed appropriately, in suits of dark brown with sober ties.

I looked back at the front, away from them. My face felt curiously still and, looking at Mom's coffin, I could feel some vast, violent emotion bubbling right below the surface.

At five minutes before the hour, Dad came in. Mr. Jones met him at the door and asked him to sign the register. Dad scribbled in the book. Mr. Jones led him up the center aisle and tried to steer him into an empty pew.

Dad said something and Mr. Jones shook his head, still pointing at the pew. Dad stepped around Mr. Jones and walked up the center aisle. Mr. Jones looked past him at me and spread his hands, helplessly.

I stood up and stepped out from my seat. Lionel started to get up and I shook my head at him, a tight smile on my face. Dad stopped dead when he saw me, his face paling. I beckoned to him and then walked to the double doors by the coffin, the ones that led out to the hearse. I opened the door and went through, Dad following slowly. As soon as I was outside, I turned left, away from the small cluster of reporters at the front of the building, away from the two attendants leaning against the hearse.

As soon as I turned the corner and was screened from anybody's sight, I acquired a jump site, then walked ten feet farther and turned around.

Dad came around the corner slowly, suspiciously. It was cool outside, slightly cloudy, but he was sweating copiously. He stopped about five feet away from me.

I stared at him, silent. My stomach was churning and I remembered things . . . bad things. He was wearing a Western suit, cowboy boots, and a string tie. The jacket parted and I could see his rodeo buckle.

"Damn your eyes! Say something!" His voice was loud and nervous. A breeze brought the smell of nervous sweat and alcohol to me.

I didn't move. Just stared at him, remembering again the night I stood over him with the heavy bottle.

"I thought I'd killed you," he said, finally. "I thought I'd killed you."

Ah. I remembered wondering if my ability to teleport was just the product of blackouts, familiar with blackouts because Dad had them so often. I almost smiled. *He thinks I've been haunting him.*

"What makes you think you didn't kill me?" I said, and jumped behind him. "Maybe you did kill me."

He flinched, turned around, and saw me there. His face was white, his eyes were wide. I jumped behind him again, grabbed him around the waist—*oh God, he's so light*—and jumped to the living room of his house in Stanville. He flailed about and I let go of him, shoving him forward as I did. He tripped over the ottoman and fell forward. Before he hit the floor I jumped back to Florida, behind the Calloway-Jones Funeral Parlor.

When I came around the corner to go back inside, Sergeant Baker leaned suddenly against the side of the building and fumbled for a cigarette. I wondered if Sergeant Washburn was working his way up the other side of the building.

I went through the doors and sat down by Lionel.

"What happened?" he asked in a whisper, a distressed look on his face.

"He went home," I said.

"Oh."

Sergeants Baker and Washburn came in again and took up their station in the back. They looked puzzled.

The service was awful. The Methodist preacher had never met Mother, had never talked to those who loved her, hadn't a clue about what sort of woman she was. He talked about senseless tragedy and God moving in mysterious ways and before it was over, I was ready to cause more senseless tragedies, starting with the pastor. He talked of Mom's deep, unshakable faith and I knew that was bullshit. Mom *had* found some measure of spirituality after going through Alanon, but she'd admitted to me that she wasn't at all sure what form or shape her "higher power" took.

The only thing that made it bearable was that I wasn't alone in my opinion. When he came over afterward to express his sympathy, I just shook my head.

Lionel was less kind, saying, while we were shuffling out to the cars, "Where did they get him?"

"Silverstein said he spoke at my grandfather's funeral. I guess Silverstein thought he'd do."

"He was wrong."

"Yeah."

There was a great deal of jostling among the press as we filed outside. Cameras clicked and flashed and whirred and reporters talked into microphones and hand-held minicassette recorders. None of them approached us, yet.

They made me ride in a limousine behind the hearse, alone except for a silent driver. I thought Mr. Adams had a much nicer limo, but I didn't say so. *What am I doing here? For Mom. You're here for Mom.*

The burial was mercifully short, attended by Lionel and the woman of the Fly-Away Travel Agency, Leo Silverstein, and sergeants Baker and Washburn. The press was there also, at the edge of the cemetery, doing things with telephoto lenses and shotgun microphones. I was tempted to jump several times in front of them and give them something really exciting to report.

A reception was arranged for a local hotel. People were loading into cars when Washburn and Baker finally stepped forward.

"Ah, Sergeant Baker and Sergeant Washburn. How nice of you to come." My voice was bitter.

That stopped them in midstride, confused for a moment. They didn't know that I'd eavesdropped on them that time in the apartment. They pulled out their badges anyway, programmed to do things a certain way. "We'd like to ask you a few questions, Mr. Rice, or is it Mr. Reece?"

"You say tomato, I say rutabaga." I took out the driver's license and flipped it at Sergeant Washburn. "Here, it's even got my fingerprints on it. Maybe they'll match up with the pottery you guys dusted in my apartment. How's your *wife,* Sergeant Washburn? Raised any good bruises, lately?"

The spinning card bounced off of Washburn's chest and dropped to the grass. He stooped and picked it up, handling it by its edges. His face was getting red and Baker was looking sideways at him.

Silverstein stepped forward, a puzzled look on his face. I turned to him.

"Sergeant Washburn and Sergeant Baker, NYPD. They wrangled a vacation in Florida to question the notorious criminal . . . me."

"Are you a criminal, David?"

All the rage burst out. "Hell, yes. I'm guilty of running away from home, of buying a fake ID out of desperation, and of using it to open a bank account. Worst of all, I'm guilty of intervening when a policeman nearly beats his wife to death! Nearly as bad as a terrorist, any day."

Leo blinked and looked at Washburn as if he were something he'd found under a rock. "Well, this hardly seems like hot pursuit. Why are you down here, gentlemen? Why didn't you just request our Florida authorities to pick him up?"

"There is the question of identity," Washburn said angrily.

"Not anymore," I said.

He nodded. "That's right. Not anymore."

Silverstein looked from the New York police to me. "Well, again, you seem out of your jurisdiction. Have you talked to Sheriff Thatcher?"

"Not yet."

"Well, then, come along, David. There's a reception at the Holiday Inn. I doubt that many of your mother's friends will be there, but there will be a lot of your grandfather's friends who wish to pay their respects."

Washburn, an irritated look on his face, stepped between us and the cars and said, "We still have a few questions."

"David, my advice, as your lawyer and," he added, looking over his glasses at Washburn, "as an officer, ipso facto, of a court which *does* have jurisdiction in this county, is not to answer these questions. Come along, we'll be late for the reception."

I spread my hands apart and shrugged at Washburn, then followed Silverstein as he walked back to the limo. When we were far enough away from them I whispered, "You're not my lawyer."

"Well, as I said earlier, I'm the executor of your mother's estate and, with the exception of a few bequests to her friends at the travel agency and Mr. Bispeck, you are the recipient of the greater part of the estate. So, in a sense, I am your lawyer. Besides, I consider myself the family's lawyer, old-fashioned as that may be. Unfortunately, you're the only member left. By the way," he said, opening the limo door, "what did you say to your father that made him leave?"

I climbed in. "I'd rather not say, actually."

He shrugged. "Scoot over, I don't think I should leave your side while the two sergeants are around. It's amazing the ameliorating effect a lawyer has on a policeman's behavior, especially when they're out of their jurisdiction. I'll come back and get my car later."

On the way to the hotel he said, "Do you have a dollar, David?"

I looked in my wallet. "Sorry. I wasn't thinking very clearly this morning. I didn't get out of my . . . room with anything smaller than a hundred."

I looked back at Silverstein. He was staring at my open wallet, which held about twenty hundred-dollar bills. "Uh . . . just how do you make your money, David?"

"Banking, banking speculation." I smiled slightly. *I speculates whether there's any money in a bank and I takes it.*

"Well, give me a hundred dollars then."

I'd read my share of Nero Wolfe mysteries. "Ah, the old lawyer-client confidentiality scam. You want to ask me some questions and you don't want to have to tell the police the answers."

He blushed. "Well . . . let's just say I want to reserve the option of not answering their questions."

I took out five hundred-dollar bills. "Might as well make it a convincing retainer."

"Can you afford this?"

"Easily."

He took a notebook out of his jacket pocket. "Let me write a receipt."

"I trust you."

"Well, thanks for that vote of confidence, but the receipt is to protect both of us. It provides a 'documentation trail,' as we say in the profession." He tore it out and handed it to me. "Don't lose it." He carefully tucked the notebook and money away. "Now, to ask a question I asked earlier today, why do they want to talk to you?"

"Washburn was my downstairs neighbor in New York. He beats his wife. I helped her get to a shelter. He started investigating me and found that I'd purchased and used a forged New York State driver's license."

Silverstein's eyebrows went up. "Why on earth did you do that?"

"I was a runaway in New York City and I couldn't get a job without ID. That's why!"

"You didn't have a driver's license from Ohio?"

"No. And I didn't have a Social Security number either. And, worst of all, I didn't have a birth certificate, so I couldn't get the others."

"Why didn't you just write off for a copy of your birth certificate?"

"Huh? You can do that?"

He laughed, then stopped when he saw the look on my face. "I'm sorry. I don't know what your circumstances were, but it just seems ironic that you broke the law without knowing there was a legal alternative."

"Ho, ho, ho."

"Is that all they want you for?"

"That's all they have on me, but . . . I'm pretty sure

Washburn has portrayed me as some kind of drug dealer."

An expression of distaste crossed Silverstein's face. "Are you?"

"God damn it! My father's an alcoholic. That's the closest I'll ever get to drug dealing. No, I'm not a drug dealer. I'm not a user either."

"Calm down. I'm glad you're not, but I had to ask. I wouldn't have disclosed our conversation, but I would have given you the retainer back." He looked out the darkened glass at the back of the limousine. "The two sergeants are still with us. I would have thought they'd split up, one to follow us, one to go to Sheriff Thatcher."

"They only have one car," I reminded him. "They may call from the hotel, though."

"Hmmm. Well, if I were you, I'd avoid being arrested. Extradition is a tricky process and you could end up sitting a long time in a Florida jail cell while I fought the procedure."

"Are you advising me to run away?"

He shrugged. "Take a vacation."

I shook my head. "You're just as bad as me."

He shrugged again. "We can lose them at the hotel. You go in for a moment, to the reception, and I'll have Walt Steiger pick you up around back. There's an exit by the men's room. I've used it many a time to sneak out of Kiwanis meetings."

"That's kind of you, but I've made my own arrangements."

"To get away?"

The limousine pulled into the hotel driveway and stopped at the door. "No, just travel arrangements, but they'll do. Nobody's going to arrest me."

I shook more hands than seemed possible for the number of people in the room. I couldn't help but wonder if someone in there was an octopus in disguise. "Yes, ma'am. Kind of you to say so, sir. Yes, I'll miss her very much. Thank you for coming. It would have meant a lot to her that you came." *God, will this ever end?*

The bunch from Sacramento rescued me after forty-five minutes.

"Mary called me from London, you know, to tell me how her visit with you went." Lionel smiled. "Christ, she was scared to go see you."

I swallowed. "It was mutual. Did she say the visit was a success?"

"Oh, yes. She was very happy to have seen you," Lionel said.

Patricia nodded fiercely. "She talked about your weekend all through the trip. Even when we were in the plane, when the terrorists were . . . well, she said, 'At least I saw Davy.' "

I lost it then. "Uh, excuse me." I stumbled blindly to the men's room, into a toilet stall, and leaned against the tiled wall, tears streaming down my face. Inside a voice screamed, inarticulate, unintelligent, but pierced through with pain. *It hurts.* I don't know why I should have been surprised.

After a few more minutes, a dozen or so deep breaths, and several blows of the nose, I left the stall, washed my face, and straightened my tie. *Time to say good-bye and blow this joint.*

There was a Florida police officer standing at the back door, the one Leo Silverstein used to avoid Kiwanis meetings. I went back into the reception hall and smiled reassuringly at Lionel and the Fly-Away girls. "Sorry."

They made noises like they understood. Over by the main entrance stood sergeants Baker and Washburn with a more senior version of the Florida policeman in the hall. Leo Silverstein was talking to them, and his hands were waving emphatically. The Florida policeman held his hands up, placating. Washburn looked angry and Baker kept looking at Washburn, a worried look on his face.

Looks like Baker is catching on.

Jane, one of the Fly-Away agents, came up to me and said, "I know this is a bad time, but I'd like to get a picture of you, to keep with my picture of Mary."

"Well, I'll make a deal. I don't have a current photo of Mom. If you send me a copy, I'll pay you for it."

She looked like she might cry. "Oh. Certainly. You don't have to pay for it. I'd like to. . . ."

I swallowed, then gave her the PO box in New York. I didn't think the NYPD had that. The utility bills all came to the apartment, but Millie's letters came to the PO box.

"Let's make it a group shot, David and Lionel and the Fly-away girls. We'll get someone else to take the shot." I pointed over the refreshments. "We can do it against that wall."

I started pushing and prodding and cajoling and in a minute, all of us were lined up against the wall, Sylvia in the middle flanked on one side by Lionel, Jane, and Patricia, and on the other side by myself, Bonnie, and Roberta. Mr. Steiger held the camera for us and took two quick shots.

"Great. Okay everybody, one giant step forward," I said, pushing us gently away from the wall. Quietly I said to Bonnie, "I'm going to step back behind. Could you close up the gap when I do?"

She looked confused. "Why?"

I tilted my head toward the police. "Please?"

"Okay," she said nervously.

I stepped back and she stepped over, pulling Roberta with her. This effectively screened me from everyone in the room.

I jumped.

TWELVE

The third day of my little walks, my tenth at Serenity Lodge, Mrs. Barton stopped by my table at breakfast in the quiet dining room.

"Everything all right, Mr. Rice?"

"It's Davy, Mrs. Barton." *That's what my mother called me.*

"All right, Davy. How is your cabin? Do you need anything?"

I shook my head. "No, thank you. Everything's fine."

She was fifty-six, a widow whose husband had died of cancer ten years before. She did grief counseling on request, but I'd only talked to her about Mom once, when I checked in. I didn't tell her how she died, though.

"Well, we like to check. What are you doing with your days?"

"I go for walks. Long walks."

"If you need anything. . . ."

"Right. Thanks."

She wandered on, stopping briefly at other tables. Most of the other guests were older, retired, but they left me alone. That was one of Mrs. Barton's rules. Guests who wanted to socialize gathered in the lodge between meals. You weren't supposed to talk to people otherwise. I stayed away from the social gatherings, the TV room, and the card parties.

I think Mrs. Barton was worried I might be suicidal.

On my way back to my cabin, I stopped by the front desk

and stared at the large-scale topographical map of Presidio County, over three thousand square miles of desert containing whole mountain ranges, but with less population than even a large town. Brewster County, to the east, was even larger, but also more populous since it held Big Bend National Park in its confines. The area was right in the middle of the northern Chihuahuan desert.

Redford, the nearest town, was on the Rio Grande, sixteen miles from the town of Presidio, thirty-four miles from the town of Lajitas on Big Bend's western edge. To the northeast was El Solitario, a circular range of mountainous terrain that made up for its lack of height by being some of the roughest and most inhospitable terrain on the face of the planet.

I'd ridden out to Serenity Lodge with the weekly grocery delivery. The driver told me that he'd driven a geologic-survey team into El Solitario. They used four-wheel-drive vehicles and were lucky if they made seven miles a *day*.

On the map, my progress to date was pitiful.

I went back to the cabin and jumped away.

The first morning I left the cabin, I walked about seven miles over the rolling desert, starting just before dawn, at six-forty, and stopping when it got too hot, about twelve. I recorded the particular piece of sand, rock, and ocotillo with the video camera and jumped back to the cabin.

After eating at the lodge, I walked back to my cabin and napped through the afternoon. According to Mrs. Barton, this was to be expected, a common reaction to grief and depression. My first week at Serenity Lodge I slept seventeen to twenty hours a day.

At five, stiff from the morning walk, I stumbled over to the lodge, had my quiet dinner, and went back to study the videotape of the morning's site. Then I jumped back out to the desert and kept walking until sunset, perhaps an hour. I could see well enough to keep walking, but I wanted enough light to record the site properly with the videocamera.

The rolling desert, with its sameness from place to place, was tricky to memorize. There were differences from site to site, but they were subtle—a weathered piece of mesquite lying so, a rock with a hole in it, a patch of lecheguia in the shape of Lake Ontario.

The second day I reached the foothills and the walking was harder. I did less than five miles, working up the hills slowly, my muscles still stiff from the previous day.

The first day I'd crossed dirt ranch roads with fresh tire tracks and "jumped" several barbed-wire fences. The second day I only jumped one fence, though I walked over several old, broken fences, torn and rusted. The kind of barbed wire was different, solid, antique. The posts on the old fences were sticks of mesquite, twisted and weathered. More and more of the terrain was defined by rock, from pea gravel to building-sized outcroppings, and the dirt roads, what few I crossed, were overgrown and washed out. There were no recent tracks.

The fifth day I twisted my ankle while working around a ledge ten feet above the next lowest ground. The sharp pain distracted me and I lost my footing and fell. It wasn't a great distance, I kept upright to land on my feet, but the thought of landing on my newly twisted ankle made me *flinch* away.

Instead of landing painfully on the scree below, I found myself standing gingerly on one foot and leaning against a bookshelf in the Stanville Public Library.

Wait a minute. Doesn't that violate some sort of physical law? Conservation of momentum or something? I limped to Periodicals and sat on a couch. The library was open, but nobody seemed to notice that I was dressed for much warmer weather.

It occurred to me that teleportation itself might violate a few physical laws. I rubbed my ankle and thought about it.

When I jump from Florida to New York, why don't I smash through a wall or something? After all, in Florida I'm closer to the equator and in Ohio, I'm closer to the pole. The earth is spinning at a thousand miles an hour at the equator. I didn't know what the difference in speed was between New York and Florida, but it had to be more than fifty miles an hour.

Why doesn't that difference in speed throw me east at fifty miles an hour when I appear in New York?

For a second I was convinced that this was likely, that the next time I jumped, I would flatten against the nearest wall as if I'd been hit by a car.

Relax—it hasn't happened yet and you've been jumping for over a year now.

Well, what is happening when I jump? Why wasn't there a frigging instruction manual?

If I didn't smash into the floor after jumping away from Texas, it meant that my relative speed didn't matter.

I remembered a book I'd read discussing Einstein's theory of relativity. I didn't understand most of it, but one thing it talked about was frames of relative motion. Even though, in Texas, I was traveling east to west at a different speed than I would travel in Ohio, and was dropping at, oh, twenty-five feet per second, I must have matched up the two frames of reference when I jumped, so there was no difference in speed, no difference in angular momentum.

The implications were interesting.

I jumped back to Texas, to the ledge where I'd twisted my ankle. I hadn't recorded it, but it was vivid in my memory.

The ledge itself was on the face of a dead-end gully that I'd found myself in. I was trying to avoid backtracking and the ledge looked like it led up over the top. It was relatively cool in the gully, perhaps sixty-five degrees, because the shoulder of a hill still blocked the morning sun.

I looked at the rock scree ten feet below me, and picked out a flat spot over to the side. I jumped to it and teetered, putting minimal weight on my twisted ankle. It was a distinctive enough jump site, with a strange cactus growing out of a crack in the rock. I jumped back to the ledge and turned, facing away from the rock.

If this doesn't work, this is going to hurt like hell.

I stepped off the ledge and let myself drop. Before I hit, I jumped to the flat spot by the cactus. There was no jarring, no thud. My ankle throbbed, but that was from standing.

I jumped back to the ledge and worked my way farther along it. After a minute, because the scree dropped sharply away, I was twenty feet off the terrain below. My heart beat fast and it was hard to catch my breath. I stepped off the ledge and the air streamed past me. In panic, I jumped to the flat spot by the cactus before I'd even dropped four feet.

Dammit!

I jumped back up on the ledge.

"Now, Davy," I said aloud. "You can drop a full second without hitting the ground below. You'll only drop sixteen feet in the first second. Give it a fair test."

I stepped off and said quickly, "One, one-thousand." The air was rushing past me, actually whistling in my ears when I *flinched* away from the rising ground and found myself crouched on the flat spot by the cactus. Again, it was like any other time I'd jumped. I felt no jarring or difference in speed.

I jumped back to the ledge and did it again, less afraid, but still nervous. To step off the ledge went against all my instincts, but I was closer to the bottom, closer to hitting, when I jumped away. Again, no problem.

My ankle throbbed though, from standing, so I recorded the site and jumped away.

After lunch, for the first time in days, I didn't feel like sleeping. Perhaps this was because I'd cut my morning hike short, but it also may have been because for the first time since the funeral, I could think about Mom without my mind shutting down. I realized I'd been in a fog for the last two weeks.

I kicked around the cabin and remembered things. Things like my first trip to New York, with Mom, and her visit to me in New York, before going to Europe. I remembered the exhibit at the Metropolitan Museum of Art. I remembered dinner with Mom in the Village.

I was able to do this, instead of shutting down, instead of hiding in the depths of slumber. I cried still and everything was still overlaid with the memory of the news footage, but I could think about her.

I was able to remember the stupid sermon at her funeral without getting more than mildly angry.

Thoughts of the funeral reminded me of Jane's promise to send me a picture of Mom. I wondered if it was there, at the postbox in Manhattan.

It was, a four-by-six photo in a stiff manila envelope. There was also a letter from Millie. I jumped back to Serenity Lodge, to my cabin, and set it on the table, unopened. My stomach churned and I felt like crying again.

The picture of Mom I put in the corner of the dresser mirror, held by the frame. She looked out at me, smiling gently, the familiar face with the stranger's nose.

"She sounds wonderful."

That's what Mom said when I told her about Millie. I opened the letter.

Dear Davy,
It's taken me a long time to write this. I'm not sure what I feel and I'm not sure what I want. If you hadn't "left" so suddenly, I probably would have said, "No. I don't want you to go away." When I'm upset, I'm just as likely as anybody to say or do hateful things. I guess I wanted to hurt you, but I don't think I wanted you to go away.

Now, though, I'm not sure. You frighten me, Davy, and you make me doubt my sanity. That's hardly a healthy thing. Also, you make me doubt your sincerity. You ran away and I thought you'd at least call, but it's been two weeks.

I'm not sure I want you to visit, but I think I'd like you to write.

Millie

I was relieved and I was angry. I picked up a piece of the Lodge's stationery and wrote:

Millie,
My mother's name was Mary Niles. She was featured on the news recently. I've been busy.

Davy

I crammed it in an envelope and wrote her name on it, then jumped to Stillwater and slipped it under her door.

The next day, after sleeping heavily, I jumped out to my last hiking spot, the ledge leading out of the gully. By my estimates, I was now some fifteen miles from Redford and almost through El Solitario's foothills.

I followed the ledge up, walking carefully. By the time I got out of the gully, my ankle was throbbing painfully, almost too painful to walk on. The sun was viciously bright and the nearest shade was thirty yards or so away. I started to limp that way, then said, "Fuck it." I couldn't see the shaded area well enough to jump to it, but I could see the halfway point. I jumped forty-five feet toward the shade. From there I could see a nice spot against a house-sized rock, complete with a smaller boulder to sit upon. I jumped again.

"Why am I walking at all?" I slapped my forehead. If I could see it well enough, and I knew where it was in relation to myself, I could jump it.

For the past several days, I'd used a particular landmark, a 4,600-foot mountain peak in the distance called La Mota, as my bearing. I studied the immediate landscape. My best route seemed to be around the ridge directly in front of me and then. . . . No, it wasn't. My best route was directly up the ridge, up a hillside more clifflike than sloping.

I studied the ground between me and the face and then jumped across it in three little hops of ten yards each. Next I jumped diagonally up the face of the hill, choosing spots to my left and right about ten feet higher than my last one. It took me less than a minute to reach the top of a hill that would have taken half a day to climb with a good ankle.

The view from the top was spectacular. It was the highest point I'd reached on my trek. I looked back toward Redford and could see the building's clustered on the road. The Rio Grande, beyond it, was hidden, but the top of its canyon was clear.

I turned around and looked toward El Solitario. It was intimidating. Even though there was less than ten miles to go, each piece of land between me and La Mota looked rougher and bleaker than the land before it.

Pity I can't see better. Maybe I could jump straight there.

See better? I quickly recorded the top of the ridge and jumped to First Avenue and Fifty-sixth in Manhattan. Twenty minutes later I walked out of a store with a large binocular case hanging from my shoulder. It was raining and the temperature was below forty degrees. Shivering, I jumped back to Texas, to the top of the ridge fifteen miles from Redford.

By lunchtime I was standing on the peak of La Mota, 4,600 feet above sea level. Around me El Solitario stretched like the surface of the moon.

I went back and had lunch and not even the sight of Millie's letter could depress me.

Well, not much.

There was a letter in the PO box two days later, sent overnight express.

Dear Davy,
My first thought was disbelief, when I found out who Mary Niles was. I didn't see the news coverage—I had midterms—but when I checked at the library, they knew all about it, down to describing the news footage. How could fate be so cruel, so viciously vindictive? I'm sure that words are inadequate at this point.

I wish that you'd come to me, though, when it happened. I don't know how you do what you do, but it seems that you could do that. . . . It hurts that you didn't come see me. I would have been glad to do what I could to help.

                              Millie
P.S. And if you can put notes under my door, why can't you give me a closer address to write?

Millie,
Thanks, I think, for your sympathy.
I did come to see you, right after it happened. Just

in time to see you welcoming Mark into your apartment. The words, I believe, were, "Thanks for coming, Mark."

I guess I can't blame you. After all, you'd told me to get lost, but, from what you'd previously said, I thought you'd have better taste.

                    Davy

P.S. Any answer can be put under the door of apartment 33. And no, I'm not there, but I'll check it every day or so. If you actually want to keep up this discussion.

I jumped to Stillwater and put my answer under the door. Even before I stood upright, I heard a hand on the doorknob. I jumped to my Stillwater apartment and shook.

I felt guilty and afraid. I leaned against the wall by the front window and watched the approach to the apartment stairway.

After a moment, Millie came around the corner, looking at the apartment numbers. I saw her stare up at my window, but the apartment was dark and the sun bright. She didn't see me. She walked on and I heard her steps on the stairway. When she reached the top, she rang the doorbell.

Oh, Millie . . .

I walked, hesitantly, to the front door and paused there, my hand on the doorknob. The doorbell rang again and I flinched, pulled my hand away from the doorbell as if it were hot. I jumped away, to Texas, to my cabin at Serenity Lodge, flopped down on the bed, and buried my face in a pillow.

Just when I thought that El Solitario was the perfect representation of my mood, bleak, blasted, ravaged, I stumbled on the first oasis.

It was a box canyon with high sides, the upper end blocked by an ancient rockfall, the downhill end stopped at a cliff's edge, dropping eighty feet or so where ancient uplift sheared the rock. Near the blocked upper end of the canyon a spring of sweet water poured forth, and ran down the length of the canyon to a small pool with no visible outfall. The pool was shaded by mesquite bushes turned into trees and trimmed with ancient buffalo grass. There were mountain goats and jackrabbits and several kinds of birds.

I spent an entire day sitting by the spring, reading, sleeping a little, and just listening to the water while I soaked my ankle.

There were two other spots of green in the midst of the desert. One was larger, two miles of valley blessed with multiple streams. In that one I saw deer droppings, the tracks of a cougar, and discarded beer cans. I got angry about the beer cans. There weren't a lot of them but it brought people into this haven and I didn't like that. I spent a couple of hours gathering them and any other traces of humanity, jumping, occasionally, to a dumpster in Stanville to dump the trash.

I may be a bank robber, but I'm no litterbug.

The third oasis was a pit, formed by rockfall and perhaps subsurface water. The walls were very high and the sun didn't shine to the bottom except at midday. The bottom was larger than the top and filled with water, except for a green island in the middle, perhaps sixty feet long by twenty wide. There were no beer cans there.

The walls were perhaps a hundred feet high, and it took me several minutes to acquire enough information to jump to the island at the bottom. It was cool there, almost uncomfortable, and the walls, towering above, were intimidating. I wondered if it would be more comfortable in the summer, when all around was hellish hot.

Davy,

Didn't you realize that the only thing I wanted from Mark was his version of the night you, well, removed him from the party? I know Mark is a sleaze. I'm not involved with him in any way, but when you vanished from in front of me, what was I to think?

I don't know if you're even human. For all I knew you fly around in a flying saucer kidnapping humans left and right. If this sort of jumping to conclusions bothers you, think how much alternative explanation you offered.

I know you're hurt, and I guess you were hurt even more when you thought I was getting involved with Mark again. But, dammit, you are doing your share of lashing out, yourself.

Millie

P.S. I still don't know if you are human, but I know that I care for you enough that you can hurt me. You did.

Several pieces of paper, crumpled into small balls of paper, were strewn across the desk. Each of them had two or three lines written on them before I discarded them. Try as I might, I wasn't able to write an answer that felt right. I swept them from the desk and into the trash can.

I considered going to her, but I was afraid to. I didn't really want to see anybody.

Earlier that day, before I picked up Millie's letter, I'd found a ledge facing south, in the depths of El Solitario. I jumped there. It was more cave than ledge, a broad shelf heavily overhung with rock, two hundred feet up a sheer rock face. It was another fifty feet to the ridgeline above and only a technical climber or a teleport could reach it.

It was thirty feet deep and relatively flat. I paced forward and stood at the edge, dry puffs of wind pulling at my shirt. I was feeling careless, apathetic. The drop would be more than enough to kill me, if I reached the bottom. The sun was almost down and there were clouds made flame and billowing orange by its rays. The rock shelf projecting above stuck out even farther than the ledge, solid, palpably heavy.

It was like the mouth of a giant, mouth poised open, massive molars ready to drop, to chew the life from me.

I liked it.

That night I started moving materials from a lumberyard in Yonkers, the one I'd dealt with before. There was a guard but he stayed near the front door and depended on the alarms. I only took mortar and some concrete dyes plus a mixing trough, trowels, and some chalk lines to mark out the walls.

The do-it-yourself book on masonry told me that working with natural stone was hard, and that projects that used ordinary brick were best to start with. I ignored that part and read the rest of the book carefully.

It was cold on the ledge at night, and I settled for leaving the materials stacked at the back, out of sight of anyone but passing buzzards.

Back at the cabin, I stared again at Millie's letter. I was still confused, still angry, furiously angry, but I knew enough, now, to know that she wasn't the cause. I penned a short note.

> Dear Millie,
>
> I'm sorry. There is too much pain right now for me to be rational. What you said about caring and being hurt makes sense. If I didn't care for Mom, her death wouldn't hurt. If I didn't care for you, your rejection wouldn't hurt.
>
> I won't be writing until I can get a better handle on things, but I'll be back. I hope that you find more good than bad in that fact. I can't give up on you without giving up on myself.
>
> > I love you,
> > Davy

There is an abandonment, an escape, that physical labor bestows.

I took my rocks from the scree at the bottom of the cliff. This was rock of the same color and texture, broken off and tumbled down by weather and time.

The mortar was hard to dye and I wasted a couple of batches before I got the proportions right. Part of the problem was that the color of the mortar was darker wet than after it had dried. I started the wall ten feet back from the edge, at the deeper end of the ledge, and I ran it forty feet long, about half the length of the ledge.

By midafternoon my back was sore and my arms ached,

but I had a wall knee-high along my ledge. I left a gap at the open end of the ledge for a doorway, but the other end butted up against the rock face. Where the mortar on the bottom rows had dried, it was hard, even from ten feet away, to tell where the cliff rock stopped and the wall began. From across the canyon, on the next ridgeline, it was impossible.

I went swimming in the box canyon oasis for ten minutes, then came back and continued working on the wall until sunset.

At night, I raided the lumberyard in Yonkers again, this time taking prehung, double-paned windows and frames, a prehung exterior door with a cut-glass window, framing timbers, and tan paint. I also took more mortar, a wood-burning stove, a stovepipe, and appropriate hardware.

After jumping these materials to the ledge—the stove was barely liftable—I spent some time at the cashier's desk working an adding machine. I left the tape from my calculations and twelve hundred dollars on the counter, weighted down by a coffee cup.

I may be a bank robber, but I'm not a common thief.

"We missed you at lunch yesterday, Davy."

"I was walking, Mrs. Barton. I guess I walked too far."

She smiled. "Well, it's probably good for you to get some exercise. I'm glad to see your appetite is picking up."

I stared at the fork in my hand. I hadn't been thinking about food, I'd been puzzling over the window frames and air-conditioning for my hidden fortress, my "fortress of solitude." Now that I saw the egg on my fork, the food in my stomach seemed to solidify in a lump, heavy and uncomfortable.

Mrs. Barton wandered on down the room. I dropped the fork and pushed the plate away from me.

Before going out to the ledge, I jumped to New York and checked the PO box, appearing first in the alleyway before walking around the corner to Broadway to the Bowling Green post office.

There was a letter from Leo Silverstein asking me to call

him. I jumped to the Pine Bluffs airport and used the pay phone.

"Mr. Silverstein, this is David Rice."

"Ah. Did you get my letter?"

"Yes."

"So, you're back in New York."

"No." I saw no reason to lie. "At the moment I'm in Pine Bluffs."

"Oh? Well, I have some business to transact. As you know, you figure in your mother's will."

I swallowed. "I don't want anything."

The image flashed in front of my eyes. The explosion, the broken-doll posture of her body, the blood and the smoke.

I can't stand to sit at the window or in the middle.

Silverstein coughed. "Well, you really should come down and hear the terms at least."

"At your office? I don't know. Have the police been looking for me still?"

"I don't know. They searched around pretty thoroughly for a couple of days, but there's a limit to how long Sheriff Thatcher is going to hunt someone whose only crime is a fake driver's license."

"I'll be right there."

I walked around the airport for a moment and watched a small single-engine plane take off. Then I jumped to the stairway leading up to Silverstein's office. There was someone on the stairs, but, luckily, he was walking down the stairs, facing away from me.

I held my breath until he'd left the building, then walked upstairs. Mr. Silverstein was standing in the reception area, looking out the window onto the square. He looked over his shoulder when I came in.

"Forget something, Joe—oh, Davy! I didn't see you on the sidewalk. How did you do that?"

"Do what?"

He shifted from foot to foot, uncomfortable. "Come on in."

Once in his office, he handed me a bundle of papers labeled, "Last Will and Testament of Mary Agnus Niles."

I looked at it and the pain surfaced, sharp and ragged. I found myself yawning, getting sleepy, my mind numbing.

Shit! I thought I was past this.

I put it down on the desk. "What does it say?"

"Essentially, with the exception of ten thousand dollars in bequests and gifts, it leaves you the balance of her estate, approximately sixty-five thousand dollars in CDs and savings, and a town house in California."

I blinked. "I guess she made good money as a travel agent."

Silverstein shook his head. "Not particularly. Your grandfather left her a good sum, especially with the sale of the house."

"Oh."

"You don't have to comment on this, and, to be perfectly honest, I'd rather you didn't, but I have the feeling that your present source of income wouldn't stand rigorous scrutiny."

He looked at me to see if I understood. I could feel my ears getting hot. He went on.

"Anyway, this inheritance would at least give you a legitimate source of income. It's a chance to get out of the gray area where you are."

I nodded slowly, reluctantly. "What will I have to do?"

"Well, the first thing you need to do is get that birth certificate. I'll handle that if you like. Then we'll apply for a social security number and a real driver's license, and I'll see about filing income tax for the time since you left your father. I don't suppose you know whether he claimed you as a dependent or not after you left?"

"I wouldn't put it past him. Uh, I don't drive, Mr. Silverstein, so the license . . ."

"Oh, well, there's nondriver's identification. You don't have to worry about that."

"What about the New York police?"

"Ah, well, funny about that. After you left the reception, Sheriff Thatcher was not inclined to pursue the matter without some sort of official request from the NYPD. Sergeant Washburn was furious, but, as of this morning when I talked to Sheriff Thatcher, there hasn't been any such request." He paused and looked out the window, stretching his arms. "I suspect, from what you told me and from Sergeant Baker's reactions, that Sergeant Washburn exceeded his authorization somewhat in coming down to Florida."

I exhaled. "Well, that's a relief."

"So," said Silverstein, "I take it you'd like to do this? Get the birth certificate and everything?"

I nodded emphatically. "Oh, yes. And do you think I could get a passport?"

He blinked. "I don't see why not. Why? Are you thinking of leaving the country?"

I looked out the window but my eyes didn't see the town square. Instead I was seeing the explosion that killed my mother, looped endlessly over and over and over. There was a feeling of anticipation, of things not yet realized. I shook the vision from my eyes and looked back at Silverstein.

"I want to go to Algeria," I said.

PART 5:

SEARCHING

THIRTEEN

"The first thing I want to make clear is that this violence, this terrorism, is not cultural. It isn't integral either to Arab or Muslim culture. I've done too many briefings for senators and congressmen who think that all 'towelheads' carry a pistol and a grenade. If you can't see beyond this stereotype, then we might as well stop now."

I felt my ears getting red. I hadn't really thought about it, but I must have been feeling something akin to this. It made me feel bad. Dad was the one that characterized people by the color of their skin.

"I don't believe that," I said. "I do have some hostility, though, I know that, but I'll be careful not to generalize."

He nodded. He was seated behind a wooden desk in a small office. The padded shoulders of his tweed jacket humped strangely when he leaned his elbows on the desk and leaned forward. One of his hands smoothed the red, fuzzy knit tie he wore with his gray shirt.

I'd taken the early Amtrak train from Penn Station in New York, down to Union Station in D.C. Mr. Anderson, from the State Department, had arranged the briefing. The man in the fuzzy tie was Dr. Perston-Smythe, an associate professor in Arab Studies at Georgetown University, and we were talking in his office.

"I can understand the hostility. However, you won't understand the Arab or the terrorism picture until you can get these stereotypes out of your head."

I nodded. "I understand."

"Consider this—there were over forty thousand Lebanese killed in the period between nineteen eighty and nineteen eight-seven. Over a million have died in the Iran-Iraq war. Less than five hundred Americans have died in the same period in the Middle East from terrorist actions, if you count the truck bombing of the Marines in Beirut, which I don't."

"Why not?"

"One of the problems with American public policy on terrorism is that our government insists on blurring the line between armed insurgence against military forces and installations and attacks on uninvolved civilians. Now, obviously attacking unarmed civilians who have no involvement with a particular political issue is terrorism. But an attack on an armed military force occupying one's homeland? That's not terrorism. I'm not saying it's right or wrong, I'm just saying that if you call that terrorism then the U.S. is also involved in financing terrorists in Afghanistan and Central America. See what I mean?"

"Yeah."

"Anyway, the point I'm trying to make is that the proportion of American dead from terrorism is way out of proportion to the response it generates. We did nothing to stop the Iraq-Iran war because we perceived it in our interests that damage be done to both of those countries. Personally I think that's inexcusable, but I'm not in the position to make government policy. Certainly both leaders were crazy with a long-standing personal grudge, but their people paid a horrible price."

"I wasn't aware that there was a personal grudge."

"Hell, yes. In nineteen seventy-five; when Hussein settled the dispute over the eastern bank of Shatt-al-Arab with the Shah of Iran, one of the unwritten conditions was that Hussein get Khomeini to stop his political activity."

"How could he expect Hussein to do that?"

Perston-Smythe looked at me like I was an idiot. "Khomeini was in Iraq. When he was exiled from Iran he went to the Shiite holy city of An Najaf. Anyway, Hussein told Khomeini to stop and Khomeini refused, so Hussein bounced him out of the country to Kuwait which promptly bounced him out of the country to France. Over a fifteen-year period, seven hundred thousand Shiites were thrown out of Iraq. There's a lot of bad feeling there. More now of course, since the war."

I blinked. "I know you're trying to give me the big picture, but what about these particular terrorists?"

"We're getting there. It's a roundabout way, but all the better for the journey. What do you know about Sunni versus Shiite beliefs?"

I'd been doing some reading, evenings, after working on the cliff dwelling at El Solitario. "Sunnis make up about ninety percent of Muslims. They believe that the succession of caliphs was proper after Mohammed died. The Shiites believe that the rightful successors descended from Ali, Mohammed's cousin, not his best friend, Abu Bakr. They believe that the rightful descendants have been assassinated and discriminated against ever since.

"Sunnis tend to be more conservative and they don't believe in a clergy or a liturgy. The only countries with Shiite majorities are Iran, Iraq, Lebanon, and Bahrain."

"That's right," said Perston-Smythe. He seemed surprised at my knowledge after my earlier ignorance. "Even among Shiites, terrorism is abhorrent. One of Mohammed's strictures calls for the protection of women, children, and the aged. One of the ninety-nine names of Allah is 'The All Merciful.' "

"All right. I accept that most Muslims wouldn't practice terrorism. I'll keep that in mind. But I want to know about the men who *do* practice it. I want to know about the men who killed my mother."

He leaned back. "All right." He opened a file in front of him. "Indications are that the hijackers of flight 932 were Shiite extremists belonging to Islamic Jihad, a terrorist group associated with Hesballah, the 'Party of God.' While we don't know who two of the hijackers were, we suspect that the leader was Rashid Matar, a Lebanese Shiite who is know to have worked with Mohammed Abbas, the organizer of the hijacking of the *Achille Lauro*. Oddly enough, the reason we believe it's Matar is his choice of your mother as his victim. With the exception of random bombings, woman hostages are usually the first to be released in airline terrorist situations.

"In nineteen eighty-seven, Matar was implicated in the beatings of several Italian prostitutes in Verona. He left the country just ahead of the police, but automatic weapons and technical manuals on various types of aircraft were found in the apartment he was forced to abandon. In early eighty-nine he was forced to leave Cairo after the beating death of a female Swedish tourist.

"Matar was also caught on an Athens Airport security camera the day before the hijacking. This is too large a coincidence." Perston-Smythe handed me an eight-by-ten photograph.

It was a blown-up shot of a newspaper photo which, in turn, seemed to be taken from a passport photo. The newspaper caption was in Italian, I thought, with only the name Rashid Matar understandable. The dots of the printing process were visible and I had to hold the picture out at arm's length to smooth out the lines of his face. He was younger than I expected, despite the reading I'd been doing. He was clean-shaven and had dark, bushy eyebrows. Though dark-complexioned, he didn't fit my image of the Arab. His nose was ordinary and his jaw somewhat weak. His face was thin and long and his ears were very flat against his head. His eyes were dark and remote.

"The fact that the terrorists not only didn't release the women, and also chose a woman to kill, strongly points to Matar, an obvious misogynist."

I waved the picture. "Can I get a copy of this?"

"That's a duplicate, you can keep it."

"Where is he now?"

"We don't know. I have some ideas, but I'm not sure."

I ground my teeth together and waited.

He shrugged. "This is purely speculation, you realize?"

"It's informed speculation," I said.

"Well, yes." He leaned forward suddenly, fingers linked

together. "An executive jet left Algeria almost immediately after the hijacking and flew to Damascus in Syria. While no comment was made about its passengers, the press in Algiers was allowed to watch it leave. The implication is that, A, the Algerian authorities promised free passage to the hijackers if they released the hostages, and B, that they were flown to Syria. This is exactly what happened after the nineteen eighty-eight hijacking of the Kuwaiti airliner."

"So you're saying that they're in Syria?"

"In the case of the Kuwaiti Airways hijacking, the hijackers traveled from Damascus back to Lebanon, overland. There they took refuge in the Baka Valley, which is the stronghold of Hesballah."

"So you're saying that they're in Lebanon."

"That's what we're supposed to think. I don't think they ever left Algeria. I have a friend with Reuters and he said that there was an area that the Darak al Watani were carefully screening at the same time the reporters were allowed to watch the jet depart. My friend has a suspicious nature. Whenever an official points one direction, my friend looks the other way. This is why he saw three unshaven men in badly fitting army uniforms climb into a truck which was driven out of the airport under police escort. He thinks that one of those men was Matar, but he didn't get a good look.

"I should think it extremely likely that they are still in Algeria."

I showed up at her door, walking from around the corner. My stomach was upset, I was nervous, and I was having trouble catching my breath, as if I'd run a long way or been jabbed hard in the stomach. My hand shook badly when I tried to ring the doorbell, and I finally dropped my hand to see if the shaking would stop. I was steeling myself to try again when Millie opened the door.

"Hi," she said quickly. Then, more slowly, she said, "It looked like you might change your mind. Are you sure you're ready for this?"

"Well, it's been two weeks." Two weeks since my last note.

"I was glad you called, but you didn't sound very sure."

I shrugged. "No. Just . . . just, well . . . I was scared." I made no move to touch her, no move to get closer. I was still scared.

She gestured toward the open door. "You want to come in while I get my coat?"

"I'll wait here. Honest. I won't leave."

She smiled uncertainly. "Okay." In a minute she was back, shrugging into a long gray coat. "Where do you want to go?" She dug in her purse for the car keys.

I wasn't hungry at all. "I don't know. Anywhere you'd like to go."

She stared at me. "Anywhere?"

"Anywhere we can get to."

She looked down at the sidewalk for a moment, then looked up at me, head raised partway, peering through her bangs. She dropped the keys back in her purse. "I want to eat at the Waverly Inn."

It was my turn to stare. The Waverly Inn was in the West Village, in Manhattan. I looked at my watch. It was six, it would be seven in New York. I didn't have a jump site for the Waverly Inn, but I could jump within ten minutes' walk.

"I'll have to pick you up," I said.

She blinked, sucked on her upper lip for a second, then said, "Okay. What should I do?"

"Just stand there."

I walked behind her and put my arms around her waist. Her hair, her scent was in my face. I stood there for a moment, until I could feel her fidget. Then I lifted her and jumped to Washington Square, by the arch. I let go of her, then grabbed her again as her knees gave way.

"You okay?" I helped her to a bench a few yards away.

"Sorry," she said. Her eyes were wide and she kept swiveling her head around to look from the arch to the buildings to the street. "I knew that you could do it, but I didn't *know* it, if you know what I mean."

"Theoretical knowledge versus certainty. Believe me, I know. Just as I know that you'll doubt it happened later, even though you experienced it now."

It was colder here than in Stillwater, probably below freezing, and the few people who were in the park walked briskly. Still, it was Friday night in the Village and things were lively. Millie stood slowly and asked, "Which way?"

I led the way down the edge of the park. On the way Millie asked about the funeral and I said it was okay. I complained about the pastor and told her about Mom's friends. Then I told her what I'd done to Dad when he showed up at the service.

"I feel guilty about it."

"Why?"

I shook my head. "I just do."

We turned onto Waverly Place.

Millie hesitated a moment, then said, "He abused you both, but I think you realize that he is capable of feeling the loss. That he loved her in some sense. By no means was the relationship healthy, but you may be feeling guilty because you feel you deprived him of his chance to grieve."

"Humph. Let him do his grieving away from me!" I lowered my voice. "You might be right. Or I just might be feeling guilty because I defied him."

She nodded. "That's possible. Oh . . . here's the inn."

There was no room at the inn, so we waited fifteen minutes, just inside the door, out of the cold, trying to avoid tripping the waiters. When Millie and I had last eaten there, we'd sat on the terrace out back, but that had been summer.

I told her about sergeants Washburn and Baker and why they'd been after me. She frowned for a moment, then said in a small voice, "You could have told me."

I looked away from her and swallowed. I didn't want to get into an argument about it.

She shrugged. "All right. Maybe I didn't give you a chance to tell me."

I almost smiled. "The encounter didn't reflect well on either of us."

The hostess led us to a table for two, wedged into a corner. I held Millie's chair while she sat.

"How do you do it?" she asked, wrapping her hands around the glass candle holder to warm them.

I pursed my lips. "Well, you grasp the back of the chair and pull it out. Once the person is seated, you push it forward while they scoot in to the table."

"Ha, ha. *Très amusant.*" She did not look amused.

"How do I do what?" I knew exactly what she meant.

"How do you . . . teleport."

I exhaled noisily. "I call it 'jumping' and I haven't the faintest idea how I do it. I just do."

She frowned. "You mean there isn't some sort of device or anything?"

"Just me." I played with the salad fork. Then I shrugged and told her about the first time. She'd heard all the gory details, but she hadn't heard how I got away. I told her some of my speculations, my attempts to find other jumpers, and some of the constraints. I told her about my revenge on Topper the attempted rapist and the guy at the transient's hotel in Brooklyn, and, finally, I told her about stealing the money.

"You did *what*?" She sat straight up in her chair, her eyes wide, her mouth open.

"Shhh."

Other diners were staring at us, frozen in silent tableau, some with forks or spoons halfway to mouth.

Millie was blinking her eyes rapidly. Much quieter, she said, "You robbed a *bank*?"

"Shhh." My ears were burning. "Don't make a scene."

"Don't shush me! *I* didn't rob a bank." Fortunately she whispered it.

The waiter walked up then and took our drink order. Millie ordered a vodka martini. I asked for a glass of white wine. I didn't know if it would help, but I figured it couldn't hurt.

"A million dollars?" she said, after the waiter left.

"Well, almost."

"How much of it is left?"

"Why?"

She blushed. "Curiosity. I must look like a proper little gold digger."

"About eight hundred thousand."

"Dollars!" The man at the next table spilled his water.

"Christ, Millie. You want me to leave you here? You're fifteen hundred miles away from home you know."

The waiter arrived with the drinks and asked if we were ready to order. "You better give us a while. I don't think we've even looked at the menu."

Millie took a swallow of her martini and made a face.

"What's the matter? Is it the wrong drink?"

She shook her head, took another swallow, and made the same face again. "It's perfect. You wouldn't really strand me here in New York, would you? I mean, I've only got fifteen bucks with me."

"Well . . . I could drop you in Central Park. Or there are certain parts of Washington Heights that would be lively about now."

"Davy . . .!"

"All right. I won't abandon you."

She looked at me strangely.

"What? I thought you'd be relieved."

"Strange choice of words." She licked her lips. "Not so much strange as too appropriate."

"Huh?"

She shook her head. "Abandonment. That's the issue, isn't it? She abandoned you again, didn't she?"

"She died. She didn't run away."

Millie nodded. "The ultimate abandonment."

I felt myself getting angry. "Excuse me a second." I got up abruptly and went to the bathroom. Someone was in it. I leaned against the wall, my arms crossed tightly, my eyes staring straight ahead and seeing nothing.

I didn't really need to go to the bathroom, but I didn't want to shout at Millie. My mother was the victim of terrorism, not someone who'd abandoned me. *Well, not this time.*

Nobody was watching so I jumped to the bathroom of the Stillwater apartment.

I felt like hitting something hard. I didn't have any plates left to break. I dropped to my knees by the bed and hit the mattress very hard, perhaps twenty times, until the heels of my hands began to ache. I took several deep breaths, then, and went into the bathroom and washed my face.

My memory of the sidewalk outside the restaurant was fresh and I returned there. The hostess saw me come in and blinked. "I didn't see you go out."

I shrugged. "Just needed a breath of fresh air."

She nodded and I went back to the table. I'd been gone about five minutes. Millie looked relieved.

"The waiter came by again," she said. "We should probably look at the menu."

The business of choosing and ordering the food got us safely through the next ten minutes. When we were alone again, Millie seemed unwilling to talk about anything serious. I guess she didn't want to scare me away again.

"I'm sorry, Millie. I'm not too rational about Mom right now. I'd rather not get into an argument about her."

Millie nodded. Her face looked pale in the table's candlelight and her hands glowed red as she wrapped them around the candle again. My irritation faded, melted like wax. She was very beautiful, very desirable. I felt tears forming and blinked rapidly. I looked away from her, toward the wall, and said, "I've missed you, Millie."

She reached a hand out and squeezed mine. Her hand was very warm. Impulsively, I kissed the back of it and her lips parted. I enclosed her hand with both of mine. She said, "I've missed you." She didn't say anything else for a moment, then pulled her hand back gently.

"I've got to tell you that I'm disturbed about the money you stole. I don't think that was right."

"I didn't hurt anyone."

"What about the depositors?"

I'd thought about this for a long time. "That bank loses that much money in bad loans every month. They make that much money in interest every day. They're a *big* bank. The money I took was small change to them. No depositor was hurt."

She shook her head. "I still can't approve of it. I don't think it's right."

I felt my face go remote, still. I crossed my arms and felt cold.

She spread her hands. "It doesn't change the fact that I still love you. I've missed you terribly. I've missed your phone calls, and I've missed your body in bed next to me. I don't know what to do about this. My loving you goes way beyond my disapproval of your theft."

I uncrossed my arms and reached across the table for her. She leaned forward and we kissed until the candle burned a hole in my shirt. Then we laughed and I held an ice cube to the burn and the food came and everything was all right.

I flew out of Kennedy to London's Gatwick South Terminal on American Airlines flight 1555. It left after midnight and arrived in Britain at 7:20 in the morning local time. It was a DC-10 and the man in first class next to me kept making stupid jokes about hydraulic fluid.

I seriously considered jumping him back to New York when we arrived in London. *Asshole.*

The weather was wet and very cold and the people talked like they were on TV. If I hadn't slept so badly on the plane, I could have listened to them for hours. My connection to Algiers via Madrid did not leave for six hours. After clearing customs, I jumped back to Stillwater, grabbed the video camera, and recorded several jump sites at the airport. Then I jumped back to El Solitario, set an alarm for four and a half hours, and slept.

The flight to Madrid was on Air Algerie. They allowed smoking on their flights and eddies of the stuff kept drifting up to me from the back of first class where four Frenchman were going at it like chimneys. Fortunately the flight to Spain was only two and a half hours and the French were replaced by nonsmoking Arabs for the next leg to Algiers.

There was some difficulty at Algerian customs. I didn't have a return ticket or a hotel reservation, so they shuttled me to the side while they processed the other passengers. I would have just jumped away except they kept my passport.

After a forty-five-minute delay they offered me the choice of buying a return ticket or posting a bond. I bought a fully refundable ticket from Air Algerie to London for the following week under the watchful eye of a customs official. I also changed money for the minimum required amount, 1,000 Algerian dinars, about 190 U.S. dollars, and declared the U.S. dollars I had, over 5,000 DA (dinars Algeriere). Only then did he give back my passport with the admonition that all money changed must be recorded on the proper form and Allah help me if I couldn't account properly for my U.S. dollars on leaving the country.

I recorded a few jump sites then walked outside. It was cold, wet, and green, with mountains climbing up from the Mediterranean. If it weren't for the men in caftans and djellabas and a few women in thick veils, I would have thought I was anywhere but North Africa. A group of chattering English walked by carrying skis. They were off to Tikjda, where "the snow was particularly good this year."

Inside the terminal, a man at an information booth directed me toward the VIP terminal. I couldn't get into that area, but at a window near the security checkpoint I could look out on the tarmac where the hostage plane sat during two days of negotiation. I wondered if I should fly to Cyprus and see the similar stretch of tarmac where Mom died.

It only took a minute or two to record jump sites, but I couldn't jump away because the beggars were thick, persistent, and grubbier than anything in New York. As soon as I paid off one set, another group would move in. Finally, I went back into the terminal and jumped from a bathroom stall.

The gates opened at 10 A.M. so I jumped Millie into Disney World at five minutes after, right in front of Space Mountain. We were the second couple aboard and we rode it three times before the line started to build up. We did Star Tours at Disney MGM and followed it with Body Wars over at Epcot.

Next we hit Pirates of the Caribbean, the Haunted Mansion, and Mr. Toad's Wild Ride. By this time, since it was Christmas vacation, the crowds thickened to the point of unpleasantness, so I jumped her to London and we took a taxi into downtown London.

It was four hours later in London, and cold after the Florida sun, but the taxi driver took us to an old hotel that served a decent high tea. Afterward, we walked by the Thames until a chill, damp fog moved up the river, and I jumped her to El Solitario.

We'd seen the sun go down in England but it was still two in the afternoon in Texas, and the temperature was in the mid-eighties. Millie took one look from the top of El Mota and said, "I thought I was handling this all pretty well, but I think I need to sit down."

I jumped her to my cliff dwelling and sat her on the couch.

In the weeks since I'd started construction, I'd finished the wall from overhang to ledge, complete with windows, door, and ducting for the wood-burning stove. I'd also built a separate enclosure at the far end of the ledge which now enclosed the largest gasoline-powered generator that I could lift. It provided the electricity for the five floor lamps I'd brought in to light the place.

I'd filled the worst spots on the floor so that it was fairly smooth, even if it did have a pronounced tilt. I'd bought several dyed sheepskin rugs and some rustic furniture made of knotty pine. At the back of the dwelling, where the overhang sloped down to meet the floor, I put a bed. At the tallest sections of my man-made wall, between the windows, I'd put more bookshelves, chocked and shimmied to be more or less level, and I was slowly filling them with new purchases.

Millie leaned back on the couch and closed her eyes. I jumped to my apartment in Stillwater and filled a large glass with ice water, then returned. Her eyes were still closed.

"Here's some water," I said, putting it on the end table.

She opened her eyes and focused on the glass, its side beaded with condensation. She sipped it and looked around, noting the natural rock above the couch and looking left and right to get the depth of the room. "Where are we?"

"Texas," I said. "It's not far from that mountaintop I showed you."

"Where did you get this?" She held up the glass.

"Stillwater."

She shook her head. "I am reminded of *A Midsummer Night's Dream.*"

"What part?"

"When Puck says, 'I'll put a girdle round about the earth in forty minutes.' "

"What a slowpoke."

"Then there's that part where the fairy says, 'Over hill, over dale, / Through bush, through brier, / Over park, over pale, / Through flood, through fire, / I do wander everywhere, / Swifter than the moon's sphere.' "

I smiled. "You know your Shakespeare better than I."

She smiled. "I was that merry wanderer of the night. I jested to Oberon, and made him smile. High school production. Great reviews, though. They wanted me to play that ass Hermia, but I stood my ground. All the guys wanted to play Puck, but I was the only one to audition who could do the first act without looking at the script."

She stood, almost timidly, and walked to the window.

The sun cast steep shadows from above and the stratigraphy of the rock was cleanly displayed on the opposite wall of the canyon, tilted at three degrees, matching my sloping floor. She leaned forward on tiptoe, to see past the edge. The floor of the canyon was just visible two hundred feet below.

"Why didn't I hear you when you popped off to Stillwater?"

"What do you mean?"

"Well, the air should rush in or something, shouldn't it? Wouldn't it make some sort of popping noise?"

I hadn't thought about it. "Well, maybe you just weren't listening well enough. Maybe it's a quiet noise."

She put her glass of water down. "Well, try it again, and we'll see. I'll pay very close attention."

"Jump away and then back?"

She nodded.

"Okay." I jumped to the ledge outside, by the generator shack. After a deep breath, I jumped back and Millie flinched.

"Well?"

She exhaled noisily. "Nothing. And it's still unnerving as hell, even when you expect it."

I reached out and hugged her to me. "I'm sorry. That's one of the reasons I didn't tell you, you know. I didn't want to scare you. I don't want to lose you. I've lost too much already."

She leaned into me, her arms curled into my chest. I rocked her back and forth. After a moment she pushed away and said, "Where's the bathroom?"

"Uh . . . it's in Stillwater."

She rolled her eyes. "Great! I'll close my eyes."

I picked her up and jumped her to my Stillwater apartment. She'd never been in my Brooklyn apartment, so the furniture and toys were new to her. I showed her the bathroom and waited in the living room.

"I just had a horrible thought," she said, after she came out of the john. "What if you took me to your house in the cliff there, jumped away, and got hurt or killed?"

The situation was unfortunately easy to visualize. There was no water or food and no way out. She'd last less than seven days. "I didn't think of that."

She shrugged. "I don't mind going there, but I don't think I want to be left there. You know what I mean? Like, if you needed to go get something, I'd want to go with you or back to my own place. Okay?"

I nodded. "Yeah. That's more than okay."

She looked around the living room and saw the video equipment. I'd told her about recording jump sites and she looked back and forth from the camera to me. "Hmmmm. Have you recorded yourself jumping? Maybe there's something to be seen in slow motion?"

"Hmm. Let's try it." I set the video camera and tripod up and pointed it at the middle of the room. I hooked the cables into my large monitor for playback and set the camera on slow-motion record.

"Where should I go?"

Millie was watching my image on the monitor. I looked at myself on the screen, then looked away, uncomfortable with the stranger there.

"Anywhere, Davy, but jump right back to where you are after a count of five?"

I jumped to the observation deck at Will Rogers World Airport. The altitude was roughly the same and it wasn't hard on my ears. I looked around, turning to see the entire deck. The place, fortunately, was deserted, and I counted slowly to five before jumping back.

Even though she was expecting me, Millie started again. "Sorry."

She exhaled sharply. "I'll get used to it. Maybe. I sure wish you could teach me how to do it."

"If I knew how . . ."

I rewound the tape and played it back at normal speed. I stood in the middle of the living room, cut off from the knees down by the framing; then I was gone. I counted to myself again, and at roughly the same moment, I appeared again.

Millie, seated on the couch, leaned forward, her elbows on her knees. "If I'd been watching this on television, I'd say it was a cheap special effect. You know, the kind where they stop the camera, have the actor walk offstage, and start filming again."

"Yeah. I'll try it on super slow." I rewound the tape and put playback on its slowest speed.

We waited, watching my image ask Millie where to jump, my mouth opening and closing in ponderous slow motion. It took over a minute to get to the part where I disappeared. One moment I was there and the next I wasn't.

"What was that."

"What?"

"Just as you jumped. There was a sort of flash, kind of."

I shook my head. "I didn't see anything."

"Back it up. Can you make it go any slower?"

"That's the slowest, but I can single-frame it, I guess." I stood by the camera and rewound to just before the jump, then started advancing using the still button and the frame advance. It took even longer to get to the point where I disappeared, but when I did . . .

"Wow," said Millie.

The video image, held wavering on the screen, had been me standing, but, from this, it went to a rough outline of myself, a Davy-shaped hole. Inside this hole was the tail of an American Airlines 727 as seen through the windows of the airport observation deck.

"What's that?"

I told Millie where I'd jumped to. She nodded vigorously, her eyes wide. I hit the frame advance again and the Davy-shaped window was gone. The scene showed my apartment living room.

"Neat! No wonder the air doesn't go 'pop.' You're not disappearing one place and appearing in another—you're going through a doorway. Or, the doorway is passing around you, since you don't move. Fast forward to the point you reappear."

When the specific point on the tape had been located, I single-framed through images of the empty living room until another Davy-shaped window appeared, slightly different to reflect my changed posture. The view was a different slice of the 727, reflecting where I had been standing when I jumped back. When I hit the frame advance again, the window was replaced by my full body.

"See?"

I nodded. "What would happen if I couldn't go through that door?"

"What do you mean?"

"Well, uh, what would happen if I were handcuffed to something too big to move? Or if I was being held by someone I couldn't lift?"

Millie stood. "Try it. Here, I'll grab you from behind and you try and jump."

I thought about it. "Uh, I don't think I like that idea. What if part of you went with me, but not the rest?"

She blinked. "Has that sort of thing ever happened to you?"

I shook my head.

"Well, it doesn't seem likely, but I must admit that the idea of having just my arms go with you is not very appealing."

"Hold on, we can try this another way."

I jumped to a novelty store on Seventh Avenue near Times Square and bought a cheap pair of handcuffs. The clerk also tried to sell me a rubber mask of Richard Nixon, very cheap, on special, but I declined.

"Well," Millie said, when I showed them to her. "This is no time for kinky sex."

I laughed. "Let's go someplace where I can lock it to something solid."

We went outside, on the porch. It was out of sight of other apartments and it had an iron railing firmly set in the concrete landing. Before I put the handcuffs on, I made sure both keys worked on both cuffs and handed one of the keys to Millie for safekeeping. Then I locked one cuff to the railing and put the other cuff on my left wrist.

"Where are you going to jump?"

"Just inside."

I pictured the living room and tried to jump. For one brief instant it seemed like I made it; then I felt a searing pain in my left arm and wrist, and I was still standing on the porch.

"Shit!" I felt like saying all sorts of other things. My wrist was bleeding from scraped skin and I felt like my arm had been stretched by a gorilla. My shoulder and elbow both ached but I didn't think either of them were dislocated. "Please unlock the cuffs," I gasped.

She took her key and unlocked my wrist. I cradled my arm to me and swore. Millie looked scared. "Bad idea, huh?"

I laughed harshly. The pain was fading somewhat and the bleeding really was just scraped skin. We went back inside, and as I washed my wrist in the bathroom sink, Millie told me what she'd seen.

"You blinked, sort of. I swear I could see the living room

bookshelf for just an *instant* but you didn't go anywhere. What did it feel like?"

"Like my left arm was on the rack. You know, pulled apart by wild horses." I was moving my elbow and shoulder more freely now, and the bleeding was reduced to a slow welling. Millie walked back to her apartment and returned with a roll of gauze and tape. She neatly wrapped the scrape.

"Well, at least we don't have to worry about you taking part of things. If you can't take it through the gate with you, it pulls you back. We should see what happens when I hold on to you from behind."

I had misgivings, but she was curious. We went out into the living room and moved the recliner back to give plenty of room. Millie grabbed me from behind, her arms around my chest under my arms. "Ready?" I asked.

She tightened her grip. "Ready."

I jumped to the bedroom, braced for resistance from behind, and almost staggered forward when I appeared in the bedroom, *sans* Millie. I heard her gasp through the open door. I walked back and saw that she was on the floor, on all fours.

"Are you okay?"

"Just off balance. It felt like, oh, you were greased, like you sort of shot between my arms like a watermelon seed. Let me try again."

I shrugged. "All right, if you want."

This time she put one arm over my left shoulder and one arm under my right arm to circle my chest bandolier style. She grasped her wrists and squeezed so hard I had trouble breathing. "Go," she said.

It was harder this time, and when I appeared in the bedroom, Millie was with me, arms still wrapped around. She gasped in my right ear and let go.

"Interesting, interesting, interesting." I turned and saw her smiling, her back to the bed. I took a sliding step forward and pushed her over. This terminated experiments in teleportation for the day, but opened the way to experiments of another kind.

Later she said, "Davy, today I've been in Florida, London, Texas, and Oklahoma. There's just one thing I want to know."

"Yeah?"

"Do I get frequent-flyer mileage for this?"

FOURTEEN

The *Entreprise Publique de Transport de Voyageurs* bus to Tigzirt was crowded with locals and smelled overly of sweat and strange spices, but the scenery, alternating between steep hills and azure waves, was lovely. The normal tourists who went to Tigzirt went by the buses chartered by the Algerian Tourist Agency or in rented Fiats. Although it was only twenty-six kilometers east from Algiers, there were many stops and the journey took an hour and a half. There were several attempts to talk to me in French, Arabic, and Berber, but I just shrugged.

At noon the bus stopped on the N24, by a bridge where a small stream poured out of the Tellian Atlas Mountains and ran to the sea. I couldn't see any buildings. The passengers and driver all poured off the bus and washed their hands in the stream. Some of them carried small rugs with them. Others knelt on the ground. All of them began praying to Mecca. After fifteen minutes of this, they got on the bus again and we drove on.

In Tigzirt the clerk at the Mirzana Hotel had some English but kept saying that there were no rooms available. I hadn't expected any rooms. I'd been told that Algeria's beach resorts are booked months in advance.

"I don't want a room," I repeated. "I am looking for someone. A guest." I put down a twenty-dollar bill on the counter. The official exchange rate made it about ninety-five dinars, but the street rate was over five times that. I wondered if the clerk knew that. I'd found out by reading the Fodor's travel guide.

The clerk took the bill and looked more attentive. "Who is it you are looking for?"

"Rashid Matar."

The clerk blinked and was still for a moment and then said, "I have no knowledge of this person."

Bullshit. I took out the photocopy of his picture and showed it to him. He blinked again, shrugged, and said, "Sorry, no."

"Are you sure?"

"Yes. Very sure." He shrugged again.

"Well, thank you for your time," I said, and went across the lobby and into the restaurant.

They gave me a table overlooking the sea and the tennis courts. The Mirzana was on a hill, well up from the beach. People came to Tigzirt for the beach or for the impressive Roman ruins or for the Byzantine basilica. I ordered mint tea and showed the waiter my picture of Rashid Matar.

He was visibly frightened and denied ever seeing him, even when I offered money. He wouldn't touch the money.

The tea, when it came, was brought by a different waiter who didn't understand English and left immediately, ignoring the picture I held up.

The tea was too sweet.

Two olive-skinned men with bushy mustaches and painfully white tennis clothes were playing on the court, the ball flying back and forth across the net as if it was shot. Through an open door I could hear the *thwack, thwack* of the rackets addressing the ball. Neither of them were Matar. There were several motor and sail yachts anchored offshore, rolling gently in small swells. And I could make out a strip of crowded beach off to my right.

I sipped my tea and kept watch, comparing every passing figure with my photo.

Matar might not be here. This was the best hotel, but there were some private residences that might be for rent. My informant had only said that Matar had been seen here.

"He was on the beach there, I'm sure of it. There were

police around, keeping an eye on things, protecting him, or the local Wali, I think."

Dr. Perston-Smythe from Georgetown University had given me a letter of introduction to Mr. Theodore, who was with the British Embassy. He took me out to the Bacour restaurant on rue Patrice Lamumba. The food was local. We finished with much better mint tea than the Mirzana offered.

Mr. Theodore spent most of his time recommending against the more or less official guides who hung around the Museum of Popular Arts and bemoaning the state of the Casbah, whose picturesqueness has long been overwhelmed by the sordid. "You see, the French left Algeria with an excellent hospital system and some pretty good public works, but the economy was driven by oil until the crash and now you have a nation with a population explosion, thanks to decent medical care, and a crumbling economy. Algeria used to be a net food exporter but now everybody crowds into the city and the desert is overtaking some of the best farmland. The Casbah is one enormous slum, now." He drank some of his tea carefully, with precision. "I'm left-handed, you know, but it never does to use your left hand to eat. Not in public. Use to make terrible messes."

About Rashid Matar he was only able to tell me that he'd been seen in Tigzirt, apparently on vacation, apparently relaxing. "There's no direct evidence, you know, that links him to the hijacking."

"Do you honestly believe he didn't?"

He smiled. "No. He's guilty all right. It's just that obviously the Algerians made a deal with him to release the rest of the hostages, and they're keeping up their end of it. They won't be sympathetic to any attempts to extradite him."

I nodded.

He looked at me almost critically. "You aren't planning anything stupid, are you? I mean, I shouldn't blame you if you were planning to kill him, but that won't work. He's the killer and they'll see you coming from miles away."

I felt my ears getting red. "I don't know what I'll do. For the time being, though, I just want to find him."

"Well, if you were a British national, I would seriously consider bundling you back home."

So, here I was in Tigzirt, where Rashid Matar had been seen playing on the beach and consorting with the Wali, the governor of the local Wilaya. I decided I'd stay in the hotel another hour, then come back the next day and try the beach. I paid the bill in dinars, then moved back out to the lobby. There was a bench just inside the main entrance with a good view of the lobby and the elevator. I took a paperback from my pocket and began to read.

There were some German tourists who came in and out, as well as a party of French. The occasional Arabs who came through looked nothing like Matar. I was about to give up when two uniformed members of the Darak al Watani, the national gendarmerie, came through the door. They went up to the clerk and he looked over at me.

Son of a bitch! I stepped to the door and went through it. Behind me I heard someone yell, *"Arrêtez! Arrêtez!"* Immediately I turned to the right and, out of sight of the cops, jumped to my apartment in Stillwater. My ears popped hard and I sat down immediately, my knees feeling weak. I heard a bus on the street and jerked.

Calm down. Do you expect them to walk through the door? They're on the other side of the planet.

I took deep breaths. Why was I so timid? I was untouchable, really. I could jump back there now, and, as long as I jumped before they handcuffed me, there wasn't any way they could keep me. I could even wait until they threw me in a cell, then jump away.

They could kill you, too. Well, yes.

Millie was at her father's home, in Oklahoma City, for the first week of Christmas break. On Christmas day she'd drive up to Wichita, Kansas, to spend the next week with her mother and her stepfather. In any case, she was busy with family and, though we'd scheduled some dates in that period, I had to leave her alone most of the time.

I jumped to Stanville, by the Dairy Queen on Main

Street, and walked slowly down the street, looking at the Christmas decorations.

There'd been a snow just after Thanksgiving and the cold weather had held, so the yards and park were covered with the stuff, dirty with blown soot and detritus. Thin dark trails, trod down to dead grass, cut across the gray snow in front of the courthouse. The streets were clear except where the snowplow had packed drifts up against the curb.

The Christmas decorations, marvels of petrochemical science, were the same plastic stars and candy canes used by the city for the last six years. The plastic fringes on the holly were looking tattered, and on one of the red stars on a courthouse lamppost someone had spray-painted REVOLUTION NOW! Somebody else had spray-painted a line through the "now!" and put, instead, ". . . whenever."

The powers of imperialist Stanville were probably trembling in their boots.

It was late afternoon in Algeria, but midday in Stanville. There were quite a few shoppers on the street. If it was this busy in our relatively sterile downtown, I shuddered to think what it was like out at the Wal-Mart. Then I saw Dad's car parked outside Gil's Tavern by an expired parking meter.

Coming up the street was the three-wheeled utility vehicle the police used for the meter maid. Mrs. Thompson, overweight and overdressed in her genuine police jacket with the blue fur collar, was writing up a BMW with out-of-state plates. I wondered if the meter had in fact expired or if Mrs. Thompson was simply ticketing the owner for sinful decadence and/or being a foreigner. Mrs. Thompson was the wife of Reverend Thompson, the Baptist minister.

I reached in my pocket and pulled out some coins. Half of them were Algerian and there were a few English 5p coins but I had enough nickels to put forty-five minutes on the meter.

Only when I saw the little arrow pointed up did I realize that I was helping my dad.

I frowned. There was a cinder block by the front door of Gil's, used in warmer weather to hold the door open. I considered picking it up and pitching it through the wind-shield of the Cadillac. I even walked over and was looking down at it when Mrs. Thompson's three-wheeled scooter drove slowly by, distracting me.

Dad must have seen Mrs. Thompson through the window, for he came through the door at that moment, looking down at silver change in his left hand. Then he saw me standing there, between him and the meter.

He looked frightened.

"Davy?"

The anger was still there, somehow increased by the shock on his face, the fear. I reached out and slapped the change from his outstretched hand. Then, as the coins bounced on the sidewalk, I jumped away, to my cliff dwelling in the Texas desert.

When I returned to Tigzirt, I dressed differently, more formally, in a tropical-weight linen suit. I avoided the hotel, and instead walked down through the village to the beach. There were a few beggars on the street, but far fewer than there had been in Algiers. The wind was off the Mediterranean and the sun was shining brightly. I hoped my description was not circulating or, if it was, I hoped it differed substantially from my present appearance.

The beach wasn't crowded and the only women in bathing suits were non-Arab. Along the water, dressed in the full-length chadour and veil, three women (who could tell?), their robes pulled up to ankle height, walked along, their bare feet in the foam. I could tell they were Saudi Arabian by the black robes and just as much tourists as the Swedes in their bikinis.

The fifteenth sunbather recognized the picture. He was French, but his English, though thickly accented, was good. "Ah, yes. The man with the bodyguards. He was staying on the big yacht." He looked out at the bay, toward the cluster of yachts anchored in the lee of the right headland. "Hmmm. It's not there. It was the large motor yacht with the blue smokestack. It was very big, at least thirty meters.

This man would come to the beach and talk to the beautiful women, to take them water-skiing."

I thanked him and confined the rest of my inquiries to this yacht. No one on the beach could tell me its name or when it had left, though several had seen it. An English-woman suggested I try the fuel dock at the harbor, by the fishing boats. "There's a couple of shops there, where all those boat people restock. The harbormaster is there, as well, and he should know."

I thanked her and walked back off the beach. I hadn't removed my shoes and sand had sifted into them. There was a low wall that separated a garden from the street. I perched upon it and emptied my shoes.

I was leaning forward to tie my laces when I happened to glance down the street to where a man stood at the corner, perhaps a hundred yards away. He had a camera with a very large telephoto lens on it, and he was pointing it at me.

Some tourist, perhaps, taking a long perspective of the street? I didn't think so. I stood and walked quickly around the corner, onto one of the narrow little streets that ran up the hill from the beach. Then I jumped to the terrace of the Mirzana Hotel.

It was directly up the hill from the fishing harbor and actually closer than the beach had been, a short downhill walk instead of the winding trek along the shore. I left the grounds of the hotel quickly, anxious to avoid the clerk who'd turned me in to the Darak al Watani. For all I knew, the police were still around as well.

The fuel dock was easy to find, the heavy smell of diesel was almost thick enough to see. The dock was a narrow finger sticking out into the harbor with a small building built onto the end. The tide seemed to be out, for the water was at least eight feet below the planking.

The two boys in attendance at the pumps didn't have any English, but they fetched an older man from the building who wore a djellaba over his Western shirt and tie.

"Ah, the big boat, the *Hadj,* from Oman. Last night they leave. They come for the, ah, fuel, and leave."

"Where were they going?" I pulled out a handful of dinars, casually, and let him see them.

He shrugged. "One moment," he said, motioning for me to stay where I was. "I ask." He went back to his office. Through the doorway I saw him pick up a phone and talk into it. Once he looked back over his shoulder at me, as if to see if I was still there. Then he put down the phone and walked slowly back.

"I talk with the port master. He no tell me, but I, ah, argue with him. He is deeficult." He looked down at my hand, at the money.

I handed him five twenty-dinar bills. "Perhaps this will help? A gift. To show my thanks."

He nodded, but instead of looking at the money, he kept looking back up the dock, toward the shore. I turned around and glanced back, but I didn't see anything. "Where did the boat go?"

The man tugged thoughtfully at his tie and said, "They go to, ah, Sicily." He didn't sound very convincing and his eyes were on my face this time, almost fixedly. I turned around.

Coming up the dock were two uniformed police, the Darak al Watani. They were walking slowly, purposefully. The dock stuck out into the harbor and there was no other way off of it that *they* knew of.

I turned back to the fuel manager, angry. He started backing away from me, smiling, getting out of range. I jumped the five feet between us and jerked the money from his hand. He flinched away from me, the smirk on his face gone. I took another step toward him and he went over the edge of the dock, into the water. The two boys started laughing.

Serves him right.

There was the sound of feet pounding on the dock. I turned. The Darak al Watani were running now, doubtless to stop my continued violence. I stepped to the very end of the dock and dropped off the end. Before my feet touched the water, I jumped away, to my cliff dwelling in Texas.

*   *   *

Later that afternoon I jumped to Union Station in Washington, D.C., and used a pay phone to call Dr. Perston-Smythe. The department secretary answered his line after four rings, which surprised me. It was Christmas Eve, after all.

"Dr. Perston-Smythe's phone."

"Is he in?"

"He's in the conference room with some visitors."

"Oh. I'm at a phone booth so I can't really leave a number. Is there a time I can reach him later?"

"I'll stick my head in and ask him for a good time. What's your name?"

"David Rice."

"Hang on."

She put me on hold. I spent the interval watching people go by the brightly decorated shops. The speakers were playing Christmas music.

An old man dressed in a plaid suit and a torn overcoat limped by. He wore filthy athletic shoes on his feet. His left foot was twisted inward, the sole of the foot facing his other leg instead of the floor, and his weight came down, instead, on the outer edge of his foot. No wonder he limped.

Behind him walked a woman dressed in a knee-length fur coat. She was staring fixedly ahead, eyes focused on infinity. When his halting pace obstructed her path, she stepped carefully around, one hand pulling the hem of her coat close to her, lest it brush against him. In her other hand she carried a large bag filled with wrapped Christmas presents.

The phone went off hold, but it was Dr. Perston-Smythe instead of the secretary.

"I didn't mean to interrupt your meeting."

"That's all right, Mr. Rice. She didn't realize that you must be calling from Algeria."

"Ah, I'm not. I'm in D.C."

"Oh? Uh, would it be possible for you to come to my office?"

"I was about to ask you the same thing."

I heard him cover the phone with his hand and say something to somebody else. Then, "How soon could you be here?"

Immediately. The temptation to jump to his office was strong. "Oh, give me ten minutes."

"Very good."

I spent the next ten minutes jumping back to Texas for some cash, then finding the old man with the twisted foot. I gave him twenty thousand dollars and hoped someone wouldn't kill him for it.

Eleven minutes after I'd hung up the phone at Union Station, I knocked on the door of Perston-Smythe's office. He opened the door himself. "Come in, David."

I started to walk through the doorway, then saw another man seated at Perston-Smythe's desk. "Oh, I can wait out here until you're done."

The other man spoke. "No. Please come in. We were waiting for you." His voice was deep and resonant, carefully modulated.

"This is Mr. Cox, David. Brian Cox."

I nodded and reluctantly walked into the room. Perston-Smythe closed the door behind me and pointed at one of two chairs. The one he took was closest to the door.

This feels wrong. "Are you sure I'm not interrupting anything?"

"Positive," said Cox. He was a tall man with a fleshy face and curly black hair cut very short on the sides. He looked like an ex-linebacker, big in the shoulder, like he could tear me in half. "What have you been doing in Algeria, Mr. Rice?"

I blinked. "What makes you think I was in Algeria?"

"Last Friday you went through Algerian customs. On Sunday you met with Basil Theodore from the British Embassy. Yesterday police pursued an American national from a Tigzirt hotel after he'd been turned in for currency violations. The American national looked a lot like you."

"Are you with the university, Mr. Cox?" Somehow I didn't think he was.

Cox pulled out a leather case and laid it open on the desk

in front of him. The picture ID within identified Brian Cox as an agent of the National Security Agency.

Shit. "What do you want, Mr. Cox? If you've been talking to Dr. Perston-Smythe, you know that I've been looking for Rashid Matar. You also know why."

"If you'd stayed in an ordinary hotel instead of disappearing from the airport washroom, I'd believe that. The embassy found no trace of you between the time you arrived and the time you had dinner with Theodore. Then there was no trace of you from that time until you showed up in Tigzirt. Who do you work for? Whose safe house did you stay in? You're not one of ours. We've asked all the other agencies. *Who are you?*"

"I'm David Rice, an eighteen-year-old American male. And I don't work for anybody." I stood up and started for the door. I half expected Perston-Smythe to rise up out of his chair and try to stop me, but he just looked over his shoulder as I opened the door.

Three men stood outside, dressed in suits. Two of them had their hands inside their jackets. The third was holding a pair of handcuffs. I shut the door.

"Am I under arrest?"

Cox ignored the question. He opened a manila folder on the desk and took out a photograph. "This picture was taken six hours ago in Tigzirt. It was developed, then transmitted by satellite to me an hour ago. That's why I was here when you called." He flipped it around so I could see it.

It was me, seated on a garden wall, tying my shoelaces. I was looking toward the camera with a suspicious look on my face. I was wearing the same lightweight suit in the picture that I was wearing now.

Cox's voice increased in intensity and he slammed his hand down on the picture. "I want to know all the answers to the questions I've already asked, but most of all, I want to know how the *hell* you got from Algeria to Washington, D.C., in less than six hours!"

I flinched back from the noise. There was a light switch on the wall, but bright afternoon sunlight poured in through the window behind Cox. No way I could jump away without being seen. *There was always this chance. You knew it from the start.* Did these men know of other jumpers? Did they know my capabilities? My palms started sweating and my heart was pounding very hard. "I want to talk to my lawyer."

"You're not under arrest."

"Then I'll be leaving."

Cox leaned forward. He almost smiled. "I don't think so." He raised his voice and said, "Harris!"

The door opened behind me.

I looked at Perston-Smythe. "Are you going to let them do this?"

Cox did smile then. "Dr. Perston-Smythe is a contracted employee of the agency. Who do you think notified us in the first place?"

I took a step toward the desk and had the small pleasure of seeing the smile drop from Cox's face. *Five witnesses. Better make it good.* I smiled then. "I have just one thing to say, then. And I hope you'll report it to your superiors, of whom there must be many."

Cox narrowed his eyes. "Yes?"

"We mean no harm to your planet," I said.

And jumped.

FIFTEEN

Neither Millie nor her father answered the phone. I took that as a good sign. I felt sure that if the NSA had gotten there, they would answer the phone, to try and trap me.

I was able to move most of my belongings from the Stillwater apartment before they came in the door. The most important things, anyway—the video equipment and my library of jump sites, all of my clothes, all of the money, and most of my books.

They were quiet—I didn't hear them on the stairs at all—but I'd piled pans against the front door and they came down with a crash. I jumped away, my arms half full of books.

I'd given Leo Silverstein the address of the apartment. I hoped they hadn't hurt him to get it. The address on my passport application had been in his law office, but, if that hadn't led them there, the funeral would have. Mr. Anderson from the State Department also knew Leo and he connected back through Perston-Smythe. Considering that they didn't break in until midnight, it seemed probable that they'd had to break into Leo's office to get the information.

I'd always suspected that the Bill of Rights occasionally had a "liberal" interpretation.

My one major concern was Millie. If they traced me back to New York and Sergeant Washburn, they might get Millie's name and address out of them. It occurred to me almost immediately after I left Perston-Smythe's office that

I should have let them take me away, put me in a cell, or let me go to a bathroom, then jump away. Anything but let them see me jump.

Oh, God, I hope they don't bother Millie.

From Will Rogers International I tried Millie again at her father's place in Oklahoma City. Millie answered the phone.

"I love you," I said.

"What's wrong?"

"What makes you think something is wrong?" I cleared my throat before she said anything. "All right. Something's wrong. Can you go out tonight?"

"It's Christmas Eve. It's bad enough that I'm going to my mother's on Christmas Day. My stepmother is already bitching that I spend most of the Christmas vacation at my mother's. After all, I'm going to pick you up tomorrow like we planned."

I had no idea how fast they would move. Or if they had already moved.

"Do you remember where we stopped for supper the first night I visited you in Stillwater?"

"You mean the—"

"Don't say it!"

The implications of my remark hit her. "Do you think this line is bugged?"

"It might be. I hope not."

"Why would it be? What's wrong?"

"Think about it."

She took in a deep breath, then said, "Before the party, right?"

"Yeah." The place I was talking about was a steak house off of I-35 on the north side of Oklahoma City. We'd stopped there for supper on our way from the airport to the party in Stillwater.

"When were you going to drive up to Stillwater?" I didn't want to mention Wichita. If they were listening they might not know where she was going.

"I was going to leave at nine."

"Meet me at the . . . at that place. I'll be waiting. If you're being followed, it should be apparent. There won't be that much traffic on Christmas Day."

I heard her swallow. "All right."

"If it comes down to it, Millie, and they didn't bug this phone, you broke up with me that time when the police called you. Okay?"

"We almost did."

"Yeah. I love you."

"I love you," she said.

I hung up the phone.

A cabbie took me from the airport to the steak house at 7 A.M. the next morning. I'd been there, but I couldn't remember the site well enough to jump to it. He didn't want to leave me there—the place was closed for the holiday and a subfreezing north wind cut like a knife—but I insisted my ride was on the way.

I'd considered going to her father's house instead, but it could have been under heavy surveillance. This seemed safer.

I jumped through the glass doors into the interior. The heat had been left on to keep the pipes from freezing. I memorized a jump site back by the kitchen, then jumped home to my cliff dwelling.

The night before, I'd used the bathroom at the Stanville Public Library before going to bed, but I deeply resented losing my bathtub/shower at the Stillwater apartment. Later, when I had time, I intended to rent a motel room, probably in Minnesota. There'd been a Western Inn near the truck stop that Topper Robbins frequented.

I set the alarm for 8:45 and tried to sleep. It didn't work. My stomach was nervous and visions of white-coated scientists with scalpels and hemostats kept running through my head.

I remembered a scene from Alfred Bester's *The Stars My Destination* in which scientists put a man in a sealed tank and try to drown him, in hopes that he would "jaunt," i.e. teleport, away from danger. He did, but I couldn't help extending the scene, to my white-coated friends putting

Millie in the tank and filling it up. "It's okay," I imagined one telling another. "If she can teleport, she'll be okay, and if she can't we won't have to waste any more time with her." In front of them the water rose higher and higher.

The alarm went off and I shuddered awake, grateful to be out of that dream. I guess I'd been able to sleep after all, but I didn't like it. I jumped to the library in Stanville and splashed water on my face in the rest room. Then I retrieved my binoculars from Texas and jumped to the interior of the steak house in Oklahoma.

Her father lived on the east side of town, but there was light traffic and it only took her twenty minutes to reach the steak house. Two other cars pulled off the same exit ramp. One drove past the restaurant and stopped on the access road; the other stopped before the restaurant's driveway. I used the binoculars. There were four men in each car.

I looked through the binoculars, then, to look at Millie, as she pulled her car into a parking place in front of the restaurant. She was nervous and had obviously seen the cars following her. She was only fifty feet away from me, but the steak house's windows were tinted and she couldn't see inside. I crouched low, pictured the backseat of her car, and jumped.

"Don't look around."

She jumped, and turned her head halfway around before staring straight ahead.

"Don't move your lips when you talk, either. Those bastards might have binoculars."

"What iv they 'ugged the car."

I hadn't thought of that. It wasn't impossible. "Was it on the street last night?"

"No. Dad 'ut it in the garage."

"We're going to have to risk it. I love you."

"You 'etter. Es'ecially with all this shit!"

I smiled. "Merry Christmas to you, too. Drive on north. Once we're on the road you can stop doing your ventriloquist impression."

She started the car again, then drove out onto the access

road. I tensed as we passed one of the cars, flattening myself further onto the floor.

"What are they doing?"

"They're looking at a map. It's a very convincing impersonation of four lost guys—should be a band name. The other car just pulled up to the steak house. I think they're going to search it. Ah, The Four Lost Guys just started up their car."

I twisted, trying to get comfortable. Millie's car had rear-wheel drive and, consequently, that hump down the floor-board for the drive shaft. I peered around the edge of the seat to the front of the car. The passenger seat and the floor in front of it were empty. I jumped to it, my legs and hips on the floor, my upper body leaning against the seat itself.

Millie started and the car swerved slightly.

"Sorry, it was uncomfortable back there."

She reached over and touched my face. I put a hand on her thigh and squeezed.

"Who are they?" she asked.

"National Security Agency. One of their agents took a picture of me in Algeria. Six hours later, long before I could have gotten there by commercial airliner, another of their agents saw me in D.C. He had a transmitted copy of the picture. I was still wearing the same clothes. They were, uh, curious."

"Aren't there planes that could have gotten you there?"

"Sure. Supersonic fighter jets don't usually carry passengers, though. I don't blame them for being curious. If I could hitch rides on military jets, I must be hot shit indeed." I paused. "The long and the short of it is that I ended up panicking. I jumped away from them in front of five witnesses."

"Ack. That wasn't very subtle."

"I know. I'm sorry. They wouldn't let me call my lawyer. I was afraid they were going to start on me with the thumb-screws and needles."

Millie made a sour face. "Well, it happened. It's all very well for you. You can jump away at the slightest hint of danger. What happens when they start in on me?"

"I hope that you won't have that problem. But I really don't know. Now that they have some idea of what I can do, they'll start that military bullshit that developed capacity equals intent."

She put her hand on top of mine, where it rested on her thigh. "What do you mean? Are you afraid they'll think you'll rob every bank in the country?"

I shook my head. "They don't know about that. Hopefully they won't draw a connection. What has probably occurred to them is much worse.

"I could kill or kidnap the president. I could steal nuclear warheads and put them in our major cities. I could smuggle vast quantities of drugs into the country avoiding any possibility of interdiction. I could jump into secure facilities, steal documents, and sell them to the Chinese. Just as bad, they could *want* me to do all those things for *our* side. You get the idea?"

"You wouldn't do anything like that, Davy."

She didn't make it a question. She said it with absolute confidence. I almost cried. I shifted over, placing my face against her leg. She ran her fingers through my hair.

"I'm sorry, Millie."

"It's not your fault. I'm not sure if it's anyone's fault. But it sure complicates things, doesn't it?"

"Yeah."

"What do you think we should do?"

"I don't know. I could jump you away from all of this. I could put a shower and bathroom in at my cliff dwelling and we could travel across Europe and the Middle East."

"Tempting, but hardly possible. I have sixteen hours of classes this semester."

I worked my hand over her leg until the fingertips were tracing up the inner seam of her jeans.

"Stop that! You want me to have a wreck?" She moved my hand off her leg. "What am I supposed to do?"

I shifted. "If you want to live a normal life, you'll have to give the impression that our relationship is over. If they were bugging your phone last night, that's out, but if they didn't, we might stand a chance."

Millie passed a slow-moving truck. I scrunched against the door so the truck driver wouldn't see me from his higher vantage point.

"I don't think they bugged the phone last night when you called."

"What makes you think that?"

"I walked my dad's dog last night, twice. Once right after you called and once before I went to bed. The street was empty the first time, but there was a van parked down the block the second time with its engine running and a guy was standing on the corner at the other end of the block. *Nobody* stands on the corner in that neighborhood. Not at night when it's twelve degrees out."

From my position on the floor, the view out the windows was strange, consisting of the tops of trees and an occasional slice of billboard or exit sign. Also, a couple of times I saw a helicopter, high overhead, moving north.

I kept my eyes on Millie's face to avoid getting carsick. "So you're saying they arrived after I called. Hmmm. Well, more and more, it sounds like you should play it cool. Do your parents know about us?"

She shook her head. "I don't like to tell them about my love life. They have, well, *opinions*. I keep it vague."

"What about your roommate?"

"No. I didn't tell her. If I told her anything, I'd tell her all of it, and I didn't think she'd believe me. Besides, she thinks you're too young for me."

I laughed. "Right now I feel very young. There seems to be a helicopter following us as well, so if the cars disappear, don't bet that you aren't still being watched."

"You're kidding!"

"Look for yourself. It's way off to the west right now, but it's been up there an awful long time. I'll stay with you all the way to Wichita, so I can get a fix on your mother's house. I wish I could see the room you're staying in. About the only time I'll be able to see you is when you're supposed to be asleep. If you go out for a walk and disappear, it won't convince them you're not still seeing me."

She nodded. "I'll park in the garage. You fix on that. This

afternoon we're going over to my sister's for Christmas dinner. The spare room is at the back of the house. I'll leave my suitcase on the bed so you know which one it is."

"What time?"

"We have to be there by four."

"Okay. I'm going to jump to the backseat and stretch out. I didn't sleep very well last night."

She put her fingers to her mouth, kissed the first two fingertips, and pressed them against my mouth. "I know what you mean. Sleep well."

Millie woke me when we entered her mother's subdivision. I transferred back to the floor of the front seat and said, "Is your escort still with you?"

"Yeah. When we got into the city, both cars closed back in. I'm starting to get mad, Davy."

I swallowed. "I'm sorry."

She shook her head. "I'm not mad at *you*. Don't apologize. It's their arms-race mentality that's pissing me off. Here we are."

She pulled into the driveway almost violently, the car rocking as it came to a stop. I crouched lower. She jumped out of the car and I heard the sound of the garage door rattling open. Then she was back in the car and pulling forward.

"Stay down. Mom will have heard the door. I'll distract her and you can get your jump site."

She got out of the car just as an interior door opened. I heard a woman say, "Right on time! How are you, honey?"

Millie shut the driver's door behind her and went forward, out of sight. Her muffled voice said, "Hi, Mom. God, it's cold in here. Did you make any Christmas cocoa this year?"

"Of course. Do you want a cup?"

"I'd love a cup. I'll shut the garage and get my stuff, if you'll put the water on."

"Coming right up." I heard the inside door shut. Millie moved past the driver's window and then the garage darkened noticeably as she pulled down the door.

"Jesus Christ," I said, climbing out of the car and stretching. Millie came to me and we kissed.

"Go on," she said, pushing me away. "You can get into the house between four and about seven. My sister's kids will have driven Mom crazy by then."

I looked around, memorizing the corner by her car. "I'll jump into your room at midnight, okay? Don't talk to me when I do. They might bug the house while you're out."

A look of outrage passed over her face. "And we're supposed to *let them*?"

I shrugged. "It hardly seems fair."

"Well, I can always call the police. In fact, that sounds like an excellent idea. When I next see them following, I'm going to call the cops. Two lone women followed by four men in a car is certainly suspicious. It will be interesting to see what happens." She hugged me. "Midnight."

"Yeah," I said, kissing her. Then I jumped.

Except for a jump back to Wichita at 4:15, I spent the afternoon napping and thinking. I wished Millie would jump away with me. I kept wondering if she was with her sister's family or had been taken away by the NSA agents.

But if I watched her, ready to rescue her, I took a chance of being seen. That would endanger her far more. It occurred to me that if I were seen elsewhere, far away, the heat might go off of her.

Dr. Perston-Smythe wasn't in his office. Unfortunately, his filing cabinets were locked and I didn't know how to break into them, much less have a desire to do so. The entire building was quiet, locked up for the holiday. On a list in the reception area I found his home phone number and address.

I took a cab.

His house was on M Street NW, a town house shoehorned in between other town houses. Before approaching the door I looked for people seated in parked cars or standing in doorways. There didn't seem to be anybody.

A woman came to the door, about Perston-Smythe's age, say forty, dressed in a green turtleneck and a red tartan skirt—very Christmaslike. She had silver hair and a lightly lined face.

"Is Dr. Perston-Smythe home?"

She looked slightly annoyed but damped it quickly. "Certainly. Come in out of the cold while I fetch him. Who shall I say is calling?"

"David Rice," I said.

She nodded. My name, apparently, meant nothing to her. She guided me into a parlor immediately off the front hall. There was a fireplace with an electric heater on the hearth. I stood with my back to it, facing the door.

Perston-Smythe took a couple of minutes to come to the room. I imagined he phoned somebody, first, before coming to talk to me. The instructions from the phone were probably "Stall him. We'll be right there." When he did come through the door his right hand was in the pocket of his tweed jacket.

"I'm surprised you would come here," he said.

I shrugged. "Well, I didn't get what I wanted when I visited you yesterday. I was hoping I could today."

He blinked. There was sweat on his forehead and he wiped at it carefully with his left hand.

"I was hoping, in particular, if you knew where Rashid Matar was likely to have gone. He left Algeria the day before yesterday, on a private yacht. It was named the *Hadj*, out of Oman."

He licked his lips.

I took a step sideways, to a chair, and he flinched and took half a step backward. I sat down slowly, with exaggerated care. "Look at it this way. If you tell me, it might keep me here longer, long enough for them to come. Who knows, maybe even long enough to capture me."

"I can't help you," he said. "The NSA is already on the lookout for the boat, but they have no idea of its destination. For all we know, it's a red herring. We don't know for sure that Matar is on the boat. He could have gone to ground in preparation for his next hijacking." He pulled his hand out of his pocket suddenly, a small automatic gripped tightly in his fist. "Don't move an inch," he said.

I didn't like the dark round spot at the end of the barrel, the one pointed at me. It made me shiver. "You've got to be kidding."

"I just got home. I spent most of the night on a polygraph machine and the rest of the time under drug-induced hypnosis. You don't think I'll shoot?"

I jumped to the hallway behind him and said, "Shoot at what?"

He jerked around, struggling to swing the pistol around. I jumped back to the chair. He looked around wildly, saw me sitting back in the recliner, my knees crossed, my fingers steepled together.

"Do you really think Matar will hijack another plane?"

His breathing came in short, sharp gasps and he held the gun with knuckle-whitening tightness. If he shot me, I wondered where I would jump to, to try and survive the wound. It occurred to me that if I was going to have dealings with the NSA I'd better acquire a jump site at a major trauma center emergency room.

"Yes, Matar didn't accomplish what he set out to do with the last hijacking," Perston-Smythe said. He pointed the pistol at the floor between us. His breathing was slowing. "How do you do that?"

"Bertol rays," I said. "Energy of a type humans have never seen before." I wondered if he'd recognize the overused "Star Trek" line. I might as well have said, "Beam me up, Scotty."

They came in the door then, not bothering with the doorbell, not even bothering with doorknob. I winced as the jamb splintered.

"Hope they buy you a new door," I said, as the first man entered the room, a small submachine gun in his arms. Before he could shoulder Perston-Smythe aside, I jumped.

The Stanville Library was closed for Christmas but that was probably for the best. I wondered how long it would be before I ended up with my picture in post offices. "Wanted, for National Security Violations." Maybe they wouldn't stoop that far. After all, public charges can be publicly defended.

I used the index of the *New York Times* on microfilm to look up the airports where aircraft hijackings had originated and ended. I'd already been to two of the airports, Madrid and Algiers. There were several more, including two in Cyprus, where hijacking deaths had occurred. I wanted to go to Cyprus anyway, to see where Mom had died.

It was slow work going through the index, finding the right spools, getting to the story, writing down the airport, and moving to the next film. By the time I was finished, it was five past midnight. I pocketed the list, put the spools carefully away, and jumped to the room in Wichita, Kansas, where Millie waited.

She was there in a long flannel nightgown, lying awake in the bed, a small light on, the curtains drawn. My worries of the afternoon faded away and I sat on the edge of her bed and kissed her. She wrapped her arms around me and I picked her up and jumped to the cliff dwelling, by the bed. I set her down.

"Cold," she said. She scrambled under the covers.

"I'll start a fire. Tell me what happened today."

She began talking as I gathered kindling and wood.

"They followed us to Sue's, my sister's, so I called the police and told them about the dark sedan with the four men that had followed my mother and myself across town and was parked outside on the street. They hit each end of the block with a car and boxed them in. Mother and I watched from the front yard.

"Anyway, they just waved some identification in front of the deputies' noses and they went away. I called the sheriff's office again, afterwards, and they would hardly talk to me. Finally they said that the men were federal agents and they weren't doing anything illegal. From his tone of voice, I think he thought I was some kind of criminal!"

The wood seemed to have caught well, so I went back to the bed and undressed. "That must have been distressful."

"Pissed me off is what it did. My brother-in-law Mark

does casework for the ACLU. He's going to file an injunction against them as soon as the courthouse opens tomorrow morning."

"Good. Serves them right. And to think I was worried about you," I said, sliding under the cool sheets to press against her warm body. I told her about my visit to Perston-Smythe and my research at the library.

"So you're going to interfere with his next hijacking?"

"If I can," I said.

"I don't like it. I'm afraid you'll get killed."

The same thought had occurred to me. "I'm going to acquire a hospital jump site, first. With my ability to jump, I should be able to survive pretty serious damage, as long as I can jump to a trauma center as soon as I'm hurt."

"I don't know. Why run the risk at all?"

I thought about Mom again, those shocking milliseconds of video on the airport tarmac. "I want him, Millie. I want him to pay. I can't not run the risk."

At five in the morning I jumped Millie back to Wichita, to sleep the rest of the morning and awake under the continued scrutiny of government agents. I jumped to London and bought a ticket to Cyprus via Rome, both hijack sites. I slept on the flight.

At Rome I used the binoculars to pick a jump site through the window of the aircraft. Then I went to the lavatory, jumped off the plane and recorded the site with video, and jumped back aboard. In Cyprus, at the Nicosia airport, I repeated the process, except that I didn't jump back aboard the aircraft. I also didn't go through passport control or customs.

I walked into the airport terminal through doors that were locked from the other side. After all, the problem is usually to keep people from going the other way. Once inside I asked at the information desk about how to get to Larnaca Airport, at the south end of Cyprus.

There was a bus, but there was also an overpriced shuttle flight leaving in the morning. I bought a ticket for the shuttle, gritting my teeth at the thought of another commuter flight, then jumped back to New York City for lunch and some more research.

My problem was this: How was I going to know when there was a hijacking? I couldn't depend on them all to be like the Kuwaiti Airliner hijacking that lasted twenty days. I had to know within hours so that I could get to the appropriate airport.

In the end I contacted a news-monitoring service called Manhattan Media Monitoring.

"Hijackings? Hmm. We already monitor that for some of the airlines and also a couple of insurance companies. Do you want copies of the print media or video of the broadcast coverage, or both?"

"Video would be nice, but primarily I just want to be notified as soon as the news breaks."

"Phone or fax?"

I realized I no longer had a phone. "I'm on the road constantly. Better if I call you once or twice a day."

We arranged payment then, several months in advance in traveler's checks. This earned me some strange looks, but they didn't say anything. I didn't give them my real name.

Cyprus is seven hours later than Wichita, Kansas. Consequently I only had two hours alone with Millie before I jumped to the Nicosia airport for my 9:00 A.M. shuttle.

I picked her up at midnight and jumped her to the cliff dwelling.

"I spent the day fighting government fascism, honey. How was your day?"

"Huh," I said, undressing. This time I'd started a fire an hour before picking her up, so the temperature was comfortable. I also bought a split of champagne complete with plastic bucket. Remembering my adventure with champagne bottles at Sue Kimmel's party, I asked Millie to open it.

"We found a microphone in the kitchen today. I called the police again and Mark filed an injunction. Some federal attorneys showed up and they're slugging it out. Mark also sent a press release to every paper and news service around." The champagne cork went *pop*. "The police were a little more sympathetic after we found the microphone. Apparently there wasn't any court order obtained. Mom was outraged."

I slid under the covers and accepted a glass of champagne. "I'd apologize except you sound like you're *enjoying* yourself." The wine still tasted like bad ginger ale.

"My that's good," said Millie, drinking half the glass. She snuggled down next to me. "I'm sort of enjoying the fight. I just wish I could get to them, though. When we go out, there they are, their sunglasses on. They don't look mad, they don't look tired, they don't even look, well, human."

I shivered. "Well, they don't think I am, either."

"What do you mean?"

I told her about my parting remark, the "We mean no harm to your planet."

She giggled. "Oh, no! Why'd you do that?"

I shook my head. "I guess I thought that they'd look elsewhere for me, you know, like in orbit or something. I was hoping they wouldn't look for a human me."

"Well, I'm not so sure you should have said that. Now the military will get in on it, I bet."

"Oh, God. What a pain." I sipped some more bubbly, then set the glass down. "I've got to jump you home in two hours so I can catch a flight in Cyprus."

She drained her glass. "Well, that's not good. We better not waste any time, huh?"

I reached for her.

The commuter flight took only twenty-five minutes. I slept through most of it. I didn't have to go through customs. I did ask, though, where the American woman had died two months before. A Turkish Cypriot with passable English pointed the spot out from a terminal window.

"Was very bad. See the gray area? That was black from the explosion. They scrub and scrub but it doesn't come clean. Very bad."

I thanked him, even offered to tip him, but he wouldn't take it. He just shook his head and went away. I hope I didn't offend him, but I didn't think about it at the time. I just stared out at the gray spot on the tarmac, numb.

In reality, the gray spot was mostly the color of the surrounding tarmac. It was only slightly discolored, but the loop of news video kept playing in my head, superimposed—a gout of flame and smoke and the twisted, broken doll body.

Oh, Mom. . . .

Will revenge bring her back, Davy? A million dead in Iran and Iraq. Fifty thousand dead in Lebanon. One woman dead in Cyprus. Will you revenge them all? What about the dead in Cambodia, Latin America, in South Africa?

They aren't my dead. They aren't my mother.

I felt sick. Too many dead, too many suffering. *Why do people do this to each other? What are you going to do with Matar when you get him?*

I blinked tears away.

I'll answer that when I have him.

PART 6:

PLAYING TAG

SIXTEEN

In El Solitario, above the water-filled pit with the little green island, I appeared on a ledge some fifty feet above the water. The walls stretched another fifty feet above me, but this ledge was over deep water. Besides, dropping from a hundred feet, you would reach fifty-five miles per hour before hitting the water. Though high divers did it, you could still break your neck if you hit at the wrong angle.

The sun wasn't high yet, and only the upper reaches of the opposite wall were lit by direct sunlight. Still, the rock was light limestone and it reflected the light well. The water below was an unblemished mirror, showing the blue sky and white walls and me.

I stepped off the ledge and dropped. It would take 1.767 seconds to reach the water, but at a little over one second, the wind starting to whistle in my ears, I jumped away, to the top of the pit, looking down at the unblemished water.

I took a deep breath. The water looked very cold and hard, like polished iron.

Again, only this time, I didn't appear on the ledge—I appeared two feet out from the ledge, in midair. Again, I dropped, jumping away before hitting the water.

I did this again and again and again.

Athens, Beirut, Cairo, Tehran, Baghdad, Amman, Bahrain, Kuwait City, Istanbul, Tunis, Casablanca, Rabat, Ankara, Karachi, Lahore, Riyadh, Mecca, Knossos, Rhodes,

Smyrna, Abu Dhabi, Muscat, Damascus, Baghdad, Naples, Venice, Seville, Paris, Marseilles, Barcelona, Belfast, Zurich, Vienna, Berlin, Bonn, Amsterdam.

I couldn't get a visa for Tripoli, in Libya, but I went anyway, not even buying a ticket, just jumping past the gate agent and the flight attendant. It was not a popular flight—the plane was half empty. I repeated the process at the other end.

I tried to do at least one airport a day, sometimes two. I would get up at two or three in the morning, jump to the departing city, sleep fitfully on the plane, acquire the new jump site, and be back by ten in the morning. Then I'd call Manhattan Media Monitoring and see if there were any hijackings.

There was only one during the month of January, an Aeroflot flight diverted to Kabul, Afghanistan, by several Soviet convicts. They'd given themselves up shortly after arrival. I didn't know what I would have done if they hadn't. I didn't have a jump site in Afghanistan at that time.

After a week of legal huffing and puffing, Millie agreed to a federal judge–supervised interview by the NSA with her lawyer present. She told me about it after I'd jumped her to the cliff dwelling late one night.

"They brought your friend in from Washington."

"Who, Perston-Smythe?"

She shook her head. "No, no. Cox, Brian Cox, the guy from the NSA with the sidewalls."

"Sidewalls?"

She touched the side of her head. "Shaved on the sides. Fleshy neck. Big shoulders?"

"I knew who you meant. I just didn't know what you meant by sidewalls."

"Ah. Well, he starts by asking where you are."

"What did he say exactly?"

" 'Where is David Rice?' I answered with the literal truth. I said I didn't know, adding that we'd broken up in November. Both of these things were true—you were off flying around Europe and we *did* break up in November."

I nodded. "Go on."

"Well, I had to lie, then. He asked if I'd seen you since we broke up. I said no. I was afraid I wouldn't sound very convincing, but I think I sounded great. I'm afraid you're a very bad influence.

"Cox then asked if I'd heard from you. I said no. I said the breakup was very nasty and that I didn't ever want to hear from you." She kissed me on the cheek. "Another lie."

I smiled and waited for her to continue.

"He asked about the cause of the breakup and I told him about the call from the NYPD. He didn't look very surprised."

"No," I said. "They had to talk to Washburn and Baker to get to you, so they've already heard their version. I wonder if they found out about Washburn's wife? If they interviewed them separately, they probably did. Especially if they polygraphed them."

Millie looked angry at that. One of the NSA's demands had been to interrogate Millie on a polygraph machine. The judge had rejected it out of hand. It didn't help the NSA's case that they wouldn't talk about the purpose of their investigation.

"Cox next asked when I'd met you, how often we'd seen each other, and how intimate we'd been. I answered the first two questions and refused to answer the last one. Again I asked what you'd done to merit this investigation. He refused to answer, so I got up to leave."

I laughed. "Vicious. I love you."

She shrugged. "He partially relented then, saying that he couldn't say why you were under investigation as it was classified. He did say he could tell me if I'd reconsider the polygraph. I didn't have time to answer—Mark and the judge practically jumped down his throat then. The judge has been on our side ever since we found the illegal wiretaps."

"Good for him."

"I felt kind of sorry for Cox. I think he wanted to know how intimate I was with you so he could judge whether you were human or not. I almost relented and told him that I wondered why you had four testicles and a marsupial pouch, but I wasn't going to bring things into the twilight zone. If I didn't know about you disappearing into thin air, how was he going to ask the question so he didn't sound like a lunatic?"

I nodded. "He has a double problem. If I'm an alien or even an unaligned human, he doesn't want to let other governments know about me. What if they got to me first? *The country that controls teleportation controls the world!"*

"God bless America," she said, dryly.

"Unfortunately, this also doesn't tell us if they have any experience with teleports besides me. Unless they said something that implied that?"

"No. Well, he did ask if I thought there was anything unusual about you, in the way you behaved. I said, 'What? Like does he speak Russian in his sleep or something? Not that I noticed.' Then I told a half-truth. I said, 'He's a nerd. A cute nerd, but a nerd. Christ, he's from Ohio. What do you expect?' "

"Owww. Which part was the truth? Being a nerd?"

She laughed and squeezed me. "You *are* from Ohio. Cox gave up then. He asked me to contact them if I heard from you and that surveillance would be withdrawn."

"Has it?"

She shook her head. "I don't know. Certainly the obvious stuff has, but the house for sale down the block, the one that hasn't sold for three years, suddenly did. Who buys a house in January? I don't know."

"So we assume they're still watching. You go back to school in two weeks. It might pay to have someone sweep your apartment for wires when you get back. Luckily," I said, letting my fingers wander a little, "I know your bedroom already."

Her back arched and she drew in breath sharply. She moved her hand down my back. "Yeah. Once school starts, you know I can't spend as much time with you. I'll need my sleep."

"But I won't be able to see you during the day, even during the weekends! It's not fair."

Her hands moved below my waist. "We'll see," she said.

* * *

After a crowded flight into Glasgow, from London, I jumped to New York, as usual, and called MMM, Manhattan Media Monitoring. We'd evolved a little ritual. I would call, the operator would check my name on the computer, and she would say, "No, nothing." I would thank her and hang up, checking again about five in the afternoon.

Today, she heard my voice and said, "Ah, Mr. Ross, we have something for you."

"Yes?" My heart began beating faster.

"An Air France 727 has been hijacked after taking off from Barcelona. It's being diverted to Algiers. We only have the initial UPI wire report. Should we fax it to you?"

My heart was now pounding and I was having trouble catching my breath.

"No. Is there any indication of how many hijackers are aboard?"

"Not in the UPI report."

"Has it actually landed in Algiers?"

"The report doesn't say, but it does say that the Algerians will let it land."

"Thanks. Well, keep an eye out for more info. I'll call later."

I hung up and jumped, first to Texas, for binoculars and a small bag of odds and ends, then to Algiers, to the airport.

Inside the terminal a barrier had been strung blocking off the VIP terminal. Darak al Watani guarded it, armed with machine guns. There was a crowd of curious onlookers but they stayed well back from the barrier. I edged along the periphery of the crowd, asking what was happening over and over again until I found someone with enough English to answer me.

"Hijackers have landed a plane, just ten minutes ago."

The man who answered me spoke with an American accent, overlaid with French. He carried a laptop computer and a camera bag.

"Are you with the press?"

He nodded. "Reuters. I was heading home after covering the OPEC ministers meeting, but I guess I'll miss my flight."

He looked around. "I wonder where they'll set up the press?" He walked off, skirting the crowd and heading for one end of the barrier. I followed at a distance and heard him speak in rapid French to one of the guards, who pointed back down the terminal. The reporter turned back and began walking briskly in that direction.

The barrier was set up before the turn into the VIP terminal, so it was not possible to see what was happening down its length. I jumped, blind, to the spot I'd visited on my first trip to Algiers. There was a group of people at the gate itself, farther down the hall.

I looked out the window and saw an Air France 727 parked out on the taxiway, perhaps a hundred yards short of the gate. The front door was open, but there was no boarding walkway rolled up to it. Through the binoculars I saw a figure in the door, a man with an Uzi-like machine gun and wearing a purple bag with eyeholes over his head. He was standing back from the door, looking out, and I had the impression he was looking into my eyes. Then he turned his head to the left, toward the cockpit, then right, toward the passengers.

When I shifted the binoculars to the cockpit windows, I could only see the pilot and the copilot, sitting very still. The shades on all the passengers' windows were drawn.

Someone shouted at me and I glanced down toward the gate. A uniformed man was talking at me, first in Arabic, then in French. I looked back at the doorway of the plane, studying each detail. I heard steps coming up the terminal, toward me. When I looked back at the voices, two Darak al Watani were walking toward me, accompanied by the other man, probably an army officer.

I looked down onto the tarmac below me. There was a baggage trailer parked in the shadow of the terminal. I jumped to it, then stepped around it, so I wasn't visible from the VIP terminal.

Using the binoculars, I studied the doorway again, waiting, hoping for my chance. I had enough detail to jump onto the plane, now, but I'd appear right by one of the terrorists. If he were the only one, that would be fine, but if there were others, I needed to know that.

There'd be a lot of dead hostages if I fucked up.

My knees suddenly threatened to give way. *What the hell do you think you're doing, Davy?* The enormity, the arrogance, and the danger of what I was attempting suddenly hit me. It frightened me, made my stomach hurt, made it hard to breathe. *Should I give up?*

Staring down at the tarmac, the same kind of concrete apron that Mom died on, drove back the doubts.

I'll be careful. Please, please, please, don't let me fuck up.

I don't know who I was talking to, but it made me feel better.

The purple-headed terrorist in the door suddenly turned and went back toward the passengers, the Uzi swinging up sharply. The entranceway was clear.

Oh, God!

I set the binoculars down and jumped.

Someone was shouting around the corner. I flattened myself against the storage closet for hanging bags that was to the right of the door. Directly across from me was the galley for the first-class passengers. It was empty. I glanced forward and I could see into the cockpit. The copilot, twisting his head to see what the shouting was about, saw me. His eyes were very wide.

I held up my forefinger in front of my lips and mouthed the word "Quiet."

He blinked several times and nodded. I noticed that his wrists were taped to the armrests of his chair. I also noticed that there was a space behind him, between the bulkhead and his seat. I jumped to it.

Both the copilot and the pilot started violently. The pilot said very loudly, *"Merde!"*

I held up my finger again, but it was too late. Footsteps pounded up the aisle. I jumped away, back to the tarmac, by the baggage trailer. I saw Purple-bag cross the entranceway headed for the cockpit. I lifted the binoculars and watched him hit both pilots in the face with openhanded slaps. Their heads rocked and I gritted my teeth.

You son of a bitch.

He left the cockpit, paused in the doorway to survey the area around the aircraft, then went back to the passenger section.

I jumped back to the cockpit.

This time the pilot started, but remained silent. When I appeared, he was staring at the doorway, hatred in his eyes. There were red marks on his face and his lip was bleeding.

Again, I held up my finger for silence. He nodded firmly. I leaned over to the copilot's right ear. "How many hijackers?"

"Three," he whispered.

"What weapons do they have?"

"I have seen pistols, machine guns, and hand grenades."

Shit.

I asked him, "Do they have the pins pulled?"

"Sometimes."

I turned and took a small dentist's mirror out of my bag of odds and ends. I pushed it slowly around the corner and used it to look down the aisle.

The cabin lights were on and the thin shades covering the passengers' windows glowed a dull orange on the side of the plane facing the sun. I couldn't see any passengers, but the three terrorists were in the aisle, two at the back of the first-class section and the other one halfway down the coach section, constantly swiveling his head around.

The first-class section was empty of passengers. I figured they'd moved everybody back to coach and they were making them keep their heads down.

Each of the hijackers had a different-colored bag on his head. Purple-bag, closest to me, carried his machine gun at the ready, one hand on the trigger, one hand on the stock. The next hijacker, Orange-bag, had his machine gun slung over his shoulder by the strap and a pistol stuck in his waistband. He was lecturing the passengers and tossing a grenade from hand to hand.

At least that meant the pin was still in.

The last hijacker, Green-bag, held his machine gun at the ready, like Purple-bag. I saw him skip back toward the rear of the plane suddenly, and strike at one of the hidden passengers with the barrel of the gun. I gritted my teeth and marked the hijackers' positions well.

Those bags were a benefit to me. They provided no peripheral vision and so, when I moved, they didn't see me.

I jumped behind Purple-bag and grabbed him, jumped to the pit, fifty feet above the cold, hard water, and let go, jumping away immediately. I appeared behind Orange-bag, his head turning to see what the brief grunt of surprise from Purple-bag meant, his hand going to the machine gun.

I grabbed him, jumped him to the pit, dropped him, and jumped away. Just before I did, I heard the splash as Purple-bag hit the water. I wondered if he would surface in time for Orange-bag to hit him.

I appeared six feet behind Green-bag. He'd charged forward from where he'd been, up the aisle. He was shouting. I jumped forward, to close the distance, but he was out of arm's reach again, still moving. *Damn.* I jumped immediately in front of him, my hand sweeping the machine-gun barrel up away from me and away from any passengers. The gun went off, carving pieces of plastic out of the ceiling, and his body slammed into mine, carrying me back, him on top of me.

Before I hit the carpeted aisleway, I grabbed him, and jumped to the pit, appearing in midair, but tumbling backward, unsettling for me, terrifying for Green-bag, who found himself facedown fifty feet in the air.

I jumped to the cliff above and watched him hit the water right next to where Purple-bag flailed weakly on the surface. There was a tremendous gout of water; then I saw Orange-bag splash to the surface sputtering. He was trying to hold on to the machine gun, but it seemed to be pushing him under. Finally he let go of it.

Green-bag surfaced then. His bag had twisted underwater and he was pawing frantically at it, trying to get it off before it suffocated him. He pulled it free and I could hear his coughing gasps for air from the top of the cliff. He'd lost his machine gun in the water.

I looked closer. Green-bag's hair was soaked and darkened by the water, but there didn't seem to be any doubt that it was blond. His face was very white, from the cold of the water, but also his natural complexion.

They made their way, weakly, to the island, collapsing in the shallows, unable to pull themselves any farther.

I jumped down to the island, waded out into ankle-deep water, and dragged Purple-bag up onto dry land by his collar. He struggled weakly, reaching for his waist. I took a deep breath and kicked him in the stomach. He stopped struggling and vomited. I finished pulling him ashore, then took a large nylon cable tie out of my bag and used it to lock his wrists behind him. Then I dragged the other two out and did the same to them.

I frisked them, taking away two pistols, three grenades, and a knife. Only then did I pull the other two bags off.

European features, light coloring. Neither one was Rashid Matar.

"Who are you?"

They stared at me, dazed, uncomprehending. The water was on the low side of 60° F. They were probably suffering from some degree of hypothermia. Hitting the water at over forty miles an hour probably didn't help, either.

I fired one of the pistols into the water near them. They jerked, more alert, the sound doubly intimidating because of the confinement of the cliff walls. "Who are you?"

The one who'd worn the orange mask said weakly, "Red Army Faction." He had a German accent.

Not Shiite extremists. Not by a long shot. I thought about asking them about Rashid Matar, but it seemed unlikely they would know anything.

It was now less than five minutes since I first moved on the hijackers. The green bag drifted to shore nearby, floated by trapped air and pulled along in the hijacker's wake. I fished it out of the water and pulled it over the blond's head. Then I put the other men's bags on.

"What are you doing?" Orange-bag asked. I pulled him to his feet. He was barely able to stand. I jumped to the first-class section of the airplane and let him collapse into a seat; then I fetched the other two as well. I brought some of their weapons back, as well, for evidence.

The passengers were coming out of their paralysis. They all looked fearfully up the aisle when I appeared, some ducking back into their seats, but none of them had ventured as far as the cockpit. The flight attendants, it turned out, were taped to seats at the back of first class.

"It's okay," I called down the plane. "It's over. Somebody cut these people free." I pointed at the flight attendants. I moved up to the cockpit and, with the captured knife, cut the pilots free. I told them the same thing. "It's over. The hijackers are tied up in first class."

The pilot looked at me, dazed, puzzled. "What should we do now?"

"Whatever you want," I said, then jumped.

I stood with the press as the plane was taxied up. The regular crowd was still held behind the barrier, but the press were close enough to see the passengers come out. I'd picked up my binoculars from the baggage cart before coming up here. I tried to stand at the back of the reporters, using them to shield me from the Algerians and the passengers.

The adrenaline was still flowing through my system and my stomach was hollow, my hands shaking. I felt like laughing but nothing was funny.

The Reuters reporter was taking pictures rapidly; he was flipping a new roll of film into his camera when he saw me. I nodded politely. He nodded back, a puzzled expression on his face, and went back to taking pictures.

A statement from the Algerian press liaison had been read aloud just before the plane taxied to the gate. It claimed that the passengers had overwhelmed the hijackers and taken them prisoner.

As the passengers went by, steered carefully away from the press by the Algerians, they joked, but the laughter sounded strained, as if it might crack easily. I recognized the sound. It was how I felt.

The crew came off last and I saw the copilot glance in my

direction, then stare as he spotted my face at the back of the group of reporters. I held up my finger again, over my lips, as I'd done on the plane. *Shhh.* He frowned and I grinned at him, then jumped.

The soupspoon was halfway to my mouth and Millie said, "Bang."

"Millie!"

She took her hand and pointed it like a gun, thumb up, forefinger extended, and pressed it against my forehead. "Bang! Too late. The first one got you in the abdomen, maybe they could have saved you, but this one got you in the brain. Too bad, nothing left to fix."

I put the soupspoon down. We were in Manhattan, in a booth at Bruno's on East Fifty-eighth, and the *zuppa de mussels* was really good, but suddenly I didn't feel like eating. "You sure know how to spoil a guy's appetite."

"We had an agreement," she said.

I nodded. "Yeah, okay. I'm sorry. It won't happen again."

She relaxed a little. "Okay. Finish your soup."

I picked up a spoonful of the stock, pushing aside the open shells of the mussels. It was halfway to my mouth when she said, "I don't want anything to happen to you, but if it does, I want you to survive it."

I nodded.

"I love you and . . . bang."

I jumped, spoon still in my mouth, to a recessed nook in the emergency room of Baltimore's Adams Cowley Shock Trauma Center. A nurse walked by but didn't look in my direction. The walls were white and I smelled methyl alcohol and disinfectant. My nose wrinkled. The smells did not go with the soup, but Shock Trauma was rated as one of the best emergency rooms in the country.

I jumped back to the street outside of Bruno's and went back in, the spoon hidden discretely in my hand and the napkin from my lap tucked into my back pocket. The waiter looked puzzled as I came back to the table. Millie smiled and kissed me as I sat back down.

We'd been playing this game ever since I described the way the machine gun had gone off during the hijacking. At any point during the time we were together, if she said "Bang" I was supposed to jump to the e-room, no questions, no delays. It wasn't supposed to matter if I was naked, eating, or sitting on the toilet.

In addition, I'd bought several alarm clocks. They were lying around the cliff dwelling, facedown. Millie reset them each night to different times. When they went off, I was also supposed to jump to the e-room.

I'd been much better about responding to the alarms, even jumping, naked, to the e-room alcove when my normal alarm woke me up one morning. A nurse screamed at me, more shocked at my sudden appearance, I suppose, than at my nudity.

It was 11 P.M. in New York. Millie, back at school, had turned in early, and I'd jumped her away to Manhattan, for our first "date" in almost a month.

"CNN did another interview with the American and the two Britishers who are willing to say you appeared and disappeared in the plane. Then they did a longer interview with a psychologist who talked about the effects of post-traumatic stress syndrome. Nobody believes what really happened."

I smiled. "Or admits it. The NSA may be suppressing some of it. Even if there aren't any teleports at the NSA, any teleports watching the news know *I* exist. If there are other teleports."

Millie shrugged. "If they exist, they may be saying, 'How stupid to be public.' "

"How did the experts explain the water? That the terrorists were soaking from head to foot?"

She laughed. "Sweat. Nervous sweat."

"Sounds like a dramatic failure of their antiperspirant."

She laughed again.

"What's the official story?"

"The original one—that a passenger managed to capture all three terrorists, but that he left the plane in Algiers instead of taking the replacement jet on to Rome."

A smile died on my face. "I really don't care who gets the credit. I just wish Rashid Matar had been aboard."

Millie frowned. "There are two hundred innocent people who are alive and well today, because of what you did. Isn't that enough for you?"

I wiggled in my seat, uncomfortable.

"What do you intend to do to him, if you catch up with him?"

"*When* I catch up with him. When, not if. And I don't know."

She shivered. "Well, think about what it would do to you to use his methods. Whatever you do, don't become like him, okay?"

The thought chilled my bones and, again, the soup tasted funny.

"Okay," I said.

She said, "Bang."

I hadn't seen Dad since before Christmas, when I'd met him on the sidewalk outside his bar, so I jumped to the backyard one evening and looked at the house. His car was in the driveway, but all the curtains were drawn. There were lights on in the kitchen and living room, none in my old room.

When I jumped to my room, it was dark and the door to the hallway was slightly ajar, spilling a thin wedge of light across the floor. There were footsteps in the dust.

Behind me I heard someone move and then a soft coughing sound, mechanical, and the world's largest bee stung me in the back of my leg.

I flinched away, jumping, appearing in the fiction section of the Stanville Public Library.

So much for all the work I'd done with Millie, I thought, twisting to look at what my hand found. It was metal, tufted with foam at the end, about an inch and a half long. I tugged it out. The needle on the end was three-quarters of an inch long and fat enough that there was blood on it. A clear liquid dripped out of the tip.

Shades of "Wild Kingdom."

The room started to spin and I jumped, dart in hand, to the cliff dwelling, where I fell forward onto my bed. I'm not sure whether I passed out before or after I hit the mattress.

In spy movies, the gallant hero wakes up after being shot with the tranquilizer dart clear-eyed and clearheaded, completely aware of his surroundings.

My first memories were of hanging facedown over the edge of the bed and puking my guts out. I think that's the first memory. From the later evidence, I must have done this several times before I was awake enough to check the time.

Fourteen hours had passed since I'd visited Dad's house. I was having trouble thinking, and the stench was making me sick again. I rolled to the other side of the bed, away from the mess, and it occurred to me that the NSA didn't have Dad under covert surveillance—they'd moved in with him.

Well, with any luck, they'd make his life *more* miserable than Millie's. I hoped they'd interrogate him on drugs. Perhaps he'd feel as bad as I did now.

I jumped to my favorite oasis; the sun was shining and the temperature was in the high sixties. I rinsed my mouth out at the spring and washed my face in the cold water.

It occurred to me that I hadn't seen Millie last night and that she was probably worried sick. I considered jumping to her apartment and waiting for her to get back from class, but I might run into her roommate or show up on their tapes if they'd bugged the place.

I was getting very angry.

There was a homeless woman at the Stillwater bus station who took my offer of a hundred dollars. I wrote the message out for her and dialed Millie's number on the pay phone, standing so I blocked the dial. When their answering machine message finished, I handed the receiver to her.

In a surprisingly pleasant voice she said, "Millie, I heard from Bruno and he's fine. He thought he had a job in a hospital, but it didn't work out. He's sorry he hasn't answered your last letter but he promises to write real soon. I'll talk to you later."

Bruno's was where we'd had dinner the night before. The homeless woman handed the phone back and I hung it up. I gave her another four hundred dollars. She looked surprised.

"Hell," she said. "I thought you were going to take the money away from me after I made the call."

"Get off the street," I said. "It's a hard life."

"Ain't that the truth."

I walked around the corner, to a hardware store, and bought a mop and bucket.

Millie wanted me to avoid Dad from then on, but all she could get me to promise was to be careful.

I showed her the dart, after jumping her to the cliff dwelling at midnight. She stared at it, then insisted on cleaning the wound. She wanted to know when I'd last had a tetanus shot.

"Two years ago."

She chewed on her lip. "That should be all right. . . . Damn! I'm really starting to hate these guys! What's that smell?"

"Disinfectant," I said, and changed the subject.

"A Pan Am 727 was hijacked on takeoff from Athens. It landed in Larnaca, on the Turkish half of Cyprus. The authorities say there is only one hijacker, but he's wired himself with explosives and the plane's fuel tanks are over three-quarters full."

"I'll call back," I said.

I jumped to Texas, than Larnaca. The press pointed cameras like cannon from the terminal. Fire trucks circled the aircraft like Western wagons under Indian attack. Where was John Wayne when you needed him? I settled in the shadow of a foam truck and used the binoculars.

The plane's doors were shut and one of the plane's engines was idling, to run the air-conditioning, I guessed. The passengers' windows weren't shaded and I could see worried faces staring out through them.

At the other end of the truck, the firemen were gathered

around the open door of the cab, listening to the radio. I moved closer until I could hear.

". . . and unless my demands are met, I will detonate my explosives, killing all two hundred and twelve passengers and crew." The voice was calm, matter-of-fact. The accent was Middle Eastern. I wondered if it was Matar, but I doubted it. He might blow up the passengers, but never himself.

I looked back at the plane. If the hijacker was on the radio, then he was up in the cockpit.

I jumped to the top of the wing, by the fuselage, near its trailing edge. I could just see in one of the windows. A terrified face looked back at me.

I held up my finger over my lips. The man blinked rapidly but didn't seem to say anything. I moved up the wing to the next window. That window and center seats on this side of the plane were empty, but a woman in the aisle seat saw me and held her hand over her mouth, then let it drop and clamped her lips shut.

I jumped into the plane, into the empty seat.

The plane stank of fear; the woman in the aisle seat jumped when I appeared, and shrieked. Down the plane, a baby cried suddenly and there was a collective gasp in reaction to both noises.

"Silence!" a voice yelled from the front of the plane. It was the voice from the radio, but I couldn't see past the partition at first class to see him.

The woman next to me held both hands over her mouth. She alternated between looking up the aisle and looking at me. I shifted into the middle seat, motioning her to be quiet. She leaned away from me, avoiding contact.

From the middle seat I could see into the first-class section almost all the way to the front galley. I couldn't see into the cockpit, but the hijacker chose that moment to walk back to the barrier between coach and first class.

It wasn't Matar. He was a slight Arab, young, with steel-rimmed glasses. At first I thought he was wearing a down vest, but I was wrong. It was the explosives, fastened to some sort of harness, wires running to detonators, batteries clipped to his belt. In his left hand he held a switch on a wire extension. His thumb was poised a quarter-inch above a small, red button. A quarter inch.

Jesus! Jump away!

In his right hand he held a pistol, a compromise, for threatening individuals rather than whole groups. I didn't care about the pistol. It was the quarter-inch gap that worried me, the little red button.

He walked past us, all the way to the back of the plane. I saw heads lower as he came by, avoiding eye contact. There wasn't any doubt who had dominance in this pack. But the eyes raised again, as soon as he was past, straining to see the explosives, the button, as if watching could somehow prevent the detonation.

A quarter-inch.

At least it wasn't a dead-man switch, a switch that would close when a person let go of it. He walked forward, headed back to the front of the plane. When he was past me I took the metal rod from my bag of odds and ends.

It was steel, a half-inch thick, twelve inches long. The bottom four inches were wrapped in cloth tape, to form a grip. It weighed slightly over one pound and was the color and hardness of the hijacker's eyes.

When the hijacker walked out of sight again, I jumped to the partition, at the edge of first class. The three men seated there jerked, but the admonition from the hijacker kept them from shouting. I motioned for silence and they blinked at me.

I used the dentist's mirror to look around the corner.

The hijacker was talking to one of the flight attendants, a stunning blonde with a very white face and spots of sweat soaking the armpits of her uniform. The hijacker would emphasize what he was saying with motions of his left hand and the stewardess would twitch in sync with the motion of the switch.

A phrase from my recent reading came, unbidden. *Insh'allah,* I thought. *If God wills.*

I raised the rod over my head, then brought it down very

fast, very hard. Before it reached the height of the hijacker's arm, I jumped.

I appeared next to him just in time for the rod to smash into his ulna, two inches back from his wrist. As I hoped, his thumb straightened, lifting away from the switch. His other fingers loosened and the switch fell free, swinging on its cord down to his thigh.

The pain must have been considerable—I'm sure I heard the bone break—but his right hand whipped the gun around very fast. The rod was moving back up then and it smashed into the bottom of that wrist, knocking the gun up as it fired. Grains of burning powder stung my cheek and the bullet burned along the top of my shoulder. The pistol fell behind him and his right hand reached for the switch.

I grabbed him then, and jumped to the pit. As I let him go, he was still twisting, trying to grab the button. I flinched away, jumping to the edge of the pit above.

He detonated five feet above the surface.

A giant hand slammed into me, lifted me off my feet, and I jumped away, even before the sound reached me, before I could land on the rocks. I staggered out from the alcove at the Shock Trauma e-room and fell to the floor. My shoulder was bleeding, my face stung, and I was having trouble breathing.

A nurse walked up to me and started asking questions, but I was still struggling to catch my breath, so I ignored her. Finally I took in a great gasp of air, followed by several progressively easier breaths.

I kept seeing the initial flash of the blast. My mind filled in the results, even though I wasn't there, from Mom's death.

"Sorry," I said. "What did you want?"

I killed him. I blew him up, just like Mom.

She saw the blood then on my shoulder, saw the powder burns on my face. "You've been shot." She turned her head and shouted, "Gurney here!"

They seemed disappointed, almost, when the source of the blood turned out to come from a shallow graze across the shoulder and the only other wounds were the powder burns. After dressing the shoulder, a nurse carefully picked the grains from my face using very fine tweezers. "If we don't get 'em out, they'll be like tattoos."

Before she finished with me, two Baltimore policeman showed up and took station just outside the door. I asked her what they were there for.

"Gunshot wound. We had to report it. You'd be surprised at the number of drug deals gone wrong that end up in this place. They don't want to talk to the cops, either, but they also want to live. We're the best, so their friends dump 'em here and leave. Who shot you?"

I shook my head slowly, carefully, avoiding tugging on the shoulder. I stared at the wall. *Dead.*

She frowned and checked my pupils again, using a small light to check the contraction, searching for a concussion. "It's not my problem. You'll have to tell them." She put down the light and dabbed the small facial wounds with Neosporin. "Not even worth Band-Aids. Keep 'em clean and they'll heal right up. Unless you get shot again."

I nodded slowly, still looking at the wall. "Thanks."

She walked out between the cops through the only door to the room. "He's all yours," she said.

They both turned to watch her walk down the hall. While their heads were turned, I jumped.

I used a full wet suit and scuba gear to recover as much of the hijacker's body as possible.

It wasn't a matter of respect for the dead—more a matter of respect for the environment. I didn't want him to rot in the water. Every time I thought about his blood in the water, my lips clamped tighter around the mouthpiece of the scuba regulator.

There were a lot of small pieces, but the blood had cleared out. An underground waterway filled the pit and an underground waterway drained it away, a fact I didn't realized until I noticed the current moving me sideways along the bottom. I carried a mesh bag to put the pieces in and I could only work at midday, when the sunlight touched the surface of the water.

The legs and arms were mostly intact and I'd found the head facedown, hair floating up like some aquatic plant. I didn't look at the face, just pushed the head into the bag, averting my eyes.

I threw up a lot.

The first time I didn't get the regulator out of my mouth and the vomit filled the mouthpiece. I was twenty feet down, about the deepest the water got, and I had to kick for the surface, choking and spitting. I jumped to the box-canyon spring to rinse the mouthpiece.

I didn't want to use the water from the pit.

On the second day, when I had as much of him as I thought I was going to find, I dumped three buckets of bluegill perch, two buckets of small catfish, and four buckets of crawdads into the water. When I'd bought the fish, the Stillwater bait supplier had lectured me on trotline fishing at great length. I'd listened to him very carefully and thanked him when he was through.

It was my hope that the fish and crawdads would find the rest of the hijacker. Call it my own form of bioremediation.

Three days after the hijacking, I left the pieces of the body on the taxiway in Larnaca, Cyprus, in a galvanized washtub, covered with clear plastic to thwart the flies. I'd considered leaving a note, explaining that his own bomb did this to him, but I thought it would be better left unexplained. If they wanted to think I'd done that to him, fine. Maybe it would deter the next hijacker.

Who picked up Mom's body?

Millie held me every night while I cried.

SEVENTEEN

There was a great deal of debate over the video footage that showed me appearing on the 727's wing. Two different news organizations captured it, though, so some sort of conspiracy was implied. The views, video on extreme zoom, only showed my back. When the galvanized washtub showed up three days later, the debate intensified.

In explanation *National Enquirer* suggested UFOs, the ghost of Elvis, and a new Anti-Hijacking Diet.

Much was made of the American origin of the galvanized tub. Torture was claimed by some, but the Cypriot autopsy said death by explosion with subsequent immersion in fresh water.

The soaking-wet terrorists from the Air France hijacking were remembered. The interviews from that incident received more airtime, along with the largely incoherent interview with the Pan Am flight attendant.

I watched a little of the coverage, read a little, but the related memories depressed me. Again, I wondered if there were any other teleports out there, watching these stories.

On Saturday, a week after the hijacking, I jumped to the Dairy Queen in Stanville and had a dip cone, seventy-three cents, please, here's a napkin. I walked across the street to the town square and sat on one of the benches with the green flaking paint. There was old, dirty snow with footpaths carved across it, but there was no wind under the gray sky and the temperature was above freezing.

Men and women walked out of the Baptist church basement in clumps of two or three. A woman detached herself from the back of one of the clumps and walked toward me.

"I know you."

I tensed to jump; then I recognized her. It was Sue Kimmel, the woman who'd given the party—the one who'd taken me to her bedroom.

"I know you," I said. I felt embarrassed. "Uh, how's college?"

Sue laughed the kind of laugh that's edged with pain. "Well, college didn't work out. I'm going to try again in the summer."

"I'm sorry. What was the problem?" Too late I thought she probably didn't want to talk about it.

She sat on the end of the bench, not close, not far away, and stretched her feet out before her. Her hands were deep in her coat pockets. "Booze. The problem was booze."

I shifted, uncomfortable.

She jerked her chin at the church. "I just got out of an AA meeting. I've only been out of Red Pines a month." Red Pines was a substance-abuse treatment center on the edge of Stanville. She shivered. "It's harder than I thought it would be."

I thought about Dad and his bottles of scotch. "I hope it works out."

"It's got to," she said, smiling again. She looked at my cone, half eaten. "Boy that looks good. Care to join me for another one?"

"Well, I'll get coffee."

She looked back at the church. "I've had enough coffee. We're very big on coffee in AA."

We walked back to the DQ and I bought her a cone and myself a small coffee. We sat at the booth in the corner and I put my back to the wall.

"Your dad's an alcoholic, isn't he?"

I was surprised at the comment and even more surprised at my first reaction—to defend him. "Yeah . . . he sure is."

"He's come to two meetings in the last month, but he left each one before it even started. He looked terrible, like he had the shakes. Somebody saw him back at Gil's later, both times. An advanced alcoholic can kill themselves trying to detox by themselves. Did you know that?"

I shook my head. "I didn't."

Sue nodded. "Yeah, the aldehydes replace neurotransmitters and if you go off booze suddenly, you're left with no little messengers, no little chemical sparks. You can go into convulsions and die. Do you see your father much?"

I shook my head. "No. I don't."

"Well, he should get into treatment. I think he even knows it, he just can't get past that last bit, that rough edge."

I sipped my coffee and didn't say anything for a moment. Then I asked, "What caused you to seek help?"

Sue looked embarrassed. "Lots of things. Secret stashes of booze. Drinking in class. Hallucinations. Like when I hallucinated at that party you came to. Uh, you did come to my party, right?"

"Oh, yes."

"Well, I had this weird waking dream where you flew out the window of my bathroom."

I stared at her.

"Don't look at me like that. I know it was crazy."

My ears started getting red.

"Anyway, I want to apologize for how I acted that night. I was pretty drunk. I've had a lot of apologies to make. We call it a ninth step."

I choked on the coffee. *Ninth step?*

When I was breathing normally again, I said, "My mom wasn't an alcoholic, but she said she was doing a ninth step with me before she left for Europe. Before she died."

She nodded. "Yeah, Alanon is based on the twelve-step program, just like AA. I was in treatment when your mom died, but my parents told me. I was sorry to hear about it."

"Uhm."

She sighed. "Hope I haven't talked too much. I tend to go on and on about it. It's like religion, you know, and I'm a new convert."

"I don't mind. Anytime."

We talked for a bit about common acquaintances and then she had to go.

"I'm glad I ran into you," she said.

"Me too," I said. I meant it.

After she left I stared into the empty cup. I wondered if Dad still had the NSA camping out at his house.

There was a pay phone by the bathrooms in the Dairy Queen, but I liked to come there. It was a pleasant part of my past. If I called from here, the NSA would camp out, hoping for my return. I went out back by the dumpster and jumped to the Stanville bus station.

The little waiting room with the vending machines seemed exactly the same as it had eighteen months previously, when I'd left to go to New York. Some of that time's fear and sadness seemed to permeate the place, coat the walls and drift in the air. I went inside and put a quarter in the pay phone.

The phone rang twice and Dad picked up the phone.

"Hello?" He sounded irritable and I knew he needed a drink.

"Hi, Dad."

The ordinary room noises that you don't normally notice went away and, with their absence, became prominent. I felt even sadder. "You don't have to cover the mouthpiece, Dad. They know to trace the call."

He stammered, "What are you talking about?"

"Go in for treatment, Dad. You've got insurance. Check into Red Pines."

"Hell, no! You know the difference between a drunk and an alcoholic?"

It was an old joke—the answer was "Drunks don't have to go to all those meetings." Before he could give the punch line I said, "Yeah. Drunks get worse until they die. Some alcoholics get better."

He said, "Fuck you."

"Get treatment."

He was silent for a moment. "Why are you running from these government men? Don't you have any respect for your country?"

I almost hung up then, angry. Then I took a deep breath and said, "I have more respect for the Bill of Rights than they do. I have more respect for the Constitution. I'm no threat to them, but they don't believe that. They probably *can't* believe that."

There was the squeal of a tire from the parking lot— nothing extreme. It was more like the sound of someone turning into a tight parking place just a little too fast, but I knew better.

"Get treatment, Dad. Before you die. Before you fuck up anybody else's life."

I dropped the phone to hang on its cord, then walked over to the hall leading to the rest rooms and stood just inside, in the slight shadow.

They hit both doors at once, four men, each carrying something that looked like a short-barreled rifle with a huge bore. *Christ! What the hell is that?* I swear there was something just visible, sticking out of the gun barrel, that gleamed in the station's fluorescent lighting. One of the men saw me then and jerked the gun to his shoulder.

I jumped.

I phoned Dr. Perston-Smythe from a phone booth on the street. I'd yet to explore much of Washington but I stayed away from the Mall. I didn't want them watching the Air and Space Museum before I had a chance to see it.

He answered his own phone and I wondered if he had an agent sitting in his office, one of those short-barreled rifles in his hand, or one of the dart guns they'd shot me with the first time, at Dad's place.

"What on earth are those nasty-looking rifles they're carrying around?"

He drew in breath sharply. "What do you want, Mr. Rice?"

"I want to be left alone. I'm not harming anyone, much less 'national security,' and you guys are going way over-board."

There was a click and someone else's voice came on the line. "Mr. Rice, please don't hang up. This is Brian Cox."

"Surely you aren't spending all your time in Dr. Perston-Smythe's office?"

"Well, no. We arranged to switch the call to me in the event you called. Dr. Perston-Smythe is no longer on the line."

"What do you want?"

"We want your services."

"No."

"All right, we want to know how you do it."

"No."

"You're already working for us. That was quite a job you did in Algiers and Larnaca. Especially Larnaca."

I felt my nose wrinkle. "Hardly. I didn't go after them for you."

He laughed quietly and I swiveled my head around, watching the streets. I wondered if he was trying to distract me deliberately, to let them sneak up. I wanted desperately to ask him if there were other teleports that they knew of, but I was sure he was capable of lying to me about that, to lure me in. I didn't want to hand him that obsession, that tool.

"Well, even if it was revenge for your mother, it works for us. We could give you Matar, you know."

Bastards. "In return for what?"

"Ah. A favor here and there. Nothing arduous, nothing unpleasant even. Certainly nothing worse than Larnaca."

I shouldn't have, but I told him, "He blew himself up. All I did was collect the pieces. Everyone on that flight would have died if I didn't."

"Oh." His voice was utterly neutral. I don't know if he believed me or not. "How can you be sure? For all you know he might have given himself up in the next five minutes. Are you sure you didn't endanger the passengers more? He might never have pushed the button if you hadn't interfered."

He was only verbalizing what I'd been saying to myself all week long.

A car was easing up the street, four men inside. Others walked the sidewalks. They were wearing long coats, the fronts open; each had one hand clamped against his side, holding something beneath the coat. They stopped fifty yards away in plain sight.

"I see your men, Cox."

"Well, they'll stay away while we talk."

"Why'd you bother? Do you think they can catch me? What is that nasty gun they're carrying around."

"Tranquilizer."

I thought he was lying. The bore was too big. "And if I'm allergic to the drug? I jump off someplace and die. You get zip."

"You should work with us. We protect the country. Is that a bad thing?"

"I'm going to puke."

"Do you want Matar?"

"I'll get him myself."

"We'll get you eventually, unless you want to stay in hiding forever."

"Aren't you afraid you'll drive me to work for the other side? *Perestroika* and all, I'm seeing less and less difference. They, at least, seem to be getting rid of their secret police. We still have you. Leave me alone."

"What about your father?"

"Do what you want to him," I said. "He deserves it."

I dropped the phone and jumped.

I spent eight hours in the air flying from DFW Airport to Honolulu. Japanese Red Army terrorists seized and held three hundred tourists outside of security at the Honolulu airport. By the time my plane arrived, it was all over.

An assault by a Pearl Harbor Navy Seal unit supported by Army Special Forces from Schofield Barracks freed most of the hostages. Casualties were "light," two tourists, one Navy Seal, and six of seven terrorists.

Honolulu was beautiful, the water incredibly blue, the mountains emerald green, but I left after acquiring a jump site, deeply depressed. One of the dead was a woman, Mom's age.

* * *

"You can't be everywhere."

I sat on a sheepskin rug, pushing sticks into the wood stove. I felt cold. Every since cleaning up the hijacker's body from the cold, dark water of the pit, I'd been unable to get warm. Even in balmy Hawaii the sweat on my skin was cold.

Millie sat beside me, her robe opened on bare skin, comfortable. I was still clothed, my coat draped across my shoulders.

"I know." I hugged my knees. The heat from the stove was almost painful on my skin, but it didn't touch my bones.

She wanted me to see a therapist, another painful echo of Mom. I didn't want to.

She shifted on the rug, leaning against me, laying her head on my shoulder. I turned my head and kissed her forehead. She spoke.

"You think that if you get Matar, you'll be done. That it will somehow make things right. I think you're wrong."

I shook my head, leaned closer to the fire.

She went on. "I think you'll find that it doesn't help at all. And I'm afraid you'll get killed finding this out. You can jump away from guns, knives, bombs, but until you can jump away from yourself, you won't get away from the pain. Not unless you face it and deal with it."

"Deal with it? How?"

"You should see a therapist."

"Not again!"

"A therapist isn't going to kill you . . . not like a hijacker. Why is it easier to get men to go to war than to see a counselor?"

"Should I just let things happen? Should I let them kill innocent people?"

She looked at the fire for a moment, then said, "There was an interview with a Palestinian on CNN today. He wanted to know why this mysterious antiterrorist didn't rescue Palestinian children from Israeli bullets."

"I can't be everywhere." I winced at what I'd said.

She smiled. "So where do you draw the line? You knew

that the situation in Honolulu had nothing to do with Shiite extremists before you left. You knew Matar wouldn't be there."

We were back where we started. "Can I just stand by? When I could do something?"

"Go to work for a fire department. You could rescue more people with less danger. I'm afraid you'll end up like the NSA if you go this route. The more you associate with terrorists, the more terrorist your behavior."

I pulled away from her. "Have I really started acting that way?"

She shook her head and pulled me back. "I'm sorry. It's my fear. Perhaps if I constantly remind you of it, it won't happen."

I slumped into her arms, curling in on myself, my head on her shoulder. "I hope so."

Athens, start of so many hijackings, was the site of the next one. An Olympia Airlines DC-10 took off for Madrid and, ten minutes later, requested an emergency landing due to depressurization. At the same time they switched their flight transponder to 7500, the international sign for hijacking.

The plane had been back on the ground for two hours when I learned this from Manhattan Media Services.

Units of the Greek Army were in place, surrounding the plane, when I arrived in the terminal. I went looking for the press, first, because I figured they would know something about the number of hijackers, their arms, and the demands.

The Reuters reporter from Algiers was there. His eyes got very large when he saw me and he stepped back from his front-row position and cut me out from the group of newsmen.

"You're the one," he said in an excited whisper. "I thought it was you from the film." He kept looking around, anxious to scoop the others.

"What are you talking about?" I wondered if this was a disaster or if I could use it.

"Don't go away. Let me interview you!"

"Relax. You attract all of your colleagues and I'll leave."

He took a deep breath, lowered his shoulders. "I knew it!" he whispered. "Why don't we go someplace quiet?"

"Aren't you forgetting something?" I said, nodding my head at the terminal window. The plane was at the end of the runway, about half a mile away.

He licked his lips. "After?"

"Depends. What's happening with the hijacking? What can you tell me?"

"So, if I tell you what I know—"

"I can ask *them,*" I said, pointing at the rest of the press with my thumb.

"Okay. Okay, take my card." He handed me a white card with the Reuters masthead, his name, Jean-Paul Corseau, and a phone, fax, and telex number. "There's three of them. They have pistols. There was a plainclothes guard who wounded one of them, but the other two killed him. In the fight, a bullet went through a window in first class. They'd only reached eight thousand feet, so it wasn't too bad, but the pilot insisted on landing. They're demanding a new plane. They wouldn't let the pilot unblock the runway, either, so they're having to route traffic to the other runways."

"Any other demands? What nationality?"

"Nothing yet. They're ETA, Basque separatists. Most of the passengers are Spanish."

"*Basques?* Since when did Basques start hijacking? I thought they went in for bombings?"

He shrugged.

"Anything else? How badly wounded is the third hijacker?"

"We don't know."

"Okay, thanks. If it works out, I'll give you something after." I looked around. Nobody seemed to be watching us. "What's that over there?" I asked, pointing back at the press.

Corseau turned his head and I jumped.

* * *

One of them stood in the doorway, looking out, wearing a long leather coat and holding a pistol in his hands. The rear door was shut and all the window shades. One of them also stood in the cockpit, just visible. He was using the radio. That left one more, the wounded man.

On a DC-10 the front door is behind the first-class section, with a partition forward that's cut by the two aisles leading forward and back. A walk-through galley leads across the plane to the second aisle. I jumped to the middle of the galley, shielded from the front by the partition and the back by the galley.

I couldn't see anyone watching the man in the door, whose back was to me, but it was possible. I decided to risk it and jumped behind him, one hand around his waist, the other covering his mouth. I jumped him to the pit and dropped him, then jumped back to the galley. I listened. Nobody seemed to have noticed. I used the dentist's mirror to look forward.

A man in a rumpled suit leaned against the front bulkhead, a strange pistol in his right hand pointed in the general direction of the seated passengers. Blood soaked the left side of his jacket, low down, and he held that arm pressed tightly against it. His face was covered in sweat and he looked very pale. From where he stood, he could see down the aisle by the doorway.

At his feet I saw the head and arm of a still body, hand outstretched, fingers pointed up, half open, almost imploring.

I moved back to the other aisle and used the mirror to examine the cockpit door.

The door to the cockpit was open and I could see the last terrorist standing there, a radio headset on his head. He stood at the edge of the door, waving his gun to emphasize what he was saying.

From my angle the only crew I could see was the pilot, sitting still, head straight forward. He had a bald spot.

I took the steel rod out of my bag. I didn't see how I could jump the terrorist on the radio away, without the other one seeing me. I lifted the rod above my head and jumped.

I appeared at the cockpit door and the rod cracked into the back of the terrorist's head. I had the vague impression that he pitched forward, but I was twisting immediately, to bring the rod down on the wounded terrorist's gun hand. I heard bone crack and cringed.

The gun fell forward and the passenger in the front seat scooped it up. The terrorist slumped to the floor suddenly, cradling his wrist *and* his side. There was blood on the wall behind him.

I looked into the cockpit. The engineer and copilot pinned the unconscious terrorist to them while the pilot pried the gun from his fingers. He looked back at the door, fear and determination on his face.

"Don't shoot," I said, smiling. "I'm on your side." I backed up and walked down the aisle, past the galley, into coach. I heard the pilot scramble out of his seat and follow. Everything seemed all right. The flight attendants were standing at the very back of the plane.

"Where's the third one?" he asked.

"Oh. I, uh, put him on hold. I'll be back with him in a second."

I jumped away, to the cliff high above the pit.

The man in the long leather coat was on the island, shivering. He'd managed to hold on to his pistol and he was standing, arms crossed, hunched forward. Water dripped from the leather coat. He kept looking from side to side.

"Drop the gun," I shouted.

His head jerked up, water droplets gleaming in the last of the midday sun. He pointed the gun at me and shouted something back in a language I didn't know.

I jumped to the top of the wall on the other side, behind him. "Drop the gun," I shouted again.

He whirled, this time firing quickly. The bullet clipped stone several feet to my left.

I jumped behind him, on the island, and hit him on the head with the rod. He screamed and fell to his knees, both hands going to his head. I hit his gun hand and the gun fell. I picked it up quickly and stepped away from him.

The gun was plastic. I'd read about them, able to pass through airport metal detectors.

He held his head and said things that sounded like swearing, whatever the language was.

I motioned for him to lie facedown and he spat at me. I raised the rod meaningfully. He winced and lay down on his stomach. I put the gun in my pocket and secured his hands behind him with a cable tie; then I stood him up and jumped him back to Athens, to the galley on the DC-10.

The captain stood there, talking to one of the flight attendants in Greek. Both of them flinched away when my prisoner and I appeared.

"Excuse me," I said. "Here's the third hijacker."

The captain nodded slowly and I jumped away.

I stayed out of sight as the passengers streamed off the plane. Two of the terrorists came off on stretchers. The third one came off surrounded by police. Behind the crew and flight attendants came one last stretcher, covered. Sad, but it didn't bother me the way the tourists in Hawaii had.

When the official statement was read to the press, I tapped Corseau, the Reuters man, on his shoulder. He turned his tape recorder in my direction and I shook my head.

"All right," he said, turning it off. "Do I get an interview?"

I thought about it. "Where is your next assignment? Did you catch this one because you were here, in transit?"

"Yes. I was on my way to Cairo."

"Where is your luggage?"

"It's already there. I'd checked it and was about to board when this thing happened."

I smiled. "Good." I walked around behind him. He started to turn, but I said, "Hold still." I looked around—nobody was paying attention. I grabbed him by the belt and jumped him, camera bag, laptop computer, and all, to the Cairo airport terminal, on the sidewalk behind the taxi stand.

"Merde!" He nearly dropped his laptop computer and I steadied him.

"You recognize where you are?"

"Yes."

"Good," I said. I jumped.

Hawaii was five hours earlier than Oklahoma, so I figured I could pick up Millie at eleven, her time, and still have a nice evening in Honolulu. I jumped there from Cairo and took a cab to the airport.

It felt funny. Except for New York City, Hawaii was the only place I'd been in the U.S. that felt like a foreign city. Even though the signs were in English, the scenery didn't fit. But it was beautiful and for the first time in weeks, I felt warm.

I spent the afternoon walking around Waikiki. I bought a Hawaiian shirt for myself and a mu-mu for Millie, and picked out a restaurant at the Royal Hawaiian. The next day was Saturday and so she didn't have to get up early.

I felt like celebrating.

At eleven, Central Standard Time, I jumped to Millie's bedroom. I was dressed in white slacks and the turquoise Hawaiian shirt I'd bought. Her dress was waiting in Texas, but I carried an orchid lei with me, to put around her neck.

The bedside light, one of those gooseneck things with a metal shade, was pushed to one side, casting the bed in shadow. I took a step forward, thinking she'd fallen asleep, when something gleamed in the shadowed bed.

I twisted to the side and something struck me a glancing blow on my leg. *Bang,* I thought, and jumped to an alcove at Adams Cowley Shock Trauma in Baltimore.

I looked down at my leg. A silver tube, six inches long, one inch in diameter, hung from my leg. At one end, a wire-thin antenna projected. From the other, a stainless-steel rod, perhaps a quarter-inch thick, stuck in my pants, then out again, two inches later, ending in a barbed point, like a harpoon of some kind. There was a clear fluid accumulating at the tip and I bent forward. The point was hollow.

Well, Cox hadn't lied. It was a tranquilizer. But *Christ,* if that barbed point had struck straight on, it would be buried in my leg and I wouldn't be able to pull it out.

There was some blood, too, but it looked like it had just grazed me, snagging in the pants. And the antenna meant it was some kind of homing device.

The picture was chilling. The harpoon would bury itself in my leg and I would jump away. Before I could get the harpoon out, the tranquilizer would put me under. And the homing device would do the rest. Could they track it by satellite?

How long before they would get here? Also, did they develop this simply for me, or were they using an existing technology for an ongoing problem, i.e., were there more teleports that they'd hunted down?

I jumped to Central Park, dark, cold, inadequately dressed in my short-sleeved Hawaiian shirt and sandals. My pocketknife cut the harpoon free. I considered smashing it.

What have they done with Millie?

I waited five minutes, then jumped again, to the truck stop in Minnesota. A large gravel truck, empty, was pulling out of the lot. I jumped across the gap and threw the harpoon into the back. I heard it clang hollowly; then the truck accelerated down the access road toward the on ramp.

I wondered where it was going.

It wasn't a pleasant night. What little sleep I got was punctuated by nightmares. Dawn found me curled before the wood stove breaking kindling I didn't need into smaller and smaller pieces.

Millie's apartment complex was lousy with NSA agents that morning, but if she was there, she didn't go to class. I watched from a rooftop, with binoculars. When I phoned, a woman answered the phone but it was neither her nor her roommate so I hung up without speaking.

In Topeka, Kansas, I phoned Millie's brother-in-law, the lawyer. I gave the receptionist a false name.

"Your sister-in-law, Millie Harrison, was kidnapped yesterday by agents of the National Security Agency."

"Who is this?"

"A friend of Millie's. They're all over her apartment complex and neither her or her roommate are at home."

"What's your name?"

"Please do what you can." I hung up.

An aquarium supplier in Manhattan sold me a two-thousand-dollar cylinder of three-eighths-inch clear Lexan plastic. It stood five and a half feet tall and was three feet in diameter. He wanted to sell me the gasketed steel bottom, with fittings for filter tubes, but I declined. I wasn't using it for an aquarium.

I jumped the tube to the cliff dwelling and promptly ruined it for holding fish by riveting two handles inside, halfway up its length. When I stood within the tube holding the handles, the tube went from my ankles to slightly over my head, shielding me all the way around.

I jumped to Perston-Smythe's office in D.C.

A harpoon hit the plastic shell and ricocheted off at an angle. Dr. Perston-Smythe wasn't in his office, but a man in the corner dropped the harpoon gun in his hand and dove at me, arms outstretched.

I jumped sideways four feet, next to the bookcase. The man passed through the space I vacated and slammed into the desk, hands trying to fend himself off at the last second. He failed and his head and left shoulder struck the edge of the desk. He fell to the floor, moaning.

I jumped out of the tube and listened at the door. There didn't seem to be anyone coming. I took the gun from his shoulder holster, then grabbed him by his belt and lifted. He began to struggle. I jumped him to the beach in Tigzirt, Algeria, and left him facedown in the sand.

I was behind Perston-Smythe's desk when he came back to his office. He was alone. I pointed the agent's gun at him and asked him to shut the door. Then, after frisking him, I jumped him to the desert, in the foothills of El Solitario.

He fell to his knees when I released him. I walked ten feet away from him and sat on a rock.

He was looking around, his eyes squinting in the bright sunlight. "How do you do that?"

If my mind hadn't been on Millie, I might have found his expression amusing. "Where's Brian Cox?"

"Huh? In his office, I suppose. Did you try him there?"

"Where is his office?"

He hesitated a moment. "Well, he's listed in the Government Directory. I guess I can tell you. He runs his own little show out of the Pierce Building, over by the State Department."

"He's not at Fort Meade?"

"No. NSA has offices all over the place. What did you do with Barry?"

"Who's Barry?"

"The agent in my office. The one on the morning shift."

"Ah. Well, Barry went to the beach. Where did they put Millie Harrison?"

"Never heard of her."

I pointed the gun at his head.

"Jesus. Honest. I've never heard of her. Are you sure I'd have a reason? Remember who you're dealing with. These guys don't tell anybody anything, unless they absolutely have to."

I lowered the gun. "I would point out that someone with my talents is very hard to run from. If I find you're jerking my string, you will hear about it."

"Honest. I've never heard of her. The only work I do has to do with the Middle East."

"Turn around."

"You're going to shoot me?"

"Not unless you make me. Turn around."

He moved slowly. I grabbed him and jumped him to the airport terminal in Ankara, Turkey, and left him.

I hoped he had his American Express card.

When I checked back at Millie's, they'd reduced the number of agents in the complex. Two men stood outside, half hidden at the corners of the building. I saw one take a radio out from under his overcoat and talk into it.

I left him at the airport in Bonn, waving his harpoon gun and trying to talk on the radio again. Airport security was closing in fast.

I don't think his radio had intercontinental capacity.

The other guard I jumped to Orly Airport outside Paris. He managed to plant an elbow in my ribs, very hard, but I held on tight and left him next to a bunch of Japanese tourists clustered around the information desk.

I handled those inside the apartment with the Lexan cylinder, drawing their fire, then jumping them away to airports in Cyprus, Italy, and Saudi Arabia.

Dad, apparently, was at work. At least the car was gone. There were only three agents in the house and I scattered them to Tunis, Rabat, and Lahore. In the process, I earned another bruised rib and a stamped instep.

I considered using the iron rod in the future, but I didn't want to risk killing someone. I was ready to take that risk when an entire planeload was at stake, but Americans?

They're terrorists in their own way.

I shivered, remembering Millie's warning. I didn't want to become like them. Even worse, I didn't want to become like my dad.

It was dark in Washington, heavy clouds blocking the setting sun, the wind cold out of the east. I went into the train station and called Perston-Smythe's number. I figured he was still in Turkey, unless he'd had his passport with him, but it was Cox I wanted to talk to.

A male voice, neutral, not Perston-Smythe, answered the phone. I said, "This is David Rice. I want to talk to Brian Cox."

There was a hesitation on the other end of the line.

"What's the problem?" I asked. "Besides starting the trace, that is."

"Mr. Cox is on another line. Can you hold a moment?"

"Don't give me that."

"Honestly—he's talking to the ambassador in Bonn. You caused the problem, after all."

Ah—the harpoon gun in the airport. I smiled.

"I'll call back."

I took the crowded rush-hour subway five stops down. The clean, fresh-smelling stations amazed me, so different from New York. On the platform I used another pay phone. Cox himself answered the phone.

"You've caused a great deal of trouble," he said angrily.

His tone of voice reminded me of Dad. For just an instant I felt like I'd done something wrong, horribly shameful. I was speechless, first with shock, then with anger.

I hung up the phone and screamed out loud, an inarticulate burst of rage. Rush-hour commuters turned and stared at me, surprised, a little afraid. A tobacco-chewing marine in uniform said, "Bad news?"

"Fuck you!" I said, and jumped to my cliff dwelling in Texas. I hoped he choked on his cud.

I screamed again, angry, furious. The man had kidnapped Millie. He had people shooting at me with sharp pieces of barbed steel and he had the nerve to say *I* was a lot of trouble? I dropped to my knees on my bed and began pounding the mattress.

God, I was frightened.

Dad arrived home from work escorted by two agents, one in the front passenger seat, one in the back. I watched from the kitchen window as he pulled the car into the driveway. I was surprised that he was driving. Considering that the NSA had been around my father now for a couple of weeks, they must know about his alcoholism. I wouldn't get into a car he was driving.

Only one of the agents carried a harpoon gun. He held it inside his coat as they walked to the house, but it was dark out, and he didn't bother to close the coat.

I jumped him to the airport in Seville just after he entered the house. The other guard I jumped to Cairo. When I came back, Dad was running across the lawn to his car.

When he reached the door, I jumped to the driver's seat

and stared out at him through the window. At the same time the car alarm went off. He yelled, pushed away from the car, and ran awkwardly up the street. I let him go and jumped back to Washington, D.C.

This time he just said, "I'm listening."

"Where is Millie Harrison?"

"In a safe place."

"Where?"

"Why should we tell you?"

I stared at the phone in my hand, then remembered to check the approaches to the booth. I was standing outside a convenience store in Alexandria. "You should do a lot more than tell me. There are much more unpleasant places your men could end up than airports. It would've been just as easy to drop them from high places. Very high places. And it doesn't have to be just your men that I take on my little trips. What would the president say if I jumped him to Colombia for a little chat? I don't think he's too popular there with certain special-interest groups. Or Cuba? It would be quite a coup: President goes on fact-finding mission. Whirlwind tour. Surprises even Secret Service."

Cox was silent for a moment. "You wouldn't do that."

"Try me."

"I don't have to. We have your girlfriend and you don't know where she is. You wouldn't do anything to jeopardize her."

"Why not? You're willing to jeopardize the president."

"I don't think I'm risking anything. Come talk to us. Help us figure out how you do what you do. We can help you. You have the right idea with this antiterrorist thing. We can get you Rashid Matar—"

I hung up the phone.

The next morning there were more guards at Millie's apartment. I jumped them to Knossos, Muscat, and Zurich. I was getting to be quite the little travel agency. I hoped it cost the NSA plenty to fly them home.

When I checked Dad's place it was empty, locked up.

The subway took me within two blocks of the Pierce Building. A government building across the street had no security and I accessed its roof with no trouble. There was a view of the side of the Pierce Building and its back entrance, the one that led to the parking lot.

The parking lot itself was fenced, with a guard at the gate. Another guard was in a glass booth at the building door. Using the binoculars, I watched both guards examine credentials. The one in the glass booth had to push a button before the building entrance would open.

Mounted closed-circuit television cameras surveyed the parking lot, all sides of the building, and even the roof.

I jumped back to Union Station and used the phone.

"Let me talk to Cox."

There was the sound of papers rustling.

"Hello."

"Let's meet."

"Good. You can come to my office."

"Don't be stupid."

"Where, then."

"Go to the Capitol reflecting pool. Walk up the middle of the grass toward the Washington Monument. Alone."

"Who's being stupid now?"

I didn't care how many people he had with him. I just wanted him to think I intended to make the meeting.

"Well, you can bring one other, but leave your weapons behind. No long coats—nothing that could hide those nasty harpoon guns. He walks behind you."

We settled for two guards.

"When," he asked.

"Right now. As you know, I'll be there before you, so play it straight. It's pretty empty on the Mall right now. I'll be able to tell if you bring any ringers in."

I heard him swallow.

"All right. It will take us ten minutes."

I hung up the phone, jumped back to the rooftop, and took up the binoculars.

He came out of the building with six other men. Some of them carried the harpoon guns. Four of the men got into a car and the other two, wearing heavy sweaters but no coats, walked toward a different car, Cox trailing, careless, expecting the real confrontation to happen at the Mall.

One of the men opened and held the back door for Cox. That's when I took him.

Cox was big and heavy, but by now I'd perfected the art of tipping them off balance and jumping. Just before I disappeared from the parking lot, I heard the agent holding the door start to yell, the sound cut off in its earliest stages by my transition to Texas, fifty feet above the cold, hard water of the pit.

I jumped to the island to watch him hit.

Water geysered from the surface, drops of spray dotting my coat. He'd tipped forward after I released him and his impact, though feet-first, was followed by his front slapping down, stomach and chest. I heard him grunt as the air was forced out of him.

It took him a few seconds to claw his way back to the surface and even longer to draw breath.

I hoped it hurt.

He didn't seem as shaken up, though, as some of the others who'd made that drop. He sidestroked to the island and actually walked out of the water.

I pointed Barry's gun at him.

"If I'm not heard from fairly soon, things are going to get very unpleasant for your girlfriend."

I turned the gun slightly to the side and fired past him, at the water. The slug skipped off the surface of the water and chipped rock from the cliff face. The noise was deafening, a palpable shock, but I'd seen explosives go off in here. I knew what to expect. Even so, I flinched slightly.

Cox jerked and his eyes narrowed.

"Take off your clothes. Quickly." I moved the gun back in line with his body.

He shook his head. "No, thanks."

I felt frustration etching at my calm expression. I fired the pistol again, this time to the other side.

Again he flinched, but he gritted his teeth and shook his head.

More and more he reminded me of Dad. *Why not. He took away a woman I loved.* I lifted the pistol over my head and jumped, bringing it down on the back of Cox's head from behind, very hard.

He fell forward like a tree.

I took a very sharp knife from my pocket and cut his clothes off. He carried two guns, but what I was looking for was strapped to his thigh, one of the silver tubes with the antenna running all the way down to his sock. It didn't have the barbed point, but it was dangerous for all that.

I jumped forty miles south, to where the Rio Grande cuts through rock between the U.S. and Mexico, and threw the tube into the foaming waters. It barely floated and I could see it bobbing along, headed for Del Rio, via Big Bend National Park.

Back on the little island I finished cutting the rest of Cox's clothes off of him, and jumped them to Central Park in New York City where I left them in a trash can by the Sheep Meadow. The guns I put in the cliff dwelling.

There are enough guns in New York City already.

Back in the pit, I rolled Cox over and checked his pupils, holding his eyelids open. They seemed to be the same size and both reacted to the light. His body was covered with goose bumps but his breathing seemed all right. The sun was shining into the pit and the temperature was in the sixties. Cox was probably better off without his wet clothes on, anyway.

I jumped to K Mart in Stillwater, Oklahoma, bought a sleeping bag, and returned. It zipped all the way open. I spread it on the ground beside Cox, rolled him onto one half, then zipped it back up, around him.

There was a swelling on the back of Cox's head that seeped a slight amount of blood. It reminded me of my mugging, when I'd first got to New York.

Again, I hoped it hurt him, but the mean thought made me feel bad. It made me feel petty. It made me feel like him.

Shit. It made me feel like Dad.

EIGHTEEN

Cox awoke to find the chemical toilet beside him and a sign that said, DON'T POLLUTE THE POND. IT'S YOUR DRINKING WATER. I also left a bottle of ibuprofen and a large glass of water. I watched him from the center of the island, lying on the ground under the mesquite bushes, and peering through the grass. I didn't want to be around him when he woke up.

Then why are you watching?

It reminded me of Sunday mornings at home. Dad would wake up with a hangover and I would walk on eggshells until he got his first two cups of coffee down. But I would hang around the house, because he needed me then. Needed me to fix his coffee, needed me to fix him breakfast. When he was hung over, there wasn't any danger of violence.

That would come later.

Cox was having trouble focusing on the note. He kept moving it closer and farther away. Finally, though, he put it down and took the ibuprofen. He moved very carefully, occasionally twisting his neck to one side, like it was stiff.

I jumped to D.C., to the subway stop at Union Station. I was going to call the NSA and start bargaining for Millie, but when I was dropping the quarter in the phone I saw a man reading a newspaper and waiting for the train. My first thought was that he might be an NSA agent, one of many scattered around the city, but then I saw the headline facing me.

"Shiite Extremists Hijack Cruise Ship." Below was a distant shot of a gleaming white ship. Side by side with that photo was a picture of Rashid Matar.

I jumped to New York and called MMM.

The operator said, "Ah, Mr. Ross, we have a lot of material for you. There's been a hijacking of a ship."

"I just saw a paper. Where?"

"It's off of Alexandria, in Egypt."

I gritted my teeth. I'd never flown into the little airport there. "There was a picture of Rashid Matar in the paper. Is he involved?"

"That is the Reuters report."

"Ah. Any numbers? How many passengers, how many terrorists?"

"At least five terrorists. One hundred and thirty passengers. One hundred and five crew."

"Why so many crew?"

"The *Argos* is a large luxury yacht. The cruise was booked by the Metropolitan Museum of Art, here in New York. It's mostly wealthy benefactors of the museum. Nearly all of them are American. There's one English couple. The crew is Greek."

"How far offshore are they?"

I heard the rustling of paper. "None of these say. The video of the ship was taken by a helicopter, but it didn't show the shore."

"Do you know where the media are? Where they're covering this from?"

"No."

"Okay, thanks."

I jumped to London. I had to change some money before I could use a public call box to dial the Reuters number on Corseau's card. A voice with a British accent said, "Middle East Desk."

I spoke quickly. "I have some urgent information for Jean-Paul Corseau. Do you know where I can reach him?"

"We can pass a message to him."

"This is for his ears only."

"I'm sorry, it's really not our policy to give out our

reporters' whereabouts. If you give me a number, perhaps I can have him call you?"

"No." I paused. "I gave him a lift to Cairo recently. Does that mean anything to you?"

He was quiet for a moment. "That wild story? He was nearly fired. So you're the chap who stops hijackings?"

"Yes."

"Why not come chat with us? We'd love to do a story."

"Jean-Paul Corseau. Now."

"How do I really know you're the one?"

"I'm hanging up. Three . . . two . . . one—"

"Okay, okay. He's staying at the Metropole in Alexandria, but the media is covering the story from Fort Qait Bey on the eastern harbor."

"Thanks."

In Cairo the airport terminal swarmed with men who wanted to change my money at very favorable rates and children who followed me crying, *"Baksheesh! Baksheesh!"* At the information desk I asked when the next commuter flight to El Iskandariya was. The woman said the daily flight had already left but that the train was very comfortable in first class, only six hours from the Cairo railway station near Ramses Square.

From what I'd read, it could take over an hour to get to the train station in bad traffic and, in Cairo, there was no other kind.

A half hour later and three thousand dollars poorer, I was airborne in a Bell helicopter, traveling northwest at four thousand feet. I'd promised the pilot a bonus if we reached the eastern harbor in under an hour.

"That's Heliopolis," he said, pointing to a section just west of the airport and, to me, indistinguishable from the rest of Cairo's sprawl. "We're flying over Heliopolis in my helicopter."

George, the pilot, was Egyptian, but he was proud of his overprecise English. I pushed the talk button on my headset and said, "Heliopolis. Helicopter. Very witty." *Idiot.* I wasn't feeling very jolly.

While they'd fueled the helicopter George told me his usual passengers were oil executives heading east to the Sinai or very rich tourists who wanted to see Giza without risking Cairo's traffic.

The helicopter swung west and George said, "Abu Rawash." He pointed down on his side of the helicopter. I found it on the map spread across my knees. He was pointing at a pyramid, but I couldn't see it from my side.

"Why so far west?"

He pointed again, this time straight ahead at a thin dark line that stretched across desert. "We follow the pipeline. Direct route, very fast."

I looked down at the map again. The SUMED pipeline ran from the Gulf of Suez at Ain Sukhna to the Mediterranean just west of Alexandria, bringing Arab oil from the Gulf countries to Western markets. Egypt had very little oil of its own, but at least it could make some revenue from its transfer, both through the pipeline and through the Suez Canal.

Off to the east of our route, where the Nile Delta gave way to the desert, I could see vegetation that was startlingly greener than the brown scrub below, a visible line that said, "The water stops here." I tracked our progress by the secondary roads we crossed. Shortly after crossing Secondary Road 7 the desert turned to dunes and we headed due north, splitting away from the pipeline. Again we approached the edge of the Delta. On the horizon I began to see the ocean.

Alexandria grew, a long strip of city along the sea. It was backed by Lake Maryut so it almost looked an island from our approach; then we were cutting across a thin strip of land and running northeast, along the shore over petroleum docks, over the western harbor. Commercial traffic and ancient dhows spotted the inner harbor with cruise ships anchored or docked.

All of the cruise ships were too big to be the *Argos*.

Then we pulled over an even thinner strip of land and passed over an ancient, weathered fort.

"El Atta," said George.

Only a little farther up the shore, on a small finger of land that protected the eastern harbor, another fort challenged the sea.

"Qait Bey." George pointed, checking his watch. I looked at mine. Fifty-seven minutes since we'd lifted off in Cairo.

"Good job," I told him, and he smiled.

He landed 250 yards from Qait Bey, at the helicopter landing pad at the Institute of Oceanography and Fisheries. I dug his bonus out of my bag, five hundred dollars, and gave it to him. Then I hit the talk button and said, "Another five hundred for one short flight."

"How long? I will need to refuel if it is very long."

"Less than fifteen minutes. Twenty at the most."

He nodded. "When? I cannot block their landing pad for very long."

I looked around the landing pad, acquiring it as a jump site. "Ten minutes."

The street was called Qasr Ras El Tin on the inset map I'd studied in the helicopter, but the street sign was in Arabic so I didn't know for sure. There was an English sign for the fort. The porter wouldn't take my admission fee in U.S. currency, so I jumped past him.

The press were easy to find, on the parapet, looking out to sea with binoculars and telephoto lenses. In the distance, a white ship with a blue smokestack was anchored a mile offshore.

Corseau, the Reuters reporter, was talking to an Egyptian Army officer. I waved at him and he broke off his conversation immediately and walked over to me, taking me by the elbow and leading me down the stairs away from the rest of the reporters.

"I talked to my office an hour ago. What took you so long to get here?"

I thought about telling him the truth, that I couldn't jump someplace I hadn't been. I didn't want them to know my limits, though.

"Held up in traffic," I said. "Astral plane all fucked up." We were winding down a small staircase, hidden from view.

I stopped him and said, "I'm going out there, but I need as much information as I can get. Hold still."

I moved behind him and he said, "Wait—"

I jumped us to the helipad.

"—a minute!" I released him and he spun around, then steadied when he realized that he'd only come about a quarter of a mile. He exhaled a deep breath. I motioned him into the backseat of the helicopter. He took a headset hanging above his seat and put it on. His eyes were large, but he'd obviously been in helicopters before, reaching for the straps and buckling himself in.

I climbed in and pointed my thumb at the sky. By the time I'd my headset on and was buckled in, George had the blades up to speed and lifted off the pad.

When we could see the ocean I pointed at the distant yacht. "A big circle, around that boat, a couple of hundred feet above the water. Don't get too close."

George nodded.

"Can you hear me, Jean-Paul?" I looked over my shoulder.

He thumbed the switch. "Yes."

"Tell me about it."

"Only if I get a real interview out of it this time."

"All right." I didn't hesitate. I wanted Matar very badly.

Corseau looked surprised, then spoke. "Yesterday afternoon they let a heart-attack victim and his wife off the ship. She confirmed that there were at least five terrorists on board. From pictures she identified the leader as Rashid Matar. They're armed with machine guns, pistols, and grenades. They also claim that they've mined the fuel tanks with plastic explosive which can be detonated at second's notice by radio control."

George reached the *Argos* and began his circle, clockwise so my side faced the ship. I used the binoculars as I listened to Corseau.

The ship was a little over a hundred yards long and about fifty feet wide. There was a bridge deck forward of the smokestack, a cabin deck with a pool at the back, and below that a level with a large sunbathing deck at the back.

There was a large radio and instrument mast sticking up from the back of the bridge deck. A line hung with miniature flags ran from the tip of the mast forward to the bow and backward to a spar that stuck up just forward of the swimming pool's yellow and brown striped awning. The way they flapped briskly in the wind reminded me of a used-car lot.

Two men with machine guns stood on the roof of the bridge deck. They were looking our way.

George looked at me, surprise on his face. "I am receiving radio direction from army authorities to clear away from the ship."

I chose a jump site, behind the smokestack, among large white ventilators. The two terrorists atop the bridge were staring at the helicopter. One of them lifted his gun and I saw the end of the barrel blink repeatedly, like he were taking flash pictures.

"Get out of here!" I kept the binoculars on the jump site, working for it, worried I wasn't close enough. The helicopter dipped and spun wildly and I was afraid we'd been hit, but it was George taking evasive maneuvers. "Back to the Oceanography Institute." I loosened the safety harness, pulled more money out of my little bag and clipped it to the preflight checklist clipboard. "There's your fee, George." I looked over my shoulder at Corseau. "Later, Jean-Paul."

I jumped.

The deck vibrated slightly and I knew that if not engines, then at least generators were running. The flags on the line above me cracked in the wind. Off in the distance the sound of a helicopter in flight was fading. Other than that I heard nothing—no gunshots, voices, cries, or whispers. I might be alone on the broad ocean.

I wondered if Cox's head had stopped hurting yet.

Using the dentist's mirror I peered around the smokestack. I could only see one of the terrorists atop the bridge. Every so often, though, he lifted a radio to his lips and spoke, the sound lost in the wind.

I wondered if he could set off the radio-controlled explosions. Or if any of them could.

At the back of the bridge deck, on the other side of the smokestack, there was a door. I jumped there, just beside it. A slight overhang prevented discovery from above. I used the mirror to peer through the entrance. A narrow, door-lined central passage led forward to the bridge itself. Nobody was in sight.

I eased my way in, checking out the open doorways with the mirror. I'd almost reached the radio room, near the bridge itself, when I heard a chair creak and a footstep scuff the floor. I jumped back to the outside, by the rear door of the deckhouse. Footsteps sounded in the hall and receded. I used the mirror carefully, in time to see a man at the other end of the passage step into the bridge and turn right.

I jumped back to the passageway just outside the radio room. The mirror showed an empty room, shelves of impressive equipment. I eased forward, past the captain's cabin, then looked into the bridge itself. Nobody. The wheel stood motionless—radar, loran, chart table unattended. A narrow stairway descended to the next deck on both sides of the bridge. Overhead I heard one of the men on the roof walking back and forth with slightly dragging footsteps.

The man from the radio room had gone right—starboard, I corrected myself—so I went down the port side very slowly, very carefully.

The stairways opened on the next deck, on the outside. I eased the port door open and walked very close to the walls, shielding myself from the two men above. This was easier said than done, because deck chairs lined the wall and I had to either step carefully over or squeeze around them. The lifeboats were on this deck, hung on davits over the railings.

A door led into an air-conditioned central compartment, large stairwell in the middle, narrow corridor running aft lined with stateroom doors. Immediately to my left on entering the interior was a door labeled CASTOR GALLERY. There were no sounds from this deck but I thought I heard something from the stairwell so I eased down it.

Fortunately, it was thickly carpeted.

At the bottom, another narrow hallway ran aft down the center of the boat. On the port side of the boat was a glass door labeled COFFEE LOUNGE. On the starboard side was a hallway leading forward, from which the noise seemed to be coming. I peered carefully around a mahogany-trimmed corner. About seventy feet forward, where the hallway opened onto a larger space, a man stood, his back to me, machine gun held at the ready. Beyond him I saw people crowded together, sitting on the furniture or the floor.

The doorway framed only a small segment of that space but there were *a lot* of people visible.

I pulled back and went into the coffee lounge on the other side of the stairway. It was deserted, a light, cheerful narrow room decorated as a café. Another glass door at the far end was labeled BAR. It also was deserted, but that door was locked. I jumped to the other side. This room was pure men's club, dark wood paneling and leather-upholstered chairs. The bottles behind the bar were all secured with little leather loops, for rough weather. A glass door at the far end was curtained.

A sign beside the door indicated that beyond it was the Golden Fleece Main Lounge. I pushed the curtain ever so slightly to one side. I was willing to lay bets that all 225 passengers and crew were crowded into that space.

The passengers were dressed formally, though rumpled. Most of the men's ties were dangling or off. Several women looked like they'd spent far too much time in girdles. Others wore men's jackets over their shoulders and leaned together. Nobody was talking.

The crew clustered together, officers and deckhands in whites, waiters and waitresses in dark uniforms, maids with aprons, cooks in more white, one with a chef's hat in his hand, barely recognizable from two days of twisting.

The captain, a white-haired man whose tanned legs were hard and muscled under his uniform shorts, sat in a chair, surrounded by his officers seated on the floor. They sat in front of the other hostages as if they could shield them from harm. The captain's face was impassive, but his hands kept turning his hat around and around and around.

The lady who'd been released the day before was wrong. There were five terrorists in the lounge, three of them holding machine guns on the crowd, and the other two in conference. That meant there were at least seven in all.

More and more, I doubted the existence of other teleports. Cox's reactions and my research seemed to point that way. Still, I sure could use a few more teleports about then.

I assumed that one of the terrorists talking was the man I'd followed from the radio room. The other was Rashid Matar.

I stared at him, eyes narrowed. My immediate, almost overpowering impulse was to jump him to just outside of my cliff dwelling, an area with nothing under it but two hundred feet of air. Well, after that, there was some rock and cactus, but the first two hundred feet . . .

Seven terrorists. My stomach hurt and I could taste bile at the back of my throat.

The man who'd been watching the radio room finished talking with Matar and left. Matar turned and I saw that he had a radio in a leather holster, like the man on the bridge roof, but that a smaller radio hung from his neck on a lanyard, black plastic with a red button on its face.

I looked at the other terrorists, to see if they had one of these. They carried Uzis and four grenades apiece, clipped to the leather harness that supported their gun belts. Extra clips of ammo hung from the backs of the belts in leather cases. While they also had the holstered radios, they didn't seem to have the bomb transmitter.

It was too much to hope that they were bluffing about the bomb. Rashid had already demonstrated his proficiency with radio-detonated explosives.

I jumped back to the coffee shop by the main stairwell and peeked through the door. The stairway was empty. One deck down was the purser's office and reception. There was a map of the ship laminated to the reception desk and I studied it carefully.

Where I stood, at reception, was on the Dionysos Deck, one of four decks with cabins. The deck above, where the passengers were being held, was called the Venus Deck. The deck with the swimming pool was called the Apollo Deck. One flight down was the Poseidon Deck, and it had less than half the cabins of the other decks, since that was the level of the engine room.

I went down, carefully, but the next deck also seemed deserted. There was a door at the bottom, behind the stairs. It said SHIP'S PERSONNEL ONLY. There was a glass porthole in the middle of it. I didn't even try to open it. I just studied the white-painted passage beyond, and jumped into it.

The background hum that I'd felt above was audible in here, the distant sound of a diesel engine. I walked faster, confident that the noise would cover my passage. I passed through another door and found myself in the engine room, on a catwalk that ran between two huge diesel engines, each taller than I was. They were still, but at the front of the compartment, the diesel generators I'd suspected ran steadily, providing power for the air-conditioning.

The chief engineer's office was forward of the engine room, a small cubbyhole filled with books and rolled-up plans. I pawed through the drawings, scattering them like autumn leaves, until I found the one that showed the diesel tanks. There were two of them, starboard and port, double-reinforced bulkheads forward of the engine compartment.

According to the plans, the tanks fronted on the outside walls of several compartments of the Poseidon Deck, including the chief engineer's office. It was the work of a moment, though, to determine that the explosives were not in there, and I worked my way forward, blueprint in hand, examining all the possible rooms.

I didn't find them. So I went upstairs at the front of the boat, still in the crew area, and found myself in the galley. According to the plans, the tops of the tank butted on the floor of the galley on the starboard side, as well as the floor of the passengers' dining room on both sides of the ship. There were no explosives in the galley.

I moved carefully into the dining room. It was directly below the Golden Fleece Lounge, where all the hostages were, and an open stairway at the forward end of the room led up to there.

There were no explosives in the dining room either.

Could it mean that Matar had been bluffing? That there were no explosives rigged to detonate the fuel?

Another possibility occurred to me. What if they'd sealed the explosives, somehow, and lowered them into one of the tanks through the fueling spigots? According to the plans, those pipes were fourteen centimeters inside diameter, almost seven inches.

Somebody was crying upstairs, and someone else began shouting. I moved back into the galley to think.

It seemed unlikely that Matar would have put the bombs inside the tanks. The double steel bulkhead would have interfered with radio transmission. It also seemed unlikely that he would have bluffed about the bomb.

I looked around. A cooking range with sixteen burners stretched down one wall of the galley, large stainless-steel pots standing. Walk-in refrigerators and freezers lined the far wall. A bank of ovens covered yet another.

Cooking range?

I flipped one of the knobs. Bight blue flames erupted from the burner. Cooking gas! Much more explosive than diesel fuel and probably closer to the hostages. I thought about trying to trace the gas lines, but instead jumped back to the chief engineer's office and searched through more drawings.

The cooking gas was kept in a large cylindrical tank behind the galley in a separately ventilated room. I jumped back to the galley and found a door leading forward. The first door on the right, a gasketed sea door with steel dogs, was labeled PROPANE GAS STORAGE—NO SMOKING.

Two massive lengths of chain secured the door, running to large security padlocks that still had the price stickers affixed. There was no inset window or bull's-eye and no way I could get past the door.

For one long desperate minute I considered going after one of the NSA guns, the real ones, not the tranquilizers, and just shooting Matar, grabbing the detonator, and jumping away.

Stupid, the idea is to avoid killing anybody, especially hostages.

Even Matar?

I looked at the plans again. There was no other way to get into the room. The ventilators were lengths of pipe, twisting, not even providing a view within.

Time to get rid of the detonator, then.

I jumped back to the closed and shrouded bar and peeked past the curtains again. One of the terrorists was taking passengers to the bathroom in relays of four. Rashid was pacing back and forth, occasionally lifting his holstered radio to speak. The detonator swung back and forth on his neck lanyard.

I jumped back to the central hall on the Apollo Deck and went back through the central passageway to the pool. There was another bar, poolside. Shielded from the terrorists on the bridge roof by the bar awning, I looked over the side. From this deck there was a drop of about thirty feet to the water below. It wasn't my pit, but it would do. I studied the railing carefully, then jumped back to the bar.

The next group of passengers went up the hallway with their guard. This left two men standing at the corners of the lounge, machine guns covering the group, and Matar pacing up and down between them.

I took a deep breath and hoped, very strongly, that Matar had the only detonator for the bomb by the propane tank.

Matar didn't have time to scream, didn't have time to even reach for the detonator. He was dropping from fifty feet up into the pit in Texas and I was back in the lounge, grabbing the terrorist next to the hallway and dropping him off the port side of Apollo Deck.

He pulled the trigger on his machine gun all the way down, until he hit the water. I was back, hidden behind the curtain in the bar, then, and I heard the distant stutter stop.

The remaining terrorist in the lounge was screaming at the passengers to get down. He was looking around wildly, trying to see in all directions at once; then, like a snake, he darted forward and dragged the captain from his chair and backed against the wall. He let his machine gun swing on its shoulder strap and pulled the pistol from his holster and placed it against the back of the captain's head, the other arm around the captain's throat.

Oh, God, don't. . . .

I was afraid he might kill him out of hand, but he didn't. He just stood there, back protected by the wall, pistol ready to splatter the captain's brains all over the lounge.

I jumped to the passageway on the bridge deck. The man on radio watch was charging away from me, forward, toward the bridge, his machine gun at the ready. I jumped forward, to the bridge, and tripped him as he came through the door. His gun went off as he fell, exploding the glass windshield outward. He fell toward the wheel and I kicked him in the stomach as he tried to catch himself. His head slammed into the post. I bent to pick him up, to drop him off the rear of the ship, and bullets tore the air over my head.

I jumped back to the rear of the ship without the wounded terrorist. That destination was already in my head. I heard shouting from the bridge deck and peeked around the awning. One of the terrorists was still on top of the bridge, but another stood on the deck below, just outside the bridge. He must have been the one who shot at me.

I jumped and an instant later he splashed into the water off the rear of the ship, followed in seconds by the terrorist on the bridge roof.

Back in the main lounge, the terrorist with the bathroom party had returned, driving them in front of him with kicks and occasional shots of his gun into the ceiling. I shivered. The situation looked very unstable. I wondered if they'd start killing passengers or settle down if I left them alone for a moment or two.

I jumped back to the bridge. The terrorist I'd tripped was getting slowly to his feet, one hand to his forehead where a scalp wound dripped red. I dropped him into the sea. He was still groggy so I opened a labeled locker and threw half a dozen life jackets over the side, then jumped back to the bar to see how things were going in the main lounge.

JUMPER 321

All the hostages were on the floor, some facedown, covering their heads, some trying to hide behind tables and chairs. Both terrorists had a hostage apiece in front of them, sitting on chairs. The captain was one of them, and an elderly woman looking incredibly out of place in a mink stole sat in the other chair. Each of them had a pistol pressed against the back of their neck, bowing their head forward as if they were praying.

Perhaps they were.

If only one of them had a gun pressed to their head, I might be able to do something.

I jumped to the dining room on the deck below and started up the stairs, walking deliberately, slowly. In my hand was my iron rod, gripped so it ran up the inside of my arm, out of sight. There was a very strong desire to take all my fear and rage out on Matar, back in Texas, leaving the remaining hostages to survive or die.

Get a grip.

I walked into the lounge, stepping over cowering passengers as if they were branches strewn across the ground. When the terrorists saw me, they must have thought I was one of the passengers.

"Get down!" the one on my right screamed. I kept walking forward, toward the middle of the ship, halfway between them.

"Get down I said!"

I could see the sweat on his face and the sweat on the captain's high forehead, captive and captor, linked in fear. I watched both terrorists carefully, my moves preprogrammed, awaiting only the right movement.

The other terrorist broke first, jerked his gun from the woman's head and pointed it at me. I jumped and the rod came down and across the barrel of the *other* terrorist's gun, smashing it away from the captain. It went off by the captain's ear and I swung the rod up, backhanded into the terrorist's face, then jumped again, to smash the gun of the other terrorist as it moved back to the woman's neck. He yelled and leaped for me. I let him grapple, then jumped to the rear of the ship, thirty feet above the waves, to let him wrestle with the water.

Back in the cabin, the captain had a gun in his hand and the terrorist flat on the floor. He was removing the grenades from the terrorist's harness. He looked up at me and smiled warily. Then someone screamed.

On the port side of the lounge, a woman in a maid's uniform lay on the floor, one hand outstretched. The carpet was red under her. I jumped to her side. *Oh, god, oh, god, oh, god.* She'd been hit in the chest by the bullet intended for the captain. I couldn't feel a pulse. *No!*

People pressed forward. "Get back!" I screamed. I hardly recognized my voice. I stooped and picked her up as gently as I could, then jumped to the Adams Cowley Shock Trauma Center in Baltimore.

They worked on her for two hours, but she didn't make it.

PART 7:

OLLY, OLLY, IN COME FREE

NINETEEN

"Next time, let me pack a bag so I can stay longer."

Perston-Smythe sounded only mildly peeved, almost philosophical about it. Out of curiosity I asked, "How did you get out of Turkey?"

"They flew me out in a U.S. Air Force jet—no passport control." His voice became a little grimmer. "What did you do with Cox?"

I turned around and scanned the approaches to the phone booth. "Cox is fine. Return Millie Harrison."

"What makes you think the NSA has her?"

"I don't have time for this bullshit! Cox *admitted* he had her. Tell Cox's boss that if he doesn't let her go, I'll start giving little trips to every NSA employee I can get my hands on. Expensive. If that doesn't work, I'll start on presidential staff."

"But—"

I hung up the phone and jumped to the cliff overlooking the pit in Texas.

Seated on the beach of the little island, Matar and Cox faced each other, several feet apart. Matar sat in his underwear, his pants and shirt spread on mesquite bushes, drying. Cox, still naked, sat on the corner of the sleeping bag, the rest of it wrapped around him. He had Matar's pistol and two of Matar's grenades. Matar had a split lip and a black eye.

I appeared directly behind Cox and pressed the cold,

325

hard end of my steel rod into his neck. The position was like that of the two terrorists from the *Argos* with their hostages seated before them. Cox stiffened and I said, "Hand me the gun."

He reversed it and passed it over his left shoulder. I put it in my coat pocket. "Now the grenades." When both of them were in the other coat pocket I jumped away, to the cliff dwelling, and added the gun and grenades to the growing arsenal on the table.

For a moment I stared at them, the plastic gun of the Basque terrorist, Cox's tranquilizer pistol, and the almost ubiquitous nine-millimeter automatics of the others.

I picked up one of the nine-millimeters in my right hand and one of the grenades in my left. Little bang and big bang. The maid on the *Argos* died of a nine-millimeter bullet passing through her aorta and semilunar heart valves. The grenade reminded me of Mom's death, but, for some reason, it reminded me even more of the human bomb. I guess the two days cleaning up his body left their mark.

Why do people make these things?

I shuddered and put the weapons back on the table.

"It is our policy not to negotiate with terrorists."

I stared at the phone, my eyes wide. I was speechless and very, very angry.

"Are you still there?" The voice belonged to an unnamed official in the NSA. Perston-Smythe introduced him as one of Cox's supervisors.

"What the fuck do you mean by that?"

"It is the policy of this government not to negotiate with terrorists."

"Do you mean to tell me that you consider me a terrorist?"

He sounded almost prim. "Certainly. You've taken a hostage."

"Terrorists," I said, gritting my teeth, "attack the innocent to achieve their goals. If you're about to tell me that you consider Cox an innocent bystander, then this conversation is over."

"Terrorists are—"

"Oh, fuck it! You want a terrorist action so you can consider me a terrorist? There's no way you can keep me out of your nuclear arsenals. Where do you want the first one to go off? The Pentagon? The White House? The Capitol building? How about Moscow or Kiev? Wouldn't *that* be interesting? Do you think they'd launch?"

His voice was a lot less prim. "You wouldn't do that."

"Well, as a matter of fact, I wouldn't. *BECAUSE I'M NOT A TERRORIST!"* I slammed the phone down on the hook and jumped.

Matar had a fist-sized rock in his hand when I jumped back. He was crouching on a grassy piece of shore, watching Cox carefully. Cox sat on his sleeping bag several yards away, apparently ignoring Matar, but his back wasn't turned.

"Food."

At my appearance, Matar shrunk back. Cox yawned pointedly but looked interested when he saw the bucket of chicken. I set it down and walked away, up the island away from them. Cox reached the chicken, piled several pieces on the lid of the tub,—and withdrew to his sleeping bag. Then Matar came up, examined the bucket, and took it back to his grassy spot.

He turned his head toward me and said, "The Colonel's original recipe is better."

I was surprised. His English was colloquial, American-accented. It disturbed me because it made him more human and violated the image I'd been carrying in my head. The monster that killed my mother shouldn't talk like a human. I remembered Perston-Smythe's lecture about preconceptions and prejudice. *Christ, Davy, are only Americans human?*

Cox finished his second piece of chicken. "How long are you going to keep me here?"

His question reminded me of his boss's comments and I regained some of my anger. "As long as necessary. If you'd like to tell me where they're holding Ms. Harrison, I might be able to speed things up."

He shrugged. "To tell you the truth, I've no idea. Some safe house. I don't even know the phone number—my secretary connected me when I needed to talk to them."

I stared at him, my face blank. I wondered if he was telling the truth. "How's your head?"

He winced. "It's okay. I could use some coffee, though."

I looked back at Matar. He sat cross-legged on the grass. His narrow face made his dark eyes seem bigger than they were. I looked back at Cox. "Does he know why he's here?"

Cox shook his head. "He doesn't want to talk to me. When he came ashore we had a little argument about his weapons."

Matar looked at Cox, then spat on the ground.

"Do you want coffee?" I asked him.

After a moment Matar nodded slowly. "With sugar and cream."

I raised my eyebrows at Cox and he said, "Black, please." I think the "please" was automatic. I turned back to Matar and said, "My mother was Mary Niles."

Matar frowned, like the name was familiar, but he couldn't place it.

"You murdered her in Cyprus. You blew her to pieces on the runway with a remotely detonated bomb." *And you don't even remember her name.*

I jumped to a New York deli and bought two large coffees in Styrofoam cups. There were no other customers and I paid with shaking hands, walked outside, and jumped back to the pit in less than two minutes.

Once again, Matar flinched when I appeared. His expression had changed—his eyes were a little wider and his mouth slightly open.

I jumped and appeared immediately in front of him. He fell back and started scrambling away from me. I set his coffee on the ground, then jumped close to Cox, handing him his coffee.

Cox jerked, but covered well. I jumped to the cliff dwelling, picked up a chair and jumped back to the island about twenty feet away from both of them. I sat down, one leg crossed over the other, and stared at them.

Matar slowly approached the coffee and picked it up carefully, like it might bite him. He removed the lid and sniffed.

"It's not poisoned," I said.

"What are you? You conjure things from nowhere."

"Perhaps I'm an afrit, a genie. Perhaps I'm an angel."

Cox watched this exchange with interest.

"Perhaps you are *Shaitan*," said Matar.

I raised my eyebrows and Cox obligingly said, "Satan."

I smiled a smile that didn't touch my eyes. The blood drained from Matar's face. "Perhaps," I said. "Welcome to hell."

"Are you ready to release Millie Harrison?"

"We don't negotiate with terrorists."

"I'm not a terrorist." I said it tiredly. "Besides, that's bullshit. The U.S. has *always* negotiated with terrorists, no matter what it's said. Why do you think we sold arms to Iran?"

"Release Brian Cox. We'll think about it."

"Millie Harrison is being illegally held. Brian Cox kidnapped her. Who is the terrorist? Who is attacking the innocent? Release her and I'll give you back Cox."

I hung up.

I brought firewood down to the island in the pit, matches, and newspaper. The wood was desert scrub, dry as parchment, and burned brightly. Matar and Cox moved close to the heat. With the sun down it was cold in the pit. I fetched my chair and sat, the three of us forming the points of an equilateral triangle. Sparks rode the smoke straight up in the still air, fading among cold pinpoints of starlight.

"Where are you really from?" Cox asked.

"Stanville. Ohio. United States of America. North American Continent. Earth. Sol System. Milky Way Galaxy." I added the last three to leave him wondering. *Are there more of me, Cox?*

He narrowed his eyes and stared at me. I shrugged and went back to looking at Matar, hunched close to the fire, his eyes darting back and forth between Cox and myself.

Finally I said, "Why? Why did you kill her?"

Matar straightened. "Why? Why does your government support Israeli fascism in Lebanon? Why did your country overthrow the democratic government of Iran to put the Shah back in power? Why do your oil companies rob our countries of their wealth and power. Why does the west profane our religion, spit on our beliefs and holy places."

My stomach hurt. "Did my mother do any of those things? I know why you're angry with my government. Why don't you attack them instead of helpless women and children? Is this honorable? Is this something Mohammed would have wanted?"

He spat into the fire. "You know nothing of honor! Your government has no honor. You are godless tools of Satan. Your mother died for a just cause. She wasn't a victim—she was a martyr. You should be proud."

I hit him in the face, jumping close and punching upward from a crouched position. My hand glanced off his cheekbone and he went over backward. I felt a sharp pain from my knuckles, then jumped again to avoid his foot as he kicked out at me. He scrambled to his feet and I drew back my arm and jumped, appearing behind him. I struck him in the lower back over his kidney. He twisted away, clutching at his side. He swung at me with his left hand and I jumped again, slapping his face with my open hand, hard as I could. Then again from another angle, rocking his head back. He covered his face with both hands and I kicked him in the groin.

He dropped to the ground and I kicked him again and again. He rolled away in a ball, covering his head, trying to cover his front with his elbows, protecting his groin with his knees. "You should be proud!" I screamed at him. "You're a martyr to the cause." I chased him, not bothering to jump, just step, kick, step, kick, until he splashed into the cold, cold water of the shallows.

Oh, Christ. What am I doing? I'm worse than Dad.

I was sobbing, tears running down my face, my arms shaking. I turned. Cox was standing by the fire, his mouth open, staring. I jumped away, to the cliff dwelling, out of sight, hiding my shame.

Wrapped in blankets that smelled faintly of Millie, I curled up on the bed. My father's face kept intruding, warped in anger. Suddenly, I sat up in bed, a stray thought stabbing deep into my core and resonating with perfect truth.

The men in the pit wre responsible for taking away the women I loved. Cox took Millie. Rashid took Mom. But then, so did Dad. . . .

His house was still empty, locked. Not even NSA. Maybe they were doing everything remotely, afraid I'd jump more agents to the Middle East. I jumped to the downtown sidewalk and found him at the end of the bar in Gil's. Through the large plate-glass window, I saw that he had a glass of amber-colored liquid in front of him and he was staring at it like it was a snake, his hands spread to either side of it, flat on the bar's surface. At one point he started to pick it up, but he jerked his hand away from it, like it was hot.

He didn't drink from the glass until he saw me walk in the door; then his eyes opened wide and he slugged it down quickly, like I might take it away from him.

"What are you doing here?" His voice was half angry, half scared. He shrank back away from me on the barstool even though I stopped halfway down the narrow room.

My hands hurt when I flexed them in my coat pockets. The knuckles of my right hand throbbed and I thought they were swelling. The pain reminded me of Matar's face as I hit it again and again. I wanted to do the same to this man.

"What do you want?" This time fear predominated, desperation rattling the voice. He was louder than before and the bartender glanced his way.

I jumped, grabbed him from behind, and released him to sprawl forward onto the sand in the pit, his face a few feet from the fire. He scrambled back away from the light and stood.

Matar was on the far side of the fire, shivering, his hands

held up suddenly, to protect himself. His wet clothes were steaming. Cox was farther back, sitting up, wrapped in his sleeping bag in the chair I'd left there.

Dad looked back and forth, bewildered. Not angry, not scared, but bewildered. This made me even angrier.

I jumped and hit him, an uppercut with my damaged knuckles that snapped his mouth shut with a click. He fell over backward and I jumped back to the fire, clutching my sore hand to my chest. Matar scrambled away from the circle of light, into the darkness.

"Is it my turn, next?"

"Huh?"

Cox sat up in the chair. "I said, is it my turn now? As long as you're in the business. Should I stand up?" He made as if to stand.

"Shut up. Sit down."

He settled back. "That's your father, isn't it?"

I glared at Cox.

Dad was sitting up, both hands on his jaw, moaning. I wanted to hit him again, even more than I wanted to keep punishing Matar.

Cox spoke again. "You've taken your time in striking back at your father. Why didn't you just kill him before? With that trick of yours, you could have made it look like suicide or at least provided a decent alibi. I mean . . . *look out!*"

There was a rustle on the sand and I jumped sideways five feet. Matar moved through the space I'd occupied, his fist-sized rock swinging down, sharp edge forward. With my evasion, he had to skip awkwardly over the fire. He turned to face me, teeth bared.

"Throw it in the water," I said.

He blinked. I raised my left hand as if to slap, even though I was ten feet away from him. He turned quickly and threw the rock underhand, away, to splash out in the darkness. I put my hand down.

"That is my father," I said, pointing. To Dad, who was glaring now, honest hatred, not bewilderment, I said, "This is Rashid Matar, the man that killed Mother."

They looked at each other, wary, curious. Dad said, "Why is he still alive?"

I stared at the fire. The flames reminded me of the blast on the Cyprus runway. "Why are *you* still alive? If you want him dead, do it yourself."

Cox stood, holding the sleeping bag around himself like an Indian. I jumped behind him and said, "Hold still." I put my arms around his waist and lifted him. He stiffened but made no move to strike. I jumped him to the parking lot of the Pierce Building in Washington, the spot where I'd grabbed him, the night before. It was snowing. The guard in the doorway's glass cage saw us and pushed a button. Somewhere an alarm bell rang.

Cox turned around and looked at me, dancing from foot to foot on the icy pavement, surprised as he recognized the building.

"Are there any more of me, Cox?" I had to ask, I had to know.

He looked surprised, then thoughtful. I'd given him some information he didn't have. Now it was time to see if he'd reciprocate. Finally he said, "No. Not that we know of."

Alone. Forever alone. My shoulders slumped and my throat tightened.

"If Millie is released unharmed, I'll stop jumping NSA people all over the globe. I'll leave you guys completely alone. If she isn't released . . ." I started to say more, but stopped. "Just release her. She never did anything to you."

He licked his lips and started to shiver. Men began to pour through the building's door.

I jumped.

They would never leave me alone.

I sat on the floor of my cliff dwelling, feeding the wood stove, a blanket wrapped around me.

It didn't matter what I did to Dad, to Rashid Matar. It wouldn't bring Mom back. She was gone, dead, worm food, just like the little Greek maid from the *Argos*. Just like the skinny Arab wired to explode. She wasn't coming back.

And would the NSA ever stop trying to use me, capture

me, or, failing that, kill me? Would Millie ever be safe? Would we ever have a chance to be happy?

I slammed the stove door and sparks flew upward, landing on the stone floor, burning minute holes in the blanket. I batted at them absently, then stood, letting the blanket slide to the floor. I jumped to the pit.

Matar was choking Dad, straddling him at the edge of the water, his hands locked around Dad's throat. Dad's hands pulled feebly at Matar's wrists. His face was dark in the firelight.

I jumped forward and kicked Matar in his unprotected ribs. He flew off Dad, into the water yet again, and clutched at his side. I think I cracked some ribs.

Dad started breathing again, deep, wheezing breaths. I grabbed him by his jacket collar and pulled him away from the water, up near the fire. Matar crawled slowly out of the water, still holding his side. He was breathing very carefully, short, shallow breaths of air.

Why did I stop him?

I considered jumping back to the cliff dwelling and getting one of the grenades, coming back, and pulling the pin. I didn't know whether I would jump away before it exploded. I didn't know whether I wanted to.

Matar's breathing regularized and he began speaking in Arabic and spitting at the ground between us. I realized that I couldn't do the grenade thing. If I killed myself and the NSA didn't know it, they might hold onto Millie forever.

Is it normal for women to enter your life and then leave forever? Oh, Millie. . . .

I jumped behind Rashid and grabbed him at the collar and waist, keeping his wet clothes at arm's length. He lashed back with one of his shoes, scraping my shin. I jumped.

We appeared outside the observation deck of the World Trade Center. Twenty feet outside, well clear of the steel and glass sides, one hundred and ten stories up. The air was crisp and cold and we dropped toward the plaza below like rocks.

Matar screamed and I pushed him away from me, letting

him flail and twist below me. The air filled my coat, flapping it like laundry on a line, slowing me slightly, increasing the distance between myself and Matar. In nine seconds we would impact the concrete below, a quick death. Slightly behind him, I'd be able to watch Matar die before kissing the pavement.

The NSA would identify the bodies and they'd let Millie go. Matar would never kill another innocent and I could stop hurting.

After two seconds the air sounded like a hurricane, tugging, numbing. After four seconds it was a steady upward pressure flattening my posture to face down. Matar was thirty feet below me and I was sliding sideways, my coat like a sail. I trailed my arms behind me, and the coat slid off as if jerked by an enormous hand. I fell quicker, closing on Matar again. The lighted fountain in the plaza grew closer and closer.

Matar kept screaming, a keening cry barely audible over the rush of the wind. The sound made me smile.

Fuck this.

I jumped the distance between us, grabbed onto his belt, and jumped back to the pit. Matar sprawled in the sand and kept screaming and screaming.

Dad was sitting by the fire. His eyes were on Rashid. "What did you—" He swallowed. His voice was raspy. "What did you do to him?"

"Sightseeing. Your turn."

He shivered. "No, that's all right."

I jumped behind him and hauled him up by the back of his shirt. He scrambled to get his feet under him. "What—" I jumped him to the cemetery in Pine Bluffs, Florida, then shoved him down again, to sprawl forward. It was after midnight but a mercury vapor light mounted over the cemetery gate brought the carved letters into sharp relief: Mary Niles, 13 March 1945 to 17 November 1989.

Dad whimpered. I reached down and pushed him flat onto the grave. With the other hand I snaked his belt out of his pants loops, then backed away.

"Remember this, Dad?" I swung the buckle back and

forth like a pendulum, the silver rodeo buckle winking in the light. I swung it suddenly back, over my head, and down. It slammed into the ground by his side and grass flew up. He flinched away.

"How many times, Dad?" I brought it down on the other side. It gouged the earth. "How many times?"

I took a step closer and smashed it again and again on the gravestone. The enameled design cracked and splintered, and the silver edges buckled. Scratches marred the stone surface. I threw the belt down in his lap.

I pointed at the grave. "Would she be here if you hadn't beaten her? Abused her? Caved her face in? Would she be in this grave if you'd stopped drinking?"

He flinched more from my voice than he had from the belt. "What kind of man are you? What sort of *creature?* What pitiful excuse for a human being?"

I took a step toward him and he started crying.

What?

"I'm sorry. I'm sorry. I'm sorry. I never meant it. I . . . I didn't want to hurt her. I didn't want to hurt you." Tears were streaming down his face.

It made me want to puke.

What do you want from him?

"Stop it! Stop it!"

He flinched again and fell silent.

"Get up."

He got slowly to his feet, one hand to his pants. The belt with its battered buckle stayed on the grave.

"Turn around."

He did and I jumped him to the parking lot of the Red Pines Substance Abuse Treatment Center in Stanville. I let him go and he turned.

"You know where we are?"

He swallowed. "Yeah."

"Well?"

"I can't! I lost my job. I don't have the insurance anymore!" The anguish in his voice was even greater than when he'd said he was sorry. It diminished him to be without his job, the same job he'd had all my life—or to admit it to me.

"You could sell your car."

"They repossessed it!" He started to cry again.

"Stop it! If there was a way to pay, would you do it?" He closed his mouth to a stubborn line.

"How many people are you going to screw up before you die? Fuck it. It's your life. Kill yourself if you want." I stood there, arms crossed.

"I didn't say I wouldn't do it. I'll do it. I was gonna do it right before I lost my job."

I jumped to the cliff dwelling, then returned, a bag under my arm. Dad followed me up the steps and inside.

It took a half hour to fill out the paperwork but Dad signed in all the right places. When it came time to discuss payment they said the average six weeks ran twelve thousand dollars.

I paid cash, in advance.

TWENTY

Cox came to the phone. He sounded tired.

"Millie Harrison and her roommate are back in their apartment."

"What?"

"They're free. Home. Safe. A federal judge in Wichita issued warrants for the arrest of myself, several of my men, and the head of the agency for kidnapping. We could have stonewalled them, but . . . I talked my superiors out of it."

"Uh, for how long? When are you going to grab them again?"

He was silent for a minute, then said, "I don't know. I don't know who else knows your identity and Millie's relationship to you."

"Well, you certainly didn't help in that area!"

He cleared his throat. "No, I suppose not. But we did release her. Think about that. An act of good faith, not unlike your releasing me."

I stared at the phone. "I'll think about it."

"You have our number." *He* hung up.

I phoned from a phone booth, still not sure if Cox could be trusted.

"Hello?" Millie answered immediately, her voice anxious.

"Any bogeymen around?" My voice was lighthearted. My eyes were full and my throat felt tight.

"Oh, Davy! Oh, God, are you all right? Are you hurt?"

"Are you alone?"

"Yes! The bastards better not come near me, either, or Mark will slap them with a—"

I jumped to her bedroom and she dropped the phone. Her bed was stripped and boxes, half packed, covered the floor. Then I didn't notice anything but the press of her body against mine, the smell of her hair, the taste of tears on her cheeks.

When we'd loosened our arms enough to actually look at each other, she said, "You haven't been eating."

I laughed. "Well, not really." I looked around. "What's with the boxes?"

"Sherry is moving out. She doesn't want to associate with me anymore. I hang out with 'questionable' people. I can't afford this place on my own."

"Some friend."

She shrugged. "We were never that close. And she was locked in a room for a week just because she lived with me."

"Did they hurt you?"

"No. They treated us with kid gloves, except for holding us incommunicado. They didn't even ask any questions after the first day."

I thought back. That must have been after I started jumping agents to Europe, Africa, and the Middle East.

"So, what are you going to do? Get a smaller apartment?"

She shrugged. "Well, if I didn't get any better offers . . . and stop grinning like that."

I kissed her.

"I'd just as soon not have to worry about goons breaking in the door. If there's anything to be said about your place, it's private."

"The rent's right, too."

She shrugged. "But you'll have to make some way for me to get out of there in an emergency. And I want a real bathroom. Stop grinning like an idiot and help me pack."

* * *

Millie looked down into the pit. Matar was seated by the smoking remains of the fire. I noticed that he'd burned the chair after the firewood ran out. He was trying to sharpen one of the chair's metal bolts on a piece of sandstone, but the hardened steel was just wearing a groove in the stone.

She whispered, "What are you going to do with him?"

"Well, I could drop him again from the World Trade Center, only this time . . ." I lowered my fist rapidly to waist height and opened it suddenly, flat, fingers extended. "Splat. Or I could drop him like I did the last time, pulling him away at the last moment, over and over again, until he loses his fear of it. Then I could let him hit."

Millie made a face. "If you're going to kill him, just do it. Don't play with him like a mouse."

"Do you think I should kill him?"

She looked away from me, at the horizon and sighed. "It's not my decision. He didn't kill my mother, did he?"

I nodded. "But it would affect how you feel about me, wouldn't it?"

She nodded slowly, looking back at me with solemn eyes.

"I thought about leaving him in the pit, just putting several years of food there, and checking on him every couple of months. He wouldn't kill anybody else."

"That's sick. You'd be obligating yourself to take care of him forever."

"Well, yeah. Besides, somebody would probably run across him eventually or he'd carve climbing steps out of the pit."

She nodded. "Give him to the NSA."

"American justice? He was wearing a mask when he killed an American citizen. I doubt he'd be convicted. When he killed the maid, he was in Egyptian waters aboard a Greek ship. Oh my God . . . I forgot about the maid. Her body's in Baltimore and they don't have any idea who she is."

"Her family . . ."

I nodded. I knew exactly how they must feel.

* * *

I arranged for Cox to meet me in the Baltimore Hospital morgue, watching carefully. He arrived alone, with the paperwork.

They put her, Maria Kalikos, in a body bag. The news media published her name, making much of her disappearance. Maria Kalikos—I wanted to remember it. I didn't want to forget. Cox signed for her and distracted the attendant while I jumped the body to Athens Airport, to the tarmac, and put it in an empty baggage trailer. Then I went back and jumped Cox to the same place.

The sun was low in the sky. It was late afternoon here, late morning in Baltimore.

He looked at his watch. "Ten minutes." He took out a knife and started to cut away the tag on the body bag, which said, BALTIMORE MORGUE.

"No problem," I said.

I jumped to Heathrow Airport.

Corseau was waiting by the New Caledonia ticket counter. He carried a camera and a tape recorder. We walked around a corner and I jumped him to Athens.

"Brian Cox of the National Security Agency. Jean-Paul Corseau of Reuters News Service. Mr. Cox will be the 'unidentified American intelligence agent.' "

Corseau looked like he tasted something bad but it was part of the deal—exclusive but limited coverage of the exchange. Cox was even unhappier about it, but it was one of my conditions. "Right," said Corseau.

"Be right back."

I jumped to the pit. Matar was ready. I'd handcuffed him earlier, wrists *and* ankles, and left him in a chair. As always he flinched back when I appeared.

I smiled and considered taking him on one more drop off the World Trade Center. No—Millie wouldn't like it.

"What was my mother's name?"

He licked his lips. "Mary Niles."

"Right," I said pleasantly. "And the maid from the *Argos?*"

"Maria Kalikos."

I hadn't taken him for any more "drops" but I'd threatened to if he forgot those names. When you're responsible for the death of someone, you should remember their name.

He screamed when we appeared on the tarmac, but abruptly cut it off when he realized he was on solid ground, not falling. I pushed him against the baggage trailer and he sat, next to the body bag.

Cox handed me a slip of paper and some Greek coins. "Call that number and tell them what gate we're at. Keep out of sight until they're gone—it's bad enough that *we* know who you are."

I was starting to like Cox. Didn't trust him a bit, but I was definitely starting to like him.

I turned to Matar. "Remember. If you escape, I will find you. If they don't convict you, I will find you. If you ever kill again, I will find you. I assure you, you don't want that."

He refused to look at me, but his face whitened.

Millie was waiting for me in the terminal, my binoculars around her neck. I'd jumped her here before any of the others. She wanted to see the exchange.

A voice on the other end of the phone said, "Metaxos."

I said, "Gate 27."

In heavily accented English, the man, Metaxos, said, "I will send them at once." He hung up.

Five minutes later, two unmarked cars and an ambulance rounded the far end of the terminal building. Millie handed me the binoculars. Four men got out of each car. Matar's face was compared with a photo and he was put in the back of one of the cars, a man on each side of him. Corseau took pictures, while Cox stood carefully behind him.

Then the body bag was opened and Maria Kalikos's face compared to another photograph. The ambulance attendants closed the bag, put it—her!—on a stretcher, and loaded the stretcher into the ambulance.

Maria Kalikos, I said to myself. I wanted to remember.

Cox shook hands with one of the Greeks and the three vehicles drove away.

"Do you want me to jump you home first?"

Millie took the binoculars back. "I'll wait. Take them first."

I kissed her and jumped back to the tarmac.

"Okay?" I asked Cox.

"Okay."

Corseau shook his head. "This isn't enough. I want an interview."

"Sorry. This is as far as I can go without endangering myself. Look at the bright side—I can be awful handy to know when you need to get someplace in a hurry."

"All right," he said, reluctantly. "I won't push it. But If you ever go public?"

"Sure," I said. "No question about it. All yours."

I jumped him back to Heathrow.

"Ready?" I asked Cox, on returning.

"We still need a better way to contact you." He sounded tired, making the argument because he'd been told to.

I shook my head. "I promised I'd check the *New York Times* classifieds. That's the most I can promise. If I see the message, I'll call. If I can help you out with quick transport, I'll think about it. But I'm not a spy. I'm not an agent."

"What'll you do, then? Hijackings only? Eventually they'll catch you. Someone may even set up a fake hijacking just for that purpose."

I shook my head. "I don't know. Maybe I'll go to work for the fire department. Maybe I'll start working my way down Amnesty International's Prisoner of Conscience list. Maybe I'll go on vacation."

"Are you sure you don't want us to watch Millie?"

I shook my head violently. "You know that you're more likely to attract attention to her than shield her. *I'll* watch her. You guys stay away."

I jumped him to D.C. and even shook his hand before I left.

I jumped Millie back to the pit. It was midmorning in Texas and the sun slanted down, not touching the water at the bottom of the pit.

"Why did we come here?" she asked.

I raised my arms. "It's over, but it doesn't *feel* over! My dad said he was sorry, but it doesn't change anything. Matar is in the authorities' hands, but . . . it all feels wrong."

She looked at me. "Did your father acknowledge the damage he did to you?"

I frowned. "Well, he said he was sorry, that he never meant to hurt us."

She closed her eyes. "That's not acknowledgment—that's 'don't be mad at me.' "

I picked up a fire-blackened stone and heaved it out into the water. It splashed just short of the cliff, spraying water on the rock wall.

"Davy, you may never get acknowledgment from him. He may never be capable of it."

I threw another stone, bigger, pried out of the sand. It only reached halfway. I started to pick up yet a larger rock, then stopped. "I tried so *hard!*"

She stood there, her mouth turned down at the corners, her eyes bright.

"Is this what you meant? That I couldn't run away from myself?"

She nodded.

"It hurts. It hurts a lot."

"I know."

I went to her and held her, let her hold me, let her squeeze my body to her, let her stroke my back. I felt sad, almost infinitely sad. Finally I pushed away and said, "I'll talk to somebody—if you'll help me find a good therapist."

"Oh, yes."

I ventured a small smile. It didn't seem so impossible, just very, very difficult.

I jumped away and returned almost immediately.

"What's that?"

"It's a lei," I said. "A Hawaiian lei made of orchids." I put it around her neck. "This is part of the custom," I added, kissing her.

She smiled. "Looks out of place in a Texas sinkhole."

I picked her up. "Well, let's go where it fits in. Hold on."

"You bet," she said.

We jumped.

ACKNOWLEDGMENTS

Teleportation is, I hope, a classic trope of science fiction, and not a cliché. Certainly without Alfred Bester's *The Stars My Destination,* Robert Heinlein's *Tunnel in the Sky,* Larry Niven's "Flash Crowd," Phyllis Eisenstein's *Born to Exile,* and even "Star Trek" 's hoary old transporter beam, I wouldn't have asked myself certain questions about teleportation—certain questions that resulted in the novel you now hold. I'll let you judge whether I've perpetrated a cliché or something new, but I freely acknowledge my debt to those who've already plowed this particular furrow.

I'd also like to thank Bob Stahl for the original question; Jack Haldeman and Barbara Denz for information on the Adams Cowley Shock Trauma Center in Baltimore; the Authorized Personnel Writer's Group: Rory Harper, Martha Wells, Tom Knowles, and Laura J. Mixon, for their support and perceptive comment; and the folks at Tor—particularly, but not exclusively, my editor, Beth Meacham, the best editor in this field.